ALL
SOULS'
DAY

ALL SOULS' DAY

Bill Morris

AVON BOOKS NEW YORK

This is a work of fiction. Names, characters, places,
and incidents either are the product of the author's
imagination or are used fictitiously. Any resemblance
to actual events, locales, organizations, or persons,
living or dead, is entirely coincidental and beyond
the intent of either the author or the publisher.

AVON BOOKS
A division of
The Hearst Corporation
1350 Avenue of the Americas
New York, New York 10019

Copyright © 1997 by Bill Morris
Interior design by Kellan Peck
Visit our website at **http://AvonBooks.com**
ISBN: 0-380-97453-3

Library of Congress Cataloging in Publication Data:

Morris, Bill, 1952–
 All Souls' Day : a novel / Bill Morris.
  p. cm.
 I. Title.
PS3563.O873975A794   1997   96-46834
813'.54—dc21   CIP

First Avon Books Printing: June 1997

AVON TRADEMARK REG. U.S. PAT. OFF. AND IN OTHER COUNTRIES, MARCA REGISTRADA, HECHO EN U.S.A.

Printed in the U.S.A.

FIRST EDITION

QPM 10 9 8 7 6 5 4 3 2 1

For my divine sisters,
Gretchen and Lisa

All Souls' Day: A Roman Catholic feast commemorating all the faithful departed. It is celebrated on November 2 and is sometimes called the Day of the Dead.

PART ONE

Sam Malloy had spent the morning waiting for the car to come out of the sky, but so far all he'd seen were refrigerators and tractors and bags of charcoal and fertilizer and cement. The sky was a sheet of metallic blue with bleached gulls swirling on it, a sky that reminded him oddly of autumn skies on Long Island when he was a boy, and the air tasted of salt water and burning leaves and the promise of cold nights to come.

But this sky, though luminously, miraculously blue, was already beginning to pulse with the first prickling heat of a tropical day. There would be no cold nights here in Bangkok, Sam knew, only the relative cool of the next few months and then the rains and the flooded streets and swollen canals, the cloying humidity and long nights when breathing the city air was like swallowing mouthful after mouthful of crushed glass. People say that dusk comes quickly in the tropics and Sam thought, not for the first time, that the heat comes quickly too, beginning with the smoke of the pre-dawn cooking fires, building steadily as the cocks begin to crow and the motorbikes begin to buzz, then hitting you in a flash as soon as the sun crawls out from behind the rooftops. Already that heat was on him. As he raised

his hand to shade his eyes from the ripening sun he noticed he
was breathing hard and his shirt was stuck to his back.

A fat white cloud galloped past and suddenly the car was
hovering above him.

"Awwwwww-right!" cried Rathavorn Saengbangpla, who
was standing at Sam's side. Like most Thais, he had shortened
his name, mercifully, for the language is larded with tongue-
twisting diphthongs and triphthongs, daisy chains of conso-
nants, arbitrary spellings ripe for shortening and improvisation.
Everyone called him Rat. He was tall for a Thai—five-eight or
five-nine—and as always he was neat as a nail. His hair, glossy
and black and perfectly combed, was a helmet of polished
metal. He was shading his eyes, too, grinning like a kid, acne-
pocked cheeks bulging, lips parting to reveal that mouthful of
scrambled teeth. When he smiled the scar on his left cheek stood
out, a perfect horseshoe of pulpy pink flesh. That scar was Rat's
half of their shared secret: They had saved each other's lives
once apiece and thus were bonded together forever. Rat had a
better grasp of American slang than any Asian Sam had ever
met, but he also had a knack for amusing blunders. Lately he'd
taken to posting handwritten signs throughout their hotel, the
White Elephant. The newest gem was "Your time to leaving
must be informed to the manager."

Rat had gotten roaring drunk with a bunch of German tourists on the roof of the hotel last night, and though he always
slept late on Sunday mornings he had risen before dawn today
and cranked up his farting Simca and insisted on driving Sam
down here to the sprawling Klong Toey docks. Rat had sensed,
in his canny way, that this was a moment he should not miss
and now, staring into the sky, he felt the utter rightness of his
intuition. "You are not lying," he said. "She is really very much
a peach."

Sam still hadn't spoken, and Rat looked over at him. "What's
wrong?" he asked.

Only then did Sam realize his eyes were moist. He swiped
the back of his wrist across them. Rat kept studying him, looking puzzled, probably disappointed by this Western show of
emotion. "Nothing's wrong," Sam said. "It's just that . . . it's

just that this is the one I've been waiting for. The last piece of the puzzle, if you know what I mean."

"I am hearing you."

Now they both looked up into the sky as the crane farthest aft on the deck of the *General Grant*, a rust-scabbed tub out of New York, swung its cargo clear of the rail and began lowering it toward the hubbub on the dock. It was hard for Sam to believe that boats like this could make it all the way across the North Atlantic, which was hell at this time of year, then the length of the Mediterranean, through the Suez Canal, down the Red Sea and the Indian Ocean, around Ceylon, past Malacca and Singapore and finally up here to Bangkok. But they did it day after day, night after night, thousands of ships coming and going. There were freighters anchored in the middle of the river, shuttling their cargo onto barges. There were freighters waiting impatiently for a vacancy on the docks, their home ports stenciled on their sterns: Panama, Mombassa, Patagonia, New York. And above these places, the ships' names: *Epoch Ace, Reefer Pegasus, Hercules, Bangbua, White Lucky.* In between these beasts, gaily painted longboats and private yachts and passenger ferries darted back and forth like waterbugs.

"Ooooo-we," Rat said with a low whistle. "Your brother does not lie about that paintjob."

No, Sam thought, my brother doesn't lie about such things. Paintjobs like this are his life. Yet Sam had to admit he was astonished by how dazzling the car looked as it came down out of the sky. When Ed had called from New York three weeks earlier to announce that the car was on the boat and the boat was on the water—and yes, he reassured Sam, he was there to make sure the dockworkers handled the car like a carton of eggs—Ed boasted that he'd matched the original two-tone paintjob so closely that the car looked just like it did the day it rolled off the assembly line in Flint, Michigan, maybe better. "You remember that crazy little bug-eyed bastard who wrote the article for *Life* magazine?" Ed had asked on the phone.

"Sure I remember him," Sam had said. "His name was Morey Caan."

"Remember how he described the paintjob?"

"Yeah, he called it 'boiled shrimp and anthracite.' "

"That's right. I don't know what the fuck that means—but this baby is pink pussy and black garter belts all the way."

Sam had wanted to call his brother a moron, a big fat thick-skulled redneck Irish moron, but that would have sounded ungrateful after all Ed had done to locate the seven cars and get them restored and safely shipped. Besides, you couldn't expect a guy like Ed Malloy to appreciate a turn of phrase like "boiled shrimp and anthracite." Ed hadn't read three books in his entire life, other than transmission manuals. He was still living at home at the tender age of thirty and he had taken over the old man's Sinclair service station and expanded into restoring classic cars and souping up street rods. He was making a "nice little bundle," as he put it, and he didn't hesitate to let his kid brother know he thought he was a fool for languishing in some tropical armpit halfway around the world and amassing a small herd of old Buicks, even if they were gorgeous enough to die for.

No, Ed couldn't be expected to appreciate what Sam was trying to do any more than he could be expected to appreciate the poetry of "boiled shrimp and anthracite," the way it so perfectly captured the essence of Bob and Sally Brunswick's Buick, the seventh and final 1954 Buick to be purchased by the seven residents of Lindbergh Street in Levittown, Long Island, the 500,000th car produced by the Buick Division of General Motors that year, an historic vehicle, the magnet that had drawn the *Life* magazine writer and photographer to Lindbergh Street with its seven identical split-levels and seven identical grassless lawns and seven identical driveways, each adorned with a gleaming gumball '54 Buick.

Sam had that frayed article from *Life* tucked in his pocket now. It was published on January 13, 1955, and for the past eight years he had carried it with him without quite understanding why. It was some sort of talisman, a challenge, a goad. Not until last year, while standing on a sidewalk in Saigon, did he come to understand that he'd kept that article because his life was pointing to the moment when he would make those seven

Buicks his own. And now, on a scalding January morning in 1963, that moment had finally arrived.

His favorite part of the article was the photograph that stretched across two entire pages, a shot of every man, woman and child who lived on Lindbergh Street—the Brunswicks, the Malloys, the Onofrios, the Tuckers, the Karpinskis, the Deckers, the Zimmers—along with assorted cats and dogs and, most important of all, those seven glistening Buicks lined up like dominoes, the sharply tipped bulbs of their front bumpers aimed at the street. The guy who lived in the middle of the block, Hayes Tucker Jr., was the local Buick dealer, and he looked like the happiest man in the world sitting on the roof of his Buick, grinning his buck-toothed grin, teeth as big as piano keys. All the kids on the block knew that Mr. Tucker had gotten drunk one night and poured a bag of sugar into the gas tank of the Brunswicks' old '42 Plymouth so they would be forced to buy a new '54 Buick from him. But the kids, being kids, never let on to the grown-ups.

The photographer *Life* magazine sent was a fat fairy named Spencer Wingo who wore a red kerchief tied around his throat. He had to climb up on a stepladder to get the picture. Sam was off to the right, sitting on the trunk lid of the Malloy family's Buick. It was hard to believe he was his mother's favorite. He was wearing a white T-shirt with the sleeves rolled up, jeans with the cuffs rolled up, white socks, loafers. Typical greaser, he realized in retrospect, with his rippling arms folded in front of his chest, an impatient sneer on his face. And why not? The day was sunny and clear, balmy for that time of year, and he could still remember smelling the sea and seeing gulls overhead and feeling impatient because he'd just gotten his driver's license and his parents had agreed to give him the Buick for the rest of the afternoon and his girlfriend, Vivien McNair, was waiting for him at her home, alone and ready.

It still struck Sam as a shame that that photograph was black-and-white. The cars all looked muddy and gray, not at all like they were, a riot of colors which, Sam learned through meticulous research, were given evocative, magical names by the Detroit stylists, names like Apricot, Tahiti Coral, Condor Yellow,

Galway Green, Cherokee Red and Malibu Blue. In Sam's mind, each color was attached to a family, and each family had its own story. The Brunswicks, who lived at the corner and bought the historic pink-and-black Buick, tended to keep to themselves, probably because Bob Brunswick had lost his left foot to frostbite during the Korean War and his wife, Sally, was afraid of her own shadow. Bob washed and waxed the Buick every Saturday afternoon. Sam's family, the Malloys, lived next door and bought the Condor Yellow (they called it "canary yellow") Buick with the black top. Sam's brother Ed treated the car as his own personal laboratory, tinkering, souping it up, doing everything in his power to turn the family car into a hot rod. The Onofrios' Buick had a Galway Green midriff with a white top and a band of white below the side chrome strip. They chose that garish green because Mrs. Onofrio was Irish and thought it was pretty, though everyone on the block agreed it was the ugliest paintjob they'd ever seen. Hayes Tucker drove a different car every week, but his favorite was the white-on-white (Dover White) Century, which everyone called The Iceberg. The Karpinskis, a loud couple prone to plate-smashing arguments, owned the most feminine Buick on the block, apricot body with white top. But Mrs. Karpinski walked out before the car was a year old and Mr. Karpinski was found dead in the front seat in the garage one morning, car windows down, garage door shut, engine idling, the needle on the gas gauge beginning to brush the E. Art and Ginger Decker were the first couple to build on Lindbergh Street and the first to buy a Buick, Cherokee Red top and body, black below the chrome line, a surprisingly sinister and flashy color scheme for people who rarely attended parties, were never seen drunk, and eventually joined the Seventh Day Adventist church. At the end of the street were Jim and Debbie Zimmer, who both died the night they were returning from New York in their Malibu Blue and white Buick and hit a patch of ice on the Parkway and rammed into a tree.

Sam knew these stories the way he knew the lines around his own eyes. The article in *Life* was written when the cars were still shiny and new, when they promised boundless joy, before history caught up with their owners.

The Brunswicks' pink-and-black Buick, trussed up in ropes like a Thanksgiving turkey, was sinking toward the dock now. The crane operator eased off a second too late and the car landed with a thud, bouncing once, then jouncing on its springs before coming to rest. A cry went up from the dockworkers. Sam winced, but he hadn't heard anything break. Suddenly, out of the shadows along the first row of warehouses, truckdrivers came sprinting toward the car. Though the sun had not yet gathered its full fury, these men had already been at work for hours and now they were busy fixing their overheated engines. Many of them had removed their radiators and were rodding them out with straightened coat hangers, filling them with lizard-green coolant, checking for leaks, chattering gaily. Everywhere Sam had gone in Southeast Asia it had been the same story. No one could afford to pay someone to fix things, so people were forced to live by their wits, to improvise. Most of these men had never seen a dentist, they bathed in café au lait rivers, they were boys for twenty years and then one day they were old men and by the age of forty most of them would be dead. But they understood that they were all in it together and they looked out for one another and they took care of their young and their elderly. Not like America, Sam thought, where kids run wild and old people wind up in warehouses. He had visited the ancient capitals—Ayuthaya in Thailand, Pagan in Burma, Angkor Wat in Cambodia—cities that attained their full glory when Europeans were living in rat-infested hovels and stacking their dead on wagons like ricks of charcoal. And while these glorious cities had been sacked and plundered long ago, Asians still planted rice as they'd planted it for thousands of years, yawning across the paddies behind water buffaloes, the way they'll be planting it a thousand years from now, when London and Paris and New York are piles of cold ash. Seeing these truckdrivers sprinting blissfully toward the Buick reminded Sam of the first lesson Asia had taught him: Anyone who underestimates these people is a fool.

By the time Sam reached the car, the mob was ten deep, everyone jabbering, speculating where the car came from. Some said Russia, some said China, some said it could not possibly have been made by humans.

"Step back! Don't touch it!" Sam barked in Thai.

The crowd retreated, and the jabbering sank to a buzzy murmur. Up close Sam could see that the car's skin wore a hazy film, a special wax Ed had discovered that protected the paint from the corrosive salt air. Ed was forever making ingenious little discoveries. He liked to brag that he'd forgotten more about cars than their father ever knew, and Sam figured he was probably right.

He grabbed the handle on the driver's door and pressed the button. The door opened like butter and a cloud of aromas—new carpet, mildew, the sea, the smells of his adolesence, the smell of sex—popped out and kissed him.

The interior was immaculate. The tops of the seats were pleated with the reddest vinyl Sam had ever seen, as red as whorehouse wallpaper. The rest of the seats were black fabric shot through with silver sparkles. New red headliner, new black carpet, arcing red-and-black dashboard. The instruments gleamed like kitchen appliances. The steering wheel was a perfect circle of red, as big as a basketball hoop, with grooves for the driver's fingers and a silver horn ring. He looked at the back seat, that womb, and it seemed to say, "Go ahead! Take off your clothes and climb in! Hurry!"

"You have come to claim?" a voice said in Thai. Sam spun. A little man in an orange jumpsuit and flip-flops was holding a stack of papers out to him, smiling. Sam placed his palms together under his chin and bowed slowly from the waist, the traditional *wai*, the gesture of greeting and respect. He took the papers and the man *wai*'ed in return and the dockworkers and truckdrivers sighed their approval.

There were forms in English and forms in Thai, everything in triplicate. Sam felt curiously pleased by this pile of red tape. One of the most appealing things about shipping the Buicks to Bangkok was that the very idea of it was so preposterous: chrome-encrusted monstrosities on streets gridlocked with compact cars, bicycles, scooters and elephants. Getting them here was a logistical nightmare, and that appealed to Sam too. What appealed to him most, though, was that people told him it couldn't be done. Even Rat, who seemed capable of anything, warned him that there were too many people to pay off, too many ways for things to go wrong: shipwreck, piracy, vandalism.

But here was the seventh and final Buick—the most beautiful Buick of them all—crouched safely on the Klong Toey dock. All the doubters had been wrong and Sam had been right. He told Rat to wash the car, and he took the stack of forms toward the long cinderblock building marked Customs Office.

Sam had once dreaded this little dance, but now he looked forward to it. This would be his final journey into the belly of the bureaucratic beast. He checked his pocket for the stack of baht notes, waved his way through a cloud of flies and opened the screen door. Fourteen heads jerked up in unison—seven pairs of diligent bureaucrats. The door closed with a *whap!* This door was opened and closed so often that an air conditioner would have been useless. There were three fans on the ceiling, but their paddles barely stirred the air. Sam knew it was best to get your business done early here, before the paper-pushers got a beery lunch in them and the room heated up and tempers began to fray.

Lt. Boonchu Lobpin had emerged from his glass cubicle at the back of the room and was gliding past the rows of desks toward Sam. Of course the lieutenant was aware the Buick had arrived. There were no secrets in Asia. His right hand was out and the familiar smile was planted on his face, the smile of a man who knew he was about to make some easy money.

"Mr. Malloy! My pleasure it is to see you again!" he said, pumping Sam's hand. Now that the boss was on the floor, Sam saw no more faces. Just fourteen heads of shiny black hair, all bent over the paperwork on their desks.

"You're looking prosperous, Lieutenant Boonchu," Sam said, releasing the hand, then tucking the papers under his arm so his hands were free to *wai*.

"Let us go to my office." Lieutenant Boonchu didn't bother to *wai*. He simply led the way toward his glass cubicle in the back, the killing floor. As he passed the rows of paper-shufflers,

Sam marveled at how particular the Thais were about pecking order. The closer he got to Boonchu's office, the more ornate the uniforms became. In Thailand everything had a rank, even the parts of the human body, the head being the loftiest, the feet the lowliest. Thus it was very bad form to point your feet at another person or touch a child on the head. And so the job of processing the American's paperwork fell naturally to the highest-ranking man in the office, Lt. Boonchu Lobpin of the Royal Thai Customs Authority, a moon-faced sausage packed into a crisp tan uniform, a man whose goverment salary was only a fraction of his net income, indeed a man whose government job was merely a license to make unlimited amounts of money through commissions, gifts, kickbacks and outright bribes. The Thais did not view this as corrupt, in the American sense of the word; they viewed it as part of the cost of doing business. Sam knew it was pointless to get upset or try to resist. He stepped onto the killing floor and sat in the appointed chair and smiled as he heard the door click shut behind him.

Sam realized he was going to miss these visits. Boonchu had acquired a strangely lofty place in Sam's life, like a favored bartender or barber, someone who understood things without having to be told. Sam watched him sink into the chair behind the desk, a high-backed, cocoa-colored throne that swiveled silently.

"You want coffee," Lieutenant Boonchu declared.

"Yes."

"Cream and no sugar."

"That's right."

Boonchu clapped his hands and a girl on the other side of the glass wall sprang into action. Sam knew the drill. She was making two cups of instant Nescafé. Java, Indonesia, was—what?—less than a thousand miles from this room, the best coffee in the world was readily available, and yet the Thais served up this pre-fab swill that was manufactured in New Jersey and tasted like a sweat sock. If you were lucky, they added a glop of condensed milk. Sam wrote it off to the fact that the Thais were Buddhists, tea drinkers at heart. But still, for people who took such deserved pride in living sensual lives, the Nescafé struck Sam as a weird misstep.

"So," Lieutenant Boonchu said when the girl had deposited the cups of coffee and bowed and gone. "Your last car is arrive . . ."

Here we go, Sam thought. "Yes, it certainly is arrive. Safe and sound."

"It is most beautiful than the others, I think."

"I agree. It's my favorite."

"Good, good." The smile was getting bigger, so big it looked like it might crack that nut-brown face. "Well, let us to start on that paperwork."

Lieutenant Boonchu took the Thai forms, Sam took the English. He could have done this in his sleep by now, and his gaze drifted up to the portraits of the King and Queen on the pale blue wall behind Lieutenant Boonchu's desk. These portraits were fixtures on the walls of every office, shop, bar, restaurant and whorehouse in Thailand. The King was dressed in a sharp silver Thai-silk suit, thin lapels, something that would have looked good on Sam Cooke. As a matter of fact, the King blew a mean saxophone. When Lieutenant Boonchu caught him staring at the portraits, Sam smiled and went back to his stack of paperwork. He knew there was no surer way to offend a Thai than to show disrespect for His or Her Majesty.

Lieutenant Boonchu attacked his forms, pressing so hard with his ballpoint pen that his knuckles turned white. Sam studied the top of his head. Like Rat's, his hair was polished metal, but it was an inferior grade, some cheap alloy, the shafts not as shiny or as dark, the comb's furrows not as orderly, sprigs popping loose, dandruff salted along the part. When he finished each page he removed the carbon copies and *bap! bap! bap!* pounded them with the stamp that made it all official and would one day make him a rich man. Sam slid his completed forms across the desk, tidy stacks of baht notes nestled between the carbon copies. Lieutenant Boonchu swept the bills into his desk drawer so smoothly Sam almost missed it, then *bap! bap! bap!* and he stood up and held out his hand, smiling more broadly than ever.

Sam rose and shook the hand. "Thank you for everything, Lieutenant."

"It is always very much my pleasure to helping an American friend." He handed Sam his copies. "The cashier is you know where. Let me know if something more I can do to you."

"I'll do that." They both *wai*'ed, slow and deep. Before Sam reached the door, Lt. Boonchu Lobpin was hard at work on another stack of those lucrative triplicate forms.

The Buick was radiant, astonishing now that it was washed and street-legal. The crowd had dispersed and Rat was sitting in the Simca reading the night's Muay Thai boxing card, circling the names of his favorites with a red pen. Since signing one's name in red was considered unlucky in Thailand, Sam wondered if Rat's use of a red pen was the reason he always seemed to lose when he bet on the bouts. Rat had been a prize Muay Thai prospect as a teenager, "The Tiger of Thailand," a sure bet to travel to Singapore and Hong Kong for the big-money matches—until he blocked a kick with his left forearm and the bone snapped like a dry stick. Rat took Sam to Lumpini Stadium once a week. Sam loved the spectacle, the way the fighters showed off their beautiful robes and then, after shedding them, showed off their beautiful bodies in a slow peacock parade around the ring. They were smooth brown vicious mayhem artists, dressed in nothing but silk boxing shorts and leather gloves, barefoot, free to punch, kick, elbow, knee, anything but bite. When Rat saw Sam coming out of the Customs Office he tossed the newspaper on the seat and sprang out of the car. "How did this go?"

"Same as always. The coffee was awful."

Rat chuckled. "You follow me?"

"Yeah. And take it slow this time, okay?"

"Yes, okay."

And so Sam fired up the Buick and dropped it into low gear and eased across the dock. The truckdrivers had put down their radiators and coat hangers and jugs of coolant, and they were lined up in the shade like soldiers. Sam pressed the chrome horn ring, and the resonant honk startled them. Laughing, they *wai*'ed in unison as the Buick passed.

The security guard at the port gate was asleep in his kiosk, which meant one less palm to grease. Sam followed the blue Simca into the Klong Toey slums, a sprawl of thatch and tin shacks laced with trenches full of brown water where women washed dishes and clothes while naked children splashed ecstatically. In the midday glare the Mosquito and the Venus, two of the more notorious waterfront bars, looked almost innocent, tawdry and defanged, with their doors shut and their neon signs dead. It seemed like a lifetime ago that Sam had first entered those raucous dives, back when he was on R&R and had money in his pocket and juice to burn. His favorite characters were the dwarf prostitute who dressed like a schoolboy in the Venus and the old Russian broad in the dirty white lace dress who sat at the top of the stairs in the Mosquito, sipping Pernod and bellowing drunkenly, "Show time in ten minutes, gentlemen! Ten minutes till show time!" while the house band played Ravel's "Bolero" and the strippers got ready to go on. Sam taught the girls English between shows and they paid him by giving him bottles of Scotch and by telling him when it was time to get under the table. The Danish sailors fought the Aussies and the Germans fought the Americans and when the chairs and bottles and fists stopped flying, as often as not, they all wound up buying each other drinks and singing arm in arm until the sun came up. Yes, Sam thought, all that was a lifetime ago.

He followed the Simca up Rama IV to Hualamphong train station, then left along the klong, a canal filled with oily black water and lined with sycamore trees. It was cooler here, a precious tunnel of shade, its floor spangled with golden coins of sunshine. This could have been anywhere, Sam thought—Saigon, or even Paris. People rose from their squatting positions, they looked up from their fruit stalls and their bowls of soup and their naps, and they stared at the Buick as it passed.

Finally, after crossing the canal, Sam followed the Simca off Charoen Krung and into the grease-bruised alleys that spun south from Chinatown. These alleys were barely wide enough for the Buick. Sam could hear the fenders brushing against pedestrians, against wagons loaded with fruit, charcoal, wicker

baskets and bricks. Bright pennants of laundry hung from every
balcony. With the windows rolled down, the car filled with the
clanging of the shops where knives and metal fence posts were
made, the hot and dirty blacksmith shops where sinewy, sweat-
slicked boys rebuilt auto parts—rear axles, leaf springs, transmissions—then stacked them by the open doorways, ready for
delivery.

This was Sam's favorite part of the city. He called it Gasoline
Alley. It was all about hot work and survival, and it had nothing
to do with tourism. He'd gotten hopelessly lost on this very
alley, Soi 22, the first time he tried to find the riverside villa
that was to become the White Elephant Hotel. He liked the
fact that it was all but impossible for the uninitiated to find
the place.

They turned right, then a quick left onto Soi Panurangsri. On
their left was the Chinese temple, its lurid red walls adorned
with sea monsters, peacocks, elephants, fat carp and deer, its
interior walls and ceiling blackened by incense smoke. This was
the home of a fierce and all-knowing god. Across the alley was
Sam's favorite noodle shop. When he tapped the horn, Mr. Hing
looked up from his chopping block and his sizzling wok, and
waved. He'd just gotten his weekly haircut, and the silver spikes
bristling on his skull made him look like someone who belonged
in a penitentiary or an asylum. Hing liked Sam even though
he was an *ang moh,* a redhead, his term for all white people; he
said the guests who stayed at the White Elephant improved the
neighborhood, which meant he could charge them triple for his
bowls of duck noodles. The lunch rush was over and the tables
were half-full and Sam could see that the cement floor was
littered with its customary confetti of shrimp tails, cigarette
butts and lottery stubs. Everyone stopped eating and watched
the Buick glide past.

When Sam turned off Soi Panurangsri the Buick's windshield
filled with a majestic view of the White Elephant Hotel. In this
grimy quarter the hotel rose up like a bleached monument to
a forgotten age. It was a rambling, stucco-walled, tile-roofed
Mediterranean villa built at the turn of the century by a Portuguese trading company that chose the site because of its river

access and its proximity to the old Customs House and to New Road, the oldest commercial artery in Bangkok. The lot was narrow but deep, running one hundred yards from the alley to the riverbank. The compound was ringed by a high wall tipped with shards of blue glass, and it stood next to a long godown, or warehouse, that was once the busiest spot on the entire waterfront. But the Portuguese left after the 1932 coup, and a distant cousin of the King's bought the villa and used it to throw parties that were legendary for their drinking, gambling, drugs, and sexual excesses. When the Prince died, Rat's father-in-law bought the compound and set about amassing a fortune baking *jan ap* cookies from a secret family recipe he had learned in his native Swatow, a seaport in Southern China. Sam had heard that Hing, a fellow Swatownese, despised Rat's father-in-law for growing so rich in that rotting old villa while he, Hing, made a modest living cooking duck noodles. But Hing was a master of the Chinese act of disappointment: The world would never know of his hurt.

Rat's father-in-law died of a heart attack in his upstairs office in 1962, and to everyone's surprise he willed the building and a chink of his fortune to Rat, who promptly summoned his old friend Sam Malloy to Bangkok. They hired a crew of Thai workers and set about refurbishing the villa from street to roof, adding Western-style bathrooms and a swimming pool and nine thatched bungalows. Rat even loaned Sam enough of his inheritance money to pay for the purchase, restoration, and shipping of the seven Buicks. The hotel was already winning a reputation as one of the secret jewels of Bangkok.

When Sam turned in to the alley that ran alongside the compound wall, he saw that Rat had the godown's last door open. Sam backed into the vacant slot, cut the ignition, and sat in the car listening to the ticking of the engine as it cooled. His dream had come true at last. The seven Buicks were now his.

2

Shwe Winn was squatting in the kitchen doorway spitting betel juice onto the brick sidewalk and watching the Thai boy who was supposed to be cleaning shrimp flirt with the Thai girl who was supposed to be washing the lunch dishes. The Thais were all alike, Shwe Winn thought, always flirting or sleeping or looking to play instead of work. The Thais worked a job until they had enough money to buy some nice clothes or some jewelry or some whiskey, and then they disappeared. No wonder the Chinese were the true rulers of Bangkok.

She sent a fresh arc of betel juice onto the sidewalk and studied the lotus flowers. They were even redder than the betel juice, redder than blood. They needed water. Shwe Winn sold the flowers to the crippled woman who lived on the alley behind the warehouse, and the woman in turn strung necklaces out of them and sold them on New Road. Everyone bought her necklaces—young men wooed women with them; bus drivers and *tuk-tuk* drivers draped them over their mirrors to protect against bad luck and accidents; people placed them in spirit houses along with offerings of food and drink and candles and incense to mollify the spirits and protect their families and homes. Thais were so full of superstitions that there would always be an appetite for lotus flowers. And yet Shwe Winn had to admit they smelled lovely, damp and huskily fragrant, and she reminded herself to water these flowers as soon as the sun was off them.

She lit a Gold City cigarette from the pack left at the pool by one of the *farangs*, a German woman. *Farangs* were always forgetting things—cigarettes, sunglasses, books, even money—recklessness that struck Shwe Winn as sinful. But she was not one to pass up free cigarettes. She didn't care if the Thais, including her son-in-law, laughed at her for being so cheap. They called betel "poor lady's lipstick" because it stained her lips red at a fraction of the cost of those tubes they sold in the department stores. Let them laugh. Her own daughters threw their money away on cosmetics, especially Ong Bui, the first-born, who was married to a rich Army general and lived in a mansion in Bangkapi and painted her face, drew on her eyebrows with a pencil, even had her hair fluffed and frizzed. Anything to look like a *farang* and please her man.

Through a cloud of cigarette smoke Shwe Winn saw Rat's blue car flash past the iron gate. Then a roar and a blur of pink and black and silver. A pink car! The *farang* had added another bright and silly monster to his collection in the godown. Her late husband, Nguan Wong, would die a thousand more deaths if he could see what had become of his godown. Not so long ago it had been a hive of activity. Coolies, both Thai and Chinese, carried the cargo off the river barges, scurried along the slick planks, loaded the godown to the rafters with sacks of flour, cans of shortening, crates of nuts—the ingredients for Wong's *jan ap* cookies, the most popular brand in Bangkok, available as far away as Chaing Mai and Korat. Back then the kitchen in the villa was full of gas ovens that produced a steady, fearful heat, full of machines that mixed the batter and molded and stamped the cookies. It was like a factory. All the workers were Chinese because they were honest and hard working, not like the Thais, who were light-fingered and lazy. And now . . . now this kitchen produced meals for tourists and the godown was full of gaudy *farang* toys, things only Americans could make and that only an American would think to bring to Bangkok.

The gate opened. Sam had his arm draped over Rat's shoulder, and Rat had his arm around Sam's waist. They were like brothers. It was unnatural, Shwe Winn thought, for a short brown man and a tall pink man to be so close. Arm in arm they passed through the hedge of canna flowers, bursting now with yellow, orange and pink blooms. Rat had planted this hedge all the way around the compound wall because, he said, its Thai name of *pootaraksa* means "the Buddha protects" and it would protect them all from bankruptcy and bad luck. Another silly Thai superstition. The men were laughing as they came toward her, and Shwe Winn realized she should be grateful that her baby girl, Jiap, had married Rat, one of the reliable Thais. Oh, he got drunk on Saturday nights and sometimes he flirted with the foreign women, especially when they showed themselves at the pool, but he worked hard and he didn't gamble and as far as she knew he had only one wife. They could have done worse, Shwe Winn reminded herself, much worse. The American was not all bad, either. He spoke fluent Thai, treated his Thai girls well, and observed Thai customs—he always went barefoot indoors, so rare for a *farang*—and he seemed to understand that he would never be fully accepted. To the Thais he would always be a *jek*, an outsider, just like the Chinese. She admired him for understanding this and accepting it gracefully. He had his dignity.

And yet she was plagued by Rat and Sam's friendship. She knew they had some secret and she knew it had something to do with the scar on Rat's face and the hitch in Sam's walk, not a limp actually, but something that stuck when he tried to bring his right leg forward. She knew their secret came from when they served together in the military, and she once enlisted Jiap to try to find out what it was. She counseled her daughter to wait till she and Rat had made love, when he was groggy and vulnerable and more likely to let something slip. But when Jiap brought it up, as casually as she could, Rat turned to ice and left their bed without a word. They had never spoken of it again, Jiap told her mother. But Shwe Winn doubted this. After all, Jiap had started acting just like a Thai: She'd taken a Thai nickname ("Jiap" meant baby chick) and she plucked her eyebrows and her armpits and she said yes when she meant no.

The two men were having such a good laugh that they nearly walked right over Shwe Winn. They stepped back in surprise. Their arms fell to their sides and their laughter died. They *wai'*ed.

"Mahndah!" Rat cried, sounding delighted to have stumbled upon his mother-in-law.

"So you have brought home one more car," she said in Thai.

"The *last* car," Sam said in Thai. He was smiling. "That's a promise, Mahndah Shwe Winn. No more cars."

"What will you do with all those ugly cars?"

"*Ugly?!*" the men cried in unison, laughing again.

"They are the most beautiful Buicks in Bangkok," Rat said.

"That's because they are the only Buicks in Bangkok," she said, spitting onto the sidewalk.

"We're going to make money with them," Sam said. But this failed to get the expected rise out of her, and the men stepped past her and into the kitchen. Rat immediately started barking at the crew to get back to work, clapping his hands, shouting threats, ending catnaps and mating rituals. Shwe Winn heard water running in the sinks, heard the banging of pots and the scurrying of bare feet. At least they listened to him. They would have laughed in her face.

Shadows had covered the bed of lotus flowers. She dragged the hose from the side of the building and, after lighting a fresh Gold City, she stood there in the shade smoking, watering the flowers, wondering how the crazy American hoped to make money with such ugly cars.

Sam had promised to telephone his brother as soon as the car arrived in Bangkok. He ate a late dinner with Nigel Colchester, the Englishman who lived alone in Bungalow 7. Everyone called him "the Major." He'd been drinking brandy since midafternoon and he wasn't making much sense. He kept bragging that he was the only soldier in the trenches at Ypres who didn't get diarrhea. When he finally staggered down to his bungalow, Sam

21

went into the godown and turned on the lights and spent an hour staring at the Buicks.

He had parked them in the identical order of the Lindbergh Street families and the *Life* magazine photograph: first the Brunswicks, then the Malloys, the Onofrios, the Tuckers, the Karpinskis, the Deckers and the Zimmers, that procession of colors that told stories, pink, yellow, green, white, apricot, red, turquoise, colors that meant war wounds, gambling debts, bad taste, greed, suicide, evangelism, terrible luck. Or was it hero-ism, steadfastness, idiosyncracy, capitalism, courage, joy and a painless quick exit? He wasn't sure. He wasn't even sure that it mattered. All he knew was the Buicks were lovely and he didn't want this day, the happiest day of his life, to end.

Shortly before midnight he switched off the lights in the go-down and went up to his room. His room was always a comfort, even late at night when he was alone with nothing to keep him company but the throb of the river traffic and the all-night hum of the alleys. This room had once been Prince Prem's personal pleasure dome, his realm of opium and marijuana and unimag-inable joys with beautiful boys and beautiful girls. The walls and floor were teak and the screened windows were high enough to afford privacy as well as a stunning view of the river. The bed, set on a pedestal, was made of gray iron, its four posts draped with a mosquito net. It reminded Sam of an altar, or a hospital, or an ark, some sort of religious medicinal seaworthy barge, a realm of pure pleasure.

Sam sat at the rolltop desk and picked up the telephone. It would be late morning in New York and he hoped to catch Ed before he went out for lunch, a typical American workingman's lunch—haunches of shiny meat, fried potatoes, limp vegetables, cakes, cobblers, pies, a recipe for an early grave.

It took several minutes for the connection to go through and then a girl answered on the second ring: "Malloy's Lawn Guy-land Resta-rations."

That Long Island accent had always been a drill bit in Sam's ear. Most people, on meeting him for the first time, were sur-prised to learn he was a native New Yorker. He took that as a compliment. No doubt this receptionist was one of those Jewish or Italian girls who spawn like salmon out on Long Island, baby fat not yet melted away, still living at home, skirt too tight and too short, way too much makeup. Ed called them his "chickens," and to hear him tell it, more than a few of them had wound up spread-eagled on the boss's gun-metal gray desk in the back office, gabbling like they'd been electrocuted.

"Hello," Sam said. "This is Ed's brother calling from Thailand." The connection was a miracle, a slight lag but clear.

"You're cawling awl the way from Tai-wan *China?*"

"Close enough. Is Ed in?"

"Please hold."

Sam tried to picture her. She probably had a pageboy haircut and thick ankles and a mustache. Those women were like oxen compared to the Thai women, who seemed to float when they walked, were always pressed and powdered, and never seemed to sweat. Ed was the male version of those Long Island girls. Though he hadn't touched a wrench or a ball-peen hammer in years—he liked to point out that he was "the brains of the operation"—he still ate like one of the boys, and as a result he couldn't see his own feet.

"Baby brother!" the voice boomed. "Whattaya know?"

"The car made it in one piece, Ed. There's a little ding on the left rear quarter panel, but Rat knows a guy who'll pound it out for us. Otherwise she's perfect. Thanks a million."

"No problem. How'd you like that paintjob?"

"Unbelievable. I'd forgotten how hot that pink was."

"Me too. Hard to believe old man Tucker sold that thing to mousy old Bob Brunswick." He chuckled. "So now what happens?"

"Now we go into business. We take out an ad in the paper and we rent them out for weddings, funerals, GIs on R&R, whatever."

"Sheesh." There was a pause. Someone shouted Ed's name. "Well, good luck, baby brother. I trust my check's in the mail."

"I posted it this afternoon. Give it two weeks."

"Say, before you run off . . ." Sam hadn't said anything about running off. Ed's stomach was probably growling and the boys in the body shop were massing for the daily lunch run, their hands speckled with gray primer and rainbows of paint, their hair peppered with blasted rust, a fate that had nearly become Sam's own. "I wonder if you'd do me a small favor."

"Sure, Ed."

"Big brother called last night."

"From Saigon?"

"Yeah. Listen, it's none of my business if you two wanna live in a coupla shit holes halfway around the world, but something's eating Charlie. He's not homesick, he's *sick*."

"Why do you say that?"

"I dunno. He just didn't sound right. Kinda gloomy and depressed—and I think he was into the sauce pretty heavy."

Sam wanted to tell him that most white men in the tropics were into the sauce pretty heavy, but he let his brother continue.

"So Sam, I was wondering if maybe you could give Charlie a call, check up on him, make sure everything's jake. He won't talk to me or the old man, but he'll talk to you."

"Sure thing. I'll give him a call tomorrow." Someone shouted from the back of the body shop. "And listen Ed, thanks for everything. The cars are gorgeous."

"Glad to do it—as long as that check don't bounce." He laughed and they hung up simultaneously, a single click.

Sam lit a mosquito coil and stripped off his clothes and stretched out on the bed. He didn't call Saigon. Not yet. He listened to the boats on the river and he watched the blades of the ceiling fan and he wondered what could possibly be wrong with the eldest of the Malloy boys this time. And he wondered if the day would ever come when the blades of a ceiling fan no longer reminded him of the monotonous *thwocking* of a helicopter's propeller.

3

Sam dreaded talking to his brother in Saigon so much that he put off making the phonecall for a week. There was no shortage of legitimate excuses. The Buicks had to be registered and insured. An ad had to be taken out in *The Bangkok Post*, which meant arranging a photograph of the cars, writing the copy, and approving the layout. The swimming pool pump obligingly died, and he and Rat had to spend two days tearing it apart and fixing the motor. A fat American guest lost her passport and was so distraught Sam took pity on her and drove her to the U.S. Embassy on Wireless Road to apply for a new one. And finally Shwe Winn's ulcer started acting up again and Sam had to take her to the only herbalist in Chinatown she would consent to visit.

It took them half a day to find the place and another half day of waiting before the good doctor agreed to see her. He had a mole the size of a penny on his chin, and the four silver hairs that grew out of it trailed all the way into his lap. Obviously a true sage, Sam thought, watching him stroke that excuse for a beard. The doctor gave Shwe Winn seven capsules of powdered deer antler and told her to take one a day, washing it down with a glass of snake wine. If her stomach pain persisted, he ordered her to return in one week. Sam figured the medicine would kill her by then. Driving her back to the hotel, he tried to imagine what could possibly be a source of worry to the old crone. Her husband had left her a small fortune when he died; she had a pleasant apartment at the hotel and a job that kept her busy without breaking her back. It was probably guilt, Sam decided, Chinese guilt: She had never produced a son, just three worthless daughters, and she would go to her grave viewing herself as the worst kind of failure.

Finally Sam ran out of excuses for not calling Saigon. Charlie was ten years older than Sam, a virtual stranger. He'd left home when Sam was in elementary school, moving to New York to work as a copyboy at the Associated Press in Rockefeller Center, a humble beginning that had led to steadily bigger things, culminating with his anointment as one of the stars of *Time* magazine's corps of foreign correspondents.

Charlie was the first person Sam had looked up after his discharge from the Navy on June 12, 1962. Two days later he knocked on the door of Room 716 at the Caravelle Hotel in Saigon. The door flew open and Charlie stood there in a bath towel, smoking a cigar and waving a snifter of cognac.

"Good God, look what the cat dragged in!" Charlie roared. Then he shouted at the bathroom door, which was shut: "Kitten, gitcher skinny yellow ass out here right now and say hello to America's newest war hero! Baby brother hath arrived!"

Charlie handed Sam a bottle of 333 beer. He looked like hell warmed over: dark tea bags under his eyes, burst blood vessels on his cheeks, the pasty pallor that comes to white men in the tropics when they drink too much and begin to fall sweatily, unprettily apart.

The bedsheets looked like freshly whipped meringue, and as soon as Sam took a sip of beer he met the reason why. A Vietnamese girl with a curtain of black hair, crimson lips and spray-on Capri jeans emerged from the bathroom humming to herself. "Heard a lot about you, sailor," she told Sam after Charlie introduced them. "You big war hero, right?"

"Small war hero," Sam said.

"He's just being modest," Charlie said, collapsing on the bed. He sounded winded from the effort of opening the beer and performing the introductions. Sam hated to think what Kitten's calisthenics must have done to his heart. Charlie reached for her, but she snatched her purse off the bed and moved nimbly for the door.

"Have to leave," she said. "Got work to do."

Right, Sam thought. Got sailors to blow. He'd been in town just two days and already he'd seen her working the bar at the Florida Club. Madame Nhu, the president's sister-in-law, had succeeded in banning decadent modern dances like the twist, but she obviously had not yet managed to stamp out the ancient art of fucking for hire. And so, in a cloud of cheap perfume, Kitten swiveled out the door and went off to work.

"Christ," Charlie said in a faraway voice after the door clicked shut. "She's a pistol, that one. Damn near broke this bed . . ."

"You foreign correspondents lead such a rough life."

The mention of his profession brought Charlie out of his reverie. He sprang off the bed, suddenly revitalized, and started getting dressed. "I'm going to take you out for the best French meal this side of the Champs Elysées—and you're going to tell me all about what happened to you out there," he announced. "But first I want to show you off to the boys at the Sunset Club."

The Sunset Club proved to be everything Sam despised about Americans on the loose in Asia. It was the regular twilight gathering of the Saigon press corps on the roof of the Rex Hotel, a chance for a dozen correspondents to watch the day die while swapping gossip and rumors and getting numb enough on 35-cent martinis to face the evening's festivities. And yet, to his surprise, Sam was initally grateful for the correspondents' company and high spirits. They helped him forget how strange it felt to be on the streets of Saigon, suddenly a civilian again, with no idea what came next.

Sam also liked the view from the roof of the Rex. He could stand by the rail and look down at the traffic swirling around the fountain. A billboard across the street showed a huge horizontal bottle of Martini & Rossi vermouth, the brand of choice among the Saigon B-girls, who loved to order the stuff at three dollars a shot so the bartender could slide them a glass of water and you, the patron, could enrich the local economy. From up on the roof the traffic cops in their white helmets and white gloves—the legendary "white mice"—looked like little wooden puppets, and the orange tiles that carpeted the city's rooftops all seemed to be rotting in unison. There was something magical about those moments when the daylight died and darkness took over the city: They were moments full of promise, the promise of unthinkable pleasures, of drowsy peace, even the seductive promise of death.

By his third or fourth visit to the Sunset Club, though, Sam began to realize he was not himself. He was sleeping twelve hours a day and his moods swung between a quiet, murderous rage and an oddly passive distraction. More than once a correspondent would be regaling him with an elaborate yarn about a hooker, or an ambassador, or an ambush, and he would have to stop himself in mid-sentence and ask, "Sam, are you still with me?" This distraction struck Sam as odd because he had spent the past two years acutely aware of his surroundings day and night, especially at night, especially when he slept.

Ultimately he stopped going to the Rex rooftop because the correspondents were a bunch of noisy bastards who asked too many questions. The worst were the hungry young ones, the guys Sam's age, because they took themselves so damn seriously. No sense of humor. They all talked about how they were in the right place at the right time, in on the ground floor of a nice nasty little war that was about to heat up and get a whole lot nastier. People were dying every day and all these guys could think about was what a great career move this was. They thought they understood the war, but Sam knew for a fact that they didn't know the first thing about it. They thought a few trips to the Mekong Delta made them experts. If only they knew how little they knew.

The man who finally drove Sam away for good was a reporter named Haversham or Halberson, Sam never quite caught it, a burly six-foot cupcake with a cocky walk and a permanent

5 o'clock shadow. One look at his face and you knew he had a hairy back. The Vietnamese must have thought he was a monster. Sam disliked him instantly, the way he stormed onto the rooftop and barked his drink order in bad French even though the waiters all spoke flawless English. Halfway into his fourth beer, Haversham or Halberson walked over to Sam, who was gazing numbly at the girls in *ao dais* floating along Le Loi on their bicycles like moths, or angels, or ghosts.

"Ladies and gentlemen," Haversham cried, though there were no women in the Sunset Club. He wrapped a big meaty arm around Sam's shoulder. He smelled of Ivory soap. "I would like to pose a question to our mystery guest, Mr. Sam Malloy."

Everyone treated this guy like royalty, for some reason, and they all swung toward the voice, bristling with anticipation.

"My question is this, Mr. Malloy: What *really* brings you to Saigon?"

"I told you. I just got discharged from the Navy and I'm here visiting my brother."

"Come, come, old boy. No one comes to Saigon to visit relatives. Surely there's more to it than that."

"Sorry."

"Well, then, I have a theory." The other correspondents leaned forward. "I believe our friend Sam here is the newest spook in all of Saigon—sent here by none other than the CIA to find out what dastardly plots we hatch every evening as the sun goes down . . ."

Sam felt his neck throb and it was all he could do not to break the man's jaw. He took a deep breath and put down his beer and walked toward the elevator. There was a scrabbling of chairs, a glass broke, someone laughed. Charlie called to him but Sam kept going, got on the elevator, and never went back to the nightly gathering on the roof of the Rex Hotel.

And now, six months after swallowing the temptation to put a newspaper reporter in the hospital, Sam asked the switchboard operator at the Caravelle Hotel to put him through to Room 716.

4

The burring of the telephone woke Charlie Malloy from a dead sleep. He looked to his left and found, to his surprise, that the bed was empty, the sheets cool. The bed still smelled of her perfume, though, like wildflowers—or was it strawberries? or gardenias? He couldn't quite place it. He swung to his right, toward the insistent burring of the telephone, and knocked over an ashtray and a half-empty bottle of beer. Cursing, he groped for the telephone and with sudden clarity he considered the questions New York could possibly have about his Ap Bac story.

He still believed, even in the dead of night, that the story was air-tight. That was a good sign. In Saigon, what you believed in the dead of night was all that mattered. He had been one of the first reporters on the scene the day after the battle at Ap Bac down on the Mekong Delta, which would be an enormous feather in his cap. He had put on his Abercrombie & Fitch bush jacket and crisp suntans for the first time and caught the second helicopter to leave Saigon at dawn. They stopped in Tan Hiep, then continued on to Ap Bac, arriving in time to see that the battle had been a disaster. Peasant homes were still smoldering.

Charlie counted twenty-three corpses of South Vietnamese soldiers stacked on top of one dike, five American helicopters twisted and bullet-pocked in the paddies. This was major news. The successes of the new H-21 American helicopters had been the big story of 1962, and until now not a single one had been shot down. On the floor of one of the choppers he saw the wallet of an American advisor who had died the day before. The wallet was open to a picture of the man's wife and infant daughter. Charlie started writing in his notebook.

Half an hour later he and Neil Sheehan of UPI were interviewing Brigadier General Bob York, a granite-jawed cracker from Alabama, when the freight-train sound of artillery fire came whistling toward them. The concussion sent bodies flying not fifty yards from where Charlie was standing, armed with nothing but a camera and a ballpoint pen and a spiral notebook.

"What the fuck?" someone muttered.

"Let's get the hell out of here!" York shouted, and suddenly Charlie found himself waddling along the top of the dike behind a general in the U.S. Army, trying to stay ahead of the "friendly" fire from some inept idiot in the Army of the Republic of Vietnam. Just when he thought the explosions were going to catch up with him, Charlie flopped into the muck, terrified and winded. He heard York scream, "Get down! Everybody down! Down!" And then there was an explosion that seared Charlie's neck and filled the trees with singing shrapnel.

As suddenly as it had started, the shelling stopped. That was war: boredom and sudden terror and then more boredom. Everyone stood up. They could hear men moaning. Jesus, Charlie thought, that could have been us. Me. It took him a minute to realize he'd shit his pants during the barrage. To clean up he quietly waded into a canal up to his waist—snakes and leeches and Abercrombie & Fitch be damned.

He snapped pictures of the downed helicopters. He talked to half a dozen American advisors, who angrily confirmed the obvious: A small, ill-equipped band of guerillas had decimated a modern army that outnumbered them four to one, an army equipped with the best helicopters, planes, machine guns, napalm, and bombs American tax dollars could buy.

Back in Saigon Charlie interviewed American Ambassador Frederick Nolting. Then he attended a press conference called by Admiral Harry Felt, U.S. Commander in the Pacific, and General Paul Harkins, commander of the troops in Vietnam. Harkins had his own ideas about what happened at Ap Bac. "I consider it a victory," he said with a straight face. "We took the objective." When Charlie led the chorus of hostile questions, Admiral Felt snapped at him, "Why don't you get on the team, Malloy?"

After the press conference Charlie had a long talk with Jon Medlin, the United States Information Service flack, who confirmed off the record that the South Vietnamese suffered eighty dead and more than one hundred wounded; three Americans died and eight were wounded. The total Viet Cong body count was eighteen dead, thirty-nine wounded. There was nothing to worry about, Charlie told himself now as he picked up the telephone receiver. Harkins and Nolting and Felt could call it a victory all day and all night, but Charlie had seen with his own eyes that Ap Bac was a good old-fashioned ass-whipping, Viet Cong-style. And that was the story he wrote, though he knew it would be even less popular with his editors in New York than it was with the American brass in Saigon.

Now he croaked into the telephone, "Yup . . ."

"Charlie, it's brother Sam calling from Bangkok. Did I wake you up?"

Charlie sank into the pillows. "No. I mean yeah. What time is it?"

"It's eleven here. Guess it's midnight there. I'm sorry—I didn't realize you were turning in so early these days."

"S'okay." Midnight. He tried to reconstruct the evening. He finished filing his story and left the cable office shortly after 6 o'clock, exhausted from a week of fourteen-hour days and yet curiously alert, as giddy as a child on the last day of the school year. He'd proven to himself—and to the doubters in the Sunset Club—that he still had a few teeth in his head. He decided to swing by the Rex for a couple of belts, unwind a little, he'd earned it. In the lobby of the hotel his eye caught a flash of blond hair at the newsstand. He waited until she paid for her newspaper and turned around. It was Anne Sinclair, Jon Medlin's assistant at USIS and one of Charlie's prize pupils during his sabbatical as a guest lecturer at Berkeley last spring. At last, he thought, the perfect opportunity to clear up a little unfinished business.

"Anne!" he called across the lobby. "Anne Sinclair!"

She spun toward the voice but didn't see him. She looked lovely and vulnerable standing there, like a deer paralyzed by oncoming headlights. Her eyes searched the crowd until she saw the hand waving. When she recognized Charlie she smiled and started toward him.

She'd arrived in Saigon shortly after he did last summer. He saw her at press conferences, at the Rue Catinat milk bars and restaurants, at ribbon-cutting ceremonies; but for some reason, possibly because he was losing his touch, possibly because he was so busy with the Vietnamese bar girls, he hadn't followed up on his promise to buy her a drink. And now she was fighting her way through the crosscurrents of people entering and leaving the hotel, and she was smiling, and Charlie was remembering that afternoon in Berkeley back in the spring of 1962.

It was the last week of classes before final exams. The semester had been just what the doctor ordered for Charlie—no deadlines, no pressure, three seminars a week plus a steady stream of invitations to uproarious cocktail parties, to scintillating dinner parties, to the bedrooms of implausibly imaginative and vigorous co-eds. Most of them were taking that new birth-control pill, and they went at it like there was no tomorrow. Of course he had noticed Anne the first day of class. It would have been hard to miss that waterfall of blond hair, the athletic legs and coltish gait of such prime sack fodder. He simply hadn't gotten around to asking her to lunch until the last week of classes, and he was delighted to find that she was bright and self-assured, full of energy and opinions. She actually had a dream. She wanted to go to work for the Foreign Service and she mentioned, almost apologetically, that her father was a "big Democrat" and he was trying to pull some strings.

After lunch they strolled along Telegraph Avenue, looking in the bookshop windows, neither of them in any particular hurry.

Charlie bought her an ice cream cone. He bought himself a pack of cigarettes. When they reached his corner, Charlie, figuring he had nothing to lose, asked if he could make her a cup of coffee. To his surprise she said yes, and he led the way up to the studio apartment the university had arranged for him to sublet.

Charlie brewed a pot of coffee with Hawaiian Kona beans and poured two cups and joined her on the sofa. They talked for hours as the sun slid across the white-washed walls and the hubbub of Telegraph Avenue drifted up from below. Mostly he told her about the benefits and hazards of working in faraway places, the loneliness, the adventure, the occasional sense of supreme satisfaction. He laid it on thick. The whole time he talked he was watching for the green light, some sign that he could slide six inches closer and start undoing the buttons of her blouse. It never came. She seemed genuinely curious about what it was like to live and work in Africa and Asia—she wanted to know about the people, the customs, the streets, even the food— and just when he finished the last cup of coffee and decided to roll the dice and go for it, the telephone rang.

"I'd better get that," he said with a groan.

"You sure?" Her head was cocked, eyebrows up. Jesus, he thought, the green light's been on all along and I missed it.

"Afraid so." He crossed the room and picked up the telephone. "Hello?"

"Professor!" It was Clem Zablocki, *Time* magazine's foreign editor, and the sugar in his voice told Charlie this was the call he'd been waiting for and the news was going to be bad. "Pack your bags, my boy. Your ticket has been punched for—you ready?"

"Yes, Clem, I'm ready."

"Saigon."

"Sai*gon?*" Charlie felt a stab of panic in his bowels. Was this New York's idea of a joke? He knew nothing about Saigon— unlike, say, Manila or Kuala Lumpur or Brazzaville or Beirut, where he knew the very best restaurants and bars, which sources could be trusted and which could not, where to find a story and where to find a girl. But Saigon? It was nowhere, most Americans couldn't find it on a map. And when he talked to some of the old Asia hands, they all told him the same chilling tale: There was a new breed of reporters and photographers in Saigon, "young huns" was the expression that kept popping up, and they weren't getting their stories the old-fashioned way, from press conferences or embassy flacks or the hotel saloon; they were going out in the paddies and the jungles, getting down in the mud with the American advisors and South Vietnamese troops, they were riding in planes and helicopters and sometimes they were winding up where the fire was very hot. "Saigon?" Charlie repeated numbly. "Clem, you've got to be pulling my leg."

"I couldn't possibly be more serious, old boy."

"Does the Proprietor know about this?"

"Of course he does. It was Mr. Luce's idea."

"Did I do something to piss him off?"

"Quite the contrary. This is his idea of a plum assignment. All his gurus—from Henry Cabot Lodge on down—are telling him that Vietnam's going to be the next big thing."

"How do you know that, Clem?"

"Because he told me so at lunch yesterday."

"Where'd he take you?"

"To the Union League Club, of course."

Charlie knew this meant it had, indeed, been a high-level chat. When the staff writers in Henry Luce's empire went out for lunch, they favored pedestrian locales such as Toots Shor's and Lindy's. But when there was something big bothering the Proprietor—Henry Luce was known as Harry to his friends and as the Proprietor to his employees—it meant a long luncheon at the swank Union League Club. So this was serious. And very, very bad.

Charlie Malloy's passport bore stamps from the world's hottest trouble spots. He'd nearly gotten short-listed for the Pulitzer Prize in 1953 for his coverage of Ramon Magsaysay's successful campaign against the communist Huk rebels in the Philippines, a performance that caught the eye of staunchly anti-communist Henry Luce and won Charlie his release from the Associated Press and his entry into the elite corps of *Time*'s foreign correspondents. His first assignment was big—Malaya during the

Emergency in the mid-fifties. He reported with great brio how the communist insurgents were flushed from the jungle and annihilated. Luce was delighted. After that Charlie landed in Lebanon with the Marines in '58. He was in the Congo in '61 when UN Secretary General Dag Hammarskjöld flew in for talks with Moise Tshombe. Fortunately, Charlie was on a three-day drunk in a Brazzaville gambling den at the time. Several reporters, including some seasoned veterans, cabled their papers that they'd seen Hammarskjöld arrive safely under cover of darkness at the airport in Ndola, Rhodesia. But there was a mixup. The white man who deplaned that night at Ndola was not Hammarskjöld. The Secretary General's plane had crashed and he was already dead. Charlie sobered up in time to get the story straight, and his career received yet another boost. His editors agreed he deserved a breather, a one-semester sabbatical lecturing undergraduates at Berkeley. Sometimes, Charlie told Anne Sinclair and her awestruck classmates, the best reporter is the one who has a sixth sense that tells him when not to write a word.

And now, after one too-brief semester of R&R at Berkeley, the Proprietor wanted him to cover some insignificant skirmish in some insignificant jungle halfway around the world. Charlie looked at the young blonde on the sofa. She was flipping through a *National Geographic* and her skirt had ridden up over her knees. The magazine contained photographs of landfills, cornfields, bats, the camels of Oman. He could see white peach fuzz scurrying up the insides of her thighs. She had said something about being a teenage tennis champion, and with those legs it was no wonder. Skull-crushers, Charlie thought. She looked up and caught him licking his lips.

"In fact," Clem Zablocki was saying, "the way the Proprietor's talking, you'd think your reporting was what whipped the commies in the Philippines and Malaya."

Charlie started to say Mr. Luce would not be entirely mistaken if he held such a belief, but every time Anne flipped a page in the magazine, her skirt rode a little higher. He bit his lip and said nothing.

"He told me as soon as you get your hat trick you can have Washington," Zablocki said.

"What the fuck is a hat trick, Clem?"

"You know, it's when a hockey player scores three goals in one game. You bag your third band of communist insurgents while you're in Vietnam and you'll be able to name your next mailing address—Washington, London, take your pick."

When Charlie hung up the phone, Anne dropped the magazine on the coffee table and stood up. She said she had to run off to her job at the library. Charlie was too devastated to put up a fight. The next time he saw her was six weeks later at a ribbon-cutting ceremony for the newest strategic hamlet in the Mekong Delta, a shameless, government-sponsored dog-and-pony show conducted under a merciless sun. And now here she was, coming across the lobby of the Rex Hotel, an *International Herald Tribune* tucked under her arm and a look of delight radiating from her face.

"How about that drink you keep promising me," she said, shaking his hand.

"Yes, it's long overdue," Charlie said. "God knows I could use a drink after the week I've just been through."

"Did you file an Ap Bac story?"

"Yeah. About broke my back." Though he was six feet tall, she was looking him dead in the eye. She was wearing oxblood pumps and a creamy, sleeveless linen dress. The hair on her arms was golden, almost white.

"Where to?" she said.

Charlie considered the gang on the roof. They would be at full throttle by now. He said, "You hungry?"

"I'm always hungry."

"I know a place in Cholon that has the coldest martinis and the best cracked crabs in Southeast Asia."

"The Diamond?"

"You know the place?"

"I love the place. And Henry Luce is buying, right?"

"Right."

Charlie hailed a taxi out on Le Loi. It was one of the little blue Renaults, as pudgy as a ladybug. *"Le Diamond, en Cholon,"* he told the driver.

He and Anne barely fit into the back seat. The hem of her dress rode up over her knees, and Charlie thought of that afternoon in his apartment in Berkeley. The wind pouring through the car's open windows was like the breath of a blast furnace, and whenever they stopped for a red light Anne patted a handkerchief against her forehead and upper lip.

Halfway to Cholon the driver pulled over and stopped. *"Un moment, monsieur et madame."* He reached into the glove box and pulled out a quart bottle of gasoline. While he poured it into the tank, Charlie caught the scent of Anne's perfume. Gardenias?

"I love the way these people get around gas rationing," she said. Charlie detected genuine admiration in her smile.

At the Diamond they drank martinis and beer and ate a gloriously messy pile of crabs and caught up on each other's lives. Then they stopped by La Cigale, where the singer, a brooding Vietnamese named Miss Yen Hung, reminded Anne of Joan Baez. Then they went dancing at Dai Kim Do, one of the city's biggest dancehalls, which was cavernous and empty and sad, thanks to Madame Nhu's ban on racy dancing. But the orchestra played some big-band numbers Charlie vaguely recognized through the martini fog, and the lights were low, and dancing with Anne Sinclair was like dancing on a cloud.

And that was the last thing he remembered about the evening . . .

"Would you like me to call back in the morning?" his brother Sam was saying over the telephone.

"No, no, no. I'm fine. What's up?" Only then did Charlie realize he had a headache, a hot pressure behind his eyeballs. He was fully dressed, except for his jacket, which somehow had wound up on the desk. He needed a glass of water.

"I talked with Ed the other day," Sam said, "and he seemed to think you were down in the dumps. Is everything okay?"

Charlie lifted the dented pillow from the other side of the bed. He held it to his face and inhaled. Yes, it was gardenias. Like dancing on a cloud . . . He tried to remember when he'd talked with his brother in New York. It was the day after he got back from Ap Bac.

"You still there, Charlie?"

"Yeah. I was just trying to remember—Ed caught me at a bad time. I'd just gotten back from the Delta. Almost got my ass blown off."

Sam laughed at this.

"You think that's funny?" Charlie said.

"No, Charlie, I'm sorry. I just didn't realize they let you old warhorses get down in the mud with the grunts."

"Very fucking funny. A guy standing ten yards away from me got blown in two. His head wound up in a tree. I was scared shitless."

"Tell me about it."

"What the hell's that supposed to mean?"

"Nothing, Charlie. Let's drop it. I guess I can tell Ed to quit worrying—you're the same ornery old fart you always were."

Charlie managed a conciliatory chuckle. "Yeah, you tell him I'm doing fine. I finished off a big story last night and then I went out dancing with *the* most beautiful girl in all of Saigon . . ."

"Same old Charlie. Go back to sleep."

"Will do. Thanks for calling."

After he hung up, Charlie swung his feet off the bed and stood up. The room spun. It smelled of ammonia and ashtrays and new carpet. Over the purr of the air conditioner he heard the thud of distant mortar fire, the wail of a siren. He was in the middle of another war, all right, and as he finished undressing he realized that the boys at the Sunset Club were right. They were all in on the ground floor of a nice nasty little war, and based on what he'd seen at Ap Bac, it was getting ready to get a whole lot nastier.

5

Talking to his brother hadn't been as bad as Sam had expected. He got a good laugh out of the thought of Charlie under fire, 225 pounds of expense-account blubber hauling ass through a rice paddy, a nice plump piece of target practice for those little fuckers in their black pajamas. He wondered if Charlie had actually seen a man get his face blown into a tree and, if so, what kind of fire he'd been under. It must have been some sort of artillery. The Viet Cong now had artillery in the Delta? Sam knew the good old days of helicopters returning from missions with arrows stuck in their fuselages were long gone, and he knew that the recent infusion of American aid had helped the Viet Cong upgrade from their bolt-action French rifles to new weapons seized from the worthless South Vietnamese army— M-1s, Thompson submachine guns and Browning automatic rifles. But artillery? In the Delta? The war must have been going even worse than Sam expected.

He turned out the light and tried to go to sleep. But he kept thinking about his brother. *I've been out drinking and dancing with the most beautiful girl in all of Saigon . . .* The women in Charlie's life were always "girls," even the ones who were his age, pushing forty, and no longer girlish in any sense of the word. Sam understood why: It was because Charlie still thought of himself as a boy, a perpetual American boy who believed that the athletic and sexual conquests of his youth happened just the other day, a man who had marched effortlessly from green ballfields to green fairways, from milkshakes to martinis, from puppy love to the latest mistress, without for a minute doubting that this procession was his birthright, his destiny. He was bred to be an ageless American boy, and it struck Sam as perfection that this boy had wound up in Saigon reporting on a war he knew nothing about, drinking like a fish, fucking as many brown girls as he possibly could, and hanging out with those noisy bastards on the roof of the Rex Hotel.

Of course, Charlie fit right in with the Sunset Club. It was his natural habitat—the lockerroom bravado, the gook jokes and war gossip and predictable laments about the bad marriages back home. Like the men who were waging this war, the correspondents covering it saw themselves as cowboys. But Sam saw them for what they truly were: lost souls on the wrong side of the world.

He could still see the 5 o'clock shadow, as blue as a bruise, on that jaw he'd come so close to breaking. To think the guy thought he was clever for thinking Sam was CIA. After that night Sam did his drinking alone, in a little corner café on Thi Sach, not far from the river but well off the press corps' beaten path. It was dark and dirty—he once saw a cat saunter across the tile floor dragging a huge rat—and the Vietnamese proprietor, Nguyen Tat Thanh, was always eager to practice his English. And best of all, it was a neighborhood hangout so there were never any Americans, which meant there were fewer kids trying to hustle lottery tickets, language books and shoeshines. It was the perfect place for Sam to forget what had just happened to him and to wait for what came next.

One evening, while drinking beer and reading the hilarious government propaganda in *The Times of Vietnam*, Sam looked up and was surprised to see an American sitting alone at the corner table writing furiously on a yellow legal pad. He had to be a reporter because he was wearing those black-rimmed glasses they all wore and a short-sleeved shirt and a thin necktie and scuffed brown wingtips. Only an American reporter would wear wingtips in Saigon. Inky curls spilled off the man's head, and he had to keep shoving them out of his eyes as he wrote. Something about this man was familiar. Sam picked up his beer and newspaper and walked over to his table. "Mind a little company?"

The man looked up, startled. The lenses of his eyeglasses were like ashtrays. He slipped the legal pad onto his lap. "Sure. I mean no. Here, have a seat."

"What's that you're working on?" Sam asked, pulling up a chair. The man was drinking Coca-Cola with ice. A brave man or a fool, Sam thought.

"It's a story . . ."

"About what?"

The eyes narrowed, like a pair of magnified fish mouths closing in unison. "That depends. Who're you with?"

"Who am I *with?*"

"Yeah, you know, which paper or wire service? Or are you government?"

Sam laughed. "I'm not with anybody at the moment."

"Oh, so you're a freelancer too. Put her there." He held out his hand and Sam shook it. It was cold and tender. The man looked down at the notebook on his lap. "This story I'm working on's for *Harper's* magazine. It's kinda technical—it's about the Commercial Import Program. You know anything about it?"

"Can't say I do. Never even heard of it."

"Do you have contracts for your articles, or are you just winging it?"

"Actually, I'm not a freelance writer. I just got discharged from the Navy—had to spend some time in the hospital. I'm hanging around with my brother till my visa runs out or I figure out what to do with myself, whichever comes first."

"I see. What's your brother doing in Saigon?"

"He works for *Time* magazine. He's—"

"You're *Charlie Malloy's* brother? Too weird!" He almost shot out of his chair. The four men playing mah-jong across the room looked up, then went back to their game.

"Yeah, I'm Charlie's brother. Is that good or bad?"

"I guess it depends. He is the most famous reporter in town now that the *Times* has replaced Homer Bigart. Then again, he does work for *Time* magazine—which means Henry Luce signs his paychecks . . ."

Sam had to laugh. "I haven't even introduced myself. I'm Sam Malloy."

"I figured. You don't even recognize me, do you?"

"No—but you look familiar . . ."

"I'm Morey Caan—the guy who wrote the article about all those Buicks on your street in Levittown."

"Aha! Stay here! Don't move!"

Sam dashed around the corner to his hotel and fetched the clipping of Morey's article on the Lindbergh Street Buicks. When he saw the two-page picture of the Buicks, with grease-ball Sam perched on the trunk of the second car, Morey howled with glee.

They sat there until midnight talking about everything—cars, rock 'n' roll, President Kennedy, Asian women, the war—while drinking glass after glass of beer and reveling in the weird coincidence of meeting in this dingy café on the far side of the world so many years after fate and a yellow Buick first brought them together. After half a dozen beers Morey confessed that the *Harper's* article was merely his cover, that the real reason he'd come to Saigon was to do research for a book on the U.S. Information Service. He and Jon Medlin, the new head of the USIS office in Saigon, had been reporters here in the mid-1950s, covering the departure of the French—in fact, Morey had taken that job as soon as he'd finished the Levittown article for *Life*. And now he was back because he was convinced that telling Medlin's story was the perfect way to tell the larger story of how America was blundering its way into this war.

"This guy Medlin's got a big-time conflict, see," Morey said. "He's all about duty and loyalty and love of the flag, but deep down he's already figured out the whole thing's rotten—the Diem regime, the South Vietnamese army, all this American money and official optimism. I'm sleeping on the sofa in his villa, and every night he comes home from work and pours his guts out. I've never seen anyone so frustrated. Eventually he's going to have to go on-the-record with somebody, or he'll explode. I'm hoping that somebody is me."

At last, Sam thought, an American who has an inkling of what's actually happening in this sad doomed land.

Later, as they were saying beery good-nights on the sidewalk in front of Sam's hotel, Morey said something that was destined to change Sam's life: "Have you ever looked out at these streets and imagined what it would look like if one of those '54 Buicks drove past?"

"No, I can't say as I have."

"Well think about it, man . . ." His voice grew dreamy. "All that chrome . . . those Dagmar bumpers . . . those creamy paintjobs . . . right here in old Asia . . . it would be *fantastic!*"

The next day Sam got the call from Rat in Bangkok, the invitation to join him in the hotel business at no financial risk. All he had to do was show up and they would be partners, fifty-fifty. Now, lying in bed on the top floor of that hotel, he knew that his chance meeting with Morey Caan was the reason those seven Buicks were in Bangkok, parked in the godown across the alley. Tomorrow the Buicks would get their first test—and Sam would find out if he was a visionary or a lunatic. He was too wound up to sleep. He felt like he used to feel in high school the night before a big game, his mind racing in maddening loops. Maybe he should have gone after that Thai woman, the new one with the short skirt and the big moist eyes and the tiny breasts, the one who'd spent the evening at the hotel bar laughing at the Major's stories while crossing and recrossing her legs and giving Sam the eye. Too late now. Surely someone had snagged her. It struck Sam as a shame that Charlie Malloy had the most influential writing job in Saigon while Morey Caan, a lowly freelancer, was the one who understood what was actually happening. Sam rolled onto his stomach so he wouldn't have to watch the rotating blades of the ceiling fan. It wasn't his problem. It was no longer his war.

6

Neh Lim was among the richest Chinese merchants in Bangkok, but that was only one of the reasons he felt so magnanimous on his daughter's wedding day. Weng Ju was his fifth and last child, and the four that came before her were all boys—good boys, as it turned out, who married into good Chinese families and went to work in the family business and had already given Neh Lim nine grandchildren, including seven grandsons, a wealth of blessings that overshadowed all of his cars and gold and jade, the big house on Sampaeng Lane, even his factory that backed up to Klong Ong Ang and produced the tin cans that were used for all the cooking oil sold in Thailand, a monopoly that had made him astonishingly rich and guaranteed the family's security for many generations to come.

So Neh Lim had decided to indulge Weng Ju on her wedding day. He allowed her to consult a famous blind astrologer and fêng shui expert in Thonburi to set the date. Since the groom was Thai, a teacher at an international high school, Neh Lim consented to a wedding ceremony that broke from tradition by blending Chinese, Thai and Western customs. The bride wore a white gown made of Swiss cloth and carried a bouquet of white orchids even though white is the Chinese color of mourning. The bridesmaids wore newly fashionable but highly unconventional pink dresses. The groom wore a dark Western suit. In keeping with Chinese custom, the groom sent gifts to the bride's family home. In keeping with Thai custom, there was a water-pouring ceremony the morning of the wedding presided over by nine Buddhist monks who chanted, sprinkled holy water on the bridal couple and blessed everyone associated with the wedding. And then, after the ceremony, the families of the bride and groom would board seven gleaming Buicks provided by the White Elephant Hotel and they would lead the wedding party's motorcade to the Erawan Hotel, where there was to be a lavish dinner followed by dancing and drinking and carousing until dawn.

Though weddings were the financial responsibility of the groom's family under Thai custom, Neh Lim insisted on paying for everything, including rental of the Buicks. He had passed his seventieth birthday, his health was beginning to fail, and he sensed that this was going to be his last chance to repay the many people who had made his life so rich and full.

Of course he invited the Prime Minister, Field Marshal Sarit Thanarat, who had come to power six years earlier in one of those bloodless coups the Thais seemed to stage with the nonchalance and regularity of birthday parties. Shortly after the coup, Sarit had awarded Neh Lim the concession on tin cans and he had taken for himself the concession on all rice sacks used in Thailand. Their fortunes had blossomed together, and Neh Lim would never forget his debt to Sarit. He also invited all the people who had contributed to his family's success and happiness over the years—the children's teachers, the neighborhood police and merchants, the lantern makers and musicians and monks and dressmakers, his many business associates. And in renting the seven Buicks from Shwe Winn's son-in-law, he hoped to do one last favor for the old woman who had married his best friend, Nguan Wong, just before they all fled China together back in 1935. The three of them arrived in this strange city, terrified and dirt-poor, and shared a tiny apartment on Sampaeng Lane. Shwe Winn had been like a second mother to

Neh Lim's boys, a nurse, baby-sitter, teacher, showering them with the affection for the sons she never had.

For Sam Malloy, Neh Lim's decision to rent all seven Buicks for the biggest social event of the season was both a blessing and a curse. He couldn't have afforded to buy the publicity the wedding would give him; but Sam had a problem that was staggering in its simplicity and complexity.

He didn't have enough people to drive all seven Buicks.

Rat was the only Thai Sam would trust. The cars were simply too big, the streets were too narrow and, to top it off, Thais drove on the left side of the road, which meant the left-side steering wheels would make it that much trickier to negotiate the city's kamikaze traffic.

Fortunately, the blind astrologer had decreed that the wedding must be held on the third Sunday in January, which meant the two new residents at the White Elephant, the American foreign aid officer Phil Greene and the Texas businessman George O'Phelan, would be free to drive two of the cars. Then there was the Major, provided he didn't have one of his crippling hangovers.

But that meant Sam still needed two more drivers. He awoke panicked on the day of the wedding, trying to think of someone he could trust. It was too late to call his brother or Morey Caan in Saigon. He went down to breakfast convinced the Buicks' maiden outing was doomed to failure, that the doubters had been right. In Asia, the ensuing loss of face would be a disaster from which he could never hope to recover.

When he entered the dining room, Jiap ran up to his table with a pot of coffee. "Great news!" she cried, pulling up a chair and filling his cup.

"Neh Lim canceled the wedding?"

"Hell no."

Sam looked at her. She never showed her face this early and she was rarely civil before noon, but there she sat, beaming. She was so pretty when she smiled, the pulpy lips peeling back to reveal pink gums and dazzling white teeth, a lurid yet curiously sexy smile. Her hair fell to her waist, so black it was almost blue, lit from within. Even Thais complimented her on her hair.

Looking at her across his steaming cup of coffee, Sam found it easy to believe she had once ruled the bars on Gaysorn Road, where she won a reputation as a sexual tornado and a heart crusher.

"American couple checks in last night," Jiap said. Her English was getting better, but she was still stuck in the present tense. "They don't even have suitcases—carry clothes on they back."

"Great," Sam grunted.

"I ask if they know how to drive and they say, sure, everybody in America know how to drive. They have not enough money to pay for room, so I put them in Bungalow 9 and tell them we work something out in the morning. Tell them maybe they run errands to pay bill. They happy with idea."

Sam felt a smile spreading across his face. Then he saw a young couple stride into the dining room. The girl's hair was dirty blond—dirty in the sense that it needed shampoo—and she parted it in the middle and held it in place with a rawhide string, which she wrapped around her head Last of the Mohicans–style. Silver bracelets jangled from her wrists. The boy's hair was a gigantic cloud of yellow steel wool, and he needed a shave. What the hell, Sam thought, we have plenty of shampoo and razors and soap. Beggars can't be choosers. He rose to meet his saviors.

Their names were Kim and Carl and they were taking a one-year sabbatical from Penn State to bum their way across Asia. They'd just come from Kathmandu by way of Mandalay and Rangoon, and after spending a few days in Bangkok they planned to cross Cambodia to Saigon, then continue on to Borneo, maybe Manila or Hong Kong. They were so enthusiastic that Sam didn't have the heart to ask if they'd heard there was a war going on in Vietnam. No sense raining on their parade. As he tucked into a plate of eggs laced with onions and garlic and thermonuclear "rat turd" chilis, Sam realized these intrepid travelers were the first people who'd ever made him feel old.

Two hours later the seven Buicks were lined up outside the wedding hall, a garish Chinese social club at the foot of Sampaeng Lane, which Neh Lim had built and paid for with cash.

The club was a refuge for the neighborhood men, a place for them to play checkers and mah-jong and gamble and get drunk while their wives stayed home. A huge crowd had gathered to stare at the cars. The signature white-on-white Buick was first in line. The driver's door had been decorated with the hotel's logo, an elephant with a crown on its head, plus the hotel's name and phone number in Thai, Chinese and English. Sam would take the bride and groom to the reception in this car. Rat would bring up the rear in the Brunswicks' pink-and-black Buick.

There were so many photographers that the police had roped them off like cattle in the shade of a flame tree. At first Sam thought the photographers had come out because the Prime Minister was attending the wedding, but then he noticed that they were all snapping pictures of the Buicks. There was even a television cameraman shooting footage. Sam was beginning to get a warm feeling about this day.

Suddenly the doors of the social club burst open and the bride and groom came trotting down the stairs, pushed by cacophonous Chinese music. They were followed by their parents, then their siblings and other relatives, and then by Shwe Winn, who had consented to having her hair curled and fluffed, a bit of vanity no one dreamed she had in her. There was a roar from the crowd, the banging of gongs and the pop of firecrackers, and suddenly someone in the wedding party, Americans or possibly Australians, started tossing rice on the newlyweds. This was greeted with a mixture of shock and horror—the *farangs* were throwing food at the bride!—and when Sam saw Shwe Winn's face he was afraid she was going to get down on her hands and knees and start scooping up the grains of rice that kept raining on her from the top of the stairs. Mercifully the Major swooped in with his arm cocked and led Shwe Winn to the fourth Buick in line, the one with the flashy Cherokee Red and black paintjob.

Sam felt better and better as he guided the white Buick down Sampaeng Lane and left onto New Road. The omens were splendid. The newlyweds were together in the back seat, cooing like a couple of doves. The Bangkok air, usually a fogbank of fumes at this time of day, was clear, almost crackling. Sam had worried about the traffic, but the wedding procession had a wedge of police motorcycles to lead the way and there were cops at every intersection blocking cross traffic so the procession could pass unimpeded. They never even had to stop for a traffic light. It was the sort of treatment usually reserved for dignitaries—the King and Queen of Belgium, or a diplomat, or the president of Firestone Tire Company. Neh Lim must have spent a small fortune just paying off the police.

The route had been chosen with great care. After passing through Chinatown, they veered toward the river, then right on Maharat Road, which took them past the white-washed, crenelated wall of the Grand Palace compound. The golden spires shot up from behind the wall, a dazzling blur in the sunshine. After circling the compound, the procession headed out Bamrung Muang Road. Sam had to step on the gas to keep up with the police motorcycles. It was thrilling to fly down a street in the heart of this congested city as crowds packed the sidewalks, gaping and pointing and laughing.

All seven Buicks made it to the Erawan Hotel safely, and as the reception rose to its full roar Sam found himself standing in front of the hotel being interviewed by reporters from *The Bangkok Post*, Agence France Presse, Reuters, UPI, even BBC World Service. More photographers snapped pictures of the Buicks. So, Sam thought, I'm not a lunatic after all.

When the interviews ended, Sam decided he deserved a drink. In the hotel ballroom the path to the bar was blocked by a bunch of drunk young Thais and by a tall white man with a pencil mustache, high forehead, and rolling waves of hair. He was gripping a cocktail, pink-eyed, a little wobbly on his pins. A Brit, Sam assumed. But the man's right hand came out and he said, in one of those indeterminate American accents that could have come from Delaware or Denver, "Good evening, Sam. I've been wanting to meet you. Alex McDougal, editor of *The Bangkok Post*."

"Nice to meet you," Sam said, shaking the hand and calling to the bartender for a beer. The drunk Thais were jostling each

other, howling with laughter, spilling their drinks. Sam wondered how long it would be before the first fight broke out.

"Did my reporter treat you decently?" McDougal asked.

"That'll depend on what he writes," Sam said, draining half
of his beer.

"Yes," he said, chuckling, "I suppose it will." Sam noticed
the hand gripping the cocktail had stubby fingers and thick, flat
nails, the hands of a workingman, not a newspaperman. Sam
got the uneasy feeling he was about to hear some kind of pitch.
"I suppose you're wondering why it is that I've been wanting
to meet you."

"Hadn't given it much thought, to tell you the truth," Sam
said, taking another long drink.

"Well, I'll tell you anyway. I've heard talk that you were
involved in some clandestine activity." The stubby fingers
strummed the sweating cocktail glass. When Sam said nothing,
McDougal pressed on. "In Laos, was it? Or North Viet—"

"Look, Mr. McDonald—"

"*McDougal.* Alex McDougal."

"Look, Mr. McDougal, you hear a lot of talk in this town and
I'm sure you've been around long enough to know that most
of it deserves to be ignored."

"No need to get defensive, sport."

"I'm not getting defensive."

"Look, Sam, it's not what you're thinking. For starters, I'm a
gentleman editor. Anything we discuss is strictly off the
record."

"We haven't discussed anything."

"I'm not speaking as a newspaper editor. I'm speaking as . . .
well, I suppose I'm speaking as a curious old spook. One spook
to another, so to speak. You see, I was with the OSS with Bill
Donovan in Ceylon at the end of World War Two. As a matter
of fact, I was on a plane on my way to Bangkok to set up a radio
network when we got word the war had ended. But I fell in
love with Bangkok the instant I stepped off that plane." Sam
was trying to get the bartender's attention, but McDougal
pressed on with his story. "I'll bet you didn't know that Jim

Thompson, the silk man here in Bangkok, was with the OSS, too . . ."

Everyone in the ballroom started applauding suddenly, and Sam saw the bride and groom coming through the crowd, heading for the exit. God bless them, Sam thought.

He set down his empty beer glass. "It's been a pleasure meeting you, Mr. McDougal, but I've got to take these two home now. They've got a marriage to consummate." He shook McDougal's hand. "And I hate to burst your bubble, but I am not a spook, I have never been a spook, and I will never be a spook. I hate fucking spooks. I was in the U.S. Navy. Sorry."

But later, after he'd delivered the bride and groom to their new home, after he'd locked all seven Buicks safely in the go-down and opened the hotel bar for the drivers who'd helped make the day such a smashing success, Sam kept thinking about Alex McDougal. It reminded him of that reporter on the roof of the Rex Hotel in Saigon. No matter how much Sam drank, he couldn't get McDougal out of his mind, that oily smile, those thick fingernails. *One spook to another, so to speak . . .* If it's true that there are no secrets in Asia, Sam told himself, it's also true that there are no facts; and therefore any rumor, especially a rumor in the hands of a newspaper editor who used to be a spook, was destined to become common knowledge and acquire the aura of fact. As the other drivers grew raucous and merry, Sam began to despair. He was beginning to understand that forgetting the past completely was as impossible as remembering it accurately.

Sam was getting blackly drunk, losing the thread of Carl and Kim's story about smoking opium in Kathmandu, when the door opened and the Thai woman with the short skirt and the big moist eyes walked up to the bar like she owned the place.

"We're closed," Sam yelled.

"The hell we are!" the Major roared. His face was as red as a cranberry. "Nok is my personal guest and she shall have whatever she pleases."

"Whisky-lah," she said, smiling at Sam.

Sam went behind the bar and poured her a double Johnnie

Walker Black. "On the house," he said. "Please forgive my rudeness."

"You are forgiven."

After two drinks she wound up in Sam's room, where she spent the rest of the night proving to him that it was possible, after all, to forget the past. At least until the sun came up.

Though she was running late for her 10 o'clock appointment at the American Embassy, Anne Sinclair stopped at the Rex Hotel newsstand to buy a copy of *The International Herald Tribune*. The paper was delivered to her office at noon, but she liked to have her own copy to take home at the end of the day so she could spread it out on the kitchen table, brew a pot of green tea, and savor the paper one story at a time. It was one of the little rituals, the little luxuries, that were becoming increasingly vital to her sanity.

As she entered the hotel lobby she realized the past two weeks had been the worst since her arrival in Saigon. Overnight the uproar over the battle at Ap Bac had turned Jon Medlin from a lamb into a monster. Two weeks ago he was the ideal boss, relaxed and encouraging, knowledgeable about Vietnam and the Vietnamese, good company after business hours, always the first to reach for the check. She could understand how he might get driven to distraction by the American reporters, by the way they stormed into his office and *demanded* information or corroboration, statistics or denials. They were such pious pains in the ass, as her father would have put it. So Jon could be forgiven for having a shorter-than-usual fuse. But why the secrecy all of a sudden? His office door, which had always been open, remained shut for the past four days. She had heard reporters shouting behind that door and she had heard Jon shouting right back.

One day, as the staff looked on horrified, he blistered the Vietnamese maid for not emptying his wastebasket often enough. The poor woman was so devastated by the loss of face that when Jon went into his office and slammed the door, she turned and, without a word, walked out into the street. That was the last anyone saw of her. The next day a grenade went off outside the building, slightly injuring an old man and the boy who was shining his shoes. Anne was beginning to understand why the U.S. State Department had just re-classified Vietnam a "maximum hardship" post.

As she stood in line at the newsstand she glanced at the front page of *The Herald Trib*. A picture of some sort of parade. Castro mocking President Kennedy for paying ransom to free captives from the botched Bay of Pigs invasion. Carl Sandburg celebrating his eighty-fifth birthday. James Meredith announcing he won't return to Ole Miss next semester. No Vietnam stories: perfect: no bad press to apologize for when she sat down with the Ambassador.

She crossed Le Loi and, after checking her watch, picked up her pace. Sweat sprang to her pores. The barbers along this stretch of Rue Pasteur were doing brisk business. They hung their mirrors on the stone wall that ran the length of the block, and some had erected little canopies so their customers could enjoy a scrap of shade while the scissors chattered and the trimmings fluttered to the sidewalk. She loved this about Vietnam, the way everything was so public. Eating, pissing, getting a haircut, even getting a tooth pulled—it all happened right out there for the whole world to see. One morning, while sitting in a café and drinking the most delicious cup of coffee she'd ever tasted, she watched a woman in an immaculate pink silk suit walk in off the street, take a knife from behind the counter, then walk outside and squat on the sidewalk and calmly slit the throats of three chickens. After draining their blood into a bowl, she tossed the flopping birds onto the sidewalk and resumed her conversation with another woman. It was so shockingly casual. And once, over on Ha Va Trung, she had walked past just as a man with pliers yanked a pink molar out of another man's mouth. Before she looked away she noticed that the man's arms were tied to the chair and a gaggle of children were standing nearby, pointing at him and giggling at his misery.

Two girls approached her now, holding hands, chatting excitedly. Their matching blue *ao dais* struck Anne as the perfect expression of the Vietnamese character—the graceful, billowing, palazzo-style pants and the tunic with long sleeves and mandarin collar, split up the sides to reveal triangular scraps of flesh above the waist. Somehow it was both sexy and supremely modest, sexy *because* it was supremely modest. No self-respecting Vietnamese woman would dream of going topless at a Saigon pool or one of the South China Sea beaches, as most of the European women and a few brave Americans did. Shedding teeth or hair in public was one thing; shedding clothes was another. Anne often wondered how she would look in an *ao dai*, and more than once she'd been tempted to walk into a shop and try one on. She was thin enough, but big-boned, too tall, and too broad in the shoulders. Besides, that was a line she had vowed not to cross. There was nothing more pathetic than a Westerner trying to go native in Asia, tricked up in sandals, an *ao dai*, a *sari*, a *pakhoman*. There was something about bone structure, about body hair and smell and movement, that could never be translated. When people tried, it was so sad and so wrong. The only thing more appalling to her was the sight—the increasingly common sight—of a Vietnamese woman strutting around the streets in a Western blouse, spike heels and tight jeans, her face painted up like she'd been burned, or beaten. Why were people so eager to adopt the ill-fitting masks of strangers?

She turned the corner onto Ham Nghi and the American Embassy rose before her: That clot of cement looked like a gigantic bird dropping. It was a firetrap with wooden floors and cramped, airless offices. Its only virtue was that there were no windows on the ground floor and steel grates covered the windows on the second and third floors, which made the building relatively grenade-proof. The Ambassador's sixth-floor office was a mixed blessing: He was well out of grenade range, but he would be the last one out if the building went up in flames.

Dodging charcoal carts, beggars, bicycles, motorscooters and a covey of orange-robed monks, she made it across Ham Nghi in one piece and pushed through the front door. The Marine on guard duty was a whiskerless boy, no older than eighteen, and Anne wondered if her brother would ever have to come over here to fight. Not likely, she told herself. Everyone was saying the Americans would be gone in two more years, certainly no later than the end of '65. Just the other night she was having a drink on the roof of the Rex when she overheard a gang of reporters singing a song to the tune of "Twinkle, Twinkle Little Star." Drunkenly they bellowed: "We are winning, this I know. General Harkins told me so. If you doubt me, who are you? McNamara says so, too." She had to cover her face with a napkin so they couldn't see her laughing.

The Marine glanced at her I.D. card and buzzed her through the bullet-proof door and she started climbing the long flights to the Ambassador's office. She hated this building. Every time she passed the drones in their cells, busy typing memos, shuffling papers and trying to climb the rococo Foreign Service career ladder, she was reminded that the only reason she was here, her only qualification for her job as assistant to the director of the United States Information Service, was that her father was the sort of man who saw to it that people owed him favors. If it hadn't been for him, she would still be in California, probably in grad school, married, pregnant—and stuck.

The odd thing about her father was that for such an ardent Democrat he'd been slow in coming around to John Kennedy. Her father liked to say that in his heart he was a New Dealer, and for this reason he favored Lyndon Johnson in the early stages of the 1960 campaign—"Mr. Fix It," he called Johnson— with his mastery of the Senate and his ties to the old New Deal. Also, her father distrusted Kennedy's money, thought Adlai Stevenson was a hopeless marshmallow, and had no feelings about Stuart Symington because he did not believe the man had a prayer of getting elected.

That all began to change with a phonecall in the spring of 1960. Anne happened to be in the front hallway at the time, and she answered on the second ring.

"Is Arthur Sinclair in?" the caller asked. What struck Anne as odd was not that the man had some sort of New England accent, but that he had called her father Arthur. Everyone called him Artie—family, friends, ranch hands, even people who feared or despised him. That had always amused Anne because her father was the least artistic, the least "arty," man she had ever known. He hadn't gone to college, and though he was well read, particularly in politics and history, he had the leathery face and hands of a man who'd spent his life outdoors, working under the scorching California sun. He was all about the nuts and bolts of things, about how an automatic transmission or a bass lure or a thunderstorm worked. While he enjoyed listening to Chopin and sipping port in the evening, what he truly loved was figuring out "what makes people tick," as he put it, what people wanted and how they went after it and why they succeeded or failed. Knowing these things was the surest way to acquire power, and in the end, power was what mattered to Artie Sinclair. He was an equally avid student of combustion engines and political conventions, and it was said that he could fix absolutely anything. Including an election. He'd been elected sheriff of Sonoma County with 51 percent of the vote in 1922, and people in a position to know said that an awful lot of Democrats living several feet underground somehow managed to vote for Artie Sinclair that year, and some of them found the energy to vote more than once.

He was one of the half dozen most powerful Democrats in California by the spring of 1960, when he stepped down as state party chairman. By then he didn't need a title (though he did retain his delegate seat to the national convention because he'd been a delegate at every Democratic convention since the party nominated Al Smith in 1928, and he intended to attend every convention until the day he died). In 1960 the handlers of all the presidential candidates took turns marching up onto the broad front porch of the ranch house near Sebastopol to seek his advice and blessing. He sat out there listening, saying very little, just staring off at the hills where his Black Angus cattle grazed and where his apples and pecans and grapes grew, those burnished hills dotted with live oaks. "My golden hills," he called them, and few people failed to understand his meaning.

He picked up the extension in the kitchen, and for some reason Anne didn't hang up the receiver in the hall.

"Hullo?" He was eating something.

"Arthur Sinclair?" the caller asked.

"Call me Artie. Everyone calls me Artie. Who's this?"

"This is Robert Kennedy, Artie. I was, ah, wondering if the candidate might stop and, ah, have a word with you when we're in California next week."

"Which candidate?" He was still chewing, obviously enjoying himself.

"My brother. Senator Kennedy."

"Senator John Kennedy?"

"That's, ah, correct." The voice was growing thin.

A lunch was arranged. Anne's mother, Esmeralda, was frantic. She may have been the daughter of the largest landowner in Baja California, she may have been able to toss off otherworldly paella and gazpacho and gumbo in the big, tile-floored kitchen at the back of the house, and she may have dazzled every powerful Democrat in California with her legendary dinner parties—but she had never made lunch for a Boston Brahmin who was beginning to show signs that he just might become the next President of the United States.

She called around and learned that the candidate's favorite food was soup and that his favorite soup was New England clam chowder. She found a recipe that called for littleneck clams, cream, potatoes and bacon—but no onions, no garlic, no pepper, no thyme. This made perfect sense to her. She believed cuisine, like character, was dictated by climate. That explained why her favorite dishes were Mexican, Spanish, Italian and creole, ablaze with spice, exuberant and full of texture like the people, hot food from hot, passionate places. Similarly, people from cold places like Boston tended to be cold fish, to keep their feelings locked away, to eat food that tasted like nothing.

The problem was that Esmeralda Guttierez Sinclair had copper pots and ropes of garlic dangling from the beams in her kitchen and a garden out back that produced dozens of herbs and spices and she was constitutionally incapable of preparing bland food. She had fresh seafood flown out from Maine and she spent two days preparing what she imagined was a typical New England feast: clam chowder, smoked bluefish, roasted oysters, crab cakes, lobster thermidor.

The appointed day, a Monday in April, fell during Berkeley's spring break. Anne had spent the vacation at home riding horses, playing tennis with her brother, studying for her upcoming exams. Even though she hadn't touched a tennis racket in months, she'd demolished her brother in three sets that morning. She was still wearing her tennis whites, was still flushed and sweaty, when she poured a glass of iced tea and joined her father on the front porch shortly before noon.

"How'd the match go?" he asked, looking up from the stock quotations in *The Wall Street Journal.*

"Six-two, six-one, six-love," she said, gulping tea and picking up her textbook on the Spanish-American War. "His backhand is so weak. I can't believe he made captain of his high school team."

Artie chortled so hard he worked up a bright oyster of phlegm, which he spat onto Esmeralda's rosebushes. "Damn Pall Malls," he said. He loved his daughter's competitive fire; it had made her a champion at tennis and gymkhana riding, and he believed it made her capable of accomplishing anything she set her mind to. He was delighted by her interest in history and political science. He believed she could have a tremendous future in politics. All she had to do was say the word.

They heard the growl of engines. They looked up as five gleaming black cars shot out of the pecan orchard and came whipping up the dirt road, powdering the row of sycamores with white dust. Men in a hurry, Anne thought. It looked like a sped-up funeral procession.

The cars stopped where the gravel lapped against the front lawn. All the doors opened at once. Anne noticed him instantly. The others were wearing dark suits, some even wore sunglasses against the brassy midday glare, but he was wearing a light blue suit. He was curiously frail, his chest sunken, yet there was something magnetic about the way he came striding nimbly across the lawn, leading the pack toward the porch.

Anne closed her book and set it on the table and watched him come. She had never seen such a sexy man—the brown mop of hair going to silver at the temples and trying to spring loose in patches; the fluid gait, the sleepy eyes, the sleekness of the man.

"Artie, I want to thank you for having us," John Kennedy said, jogging up the stairs with his right hand out, his left hand smoothing his jacket. "A lovely place you've got here."

"Thanks, Senator. Pleasure to have you." Artie shook the hand without getting out of his rocker. He didn't have to stand up. These men were the supplicants, and Artie Sinclair could make a dozen phonecalls that would virtually guarantee the candidate of his choice every county north of the Golden Gate Bridge. "This is my daughter Anne, Senator. She's a sophomore at Berkeley. She was all-state in tennis in high school, but she's too damn busy with her history books to pick up a tennis racket nowadays."

The Senator turned to her, and in her sleeveless shirt and pleated skirt she felt suddenly naked. She shook the offered hand, mumbled that it was a pleasure to meet him.

"You really ought to read Mock Twain's view of that war," he said, motioning toward her textbook.

"I beg your pardon?" There was a roaring in her ears and she heard the newspaper crinkle and sensed that her father was listening closely.

"Mock Twain," Kennedy repeated. "He had a slightly different view of the Spanish-American War than you get from most textbooks. He wasn't too happy that we killed a million Filipinos, for starters. I think he had a point."

The screen door opened into the stunned silence and Esmeralda came out of the house dressed in a brilliant, hand-embroidered peasant dress. Anne knew she hadn't slept the night before, but she looked radiant. She clasped the candidate's hand with both of hers and pumped it so long Anne was afraid she would never let go. "It is a great honor to meet you, Senator. I am so pleased to see a Catholic running for the American presidency."

Artie cleared his throat and announced he was hungry and led the way inside. Anne, after putting on a sweater, sat beside her mother. She was facing Robert Kennedy, whose buck teeth and jerky movements reminded her of a chipmunk. Artie and the Senator sat at opposite ends of the table, and as the food was brought out they engaged in a freewheeling exchange. Artie was impressed by Lyndon Johnson's record in the Senate; Kennedy was not. Artie thought Richard Nixon was a shoo-in for the Republican nomination; Kennedy said his great worry was a draft-Rockefeller movement. Artie said he'd heard the name of Margaret Chase Smith mentioned as a possible Republican vice presidential candidate; Kennedy countered that while he had the highest respect for "the lady from Maine," he believed an electorate that was so resistant to a Catholic presidential candidate was not yet ready for a female vice president. Artie thought John Foster Dulles was a moron; Kennedy agreed, but he quickly added that, given the flavor of the Cold War rhetoric of the 1950s and the victory of the Chinese communists and events in Korea, no candidate could afford to appear even slightly soft on the global communist threat. Anne noticed that her father's eyes were dancing.

Esmeralda wasn't even listening. She was holding her breath, waiting for the Senator's verdict on her chowder. He sloshed a spoonful around in his mouth, closed his eyes, swallowed. Anne could hear the grandfather clock ticking way out by the front door.

"Let me, ah, see here, Esmeralda," he said. "Cayenne pepper . . ."

"Yes."

"Paprika . . ."

"Yes."

"And ah . . ." He took another spoonful, swallowed. "And now I'm stumped. Is that cardamom I'm tasting?"

"No, Senator, it's thyme."

"Thyme! Of course! Well, it's delicious, best chowder I ever tasted. Bobby, make a note to get Esmeralda's recipe—provided she doesn't mind divulging state secrets."

"Of course I don't mind." She was beaming as Bobby Kennedy took out a notebook and jotted himself a reminder to get the recipe.

After lunch they all went out to the porch and spent the rest of the afternoon talking. By the time the black cars roared back down the dirt road, Artie Sinclair was sold. He knew that since 1956 John Kennedy had spoken to more Jackson Day dinners than anyone else in the party, had cultivated the grass roots, had built an impressive network among precinct workers, delegates, county and state chairmen, city bosses, union brass. He may not have known cardamom from thyme, but he had read Mark Twain's denunciation of the Spanish-American War and he was acutely attuned to the political importance of standing up to the communist threat, whether it came from Cuba, Berlin, or Laos. Besides, he was handsome, witty, charming and rich. Artie had never seen his wife and daughter struck dumb before by a mere politician. Yes, John Kennedy had a ton of the quality Artie looked for in a candidate: He was, despite his Catholicism, supremely electable.

Though Kennedy didn't carry California in the November election, the margin of defeat was microscopic—half of a percentage point—and it *was* Nixon's home state, and Kennedy's campaign in the Far West *was* managed by his idiot kid brother Teddy. Artie had led the charge at the convention in Los Angeles that had pushed Kennedy onto the ticket, and in early autumn he'd helped orchestrate a whistle-stop campaign swing from the Oregon border to San Francisco. The crowds had been large and responsive, the press had been favorable, and the candidate had found his voice. The northern half of the state voted solidly Democratic while the south, as expected, went Republican. It was a valiant, bare-knuckled fight, the kind the Kennedys seemed to relish. So when the President-elect called to thank Artie for his help and to let him know that Esmeralda's clam chowder would be a staple in the Kennedy White House, Artie reminded him of his debt. And when Anne graduated from Berkeley in the spring of '62, Artie called in that I.O.U.

And now Anne was climbing toward the office of Frederick Nolting, U.S. Ambassador to the Republic of Vietnam. She paused halfway up the last flight of stairs to catch her breath and compose herself. Couldn't they put an elevator in this rat trap? She realized she hadn't exercised in months—the heat made the very thought unpleasant—but she renewed her vow to start swimming every day at the Cercle Sportif.

As her breathing returned to normal she heard a door slam, then a man's voice coming from the waiting room at the top of the stairs. "So how's the Ambassador this morning?" It was Charlie Malloy, the man who'd taken her out dancing the other night and gotten so falling-down drunk she had to pour him into his bed at the Caravelle Hotel.

"The Ambassador's just fine," another man said. "He told me the war's going splendidly. That's a direct quote, by the way. 'The war is going splendidly.' And he kept a straight face when he said it."

"That's odd," Charlie said. "I had a nice little six-hour chat with President Diem yesterday—and he told me exactly the same thing!"

They laughed heartily at their little joke. Anne still couldn't place the second man's voice.

"So how is His Royal Highness these days?" the voice said. "In good health, I trust."

"Seems to be unchanged. His eyes still wander off in different directions and he still chain-smokes and talks nonstop. But I finally figured out how to get in a question when he starts ranting like that."

"Oh?"

"You wait for him to light the next cigarette—and when he's inhaling, you pounce. It actually worked three times. I got three quotes I'll be able to use when I file!"

Another burst of laughter. When it died, the second voice, cordial till now, had a sudden edge to it: "By the way, Charlie, I saw your piece on the battle at Ap Bac."

"Yeah. Pulitzer material."

"I realize you're kind of old-school and all, and that you work for *Time* magazine—but how can you look yourself in the mirror in the morning after writing shit like that?"

"What's that supposed to mean?"

"You know, that crap at the end of the piece about how the American advisors are pleased with the progress of the war, how they're still way out in front of the V.C. Jesus Christ, man, you were *there*. You talked to York and Vann. You saw the choppers and the bodies and the fucked-up artillery exercise—"

"For your information, Dave, I didn't write that last paragraph. My editors in New York wrote it. If you've got a suggestion how I can wave a wand and make them stop adding bright little nuggets of optimism to my stories, please let me know. I'm all ears."

"You might try threatening to resign, at least rattle a few cages. It might actually do some good."

"Then again, it might not."

"You'll never know until you try."

"Gee, Dave, thanks for all this free advice. I really appreciate it—especially coming from a veteran correspondent like yourself. As I hear it, you've been posted in Mississippi and Nashville and the Congo, which means you've worked in a foreign country a grand total of—what?—once? Unless you consider Mississippi a Third-World country, which I do. So I guess that means twice, right?"

"Very fucking funny, Charlie. Maybe your problem is that you've been posted in a few too many foreign countries and you've lost your edge, if you ever had an edge. Which I'm beginning to doubt."

And suddenly the man was storming down the stairs toward Anne, a scowl on his face. He thundered past her without a word and was gone. It was David Halberstam of *The New York Times*, one of the main reasons Jon Medlin was coming apart at the seams. What was with these young correspondents? Anne wondered. She'd read Charlie Malloy's article in the current issue of *Time*, and she thought it managed to be both tough and fair. He called Ap Bac a "brutal" defeat, noted that the Viet Cong were better armed than ever, more willing to stand and fight, less likely to melt away at the sound of a helicopter or the sight of an ARVN platoon. What was so terrible about quoting an American advisor as saying we were winning the war? It was true, so why not put it in the story? Hadn't Halberstam and that crowd read any history? Didn't they know what Ho Chi Minh and Vo Nguyen Giap had done to the French? Didn't they know what Mao was doing in China? Didn't they know that the communists had their sights on much more than South Vietnam?

She climbed the last stairs and stepped into the waiting room. Charlie Malloy was sitting on the sofa smoking a cigarette and flipping through the new issue of *Stars & Stripes.* He hadn't heard her come in. He was wearing a crisp poplin suit, and his freshly watered hair was combed straight back into tight silver curls that sizzled along his shirt collar. He had on sheer socks and woven tan loafers, probably Italian, definitely not American, nothing like the scuffed clodhoppers the other correspondents wore. For the first time she noticed he had tiny feet, which may have explained why he was such a lithe dancer even when he was too sozzled to walk in a straight line. Though he was overweight, pot-bellied and jowly, sort of pickled-looking, she found him sexy. He was a good dancer and a better storyteller, a man who could talk with equal ease about jazz, French wine, the virtues of Islam, and the blending of English and Moorish influences in the architecture of Kuala Lumpur. He spoke smatterings of a dozen languages. It was this zest for the finer things in life that made him attractive to her. She could still taste that coffee—Hawaiian coffee—he made after taking her to lunch in Berkeley.

Then again, maybe it wasn't his coffee or his clothes or his conversation; maybe she simply had a thing for older men, a suspicion that began to take root in her mind the summer before her senior year when she went to Europe with a group of Berkeley students. They were supposed to be touring cathedrals and museums, but Anne found she was far more interested in the middle-aged European men she met by chance in out-of-the-way places, like the man she bumped into in the café across from the Prado in Madrid, that charming man who bought her tapas and glass after glass of port and told her of fighting

Franco during the Civil War and then took her to his apartment, where they proceeded to break his bed, then shifted to a chair—he sat, she straddled him—and they proceeded to break that too . . .

"Hello, Charlie."

He spun so fast the ash from his cigarette splashed to the floor. "Why, hello, Anne. What a pleasant surprise." He stood up, stabbed his cigarette into an ashtray full of white sand. "What brings you to the fortress?"

"Got a 10 o'clock with the Ambassador. Have to fill him in on the wonderful propaganda films we're finishing up this week."

Charlie looked at his watch. "I was supposed to see him at 9:30, but Hot Air Halberstam ran over by half an hour."

"He's such a jerk."

Charlie didn't seem to hear her. He was studying one of his tiny Italian shoes, like a man about to make a sales pitch. Then he looked her in the eyes and said, "Listen, Anne, about the other night . . . I hope I wasn't—I realize I had a little too much to drink—I hope I didn't do . . ." He ran out of steam and looked back at his shoe.

"Do what, Charlie?" She was grinning.

"You know—anything out of line. I was pretty well gone."

"You sure as hell were. And if you're wondering whether you tried to do anything *sexual,* the answer is no. Frankly, I don't think you could've gotten it up with a bumper jack."

He looked up from his shoe so sharply his whole face wobbled, the jowls, the bags under his eyes, the plump red lips. He looked stricken. "Did you say bumper jack?"

"Miss Sinclair!" It was Louise Bullock calling from the far end of the room. "The Ambassador's ready to see you. Mr. Malloy, you'll be next."

"Thanks, Louise," Anne said. "Be right there."

"Did you say bumper jack?" Charlie repeated.

"Don't take it so hard," she said, patting his arm. "You were a perfect gentleman and I had a marvelous time. If you asked me, I might even let you and Mr. Luce take me out again sometime."

She was smiling as she strode across the room. Men were so

easy to shock because they were so full of themselves. By the time she reached the Ambassador's frosted-glass door, her thoughts had turned to the job at hand: She was under orders from Jon Medlin to tell the Ambassador that the three new USIS propaganda films would be ready by the end of the week and that they were Oscar-caliber efforts. The first film urged the peasants to stop urinating in the village wells; the second showed them the best way to grow big healthy turnips; the third promised them that government soldiers would no longer steal their chickens or their rice. It wasn't art, Anne had to admit, but the Viet Cong were no better. They'd started distributing pamphlets that claimed Americans loved to eat the fried eyeballs of Vietnamese children.

When Anne emerged from the Ambassador's office an hour later she was exhausted. She'd spent the first ten minutes going over the progress of the new propaganda films and the next fifty minutes listening to Frederick Nolting rage against the press coverage of the battle at Ap Bac, which he called "negative, distorted, inaccurate, vindictive, mean-spirited and damaging to the cause."

When he got wound up like that he tried to suck the filters off his Tareytons and his face got flat, kind of mashed-looking, and very red. In such moments she found it easy to believe he had once been a peanut farmer in Virginia because he looked like a man who'd been out in the sun too long. When his rant passed the half-hour mark her attention began to drift—she may have agreed with the essence of what he was saying, but she'd heard it all before—and her gaze wandered to the view the Ambassador had from his desk. The highest official from the most powerful nation on earth looked out his window to the filthy back terrace of the neighboring apartment building: a busted television set with a coat-hanger aerial, a clothesline sagging with wash, and a Buddha shrine ringed with parched flowers and scorched joss sticks. So this was what a Virginia Gentleman's brilliant career with the Foreign Service led to: an office on the top floor of a fire trap with a panoramic view of a slum.

When the session finally ended, Anne found Charlie still sitting on the sofa, still immersed in *Stars & Stripes*. It must have been a hell of an issue, she thought. "He's all yours," she told Charlie. "And I hope you remembered to wear your flack jacket. He's loaded for bear—and you're one of the bears."

"You look beat," he said, rising from the sofa.

She wanted to say, *And you look like you've been hungover for the past fifteen years.* But she said, "I'm not beat, Charlie, I'm exhausted. I haven't had a full weekend off since I got here six months ago. I need a vacation."

"How about dinner instead? Henry Luce is buying."

"Can't make it tonight, I'm afraid."

"Then how about tomorrow?"

"Sure. Why not."

"Let's meet at the Continental at seven. We'll have a drink and figure out what we're in the mood for."

"Sounds good. See you then."

As she turned to leave she noticed he was staring at her—the sonofabitch was staring at her breasts. Before she could say anything, he cried, "Holy shit! Is that today's *Herald Trib*?"

She looked down at the newspaper cradled under her arm. So he wasn't staring at her breasts, after all. He was staring at her newspaper. She handed it to him.

"Look at this! These belong to my kid brother!"

She looked at the photograph on the front page. It was a parade of seven cars—seven very big, very shiny, very fat old American cars—driving past some sort of castle wall. She read the caption: "Bangkok Wedding Party—Seven 1954 American-made Buicks carry the bride and groom and their wedding guests past the Grand Palace in Bangkok on Sunday. The Buicks are owned by Sam Malloy, a former U.S. serviceman, and Rathavorn Saengbangpla, a Thai businessman. The two are partners in the White Elephant Hotel. It was the inaugural outing for the Buicks, which can be rented for any occasion. (Reuters)"

"Your brother owns those cars?" Anne said.

"Yes! On the block where our father lives in Levittown, everyone bought a new Buick back in '54—and my brother just bought them all and shipped them to Bangkok. Oh, this is too much . . ."

Anne noticed he'd broken out in a sweat, despite the air-conditioning. She was afraid he was going to start weeping, but Louise Bullock announced that the Ambassador was ready for him and he buttoned his jacket and hurried off. Anne took another look at the photograph. She had to admit that those cars looked truly weird passing in front of the gold-plated spires and soaring statues of the Grand Palace.

As she started down the stairs she renewed her vow to start swimming after work. And she would wait for Jon's mood to improve and tell him she wanted a long weekend off, maybe go to the beach during the Tet cease-fire, maybe get out of the country altogether, go to Hong Kong or Singapore, away from Saigon's intrigues, its pushy correspondents and grenades and paranoia.

When she reached the second-floor landing she almost ran into a woman chugging up the stairs hugging a stack of leather-bound volumes. It was Lois DeVries, head of the Embassy's communications center, one of those career Foreign Service matrons who had been stationed all over the world without bothering to learn a single foreign language, who socialized only with Americans, who knew everybody's business before they knew it themselves. The last person in the world you would want as an enemy.

"Oh, Anne!" she huffed. "I didn't even see you coming."

"They promote you to librarian, Lois?"

"Ha. I wish." She had a new hairdo, tight brown curls that looked like a ball of twigs. She was not an unattractive woman, but she worked hard at being plain—always a shapeless, neutral-colored dress, flat shoes, and now that menopause hairdo. Anne learned at an Embassy reception that Lois had been married once, years ago, but the man walked out on her, just disappeared one fine afternoon into the streets of Cairo and was never seen again. "No," Lois said now, nodding toward the volumes she was carrying, "I got stuck with moving these damn things."

"What are they?"

"Old cables and memos, the usual crap. Once they get to be a year or so old we put them in storage—where they belong.

Out of sight and out of mind." Suddenly she brightened. "Are you real busy, Anne?"

"Uh, not really . . . I've got a lunch appointment at noon . . ."

"Would you be a doll then and help me carry the rest of this junk up to the fifth floor? That new girl from Boston called in sick today—I think she's got her monthly—and I'm swamped. I've got cables to send to Washington that are already two hours late."

When Lois DeVries asked you for a favor, you did not say no. "Sure," Anne said. "Be glad to help."

And so she pitched in and helped carry the volumes from the cable room on the second floor to the storage locker on the fifth floor. It was strenuous, monotonous work, and after half an hour Lois bailed out on her, claiming she had to get that backed-up cable traffic moving to Washington. One of the first things Anne had learned about the Embassy was that the cable room was the umbilical cord to Washington and that Lois De-Vries was the goddess of the cable room. She saw everything that came and went, including the "eyes only" traffic, and as a result she knew everything about everybody.

After half a dozen trips Anne started taking breathers in the cool privacy of the fifth-floor storage locker. As she waited to catch her breath she started browsing through the big leather volumes, scanning the clipped prose of cables that conveyed the minutiae of protocol decisions, policy shifts, personnel changes. She came upon an item entitled "Cablegram from Elbridge Dur-brow, United States Ambassador to Saigon, to Secretary of State Christian A. Herter, Sept. 16, 1960." Her mind drifted back. In September of 1960 her father was busy arranging John Kenne-dy's whistle-stop tour of northern California . . . and Anne was beginning her junior year at Berkeley and dating that Beat poet she'd met at City Lights bookstore in North Beach . . . God, he could put away the booze . . . She scanned the cable, expecting more of the same dreary prattle. But as she read, her eyes grew wide:

> Conditions here are by no means normal. Diem govern-
> ment is in quite serious danger in South where Commu-

nist infiltration is increasing so rapidly . . . Rumors about
Mr. and Mrs. Nhu are creating a growing dissension
within country and seriously damage political position
of Diem government . . . secret police methods of repres-
sion and control . . . If Diem's position in country contin-
ues deteriorate as result failure adopt proper political,
psychological, economic and security measures, it may
become necessary for US government to begin consider-
ation alternative courses of action and leaders in order
to achieve our objective.

Her heart was hammering her rib cage now. This cable was
written back in 1960, more than two years ago, and yet she had
heard nothing but praise for President Diem from everyone in
the U.S. Mission. The war was going swimmingly, they all said.
We'll have everyone home by '65, they all said. Ngo Dinh Diem
is the Churchill of Asia, they all said. So not only was the official
optimism about the war a lie, but the Embassy and State Department had spent years discussing the wisdom of removing a
leader they publicly lauded as a great patriot and ally. Anne
could see, in sudden shocking detail, in the dry prose of the
cables, that Washington regarded Vietnam as nothing but a
chessboard and the Vietnamese as nothing but pawns, to be
manipulated at will.

She continued reading until she came to a typed memo, "A
National Intelligence Estimate Prepared by DIA for JCS and
President." It was dated March 28, 1961—several months after
Kennedy's inauguration. Her eyes flew across the page:

. . . *extremely critical period for President Ngo Dinh Diem and the
Republic of Vietnam lies immediately ahead . . . more than one-half
of entire rural region south and southwest of Saigon, as well as some
areas to the north, are under considerable Communist control . . . the
Viet Cong's strength encircles Saigon and recently has begun to move
closer to the city . . .*

"How's it coming?" Lois DeVries was standing in the
doorway.

"Fine!" she said, slipping the volume into the cabinet, her
heart racing. "Just trying to catch my breath!"

"Well, I got all the cables sent. I'll help you finish up." She looked at the half-full cabinet and clucked her tongue. "What a lotta crap."

Anne was in a daze as she followed Lois down to the second floor, and she remained in a daze until she left the Embassy a few minutes before noon and was swallowed up in the jostling, braying, frantic streets of Saigon, a city that didn't even realize it was encircled by the Viet Cong.

8

The wedding of Neh Lim's daughter was such a publicity coup for the Buicks—they appeared in newspapers and in magazines, on radio and television shows from New Delhi to Melbourne—that Sam Malloy was able to cancel his ad in *The Bangkok Post*. Every day the cars were rented out by diplomats, tourists and Thais, by Chinese businessmen and the growing number of American G.I.s who were flooding into Bangkok because the city was winning a richly deserved reputation as the dream R&R destination.

At first Sam didn't want to rent to servicemen because he knew all about the young American male's capacity for deep mayhem when he was relieved of duty in Saigon and turned loose in a candystore like Bangkok. He had visions of vomit-spattered upholstery, shattered windshields, stolen hubcaps, slashed tires. But Rat persuaded him that a G.I.'s money was as green as anyone else's, and he promised to send a message, "clear and loud," that it was not wise to abuse a Bangkok Buick.

One evening Rat gassed up the canary-yellow Buick and drove out to Don Muang to pick up three crew-cut American sailors who'd just flown in from Saigon. They'd spent the day unloading AD-6 fighters from the USS *Core* onto the downtown docks, and they were determined to make use of every last minute of their 48-hour shore leave. After Rat read them the riot act about the car, he headed for the Why Not on Sukhumwit Road, which, like dozens of other Bangkok nightclubs, claimed to employ "the most beautiful and gracious hostesses in the world." All the way into town the sailors socked each other and bounced up and down and chanted, "We're gonna get laid! We're gonna get laid!" When they piled out of the car in front of the Why Not, a barker in an oversized tuxedo sprang off the curb and stuck a plastic menu in their faces and started ticking off the delicacies available inside: "Girl-girl, girl-boy, girl-boy-girl, shampoo, private dance, trapeze show, two-girl massage . . ."

Two of the sailors plowed inside, but the third paused and unzipped his pants and started pissing on the Buick's right rear moon hubcap. "I thought I tell you about such kind of crap," called Rat, who was in a good mood and was going to give the kid a break if he agreed to clean up his mess. But the sailor waved his free hand and kept pissing and said, "Yeah, yeah, yeah, Papa-san, but when a man's gotta go, a man's gotta *go*."

Rat calmly set down his newspaper, slid out from behind the steering wheel, walked around the back of the car—and kicked the kid's nose up into his brain. He was stretched out there on Sukhumwit Road, unconscious, bleeding like a faucet, pissing feebly on himself, when his shipmates came charging out of the club. They, too, won free one-way tickets to Siriraj Hospital: One wound up with three broken ribs and his jaw wired shut; the other lost two teeth and the sight in his right eye (and, as a result, a general discharge from the U.S. Navy). The police declined to press charges, and word got back to the Americans stationed in Vietnam that if you went to Bangkok on R&R and rented a Buick, you should not, under any circumstances, do anything to piss off the man behind the wheel.

After that there was no more trouble. Sam's biggest problem was keeping up with demand. The booking, driving and mechanical work proved to be a full-time job. Little things were forever going wrong—a generator burned up, a radiator hose

sprang a leak, a fuel pump died—and since he couldn't afford
to wait for spare parts from New York, he was forced to improvise. He never would have been able to pull it off if it hadn't
been for Rat and the Major. Rat's help was expected; the Major's
came as a pleasant surprise.

Nigel Colchester ("the Major" was a term of respect, not military rank) was one of those Englishmen who came out East as
a young man after serving in the Great War and spiritually
never went home again. The farther he got from London on his
initial voyage, the happier he became, like a lily opening to the
sun. Every time he paused he found he was as intrigued by the
natives as he was repelled by the emblems of a wilting empire.
In the English clubs he visited, from Bombay to Rangoon to
Singapore, the talk was always the same. Niggers and Chinamen
and yellow-bellies and mahouts—the whole bloody bunch of
them was showing altogether too much cheek. Half of them
didn't even salaam anymore when you passed! And now the
office babus were acting like the rulers, damned insolent
ticks . . .

Those Englishmen, with their resentments and their afternoon
oolongs and pink gins, struck the Major as profoundly sad. They
would never admit that they were as doomed as the empire
itself, that all they would have to show for their twenty or thirty
years of service on the far side of the world was a narrow mind,
a ruined liver and a pineapple backside from thousands of evenings spent in wicker chairs. The two most visible achievements
of the empire, it seemed to the Major, were the railroads and
the stout prisons sprinkled from Gibraltar to Hong Kong. The
worst he ever saw was the Cellular Jail in Port Blair, in the
remote Andaman Islands off Burma. Its thick-walled cells, radiating like spokes from the central guard tower, were packed
with Indian freedom fighters. And the porches and towers were
so crisp and correct, so very English, splendidly white-washed
under the unblinking tropical sun.

As soon as the Major stepped off the boat in Bangkok he
knew he had found his true home. Siam, alone among the nations of Southeast Asia, had never been colonized by a European power. The Siamese, as a result, had a gorgeous go-to-hell

attitude toward the white man. "Europe is a boneyard," the Major wrote to his parents in Cornwall, "and the Near East is nothing but dagoes and smells. But the Far East—Siam espe-cially—ah, the Far East is natives and *scents*."

He had arranged in London to go to work for a British timber company, and he spent his first years logging teak up near Korat, the gateway to the impoverished *issan* region of northeast Siam. It was so remote that news of the 1932 overthrow of the absolute monarchy in Bangkok did not reach them for three weeks. Now, thirty years later, the Americans were busy ex-panding the Korat airbase, adding hangars and barracks and depots, lengthening the runways, getting things ready for their very biggest bombers.

The life of the teak-wallah in the '20s and '30s was hard, but it suited the Major. After all, few discomforts could match what he had endured during the Great War, and here, for the first time in his life, he was not suffocated by public school and pub chat and the Queen, the drizzly weather and bland food of home, the unspoken expectation that a minister's son from Corn-wall who had attended Eton and Oxford would amount to something. Instead, Nigel Colchester had gone to Siam, and when he got there he had disappeared.

"It wasn't the war that made me a man. It was that twelve-year chukker up near Korat," the Major would tell anyone who was willing to listen. And part of the beauty of living at the White Elephant was that there always seemed to be fresh ears at the open-air bar, under the lazily twirling ceiling fans. "In its way, logging teak was far more grueling than fighting in that ghastly war. All you had to do in the war was follow orders, keep your head down, and pray. But the jungle made you think. An elephant with a broken leg twenty miles from the nearest town is a problem that requires a certain amount of . . . *imagination*. And then there was anthrax—those village cattle were simply stiff with it—and sweat bees and blackwater fever and tick typhus. God, there were a bloody million ways to die!"

But the life of the teak-wallah had its rewards, too. In the evenings, when he was in from the jungle, he joined the other

Europeans for tennis and dinner and bridge in their informal club, and sometimes those evenings stretched on pleasantly for hours, fueled by gin and whisky and beer. They were a decent lot, not like those loudmouths he'd encountered on his way out East. There was never any talk of coolies or yellow-bellies or niggers because these people were all misfits in their own ways, people with secrets, people who would not have fit in with polite society in Hong Kong or Mandalay. Occasionally Thais and Chinese were welcomed at table, provided they had good manners and something interesting to say. In its way it was a hugely democratic little world.

It was here that the Major met Virginia Finch-Haden, the niece of the timber company's superintendent, a young, well-made woman with a delicious laugh and a crown of chestnut hair. She shared the Major's passion for horses and his determination never to return to England. They were married in 1934. He built a large bungalow on the edge of the European settlement, and Ginny planted a garden around the tall jacaranda tree, a garden that gave them the best of England without giving them England itself, rich gushes of larkspur and hollyhock and petunia, which Ginny watered so religiously they never succumbed to even the fiercest Siamese sun.

One Christmas Ginny bent to family pressure and returned to London for her father's funeral. Left alone, the Major cobbled together what he would remember years later as a thoroughly satisfactory holiday feast: "A tin of pâté foie gras, a tin of Heinz tomato soup, a tin of Hunter's Handy Ham, the inevitable chicken—and with the help of a spot of Guinness and port, it made an excellent tiffin." It was this ability to improvise, to embrace the grandeur of small pleasures, that made it impossible for him to imagine trading his simple life in Thailand for a life of dreary respectability in England.

He tried once, and it was a disaster. Ginny bore a son after returning from her father's funeral, but at the age of six the boy drowned in Ta Kong Stream when his boat capsized and he became tangled in the spongy petals of water hyacinths. Ginny never recovered. Her health began to deteriorate—she lost weight and became vulnerable to fevers—and the Major moved her to Bangkok, where she could get reliable medical care and he could get steady work teaching English at Chulalongkorn University. She died during the influenza epidemic of 1957, on the very day Field Marshal Sarit Thanarat came to power. As the Major had promised, he flew her remains to England for a proper burial beside her father in the graveyard behind Christ Church, Spitalsfield, in the grimy East End of London.

After the funeral the Major, afraid of the memories that awaited him in Thailand, wandered the streets of London, ringing up old Oxford acquaintances and seeking out familiar pubs. But he felt pitiful and lost. One drizzly afternoon, while getting pissed on Guinness by himself in a pub off Piccadilly, he looked out the window and saw Flory and Boyle staring in at him. At first he thought he was seeing a pair of ghosts. Flory and Boyle had shared a trench with the Major for three weeks of unimaginable hell at Ypres in 1914. They charged into the pub and stood drinks the rest of the afternoon, and the three old warriors got merrily blind as the daylight leaked away. Flory, now a dentist, and Boyle, a salesman of dry goods, teased the Major for having led a charmed life in that trench at Ypres. Nothing scratched him—not bullets, mortars, star shells, grenades, flamethrowers, not bayonets or daggers or tomahawks. He never even got diarrhea! They roared at this. They roared at the memory of the feet of buried soldiers protruding from the walls of the trench. They roared at the memory of slaughtering more than 30,000 German recruits, mostly recent college graduates. They even roared when Boyle reminded them that the one German worth killing at Ypres was the one who got away, that little bastard Adolf Hitler.

By the end of the night the Major understood that he had lost interest in playing the game, the great elaborate game of being a certain sort of Englishman. So he returned to Bangkok and got back his teaching job and settled into a small apartment near Lumpini Park. He was alone but not lonely, happy to be back among people he understood and loved, people who shared his joy when the mechanical world failed them, people who were amused by a power outage, a flooded street, a broken-down bus, people who believed in the spirit world and the mystical power of numbers and stars and good deeds, who distrusted banks and trusted their own senses, who preferred bloodshed to neurosis. The Thais, like the Major, cared a great deal about shame and not at all about sin. And the streets of Bangkok could not have been more unlike the flannel-gray streets of London: These streets were a mad, around-the-clock carnival where people were always boiling noodles, mending pants, making dentures, hawking Buddhas, shaving pineapples, catching naps, stirring woks, and eating, always eating, eating at noon and midnight and dawn, eating noodles and soup and coconut cakes, eating fish and rice and duck and pork laced with garlic and ginger and chilis, food that made your eyeballs sweat, food that could make you hallucinate, food that made you know you were alive.

When he heard that Prince Prem's old riverside villa was being converted into a hotel, he decided to investigate. He spent an entire afternoon wandering in circles, unable to find the place. Just when he was about to give up and return to his apartment, he looked up from the choked, greasy alley and there it was. He had walked past it a dozen times without recognizing it, and now he understood why. The main building, separated from the alley by a glass-tipped wall and a massive banyan tree, used to be a mossy yellow, the color of rot and loving neglect. Now workers were busy painting the walls white. The place look distressingly clean and new, almost antiseptic.

In the familiar foyer the Major received another surprise. A tall white man, speaking Thai, was ordering a crew of workers to give the wall that ran along the alley one more coat of whitewash, and then they could quit for the day.

"I should like to speak with the manager," the Major said.

"You got him." The man extended a paint-speckled hand. "Sam Malloy. What can I do for you?"

An American no less, the Major thought, a big blustery handsome American. Probably a football star. God help me. But he had gone to all this trouble, so he introduced himself and pressed on. "I used to come to parties here a good many years ago, back when Prince Prem was still alive—"

"Some wild times, I'm told."

"Quite. But I'm afraid the Prince was a regular martyr to booze. And gambling. And, for that matter, to young women and younger boys. Perfectly charming fellow for all that, of course."

"Of course."

"At any rate, I hear you've built bungalows."

"Yes, nine altogether. They're not quite finished—we don't expect to be open for another two weeks or so."

"Are they air-conditioned?"

"Afraid not. Just ceiling fans, window screens and mosquito coils—or a net if you prefer."

"Splendid! Can't stick air-conditioning. Damn things always give me a cold. I say if a man wishes to live in the tropics, then by God he should be willing to live in the tropics. Would you be good enough to show me one of your bungalows?"

The Major spent that night in the only finished bungalow, Number 5, the one in the corner of the compound nearest the sights and smells and sounds of the Chao Phraya River. In the morning he announced he had found the spot where he intended to spend the rest of his days. He paid a year's rent with cash.

Settling into the riverside bungalow was a rebirth for the Major, the beginning of his brilliant twilight years. Scarlet and salmon bougainvillea tumbled off the thatched roof like tongues of flame, and he spent long leisurely hours sitting on the veranda watching the river traffic, reading, talking to the geckos, the bright green lizards that took up permanent residence on the sunny steps and were said to bring a dwelling good luck. He decorated the interior of the bungalow with silks and his vast collection of books and the statuary he'd picked up over the years on his upriver trips with his friend Jim Thompson, the silk man. He swam twenty laps every morning in the hotel pool and he had cocktails every evening at the open-air bar, where the barmen laughed at his jokes. He usually ate dinner in the hotel dining room, which boasted Shwe Winn's cooking, the best Chinese the Major had found in Bangkok. He was frequently invited to the homes of his many friends: Thai and

European and American colleagues from the university; Jim Thompson; Kukrit Pramoj, who published the irreverent daily newspaper, *Siam Rath;* and Alex McDougal, founder of *The Bangkok Post.* It was, he told people, a good life for an old expat.

He developed strange new tastes. The first thing he read in *The Bangkok Post* after his morning swim was Sheilah Graham's column, and he became slavishly addicted to Hollywood gossip. The grandeur of it was what hooked him—the larger-than-life stars, the gargantuan egos, the box-office smashes and the box-office flops, the alcoholism, drug addiction, homosexuality, infidelity. It was epic. It was Roman. It was America's version of royalty, and it was so much more energetic and democratic, so much more interesting, than the British brand. The Major was a sponge for news of Hollywood. He knew that the biggest box-office draws were Doris Day, Rock Hudson, Cary Grant, John Wayne, Elvis Presley and Liz Taylor. He was outraged that Tony Curtis married an 18-year-old tart of a German "actress." He was disappointed that a great talent like William Holden allowed himself to be paired with a bit of fluff like Kim Novak in a nothing picture like *Picnic.* He was thrilled that a crew was coming to Thailand to film *Tarzan's Three Challenges.*

The only thing missing from the Major's life was a challenge. And then the Buicks arrived.

In Korat he had earned a reputation for infinite resourcefulness, but modern Bangkok had less and less use for such virtues. Though the Thais had never been colonized by Europeans, though they didn't have stout jails and tea plantations to remind them of the British or tree-lined boulevards and rubber plantations to remind them of the French, the Major was dismayed to see that the Thais' appetite for Western things was becoming ravenous. By 1960 Bangkok was beginning to drown in air conditioners, transistor radios, cheap magazines, electric shavers, fluoride toothpaste, gas hot plates and, it seemed, more cars and trucks every day. Split-level houses were replacing lovely old wooden Thai homes like Jim Thompson's. Trees were being cut down and klongs, the canals that were the lifeblood of the city, were being paved over. It was not unusual to see Thai men in Hawaiian shirts and Thai women in stretch pants.

The Major's initial reaction to this ghastliness was to blame it on the American dollar. Every day the newspaper seemed to contain stories about new U.S.-backed aid programs and road projects. There were pictures of grinning Thai officials receiving Westinghouse road graders or John Deere tractors, signing contracts, breaking ground with silver-plated shovels. Some of the money went directly into the pockets of government officials, and some of it trickled down to the city streets. All over Bangkok four- and five-story apartment buildings were shooting up. Before the paint was dry, families moved in, perfuming the air with their cooking, festooning the rooftops and balconies with their television antennas and gaudy laundry and birdcages. What powerful empires had been unable to do for centuries, the almighty dollar was doing overnight, with ease.

This sudden abundance of consumer goods made fixing the Buicks a relative breeze. When a generator burned up, for instance, the Major led Rat to some refrigerators he'd seen men dumping behind the gravel pits next to the Royal Thai Navy compound, not far upriver from the hotel. In years past, no Thai would have dumped a refrigerator without stripping it of every useful or resalable part. But the motors were intact, and the Major removed them, then paid a boy five baht to unwind the copper wire and wind it into the Buick's generator. It wasn't a work of art, but the car fired up on the first try.

"I'll be damned . . ." Sam said when the Major summoned him to inspect the car. "The engine's quieter than it used to be. Major, you're a genius."

"Nothing to it," he said. "I'd say this calls for a small libation, what?"

"But Major," Rat said. "You always say white man must never drink before sunset in tropics."

"Oh, rot that," the Major said, laughing, and led the way to the bar.

After the barman poured them three perfectly foamless glasses of Singha beer, Sam said, "Major, I was just on a long-distance phonecall to Los Angeles. I believe I've got the perfect assignment for you."

"Oh?"

"Does the name George Englund mean anything to you?"

"Sorry."

"Well, George Englund is the producer of *The Ugly American*, that movie they shot here last year. Your buddy Kukrit Pramoj—"

"Yes, yes, yes, Kukrit played the Prime Minister of Sarkhan—and got a free trip to Hollywood in the bargain. Said the place was perfectly beastly. Just the other day he told me the movie's going to be beastly, too."

"Maybe so. But George Englund's assistant was calling from Universal Studios to let me know the world premiere is going to be here in Bangkok on March twenty-fifth—and Marlon Brando has expressly requested two things. One, he wants to stay in our very biggest bungalow; and two, he wants to be picked up at the airport and driven around town in our very best Buick. I guess Kukrit sent him a newspaper clipping about the Buicks or he saw an article in an American magazine."

"Oh, what awful fun!" the Major cried. "You aren't pulling my leg, are you, old boy?"

"Cross my heart," Sam said. "The great Brando will be our guest of honor. And naturally you'll be his personal driver and guide—if you're interested."

"Interested? Good Christ, I'd kill for the chance to meet the man!"

And so it was settled that the Major would be Marlon Brando's personal chauffeur and tour guide when *The Ugly American* had its world premiere at Bangkok's Chalerm Thai Theater.

9

For weeks after discovering the truth about the cable traffic at the U.S. Embassy, Anne Sinclair remained in a trance. It was as though a single thread had come loose and suddenly the whole tidy fabric of her world was unraveling and there was nothing she could do to stop it. She considered calling her father, but she knew what he would say. He would tell her that she'd been out of college less than a year and that she was working for bright, dedicated men who had spent long, sometimes brilliant careers forwarding the interests of the United States around the world. They knew what they were doing. They saw the big picture. Trust them.

She considered spilling it out to Jon Medlin, who had begun showing signs of his old self. He took the USIS staff out drinking one night at La Cigale, and the evening was so delightfully devoid of shoptalk that she didn't have the heart to break the spell. When she arrived at the office the next morning Jon's door was shut and it remained shut till noon, when he walked out and handed her a stack of reports. It was the weekly PI-REPs, pilots' reports of casualties which they gleaned by buzzing battlefields at treetop level after the shooting had stopped.

The reports were a joke and everyone knew it, but as Jon handed her the stack he said, "Dress these up real pretty. The Ambassador wants to see them at least an hour before his five o'clock press conference."

"You're joking, right Jon?"

"I most certainly am not joking," he snapped. "This Mission's job is to bring about progress in the war, and that means our job in this office is to report progress in the war. So find the progress in these numbers and write it up. Understood?"

"Understood." And that was the last time she considered sharing her secret with Jon Medlin.

That evening, after completing a report full of ingenious and patriotic lies, Anne walked directly from the office to the Cercle Sportif. In keeping with her vow, she'd been swimming twenty-five laps every day after work. She always wore her black, one-piece swimsuit because she was aware that the men lounging around the pool—Vietnamese and American military officers, French diplomats, businessmen, a few journalists and stray tourists—were there to suck on iced drinks and ogle the young women in bikinis. And it was quite a show. But Anne was not there to be ogled. She was there to swim and she loved the way her muscles unknotted and her mind emptied out as she carved her way up and down the pool. This evening the air was steamier and the water even more refreshing than usual and she lost count of how many laps she'd swum and her thoughts drifted back to a casual remark Charlie Malloy had made while they were having drinks last week at the Paris Bar on Rue Catinat. The conversation had come around to *The International Herald Tribune*'s front-page picture of the Buicks Charlie's brother had shipped to Bangkok, and Charlie had said, "He's a funny kid, that baby brother of mine."

"Funny how?" Anne asked. She was watching a boy hawk newspapers across the street, wondering if he'd ever thrown a grenade.

"Well, when he got that early discharge from the Navy last year he stayed with me at the Caravelle for almost a month— slept on the floor like a dog. No matter how often I asked, he wouldn't tell me what he'd done for the Navy or why they gave him an early discharge. It was almost like he had something to hide. It was spooky."

"Everyone has something to hide, Charlie."

He ignored her remark. "One night Halberstam got drunk on the roof of the Rex and walked up and put his arm around my brother's shoulder and announced he thought Sam was CIA. The look on Sam's face scared the living hell out of me."

"Why?"

"I thought he was going to tear Halberstam in half."

"Halberstam's a big boy. I'm sure he could've taken care of himself."

"You don't know my brother. He boxed and wrestled when he was a kid, never took any shit off anybody. Tough as nails, mean almost. And I think the Navy did something to him that made him even tougher and meaner."

"Why do you say that?"

"Something about the way he acted when he was here, always sizing people up, never saying much. Like he was smoldering inside, ready to explode. I know one thing—I was glad when a buddy of his asked him to help manage that hotel in Bangkok. He was starting to give me the creeps."

Anne stood up now in the shallow end of the pool. She was breathing hard. As she waited to catch her breath she looked down to the deep end and to her surprise saw Lois DeVries, wearing a red two-piece bathing suit and a black swim cap. Lois executed a perfect jackknife off the high dive. Anne watched as Lois emerged from the pool, climbed back up the diving board, and did a perfect one-and-a-half back flip. She followed this with a swan dive, a full gainer, a single flip, another jackknife. Anne was transfixed. So were the men stretched out in the lounge chairs under the coconut palms. They had stopped whistling and calling to the girls who passed; they watched Lois in reverent silence. When she picked up a towel and walked toward a chair in the far corner of the deck, there was a burst of applause from the men. Lois ignored them. Anne was surprised that Lois was in such good shape for a woman in her forties—long firm legs, flat stomach, strong back. She was even tanned. In that two-piece swimsuit, with her bird's nest of hair tucked inside the black cap, she looked sleekly sexy. Anne climbed out of the pool and started walking toward her.

"That was quite a show," she called out.

Lois spun. She had removed the cap and was toweling her hair. "Oh, hello, Anne. I didn't even know you were here." She twisted the towel around her head.

"And I didn't know you were an Olympic diver."

"Oh, that. That's just something to help me keep my sanity."

"What—showing off for those sex-starved men keeps you sane?"

Lois gave her a startled look. But when she realized Anne was joking, she laughed. "No, it's got nothing to do with those men. There's something about diving that makes the world go away—all the pressures, the war, everything. It's been like that since I was a girl. I used to spend whole days diving. Lately it's been coming in handy, believe me."

"Tell me about it. I've been swimming laps every day after work. I think it's saved my life."

Lois picked up a canvas bag and started walking toward the changing rooms. Anne walked beside her. "Tell me something, Lois, have all your postings been as strange as this one?"

"God no. This one's been the worst by far—the way this place works on your nerves. I despise it."

They looked at each other and something passed between them. It was electrical, Anne thought, a current of shared understanding.

"Well," Lois said, "guess I better get changed. The Ambassador and his wife actually invited me to their house for dinner tonight."

It struck Anne that this woman was not anti-social, that she was not even particularly unfriendly. She'd been wounded by life, by a man who left, and she was not going to allow herself to get hurt again. She was shy and she was lonely, but that was simply her way of protecting herself.

"Say, Lois, I was wondering . . ." They stopped walking. "I've learned how to make some fairly edible *coq au vin* and I was wondering if maybe—if you might like to come over to my place for dinner sometime?"

Lois paused. Then she said, "That would be nice. Yes, I'd like that."

"Tomorrow night?"

"Um, sure . . . why not."

"Is eight o'clock good?"

"Yes, eight's fine."

And so after work the next day Anne did not go swimming at the Cercle Sportif. She went to the butcher, to the *boulangerie*, to the vegetable stall at the corner, and she hurried home and spent two feverish hours in the kitchen. At precisely 8 o'clock there was a knock on the door and she called, "It's open!" and Lois DeVries walked into the apartment.

She looked different somehow—and Anne wondered if this was only because she'd seen her in that red swimsuit and black cap, her tan skin wet and gleaming. Lois was wearing an embroidered peasant dress that made Anne think instantly of Esmeralda's dress the day John Kennedy came to the ranch for lunch.

"Come on in," Anne said. "Don't you look nice."

Lois had stopped in the middle of the living room to study the map on the wall over the sofa, a yellowed map of Vietnam when it was part of the dying French empire, a country of three equal parts: Tonkin, Annam, Cochin China. When Lois heard Anne's compliment, she looked down at her dress. "Oh, thanks. I got this thing for a dollar when I was posted in Tegucigalpa." She looked back at the map. "Where'd you pick that up?"

"Isn't it fabulous? It belongs to my new roommate. It was hanging in her last apartment when she moved in—apparently some Frenchman left it behind when he moved out."

"That yellow color is perfect. It *feels* like Saigon—humidity and rotting garbage."

"Would you like a beer or a glass of wine? I've got Chablis and a pretty decent Burgundy."

"I prefer white wine."

They had a drink on the balcony that was suspended above the alley. It was Anne's favorite spot in the apartment—removed from the alley yet close enough for her to smell the garbage and the cooking smoke, close enough for her to hear the old women whispering in the doorways, the trill of the ice cream vendor's bell, the slap of sandals on the wet pavement.

"So who's this new roommate?" Lois asked, studying the alley.

"She's an Australian journalist, a fascinating woman. She came here because her boyfriend's company got the contract to build a waterworks in Dalat. Two weeks after they arrived from Sydney he drove over a land mine on his way to work—killed him and both passengers. But she decided to stay and now she's writing an article about an orphan boy who lives on the streets in Da Nang. She's up there now, won't be back for a couple of weeks."

"You could spend the rest of your life writing about orphan boys in this godforsaken country."

"That's exactly what Rosalynn says. She calls them 'the ninety-five percent that don't count.' "

"I like that. 'The ninety-five percent that don't count.' " Lois emitted a single bitter bark of laughter and drained her glass. "It's nice up here, almost like you're invisible."

"I used to think I was invisible too, but I figured out that everyone in that alley knows we're up here. There aren't any secrets in Saigon." Even as she was saying this, an old Vietnamese man in a beret smiled up at her from the alley. He walked with a cane and had a tuft of white billy-goat whiskers trailing from his chin. *"Bon soir, mademoiselle!"* he called up to her.

"Bon soir, Monsieur Trung," she called down to him. *"Votre chapeau est bien gentil."*

He doffed the beret and bowed. *"Merci beaucoup!"* Then he shuffled up the alley.

When he disappeared, Lois said, "What was that all about?"

"He runs the grocery around the corner. I was complimenting him on his new beret. I'm teaching him French and he's teaching me Vietnamese."

"You're actually learning Vietnamese?"

Anne realized this was not a question; it was a reproach. "Yes, I'm trying to learn Vietnamese. Is that so awful?"

"No, it's not awful. It's just that—why on earth would you want to learn such an ugly language? I can understand studying

French or Spanish—but Vietnamese is useless. And it sounds like a bunch of grunting animals."

"I'll tell you why I want to learn the language, Lois—because I live here. Because this is *their* country. Are they supposed to learn English just because you and I showed up?"

"No, I suppose not," Lois said wearily, as though she didn't have the energy for this argument with a naive little girl. "But I do suppose I could use another drop of that Chablis."

They ate at the table on the balcony, with candles and lanterns flickering in the alley below them and cooking smoke drifting up into the star-speckled sky. Anne was pleased with the way the meal turned out—*coq au vin,* French-cut green beans, baguettes, then salad and Camembert cheese. Lois ate two helpings of everything, and the way she put the wine away made Anne glad she'd bought two extra bottles.

Lois asked for a glass of port instead of coffee and dessert, and Anne decided to skip the tarts and have a glass of port with her. They didn't say much. Lois chain-smoked and bit her lip constantly. They watched the alley come to life as it did every night, rejuvenated by the darkness and the cooler air. A river breeze washed this part of the city.

Three girls passed in *ao dais,* blue, yellow, white, holding hands. They moved so fluidly they seemed to be joined together, a single organism. Anne watched them until they reached the street and turned the corner. "Never dressed carelessly," she said, "never the wrong word, never prey to untidy passion . . ."

"I beg your pardon," Lois said.

"Those girls. They reminded me of a book I'm reading, a book about Saigon."

Lois lit a fresh cigarette and said, "How much rent you paying?"

The bluntness of the question surprised Anne. "Not a lot. The landlord lives on the ground floor—Mr. Hing, he's Chinese. We call him Slumlord to the Stars. This building has a little bit of everything. There's a French car dealer one flight down who supposedly imports a whole lot more than Citroens. There's a Vietnamese couple across the hall who fight like cats and dogs, and an old man at the end of the hall who owns an opium den behind the cathedral. Everyone says he's Viet Cong."

"Jesus." Lois shook her head and exhaled smoke. Another reproach. Learning the language was bad enough, she seemed to be saying, but going native like this was too much.

"Where do you live, Lois?"

"In the American compound over on Nguyen Thai Binh. I can walk to work—and it's paid for." She seemed to realize this sounded harsh. "Then again, I don't get to watch the world go by like this. It's very nice."

Anne refilled their glasses. She knew she might be making a terrible mistake, but she had to do it. She said, "Lois, there's something I've been wanting to tell you. Remember a few weeks ago when you asked me to help you carry those old cables up to the storage locker on the fifth floor?"

"Yes."

"Well, I realize I probably shouldn't have done it, but I read some of them."

"Did they bore you to tears?"

"Actually, I found them fascinating. There was one from Ambassador Durbrow back in 1960 that mentioned problems with Ngo Dinh Nhu's secret police. It almost made it sound like the communists were winning the war."

Lois waved her hand as though she was disappointed by such a tepid revelation. "That's old hat. Durbrow got shipped out precisely because he rocked the boat. When Kennedy got into office he decided he wanted an ambassador who was gung-ho, which is why he picked Nolting. But that's not news. You want to hear some news?"

"Yes."

"Now the boneheads in Washington are getting tired of Diem—and there's been talk that Nolting might be on his way out because he's so pro-Diem. They're talking about bringing in someone who'll make Diem and Nhu straighten up and fly right."

"My God, Lois."

"That's not the half of it. You know whose name keeps coming up?"

"I have no idea."

"Henry Cabot Lodge."

"But he's a . . . *Republican*."

"That's the whole point. Lodge is perfect for those devious bastards in the State Department. He's respectable, he's patrician, he won't take any crap off anybody—certainly not a couple of flakes like Diem and his brother—and best of all, if the whole thing falls apart the State Department has a handy scapegoat. A Republican scapegoat."

They drank another glass of port in silence. Anne could see her tidy world unraveling faster than ever. "Tell me something, Lois. Do you believe we're losing the war?"

"I'll put it to you this way." She was beginning to slur her words. "It's hard to say who's winning and who's losing on any given day. The only fact in this country is that there are no facts."

"That's what Jon Medlin's always saying."

"Well, he's right about something for once. But I will tell you this much—I see the raw CIA data from the field, I read the American advisors' reports before MACV dresses them up for the press, and things aren't going half as well as Washington thinks they are."

"Why doesn't someone just tell them the truth?"

This, finally, was too much for Lois DeVries. "My dear girl," she said, exhaling twin tusks of smoke, "you've been here how long? Six months?"

"Closer to eight."

"That's plenty long enough for you to have figured out the First Commandment: Thou Art Part of a Machine and Thou Shalt Tell the Machine What the Machine Wants to Hear. In this case the machine wants to hear that the communists are being defeated and that the South Vietnamese are in love with Ngo Dinh Diem, so every American in the country who wants to keep his job winds up saying just that. I know for a fact that there are several American advisors down in the Delta who are about to go stark raving mad because they can't get anyone to believe that the military situation is going to hell in a handbasket. I feel sorry for those men. They're dedicated and they're brave, but they're doomed to being ignored—or worse, they're doomed to being punished for telling the truth. Their futures do not look bright."

"So there's nothing anyone can do?"

"I'm afraid not. All we can do is muddle through and hope for the best. The funny thing is, it just might work out in the end. I've seen weirder things happen." She looked at her glass and was surprised to find it empty. "And I've had too much to drink. I'd better run along."

On her way out Lois paused and picked up the book that was open, face-down, on the sofa. *"The Quiet American*. Is this the movie Marlon Brando's going to be in?"

"No, that's *The* Ugly *American*. Different story altogether."

"Oh. I haven't read a book in months. I find I can't concentrate anymore." She was staring at the book, wobbling slightly. She seemed distressed by the fact that she couldn't concentrate anymore. Watching her standing there, frowning and wobbling, Anne realized that Lois DeVries was unraveling, too. She felt the desire to make it all stop—the lies, the frayed nerves, the rising scent of doom.

"Let's go to the movies together sometime," Anne said brightly.

"I'd like that. But first I want to have you over for dinner. And, Anne . . ."

"Yes?"

"Let's keep what was said here tonight between us, okay?"

"Sure."

"Thanks for a wonderful evening. I needed it."

Anne went to the balcony and watched Lois walk down the alley, past the whispering old ladies squatting on their haunches, past the flower vendor and the boy selling lottery tickets. At the corner Lois flagged a trishaw and haggled with the driver, using hand signals, then she climbed aboard and waved to Anne and was swallowed by the night.

10

Her swimming regimen and her budding friendship with Lois DeVries did not fill the hollow place in Anne Sinclair's life, so she decided to set out on a literary pilgrimage.

She had first encountered Graham Greene's *The Quiet American* in a course on postwar British fiction during her freshman year at Berkeley. At the time she was left cold by the novel, the story of Thomas Fowler, a burnt-out, fatalistic, opium-smoking British correspondent in Saigon in the early 1950s who loses his Vietnamese mistress to Alden Pyle, an American innocent, a boy from Boston who has come to Asia to spread the gospel of democracy and instead winds up bringing misery on everyone, especially himself. When Anne's new roommate moved in, the first things she unpacked were the yellowed map of Indochina and a dog-eared copy of *The Quiet American*. Anne reread the book in a state of growing ecstasy.

In the evenings, after swimming her laps, she found herself prowling the streets of the city, retracing the steps of Greene's characters, delighted that so many of his details still rang true a decade after he wrote them. Saigon, she was beginning to see, was a city that existed outside of time. From the roof of the

Majestic she watched American ships unload helicopters and bombs, just as Fowler had done. The building that used to house the French *police sûreté* was now some sort of barracks for Nhu's secret police, but the courtyard wall was still topped with wrought-iron spikes and it still smelled of urine and injustice, just as Greene had written. Looking up from the street, Anne could see the ceiling fans twirling behind the open shutters, could see the hard chairs, the moths circling the bare globes of light. There was a man sitting with his back to the window, and it was easy for her to believe it was Vigot, Greene's fictional French police inspector, slouched in the cigarette smoke and heavy heat, wearing a green eyeshade and reading Pascal the night Fowler was brought in for questioning after Pyle was found under a Saigon bridge, a stab wound in his chest, his lungs full of mud, suddenly a very quiet American.

Of course barbers still cut hair and dentists still pulled teeth right out on the sidewalks. Anne walked the length of Rue Catinat dozens of times, and the only detail from the novel she disagreed with was Fowler's description of Notre Dame as "a hideous pink cathedral." Anne found the church lovely. But then, Fowler was scornful of all expressions of godliness, and Anne, so far, was not.

In fact, Fowler detested all ideology, all *ism*'s, almost as much as he detested Americans like Pyle, men born to a world of dude ranches and skyscrapers and express elevators, of dry martinis and chicken sandwiches on the *Merchant Limited.* But Pyle had his virtues. He drove a Buick, and Anne, thinking of that parade of Buicks in Bangkok, liked him for that. Fowler disliked Ike, and Anne, being a good Democrat, liked him for that. The thing she liked best about Fowler, though, was that at the outset of the book he refused to become *engagé,* as he put it, refused to choose sides. He said he was an impartial observer, a reporter, a man with nothing to gain and nothing to lose. By the end of the book, however, he realizes he has a great deal to lose—and he realizes how terrified he is of losing his mistress and being alone—and so he is forced to choose, to act, to live in the world of untidy motives and even less tidy consequences.

Her favorite passage in the book was the day Fowler and

Pyle drove out to Tay Ninh, eighty kilometers northwest of Saigon, for the festival at the Caodaists' Holy See. It was a day that began in sunshine and nearly ended in disaster. When she'd read the book back in college, Anne assumed the Caodai religion was something Greene had cooked up after a few too many pipes of opium. But soon after arriving in Saigon she learned that it was an actual, if fantastical, creed—a hash of Confucianism, Buddhism and Christianity built around the odd saintly trio of Victor Hugo, Joan of Arc and Sun Yat-sen. The Caodaists had their own standing army back then, armed with bolt-action rifles and mortars made out of car exhaust pipes. Anne knew her literary pilgrimage would not be complete until she'd seen the Holy See.

Though USIS regulations strictly forbade it, she borrowed her roommate's car, a battered gray Austin, and set out early one Sunday morning, giving herself plenty of time to make the round trip before nightfall. She filled the gas tank so she wouldn't wind up stranded all night in no-man's-land, like Fowler and Pyle.

Saigon was soon behind her and she was moving through dusty towns, honking the horn to alert the bicyclists, water buffaloes and children, the old ladies balancing buckets of water on the ends of long poles. The French had built a guard tower at every kilometer post out here because at night they withdrew into their little fortresses, ceding the country to the Viet Minh until sunrise. Not unlike the war today, Anne thought. She passed several Caodai churches, pale blue with the all-seeing eye of God above the door, then vast stands of rubber trees. She thought of the recent night when a drunk, ruined old Frenchman had plopped down on the barstool next to hers at the Continental Hotel and spent an hour regaling her with the glorious achievements of France's *mission civilisatrice* in Indochina. The French brought their penal code with them, the man said, and it was a vast improvement over the Vietnamese code, which required that thieves be beheaded and that adulterous women be trampled by elephants. The French also created monopolies on alcohol, salt and opium, and they made a fortune exporting rice. This particular Frenchman was a superintendent at a Michelin rubber plantation not far from where Anne was now driving, and he freely admitted—he practically boasted—that during his tenure between the world wars, he'd lost one-fourth of his Vietnamese workers, more than 12,000 people, to malaria, dysentery, malnutrition and exhaustion.

She reached Tay Ninh just before noon. The sun was fierce and she was hungry and dusty and tired, but she drove directly to the Holy See, parked in the shade of a peepul tree, and bought a bottle of cold Green Spot soda from a vendor. She downed it in three gulps, then started walking toward the cathedral.

The grounds were decorated with bronze fish, deer, turtles and what appeared to be car radiators. Nothing had quite prepared Anne for the church itself, though Greene had invoked the name of Walt Disney and had used words like "technicolour" and "fantasia" to describe it. In the main sanctuary the walls were yellow and the pillars were pink, entwined with dragons and supporting a sky-blue ceiling studded with stars made of faceted glass. The focus of the room was a huge globe decorated with the ubiquitous eyeball in a pyramid. Only then did Anne realize the eyeball was copied from the back of the American dollar bill.

A woman in a white robe shooed all visitors to the balcony that ringed the room. An orchestra began playing—the twang of string instruments mixing with the thump of drums, gongs, horns, chanting, a cloud of incense. Birds flitted through the open windows. The priests and cardinals filed in, wearing pointy hats and gowns of white, yellow and blue silk. It was like a Ku Klux Klan rally, Anne thought, or some snake-handling Holy Roller cult with a big budget and a lunatic for an interior decorator.

When the mercifully short ceremony ended, she went outside and bought an ice cream and sat in the shade savoring it. It tasted so good in the heat that she was able to ignore the cloud of flies humming around her head. She dreaded starting the drive back to Saigon. The sun was vertical now, the air dead. She prayed the car would make it. For the first time she realized how unwise this impulsive little trip had been. As she stood up and started for the car, a man called to her. "Excuse me? Ma'am?"

She turned. A crew-cut whiskerless American boy, dressed in a sportshirt and shorts, was walking toward her. The sunburned face looked familiar. It was the Marine who checked credentials inside the front door of the U.S. Embassy. Luckily he didn't seem to recognize her. "Do you speak English, ma'am?"

"Yes, I do."

"We was wondering if you'd do us a favor." He looked down. He was holding a cheap camera in his big pink paws. "My buddy and I was wondering if you'd mind taking a picture of us with our girls. Right there—in front of the church."

"Of course not. I'd be delighted."

The two buzz-cut boys stood like bookends with the two Vietnamese girls squeezed between them. Anne ordered them all to say "Cheese!" and as they giggled and grinned she snapped three pictures. They thanked her profusely, then climbed into an unmarked dark blue Jeep.

The Austin fired right up and Anne started back to Saigon, driving faster than she had on the way out. She still had plenty of gas and the engine was running cool. A few miles out of Tay Ninh she had to swerve to miss a hairless, scab-encrusted dog that darted in front of her car, and when she checked her rear-view mirror she saw the dog standing in the dusty road, scratching itself. The dark blue Jeep approached and it, too, had to swerve.

Before long Black Lady Mountain rose up on her left, and she felt reassured that she was making good time. She told herself no one would find out she'd broken regulations. In one town she passed a café where a dozen uniformed South Vietnamese soldiers were drinking beer, their rifles on their laps. They all stopped talking and watched her pass.

As the town faded into the haze she checked her mirror again. The Jeep was still behind her. She tried to sing the new Sam Cooke song, "You Send Me," but found that her mouth was too dry and she couldn't concentrate on the words.

She crossed a bridge that spanned a canal, then slowed as she entered another small town, another town like every other town, the same water buffaloes, the same bicycles and half-naked brown children, the same dust, the same pitiless sun. She looked in her mirror. When the Jeep rose onto the bridge it suddenly shot into the sky on a ball of orange flame, coming apart, then raining sheets of metal, tires, pieces of burning bodies that bounced when they hit the road. Only then did Anne hear the explosion and feel the concussion.

Pigs were squealing, people screaming, panicked water buffaloes lurching in front of her car. Anne had to stop. A water buffalo slammed into the passenger's side of the car, shattering the rear windshield. She screamed. Then, without thinking, she started honking the horn and inching the car forward. Moving seemed crucial to survival. The crowd parted and she eased forward, muttering, "Please oh please oh please oh please . . ." She kept honking, kept moving, and soon she was escaping the town.

It turned out she was only a few miles from Saigon. Soon she was passing Tan Son Nhut Airport and re-entering the familiar honeycomb of the city streets. Nothing seemed out of the ordinary. People were buying food at the stalls, drinking beer in the cafés, squatting in the doorways. Traffic was light, and in no time she was parking in the alley under her balcony and shutting off the engine. Only then did she realize the back seat was covered with shattered glass and she had sweated through her shirt. She was still breathing hard. Though the car was unbearably hot, she couldn't move. She couldn't let go of the steering wheel. She kept seeing those burning bodies falling out of the sky. Finally she leaned forward and rested her forehead against her hands and began to weep.

11

Mercifully for the Major, the weeks before the premiere of *The Ugly American* were so hectic he didn't have time to fret about his impending meeting with the great Brando. The Automobile, Truck and Accessories Exhibit brought in several planeloads of executives from Detroit. The Major spent the week shuttling three General Motors executives all over town in the red-and-black Buick. They called the paintjob "lipstick" red, which the Major found rather poetic, but they were big loud ham-fisted men who seemed to stay drunk twenty-four hours a day.

Then the city shut down for Songkran, the traditional Thai New Year and the Major's favorite holiday. In the mornings he rose early to watch people making merit—offering food to monks, releasing birds into the air and fish into the rivers and klongs. He attended a parade of the Phra Putta Sihing image of the Buddha, which passed through the streets once a year so crowds could splash scented, purifying water on it. He even ventured across the river to Phra Pradaeng, a Mon community where the parade was said to feature the most beautiful Miss Songkrans in all of Bangkok. It proved to be true, though the Major caught a cold after a long day of being doused with purifying water, which the gleeful Thais dispensed from buckets, plastic bags, garden hoses, even plastic pistols imported from Hong Kong.

After Songkran, a gang of Sony executives rented the Buicks for the International Trade Fair, which drew half a million people to Lumpini Park to ogle foreign watches, radios, cameras and cars, most of them made in Japan. The Thais found this cornucopia of cheap gadgets irresistible. On the fourth day of the fair, a freak rain shower turned the park into a quagmire. The turquoise-and-white Buick sank to its axles, and the Major had to pay a man on an elephant ten baht to pull the car out. And then, of course, there was the growing legion of American servicemen on R&R who wanted to travel in style to the Fantasy Bar, the Ramble House, the Sani Château, the Boom Boom Room and places that were springing up so fast it was impossible to keep track of their names.

Finally the big day arrived and the Major found himself standing with his friend Kukrit Pramoj and the Universal Studios advance man in a giddy mob at Don Muang Airport. The Major was dressed in a starched shirt, poplin suit and white bucks. He was trying to look dignified, but he found the excitement of the crowd infectious. He was standing in a sea of reporters and photographers and tourists and young Thai women who obviously had spent hours getting buffed and painted to perfection for this rare chance to glimpse a Hollywood movie star. The young ladies were actually jiggling. Even his distinguished friend Kukrit—a member of one of the finest families in Thailand, a graduate of Queen's College at Oxford, a banker, soldier, teacher, Finance Minister, monk, newspaper editor, pundit, novelist and, now, movie star—even Kukrit was trembling with anticipation.

When the Pan Am jet parked outside, half an hour behind schedule, a roar went up from the crowd. The jet's door popped open and a man appeared at the top of the stairs. But it was not Brando. It was a bewildered Japanese tourist, and he was soon followed by his wife and three children, then by dozens of other tourists from all over the world. Just when the crowd was beginning to despair, a fresh roar went up and there stood

Marlon Brando, the man who had played Marc Antony and Terry Malloy and Napoleon, the original wild one, the greatest talent Hollywood was ever likely to produce—though the Major got the unsettling impression watching Brando play Fletcher Christian in *Mutiny on the Bounty* last year that even a genius was capable of going through the motions. He was dressed in a short-sleeved white shirt and a black necktie and black pants. His hair was mussed. He looked like a waiter who'd just been jolted awake from a nap. The Major was appalled.

The rest of the mob didn't seem to mind. They poured out onto the tarmac, led by the men with cameras and notebooks. The Universal Studios man instructed the Major to pull the Buick up in front of the terminal while he guided Brando through interviews and autographs and Customs.

An hour later the Major was sitting in the pink-and-black Buick reading the Singapore cricket scores when the terminal door opened and three policemen elbowed their way through the crowd and ripped open the car's passenger door. Marlon Brando ducked into the back seat, followed by an almond-skinned girl in a floral wrap dress with a red hyacinth in her hair. Kukrit climbed into the front seat. The Major had trouble taking his eyes off the girl—she was just about the most delicate thing he had ever seen—but Brando was holding out his slab of a right hand. "Thanks for waiting. I'm Marlon and this is Supi. We met yesterday in Hawaii—her English ain't so good."

"And I'm Nigel Colchester. They call me the Major." He shook the hand. It was strong as a vise, but soft. "Where to, Mr. Brando?"

"Marlon."

"Where to, Marlon?"

"The hotel. I wanna take a swim and a nap. They got a pool, don't they?"

"Oh yes. Quite."

All the way into town Kukrit and Brando reminisced about the time they'd spent together in Hollywood. Supi didn't utter a word. The Major was so busy studying Brando's face in the rearview mirror that he almost caused half a dozen accidents. Brando looked younger than the Major had expected. The

103

smooth skin and fleshy lips, the scrambled hair, the sleepy eyes—it was the face of a groggy, overgrown boy.

Kukrit was talking about Brando's remarks to the press back at the airport. "I was most amused by the way they kept asking about the movie and you kept talking about the American Negro. It was the same when I got back from Hollywood. All they wanted to know about was what it was like to be a movie star."

"What'd you tell 'em?" Brando asked.

"Well, I tried to tell them about that lovely reception Burt and Norma Lancaster hosted for Reverend King, but they weren't interested in racial matters. They wanted to know about life on a movie set. So I told them I had my very own trailer, just like Mr. Marlon Brando's, with carpet and air-conditioning and gin flowing from the tap."

"Hoo-hoo!" Brando slapped his thigh.

"I told them about how the script girls and dressers mothered me—which was the truth—fetching me sandwiches, giving me records to play in my hotel room, telling me where to go for weekends and vacations."

"That's the sorta crap the press cares about."

"Indeed it is. They didn't want to hear about how the air turned orange in Los Angeles, or about how people in the movie industry are doing everything in their power to help Reverend King."

"Or about how we're on the verge of a race war."

"Heavens no," Kukrit said, chuckling. "All they care about is what kind of gin flows from the taps on a Hollywood movie set."

Marlon Brando had hoped to find some peace and quiet by staying at an out-of-the-way hotel instead of a customary movie-star address like the Erawan or the Oriental, but the White Elephant was under seige. Sam had to put a chain and lock on the alley gate, and he stationed Rat at the main entrance to make sure no uninvited guests slipped into the compound. The place took on a circus atmosphere—photographers climbed trees, hoping to get a candid shot; people bounced up and down in the alley, trying to peek over the wall; guests who never went swimming suddenly spent entire afternoons poolside, pretending to read magazines while they kept an eye on the door to Bungalow 9; women on the telephone offered huge sums of money for the chance to rent a bungalow or simply make a dinner reservation.

On his first night in town Brando was the guest of honor at a bash thrown by Universal Studios at the Oriental Hotel. On his second night he was received by the King and Queen at Chitlada Palace. On his third night he attended the world premiere of *The Ugly American* at the Chalerm Thai theater, then a reception, then a press conference, and then he said he wanted to go somewhere quiet and have a nightcap. The Major suggested the roof of the White Elephant. Brando loved the idea.

They dragged Sam and Rat and Jiap up to the roof with them and had the barman send up bottles of beer, whisky, brandy, soft drinks, ice. They lit candles and mosquito coils. Brando collapsed onto a lounge chair and gazed numbly at the river, at the sprawling lights of Thonburi and, to the north, the spotlit needle of the Temple of Dawn. Supi knelt by his side and sat on her heels. She hadn't said three words in the past three days, and the Major thought she became more radiant by the hour.

"It really stunk, didn't it?" Brando blurted to no one in particular.

This was greeted by silence. Finally Kukrit said, "You mean the movie?"

"Yeah, I mean the movie."

"It was pretty dreadful, all right," Kukrit said. "Although I thought I had my moments."

Everyone laughed, including Brando, and the tension eased.

"The one thing you must remember, Marlon," Kukrit said, "was that the pay wasn't too bad."

"The pay was fantastic," Brando said. "That's the only reason I did the lousy picture."

"Come, come now," the Major said. "It wasn't so altogether dreadful. I thought the Colonel Hillandale character had certain virtues—considering that he worked for the CIA. At least he didn't buy into that 'inscrutable Orientals' rot."

"I thought having him hold a diploma from the Chungking School of Occult Science was a nice touch," Kukrit said, and everyone laughed again.

Suddenly Brando started mimicking the voice of Colonel Hillandale: "Every person and every nation has a key which will open their hearts. If you use the right key, you can maneuver any person or any nation any way you want." Brando turned to Sam. "What do you think about that, Sam? You think you can maneuver nations any way you want?"

"I suppose that depends on the nation," Sam said uneasily.

"Well," Brando said, "let's start with the nation of Sarkhan from this shitty movie I just got paid a bundle to make. I played the American ambassador to Sarkhan and Kukrit played the Prime Minister." Rat and Kukrit were chuckling, but in the candlelight the Major could see that Brando's face was as cold as stone.

"I've never been to Sarkhan," Sam said.

"It don't exist. It's a state of mind."

"I haven't read the book or seen the movie yet. I had to work the desk last night."

"Well then," Brando pressed, "since the country of Sarkhan is obviously supposed to be Vietnam, let me ask you if you think America can maneuver Vietnam any way it wants to. You been to Vietnam, right?"

"Oh yeah. I've been to Vietnam."

"Well?"

The thrum of the river traffic suddenly seemed very loud to the Major. He could hear the distant pop of firecrackers up toward Chinatown.

"Let me put it to you this way," Sam said very slowly. "Anyone who takes the Vietnamese communists lightly is a fool. And from what I saw over there, our government is taking them very lightly. We seem to think that all we have to do is show up with enough money and enough people and enough hardware and we'll get whatever we want."

"And we're wrong?" Brando said.

"Dead wrong."

"What exactly did you see over there that makes you so sure?"

A shrill voice barked, "That's enough, Sam!"

Everyone turned. It was Rat who had spoken. He was glaring at Sam, glaring at him with such fury that everyone looked away.

"I say," chirped the Major into the prickly silence, "I have a question for Kukrit and Marlon that has nothing whatsoever to do with Vietnam. On the way in from the airport the other day you both mentioned something about a reception hosted by Burt Lancaster for a Reverend King. I know who Burt Lancaster is, of course, but who is this King chap?"

Kukrit pounced on this, launching into a long story about the night they were invited to Burt Lancaster's palace in Beverly Hills. Governor Edmund G. Brown sent out the invitations. After everyone had a few drinks, a very brassy man, some sort of show-business lawyer, told the crowd that it cost $1,000 a day to run the Southern Christian Leadership Conference, Martin Luther King's civil rights organization. The man wanted money on the spot. Kukrit was astonished by such cheek; he was even more astonished when Paul Newman took out a checkbook and wrote a check for $1,000.

"I couldn't believe the man had brought his checkbook to a party!" Kukrit cried.

"You gotta carry a checkbook," Brando mumbled. "Nobody in Hollywood carries cash." The Major noticed he was gazing distractedly at the Temple of Dawn.

"At any rate," Kukrit went on, "after that, people were tripping all over themselves to donate money to Reverend King. John Forsythe and Lloyd Bridges wrote checks. Polly Bergen and Tony Franciosa wrote checks. Marlon Brando wrote a check for, what was it, $5,000 . . .?"

Brando grunted.

"And not to be outdone, Sammy Davis Jr. matched the pot by writing a check for $20,000!"

Brando, apparently, had heard enough about the largesse of the Hollywood movie colony. As he stood up, Supi rose simultaneously, like his shadow. "We got an eight-o'clock plane in the morning," he said. "Major, you gonna run us out to the airport?"

"I should be delighted."

And with that, the great Brando was gone. For the Major, it was an unsatisfactory conclusion to an unsatisfactory day—to three unsatisfactory days. When the others went downstairs he mixed himself a fresh gin and tonic and sat watching the river. He kept hearing Marlon Brando say the only reason he'd made *The Ugly American* was because the pay was fantastic. He kept thinking of Brando writing a $5,000 check for a Negro minister. And he kept seeing the look on Rat's face when he had commanded Sam to be silent. It was a look the Major knew well: It was the look of a man whose blood was on fire, a man who was capable in that instant of murder, or worse. Much, much worse.

PART TWO

12

Anne Sinclair arrived in Bangkok the day after the Marlon Brando circus left town. Charlie Malloy had arranged for her to stay free at the White Elephant and for his brother to pick her up at the airport. Charlie assured her she wouldn't have any trouble finding Sam. "Just look for a well-preserved version of me—ten years younger and maybe ten, fifteen pounds lighter."

Anne was in line at Customs when she spotted Sam. He was standing behind a bright yellow fence in the upstairs arrival lounge, scanning the crowd. The first thing she noticed was that he was shockingly handsome—nothing at all like portly, dissolute, lovable Charlie. In fact, it was hard to believe the two men were related. Sam had a full head of inky black hair, a solid jaw, the coiled body of an athlete. There was no fat on him. He was easily forty pounds lighter than Charlie, not the advertised ten or fifteen. If he was ten years younger, that meant he was in his mid-twenties, but there was something about his eyes, a darkness, a weariness, that made him look much older. She noticed a slight stoop in his posture, as though that long liquid body were bending under a terrible weight. Only when he started walking along the yellow fence did she notice the thing most people noticed first about Sam Malloy: the hitch in his walk. This beautiful man had been damaged somehow, and by the time their eyes met and she'd waved to him, she had vowed to find out what had done this to him.

When she cleared Customs and reached the top of the stairs, Sam snatched her bag and held out his right hand. *"Sawadee kaa,"* he said. "Welcome to the Venice of the Orient."

"Thanks for coming out," she said, shaking the hand. Shaking Charlie's hand was like gripping a fish; shaking this hand was to feel the perfectly sprung sculpture of muscle, tendon and bone. The sockets of his eyes may have been dark, their corners webbed with the beginnings of wrinkles, but his irises were a blue she recognized immediately: They were the blue of the California sky. It was almost unbearable to look into those eyes, and as his hand released hers she looked away and realized she was off balance. Her flight had been choppy—they had flown through a rain squall—and now the floor seemed to be shifting beneath her. She had prepared a quip for this moment, but she could not begin to remember what it was.

"So how was your flight?" he asked, starting for the exit. The hitch in his walk was more obvious than before, but his strides were so long she had to hurry to keep up with him.

"Just fine," she lied. For some reason it seemed important that this man not think of her as a complainer.

He stopped just before the exit and slapped his forehead. "I'm sorry. I didn't even think to ask—is this your only luggage?"

She had to think. "Um, yes. Yes it is."

"Well, for once, my brother was telling the truth."

"The truth? About what?"

"He told me you'd probably pack light."

"Oh."

"He also told me you're the most beautiful woman in all of Saigon. Charlie says things like that about a lot of women—but this time it's obvious he was telling the truth."

He was holding the door open for her, and she could feel her face flush as she walked out of the air-conditioned terminal into the steambath of the Bangkok morning.

They crossed an acre of parked cars, sunshine exploding off

their windshields, and when Anne saw the pink-and-black Buick floating in that sea of puny Vauxhalls and Datsuns and Fiats, she thought of how a thoroughbred looks in a corral full of quarter horses: almost like a creature from a different genus.

"Oh. My. God." She was circling the car, her mouth hanging open. "It's so *pink*. And all that *chrome*. It's gorgeous! That picture in *The Herald Trib* didn't begin to do it justice."

"Black-and-white pictures never do." He was standing back and smiling, admiring her admiring the car.

"I just realized something," she said. "I went to my senior prom in a car just like this." She bent down and examined the back seat. "Yep, same exact car. Wait! Don't tell me! It's a Buick . . . a nineteen . . . fifty . . . *five*."

"Close. It's a fifty-four."

"The one I went to the prom in was turquoise with a white top." She was still studying the back seat. "The upholstery was just like this—turquoise on top, then black the rest of the way down."

"They call that turquoise 'Malibu Blue.' I've got one of them, too."

"How many do you have altogether? Five?"

"Seven."

"Where do you keep them?"

"Back at the hotel."

"What the hell are we waiting for?"

Anne was so thrilled to be away from Saigon, so delighted by the car's plush interior and the gleaming arc of the dashboard that she forgot her anxiety at the airport. Even the ugliness of the Bangkok outskirts, the shattered pavements and muddy ditches, the snarled traffic and sooty air, couldn't dampen her delight at being away from the war, even if it was only for a weekend. She was studying a gold-roofed pagoda surrounded by thatch and tin shacks when she heard Sam's voice. ". . . pretty exciting."

"I'm sorry," she said. "I was admiring that incredible pagoda back there. What were you asking me?"

"I said that from what my brother tells me, your job in Saigon sounds pretty exciting."

"Not really. Most days I feel like a glorified typist. But I did just finish working on a pretty amusing propaganda movie. And I'm learning a lot about how the Embassy and the State Department work. That part's fascinating. I can't believe some of the stuff that goes on . . ."

"What's the movie about?"

"It's about the patriotism of President Ngo Dinh Diem. I got to visit his birthplace up in Hue, which is a beautiful city on the coast. I even met the tailor who makes his white sharkskin suits. Crazy old coot smokes opium from dawn to dusk."

"Diem smokes opium?"

"No, no, no," she laughed. "His *tailor* smokes opium. I have been hearing rumors, though, that Diem's brother smokes like a fiend."

"Did you get a chance to ask any peasants what they think about Diem?"

"Actually I did try. But the first six people I asked all gave me a blank look and said, 'Who is Ngo Dinh Diem?' That didn't make it into the movie."

"When I was in the central highlands we asked some Montagnards what they thought about Buddhism. They said, 'Is Buddhism a disease?' "

When she stopped laughing she said, "What were you doing in the highlands with Montagnards?" She instantly regretted it. He flinched and then there was a long silence.

Finally he said, "Ask one of your friends in the Embassy. I'm sure they know all about the recruitment and training of the 'Yards. It's old news."

"You were in the Navy?"

"That's right. Listen, I'd rather not talk about the war if you don't mind. It's ancient history, as far as I'm concerned."

"Suits me. I'm here to forget it, too."

He turned right at the Victory Monument, a rotary as treacherous as any in the world, then left at Chitlada Palace. The traffic slowed to a crawl. Pedestrians spilled off the sidewalks, hawkers approached the car offering flowers, fruit and newspapers.

Sam pointed out the sights as they inched along—the construction site of the new National Library, then Thamasat University, then the Grand Palace with its crenelated wall, which Anne recognized from the picture of the Buicks in *The International Herald Tribune*. It looked like a walled silo full of gold-tipped missiles.

At one intersection the traffic came to a standstill and they didn't budge for twenty minutes. Sam shut off the engine and then, chuckling, pointed out the source of the problem. The traffic cop was sitting in his kiosk in the middle of the intersection, dressed in his natty brown jumpsuit, white helmet and white gloves. But he wasn't directing traffic; he was drinking from a pint bottle of Mekong whisky. The traffic light changed half a dozen times, but no one moved an inch.

"Welcome to Bangkok," Sam said, still chuckling.

Finally the jam eased. When they reached Chinatown, Sam asked Anne if she was hungry.

"I'm always hungry."

"Do you eat the local food?"

"I love Vietnamese food. But I should warn you, I do have my limits. I haven't worked up the nerve yet to try bull penis or raw duckling eggs or dog meat. I still have a little trouble with the concept of Lassie as one of the four basic food groups."

Laughing, he turned off Songwad Road into an alley that seemed inadequate for the Buick's bulk, then he eased into a slot beside a noodle shop that looked across the alley at a red-walled Chinese temple. Anne thought the temple was on fire, but when she stepped out of the car she realized it was the incense. It smelled like burning tires.

Mr. Hing personally delivered two steaming bowls of his specialty to their table, *kuay-tiao ped*, duck with noodles. Hing never passed up the chance to get close enough to smell an *ang moh*, especially a female one with hair like polished gold who towered over him.

"I hope you enjoy," he said in English. He *wai*'ed slowly and deeply enough to get a good look at the long brown legs tucked at an awkward angle under the low table.

"Mr. Hing," Sam said, "this is Miss Sinclair. She's an American visiting from Saigon. A friend of my brother."

"Ohhhhh," Hing said. "You know Mr. Charlie?"

"Yes, I do," Anne said. "He's a very good friend of mine."

"Number one," Hing said. "Always hungry."

"Right," Sam said. "I was just telling Miss Sinclair that you make the best *kuay-tiao ped* in Bangkok because you simmer the stock for two full days."

"Three," Hing said, holding up four fingers.

"Sorry. Three full days. I see you just got a haircut."

Hing patted the silver bristles on top of his head. The sidewalls were shaved right down to the scalp. "Leave too much on top," he said.

"It looks terrific."

"Very handsome," Anne agreed. Hing was wearing cheap plastic sandals, and she noticed that his feet were filthy, his toenails yellowed and cracked. Her compliment sent him waddling back to his wok with a thousand-watt smile on his face.

"Jesus," she whispered through the steam rising from her soup bowl, "where do these Chinese guys get their hair cut? It's the same thing in Saigon—they all look like they've been attacked by a blind man with a pair of hedge trimmers."

"I know," Sam said. "My guess is that they're too busy worrying about money to give a damn what they look like." He reached for the tray of four glass condiment jars—sugar, fish sauce, dried chili flakes, and chili slices floating in rice vinegar. He spooned chili flakes into his bowl, then pushed the tray to her. "Careful. You overdo the chilis and your eyeballs melt. Guaranteed."

She filled the tiny spoon twice with red flakes and, for good measure, added a dose of sliced chilis. She followed Sam's lead, using the chopsticks to pile the noodles onto her soup spoon, then slurping it all down, sloppily and noisily. Hing brought two tin cups of iced tea and gave her an approving smile.

They ate without talking, slurping and gasping and inhaling broth until their eyes glazed over and they had to pause for cooling gulps of iced tea. Anne reached for the roll of toilet paper that served as napkins. After patting her eyes and brow, she kept on eating. Sam had dreaded this three-day assignment of entertaining his brother's latest catch, but already he could sense that this was not going to be the chore he'd anticipated. She was what the Major would call "rather an exceptional bit of stuff." Everything about her was sexy, including that mustache of perspiration on her upper lip, the way she attacked her food, her openness to new things. It hardly mattered that she was blond, enormously easy to look at and nearly six feet tall. She had something more important than looks: She had spirit and she had a sense of humor: She had trouble with the concept of Lassie as a basic food group. Sam realized how long it had been since a woman had made him laugh.

"So tell me," he said, "are you going to be the woman who finally makes an honest man out of my brother?"

"You mean Charlie?"

"Yes."

"Look. Charlie's a teddy bear—a teddy bear with a big fat expense account who knows all the best restaurants in Saigon. He takes me places I couldn't dream of going on my salary." She paused. "Don't get me wrong. I'm very fond of your brother and we have a wonderful time together. God knows he puts the other American reporters in the shade. But it's strictly platonic between us, if that's what you're asking."

Yes, Sam thought, that's what I was asking. In addition to her other virtues, she was nobody's fool. "So you've met the esteemed members of the American press corps?" he said.

"Met them? I deal with them every day. Biggest bunch of self-important assholes I've ever met—except your brother, of course."

"Of course."

"I understand you and Halberstam almost got into it."

"Halberstam?"

"David Halberstam—*The New York Times* correspondent. The guy on the roof of the Rex Hotel."

"Oh, him." Sam managed a laugh. "That was nothing, just a little misunderstanding."

"About what?"

"He was being nosy, as usual."

"I hear he thinks you're CIA."

"He thinks everybody's CIA. He probably thinks you're CIA."

"Well, are you?"

"Hell no. I was in the Navy. They gave me a job to do and I did it and got out."

"Charlie says they gave you an early discharge. What for?"

He was studying a poster on the far wall urging him to drink Ho Yan Hor herbal tea because it "keeps away heatiness." When he heard her question his head snapped toward her. His eyes had changed. They were no longer the soft, cloudless California sky; now they were ice. "I had some medical problems. Getting out early was the best thing that ever happened to me. I don't want to have anything more to do with that mess as long as I live."

"You mean the war?"

"Yes, I mean the war."

"It's a mess?"

"It's beyond a mess. It's a disaster waiting to happen. It's only a matter of time."

"That's funny. Everyone I work with seems to think we'll have it mopped up in time for the election next year."

"They're either blind or they're lying. Or both."

"What makes you so sure?"

"Let's drop it . . ." He put down his chopsticks and spoon and pushed his soup bowl away. "You certainly do have a curious streak."

"Thank you."

"You remind me of my wife."

Now she set down her chopsticks and spoon. "You're married?"

"I should say you remind me of my ex-wife."

"Oh. So you *were* married." She picked up her chopsticks and spoon and resumed eating just as Hing arrived to refill their teacups.

"Soup good?" he asked.

"Mmmmmmmm," Anne said through a mouthful of noodles.

When Hing wandered off, Sam said, "Yes, I was married once. Once too often."

"What happened?"

" 'What happened?' That's such a simple question . . ." But how could he look into Anne's eager amber eyes and explain to her that he and Vivien McNair were the sort of high school sweethearts who became inseparable the moment their eyes met in the back row of Mr. Jorgensen's geometry class on the first day of their junior year at Hicksville High School? Joined at the hip, he would say later, much later, when he'd learned to laugh at the thoroughness of the catastrophe.

Vivien was strawberry blond and stupendously brainy, certain to be class valedictorian, captain of the cheerleading squad and editor of the school newspaper, Most Likely to Succeed, in the opinion of her peers, one of those flawless American girls who seem minted for a long and sunny life. And in Sam Malloy, he realized much later, she had found the perfect antidote to her too-perfect world: He was dangerous, his family had moved out from the city a year earlier and settled in Levittown, on the wrong side of the Parkway, and already he was captain of the basketball team and an all-state wrestler, a Golden Gloves boxer who had the smoldering intensity of a caged, pacing animal. The boys from her neighborhood in Oyster Bay played golf and tennis in the summer and worried about getting into the right colleges; Sam was a surfer and a lifeguard and he spent his spare time souping up cars. The very day they met she launched a methodical campaign to tame him to her uses, employing every weapon at her disposal: her mind, her looks, her convertible, her considerable wits. He didn't have a prayer. Again, it was much later before he understood these things, and by then it was much too late to do him any good.

Of the half dozen colleges that wanted her, she chose Barnard, and he followed her to New York because it seemed like the thing to do, better than hanging around Levittown and going to work in his greaseball brother's garage. College had never struck him as something worth wasting money on, so when the faint hope of a basketball scholarship to Hofstra fell through, he shrugged it off and took a job tending bar at the West End on upper Broadway. By then, the fall of 1956, the place was thick with Columbia undergrads, weekend beatniks and bad poets. Sam loathed them all. On bad nights he swore he would rip out the eyeballs of the next person who mentioned Rimbaud or Nietzsche.

He was miserable but he was also in love, in love with Vivien's waterfall of hair and her hard white teeth and her high laugh, in love with her smooth brown body that led him on and drove him to a frenzy but never let him all the way inside. That, she would say, chortling, pushing him off a sofa or bed at the last possible moment, she was saving for her wedding night.

By her sophomore year she had honed her rebellious streak and added a taste for alcohol and marijuana and uppers. She simply *adored* the vodka gimlets he slipped her, free of charge, at the West End. She argued with her parents constantly. She started skipping classes and riding the subway downtown to Greenwich Village coffeehouses and jazz joints and poetry readings, sometimes staying out till dawn, sometimes for days. It made Sam panicky, terrified he was losing her. One raw rainy night, after he closed the bar and locked the doors, he poured her a double vodka gimlet and took a deep breath and asked her to marry him. It seemed like the solution to all of his problems. "Why not?" she said, staring at the rain lashing the plate-glass window. "It'll be a kick." Only when she knocked over her drink did he realize she was drunk.

But they went through with it the summer before her junior year. She agreed to submit to "the works," as she put it, because there was still a good bit of the princess in her and because her parents made any other course unthinkable. Their daughter may have been marrying beneath her station, but she was going to do it in the proper style.

The ceremony was held at the First Presbyterian Church in Oyster Bay, which had never before accommodated such a weird mash of North Shore society matrons, Greenwich Village bohemians, Wall Street finance barons and Sam's Levittown clan with their cheap clothes, ghastly perfumes and children who seemed incapable of being quiet or still. The reception was held at the Cold Spring Harbor Country Club, and the affair was pleasant, if a little stiff, until Sam's brother Ed, the mechanic, started getting loudly drunk by the buffet table.

"You sonsabitches all need a bath and a shave!" he bellowed at a clot of black-clad refugees from the Village. "And look at your clothes—this is a wedding, for chrissakes, not a funeral. Buncha fairies." He had a glass of beer in one hand and a dozen chilled shrimp in the other. There were black arcs of grease under his fingernails. He was popping the shrimp into his mouth like salted peanuts.

"Aw fuck off, you fascist," said a man with a goatee.

Ed put down his beer glass and dropped the shrimp on the carpet and threw a punch that missed by a yard and caught a waiter between the shoulder blades, sending his tray of freshly poured champagne glasses exploding against the wall. There was a brief scrabbling of chairs, then three waiters hustled a cursing and flailing Ed Malloy out a side door and dumped him in the parking lot. It was, the Village crowd agreed, the highlight of the reception.

That night the honeymooners flew to Miami, then rented a car and drove to her parents' beach house in West Palm. They consummated the marriage in her parents' four-poster bed. Sam was so happy he didn't realize Vivien had gone through with the wedding largely to spite her parents, a Wall Street dad and charity-ball mom, the sort of glossy suburbanites who think of themselves as America's royalty.

The newlyweds moved into a fifth-floor walk-up on a shabby block of West 100th Street near Central Park, and Sam got a job in the mail room at the General Motors building while Vivien, suddenly serious about school, plunged into her new major in Modern American Literature. Within a month Sam began to sense he'd made a terrible mistake; he woke up every morning with a sick feeling in his stomach, a feeling he recognized as dread. Overnight he felt old. It was bad enough that Vivien, the world's most inventive tease, proved to be an unenthusiastic and unimaginative lover; it was worse that suddenly he could see their future in chilling detail. She would get her degree and then land some suitably hip job, probably in publishing; she would quickly grow tired of living in a borderline slum and hearing nothing but Spanish in the corner grocery and always being broke; and after the romance of New York wore thin, as it invariably did, she would insist they flee the city and settle in the suburbs because her family's money would win out in the end, because that kind of money always won out in the end. To Sam the suburbs meant an inevitable procession from cookouts to cocktail parties to baby strollers; some numbing job, probably in her father's firm; and a two-week vacation with her parents at the Hamptons every summer. Vivien was writing a paper about a book that perfectly captured the way he felt. It was called *Death on the Installment Plan*. At the age of twenty-one he already felt tired and old. It occurred to him that he had never had an adventure in his life.

He started running. He dug out his old black high-top Converse All Stars and his burgundy-and-gold Hicksville Hurricanes sweatsuit, and every evening, after riding the underground cattle car home from midtown, he suited up and pounded around the cinder path that circled the reservoir in Central Park. He was astonished by how out of shape he was, how rubbery his legs felt, how easily he became winded. He wasn't old yet, but as he huffed around the reservoir he understood for the first time that he was no longer a kid. Things would not come so effortlessly from now on.

But he stuck to his regimen and soon he was doing two laps around the reservoir every day, then three, then six, and he could feel his wind coming back, his muscles hardening. Eventually the park began to bore him and he took to the streets, running west to Riverside Park, then south along the banks of the Hudson. He loved running alongside the river. Its smell reminded him of something, something he had lost and could no longer name. He felt a mystifying but powerful need to remember what it was, and he vowed to return to the river every day until he did.

Two weeks later it hit him as he flew past the boats bobbing at the 72nd Street basin: He loved the river's briny smell and its silver light because these things hinted at salt water and the vastness of the sea and they reminded him of his boyhood, when he rode his bike to the shore and fished in the tidal creeks, hunted for birds' eggs and turtles and dead fish in the sawgrass, breathed the lovely stink of salt water and seaweed and mud.

Even as a boy he sensed the power of that smell. It was the smell of the beginning and the end of life. Later, as a teenager, he spent his summers as a lifeguard at Jones Beach, learning to skin-dive and surf, flirting with the city girls, spending so much time in the water that the smell was in his nostrils even when he slept. And now that smell was in his nostrils again, and for the first time since returning from his honeymoon he felt it might be possible for him to escape the prison of his life in New York.

One day, after running even farther downtown than usual along the river, he was walking home through Hell's Kitchen, soaked with sweat, breathing hard, when he came upon a sign that said "Sal Stillman's Gym." Without thinking or knowing why, he pushed through the chipped green door. Even as he walked toward the familiar sounds—the tattoo of a skip rope, the *thwapety-thwapetry-thwapety-thwapety-thwap!* of leather gloves on a light bag, the grunts and thuds of two fighters sparring— he knew he was walking into a dream that was going to change his life.

In the ring, under a single hooded lightbulb, two teenagers were sparring while an old man in a gray sweatsuit leaned on the ropes and shouted insults at them.

"Hit him, Freddie! I seen girls punch harder'n dat!" And when the kid, a Puerto Rican, threw a roundhouse that missed, the old man shouted: "Oh, cut it out already. That breeze! I'm gonna catch my deatha cold!"

Sam recognized the sound of genuine affection in the man's hectoring. He had a paunch, a halo of frizzy gray hair, and charcoal pouches under his eyes. Minus fifty pounds and a dozen years he could have been Jimmy Goins, the man who'd trained Sam to two Golden Gloves titles, the man who'd sensed something rare in him and polished it until he became that most dangerous of fighters: a fearless counter-puncher, a hit-me-and-I'll-hit-you-back boxer.

When the sparring ended and the old man finished insulting both fighters, Sam walked up to him. "Excuse me, are you Sal?"

The man was busy studying the next two fighters slipping

through the ropes, and the voice surprised him. "Yeah, I'm Sal. Who needs to know?"

"I'm Sam Malloy." He held out his hand. Sal shook it like it was a piece of spoiled meat. "I used to box Golden Gloves a few years back—and I was wondering—I've gotten rusty, but I'd like to get back into it, at least do a little sparring."

"Where you from?"

"Right now, 100th Street. On the West Side."

"No, I mean where'd you box Golden Gloves?"

"Levittown. Out on Long Island."

"Hey!" Sal shouted, loud enough for everyone in the gym to hear. "We got us a *suburban* tough guy here!" Howls and whistles and catcalls.

"I can box."

"All right, kid. Come back next Tuesday at six. We got all the gear. Alls you gotta do is box—and pay five bucks a night, stay as long as you like, work out, whatever." Then he turned to the two men in the ring, grown men about Sam's size. The old man clapped his hands. "Whadda we got here? The Glass Jaw and the Low-Blow Artist. Oh, this oughta be rich!"

For the next week Sam shadow-boxed, skipped rope and did sit-ups in addition to his running. When he finally stepped into the ring at Sal's Gym, he found himself peering through his headgear at the mashed face of a café au lait Negro with a flat nose and rat eyes, a vicious face.

Sam felt him out for two rounds, sensing he was all about attacking, no finesse, more of a puncher than a fighter. Sam felt light on his feet, plenty of wind, strong, no fear. The running was paying off. In the third round he started doing what he had always done best—letting the occasional punch land and, as soon as it did, lashing back at his off-balance, unguarded opponent, drilling him with crisp combinations, body blows, jabs, punches that surprised as they punished. After the fourth round the Negro's knees were wobbly and Sal called it off. Sam left the gym feeling exhilarated, more alive than he'd felt in years.

As he became consumed by the twin passions of running and boxing, Vivien spent longer and longer hours in the Columbia library or locked away in the spare bedroom working on her thesis. She told him she was writing about John O'Hara. The name meant nothing to him.

To fill the empty nights he started prowling the city's waterfronts, the Hudson and East River piers, the Brooklyn Navy Yard, Staten Island. He studied the boats—freighters, barges, cruise ships, tugs, an occasional destroyer. If it floated, it fascinated him. He talked to sailors and merchant marines and dockworkers. He drank in waterfront bars with deck hands, bosuns, engine-room wipers, third mates. They all moaned about the boredom and the danger and the bad food, and yet, at the slightest prodding, they told stories that made Sam's blood race. Stories about seeing whales off the coast of Colombia. Or the time pirates with machetes boarded the ship in the Strait of Malacca. Or the gorgeous whore in Bangkok who turned out to be a man. Even their stories about chipping rust beat anything Sam ever heard at the West End. Something about the sea kept calling these men back, and Sam felt the first stirrings of a desire to find out what it was.

One hot summer Saturday when Vivien went out to the Hamptons to swim in her parents' pool, Sam wound up drinking beer and watching the Yankees game on TV in Haley's Taproom, a windowless dive across the street from the Brooklyn Navy Yard's main gate. He fell into a conversation with an Italian kid from the neighborhood, an engine cadet at the Merchant Marine Academy in Kings Point who was happy to explain the intricacies of getting a seaman's card as long as Sam was willing to buy the beers.

In the bottom of the sixth inning, the door banged open and a gang of Danish sailors, big guys with yellow hair and leathery faces, stormed in and started slapping the bar and yelling at the bartender to bring them beer, whisky, schnapps. About the time they were getting merry and argumentative, the door opened again and two men walked out of a pool of golden sunshine into the gloom of the bar. They had shaved heads, and though their clothes were baggy, Sam could tell they were crushers. Not anyone to mess with.

When the two men were halfway through their first beers,

one of the Danes, a six-foot-tall fire hydrant with an earring and no front teeth, walked over and started rubbing the tops of their heads. The men didn't move. "Iss smooze!" the Dane announced to his shipmates, who roared their approval. Then he picked up one of the men's half-empty beer glasses, chugged it down, gargled the last of it briefly, and spat it into the bigger man's left ear. Sam and the Italian kid instinctively stood up and moved sideways for the door. Before they got there the man with the beer leaking down the left side of his face jerked his elbow into the Dane's throat, sending him staggering backward, gasping for air. The two skinheads rose without a word and stood shoulder-to-shoulder and waited for the sailors to attack. As they did, the two men felled them with lightning kicks to the face, with hand chops, elbows, knees to the groin, two-knuckle punches to the eyes and, as a finale, the butt of a hand driven up into the last man's nostrils, shattering his face and dropping him to the floor, where his shipmates were kneeling, writhing, clutching their faces and groins, spitting, moaning. It had taken all of thirty seconds. The two men paid for their beers and walked slowly back out into the sunshine.

"Who the fuck were those guys?" Sam asked.

"Hell if I know," the Italian kid said.

"Navy Frogmen," the bartender said, picking up the telephone and dialing the police. "Musta just shipped in."

Sam had never heard of Navy Frogmen before, but the following Monday he took a cab to Times Square during his lunch hour and walked into the Navy recruiter's office. Behind the desk, intently studying the Yankees box score, sat a ham-faced petty officer in a crisp white uniform who looked like he'd never left the air-conditioning or set foot on a ship. His black shoes were brilliantly shined. He showed Sam a brochure about Underwater Demolition Team Frogmen, and Sam felt the hair on his neck tingle as he read. Frogmen jumped out of planes and helicopters, they swam underwater for miles, they were experts in hand-to-hand combat, they blew up bridges and sometimes they shot people, but usually they worked on the sly—invisible, silent and very deadly. Sam thought of his boyhood summers, when he could smell the sea in his sleep. He thought about his job in the airless mail room in the basement of the General Motors building and his twice-a-day rides in those stinking underground cattle cars. He thought of those two guys with the shaved heads kicking unholy ass in Haley's Taproom. And finally he thought of his wife, who grew frostier and more remote every day, locked in her room writing about someone named John O'Hara.

"So how do I become a Frogman?"

The chief petty officer looked at him hard. "Son, during boot camp they're going to ask you a lot of questions. They're going to find out what you can and can't do. You say you're a good swimmer, and if you really love the water and aren't afraid of some rugged training—and I do mean rugged—then they'll cut you orders to try out for one of the teams."

"Just like that, hunh?"

"Just like that."

Sam didn't believe him, but he believed in himself, believed he could survive any training the Navy had devised. He took the brochure home to talk it over with Vivien. Before he'd said ten words, she went into orbit.

"You want to join the fucking *Navy!?*" she howled, hurling a copy of a book called *Butterfield 8* against the bedroom wall.

"Not exactly. I want to be a Frogman."

"A Frogman? Is that like Batman? Or is it closer to Superman?"

"Neither."

"Have you lost your fucking mind? We happen to be married."

"Thanks for reminding me."

"And you want to run off and become a Frogman and leave me here alone for four years?" She started pacing. "I should've listened to Mother. She was right—she said from the start that you were nothing but a white-trash greaser who didn't care about anything but sports and cars and getting laid. She said you'd leave sooner or later."

"I'm not leaving you. And there's nothing wrong with getting laid—you ought to try it sometime."

"You're disgusting."

It went back and forth well into the night, all the resentment, all the poison, all the loathing they felt for each other pouring out in a river of escalating rage. They shouted. They cursed. They wept. When she started throwing things, books and plates and ashtrays, he left the apartment and spent what was left of the night walking the streets. When the chief petty officer showed up at his Times Square recruiting office the next morning at 8 o'clock carrying a bag of doughnuts and *The Daily News*, Sam was waiting on the front stoop, bleary, disheveled, and ready to enlist.

They sent him to boot camp at Great Lakes, Illinois. For the first two weeks he wrote a letter to Vivien every day, telling her that if he didn't get on one of the Underwater Demolition Teams he would refuse to become a part of the black-shoe Navy. He would go AWOL if he had to.

She never wrote back, not one word. Already he was bored with the routine of boot camp, but fortunately there were ample opportunities for him to demonstrate his potential to become a gifted killer. He was the camp's best swimmer, second-best runner, easily the best boxer. At the end of boot camp, to no one's surprise, he was assigned to UDT training at the naval amphibious base in Little Creek, Virginia. Instead of going directly there, he decided to go to New York to break the news to Vivien in person.

He wasn't surprised to find a Cuban couple living in the apartment on West 100th Street. A day of prowling the Columbia campus and Broadway bars produced a few leads, and that night he found her in Little Italy, sharing a cold-water walk-up with a poet named Gregory, no last name asked for, none given. She had chopped her gorgeous hair halfway up her neck and she'd lost weight. Her skin was as white as an eggshell. She didn't invite Sam into the apartment. She asked him for a divorce before he could tell her his news, then handed him a stack of papers. He signed them right there in the hallway that reeked of radiator steam and cat piss. After exactly one year, six months and three days of holy matrimony, he was a single man again. He skipped down the stairs feeling airy and light, like a man who'd just been sprung from jail.

How could he possibly hope to explain all this to those amber eyes that looked at him now across the cooling bowls of *kuay-tiao ped*? He couldn't imagine where to begin. So he said, "What happened? Nothing happened. We got married too young for all the wrong reasons and it didn't work out. Period. Oldest story in the book."

She wanted to press him for details, but she'd already seen how quickly his eyes could turn to ice, so she decided to let it go. Another time, she told herself. No need to rush.

When Hing brought the change to the table and bowed stiffly, Anne noticed Sam was covering a smile with his hand. She waited for Hing to leave, then asked, "What's so funny?"

"I've never seen Hing so polite and attentive. He's usually about as friendly as a rattlesnake. I think he likes you."

"He probably doesn't get many blond customers."

"Certainly none as beautiful as you."

"Stop that." She slapped his arm playfully. "You're making me blush again."

"Again?"

"Cut it out right now, Sam Malloy. I thought you were going to show me the rest of your Buicks."

"Let's go."

Hing and his wife and their four children stopped working and stared at Anne and Sam as they left. The Hings didn't move until the two giant *ang mohs* had climbed into the Buick and it slid past the shop with the sign, written in Chinese, Thai and English, for "FONG: Piles Treatment and Acupuncture." When the Buick disappeared into the next alley, Hing, remembering himself, clapped his hands and shouted at everyone to get back to work.

13

It was hard for Anne to believe someone had shipped these seven cars halfway around the world. Tucked away at the end of the alley, the garage was like a secret museum bristling with chrome and wide whitewall tires and moon hubcaps and rainbows of gleaming steel. She had to remind herself she was in Bangkok. She thought of a Somerset Maugham story she'd read recently in which he claimed that the cities of Asia are all alike because they give you nothing, and after you leave them you can't shake the feeling that they have some secret they've kept from you. Well, she had discovered one of Bangkok's secrets, a long shabby unassuming warehouse that happened to be full of the most beautiful cars she had ever seen.

"You like them?" Sam was beaming, a father proud of his brood.

"No, I love them. I was just thinking they look good enough to eat."

He locked the godown and she followed him through an iron gate, down a path lined with lotus flowers that led to the villa's broad front porch. The porch faced the pool and the bungalows and, beyond the wall, the river. There was only one couple at the pool, a pot-bellied man in a skimpy bathing suit and a woman with meaty arms. Their skin was oiled and deeply tanned. Germans, Anne supposed.

She walked halfway down to the pool and turned to get a better view of the villa. "My God, Sam, it's beautiful . . ." The long, wraparound porch on both floors, the tall shuttered windows, the tile roof—it was unlike anything she had seen so far in Bangkok. It would have fit better in Saigon, except that it was white instead of the standard pale yellow, and it wasn't mossy and sagging. It was dazzling, plumb, true, fresh-faced yet pleasantly aged. Her eye landed on something to the right of the villa, in the sunny southeast corner of the compound. She started toward it. "What in the world . . . ?"

Sam followed her to a miniature building that looked like a cross between a doll house and a temple. It stood on a pedestal and was surrounded by pieces of cake, burning sticks of incense, flowers and a bottle of red soda pop.

"This is the spirit house," Sam said. "It's where the *phra phum* live—the spirits of this place. If you don't have a spirit house, the spirits might get into the main building and cause all sorts of problems. And you'll notice it's in the sun. The spirit house must never be shaded by the main house."

Most Westerners, upon learning about Thai spirit houses, either chuckled condescendingly or laughed out loud. But Anne was holding a hand to her throat and staring. He could see she was smitten.

He pointed out the towering banyan tree behind her, its bark as coarse as an elephant's hide. The trunk was wrapped with long purple scarves, and at its base was a single flower, a burning candle and a joss stick. "The *thepparak* that lives in this tree protects everyone who enters the big building," Sam said. He glanced at the flower and candle and joss stick. "As you can see, we try to keep it happy."

They left their shoes with the dozens of other pairs on the porch. In the lobby Sam introduced her to his partners, Rat and his wife Jiap, who *wai*'ed deeply and said it was a great honor to have her stay with them.

"If there is something we can do to you, something at all, please give us the ring," Rat said.

"I certainly will," Anne said.

She followed Sam up two flights of creaking teak stairs. It was like ascending into a dream. The building was cool and it had a pleasing, cocoon-like gloom. They stepped out onto the porch that wrapped around the building. From this height she had a much better view of the river, and she was astonished by the gaudy pandemonium of boats darting back and forth, narrowly missing one another.

Anne's room was at the far end of the villa's top floor, above the alley and the garage full of Buicks. The shutters were closed and the room was cool and dark, with a parquet floor, a teak chair and desk, a bouquet of yellow and orange flowers by the bed. The bed was covered with a bolt of shimmering silk—indigo, gold and crimson.

Anne drank it all in for a moment. Then she walked over and picked up the flowers and smelled them.

"They're canna blossoms," Sam said. "They're from the hedge Rat planted all the way around the inside of the compound wall. Their Thai name is *pootaraksa,* which means 'the Buddha protects.' The Thais believe that if you plant them around your home, you'll be protected from harm and bad luck."

"How charming. Do they work?"

"I happen to think so."

He had placed her bag on the chair and was standing in the doorway. "There's a bar and a restaurant on the ground floor. Jiap's mother does the cooking and it's usually very good. Or if you'd like, we could go out . . ."

"I think I'd like to go for a swim."

He mimicked Rat's voice: "Let me know if there is something I can do to you."

"I certainly will. Thanks for everything, Sam."

She changed into her bathing suit and went back downstairs. The Germans were gone, so she had the pool to herself and she started doing the backstroke without bothering to count laps, luxuriating in the cool blue water, the sun's dazzle, the realization that it would be days before she would have to write another press release or lie to another American reporter. She could still taste Mr. Hing's soup—it was so simple, yet there were dozens of flavors humming on her tongue, garlic, ginger, chilis, the rice noodles, the briny duck. It would be days before she would have to worry about grenades or sit on her balcony with Lois DeVries and a bottle of wine, listening to the latest horror story from the Embassy's cable traffic. Anne pushed such thoughts from her mind. She felt the sun baking her eyelids. She tasted Mr. Hing's soup. She kept doing the backstroke until her arms and legs gave out.

As she was toweling off she noticed a silver-haired man sitting alone on the porch of the last bungalow, reading a book. He had a trim mustache, which he twirled as he read. He seemed perfectly content. She breathed the perfume of a frangipani tree and realized all of it—the pumping of her heart, the daubs of color from the bougainvillea and the canna hedge, the hot sun on her skin—it was the first moment of true peace she had felt since arriving in Asia.

The spell was broken when four Japanese men came scurrying down from the villa and shed their robes and stretched out on lounge chairs. They all lit cigarettes and started talking at once. Their skin had the texture of candle wax.

Anne went up to her room and closed the shutters. She considered taking a shower and putting on fresh clothes and going for a walk, but as soon as she stripped off her bathing suit and stretched out on the bed and closed her eyes, she knew she wasn't going anywhere. The sheets were cool. The ceiling fan sent a soft breeze washing over her. Her mind emptied. She could hear the twang of cicadas, but it seemed to come from very high up, from very far away, part of a hot afternoon that couldn't touch her here in this cool cocoon.

She awoke in the dark. The first thing she realized was that she was hot. Her hair was matted to her forehead, her skin was slick, and she was wet, very wet between her legs. She'd been dreaming, and though she couldn't remember the details she knew it had been a sexy dream: She had had an orgasm in her sleep. She couldn't remember feeling so deeply rested.

After a hot shower—the water pressure surged and faded continuously—she put on a sleeveless, cream-colored cotton dress, pulled her hair back, and gathered it in a tortoise-shell clip. She decided against makeup. She spent a minute looking for her espadrilles before she remembered they were lined up with everyone else's shoes on the villa's front porch.

When she stepped barefoot onto the cool tiles of the side porch, where the bar was, she was surprised to find half a dozen people, including Sam and Rat and Jiap, seated around the largest table. They all lit up when they saw her, as though they'd been waiting for her a long time and were delighted their vigil was over at last.

"I went out like a light," she told Sam. "I didn't realize how tired I was . . ."

He introduced her around. The Major was the natty, silver-haired Englishman with the wiry eyebrows and trim mustache who'd been reading on the porch of the corner bungalow. George O'Phelan and his wife, Jill, were two sweaty over-fed Texans. The hotel's most recent arrival was Phil Greene, a gangly American about Anne's age with pimply skin and an Adam's apple the size of a golf ball. He had a nervous laugh. Rat and Jiap were still smiling, and they *wai*'ed as Anne sat down.

Sam called for a fresh round of drinks, and Anne asked for a gin and tonic. As she settled into her chair she realized everyone was staring at her. She was still feeling groggy and dislocated from her nap—she'd always been slow to wake up from naps and the heat of Asia made it worse—and now she couldn't think of anything to say. It was the Major who came to her rescue.

"Perhaps you can settle this for us, Anne," he said. "We've been debating whether or not someone in show business is entitled to an opinion on the affairs of the real world."

"I'm afraid I don't understand." She felt intensely uneasy. She took a deep drink of gin and wished Rat and Jiap would quit beaming at her.

The Major slapped the front page of *The Bangkok Post*. "Marlon Brando, my dear girl. He left town yesterday—after getting in a few parting shots." The Major picked up the paper and read aloud from the front-page story: " 'Speaking to reporters before boarding his Pan Am jet to Hawaii, Brando once again sounded the theme of his three-day visit to Bangkok—the troubled state of race relations in his native land. "I think in the American South today we have a situation that has brought a great deal of shame on us as a nation." ' "

"Marlon Brando was in Bangkok?" Anne said. Already the gin was reviving her.

"He stayed right there in that first bungalow," the Major said. "I drove him all over town. Marvelous chap. He told me he once joined a civil rights march in Oakland, California, and a crowd of white hecklers showed up. They carried signs that read 'Marlon Brando is a Nigger Lover,' beastly things like that. And he pointed out that the American government has spent four and a half million dollars on police protection for that Negro boy at the University of Mississippi. Oh, what's his name—?"

"James Meredith," Sam said.

"Quite right. James Meredith."

"And here's what I say," said George O'Phelan. His face was shiny and pink in the evening heat. "I say who gives a damn what some movie star thinks about the niggers? Let him stick to making movies."

"I certainly don't care," said his wife. She, too, looked like she was about to melt from the heat. She was wearing a garish silk cocktail dress and a rope of pearls, and Anne realized she was so drunk she was in danger of sliding off her chair. Anne had seen the type dozens of times at Embassy functions in Saigon: the American wife in Asia, coming apart right before your eyes.

"So you see, we've been having a perfect row," the Major said. He was smiling, and Anne could see his eyes dancing under that wiry white hedge of eyebrows. He tugged at his mustache. "At any rate, we're delighted to have you with us. You've had a first-hand taste of a situation that's of great interest to us all."

"I have?"

135

"Why, yes—you *are* part of the American war effort in Vietnam, aren't you?"

"Yes, of course." She noticed Rat had stopped smiling and Sam was staring at her. She took another drink of gin.

"So you're on the scene in Saigon. That's perfect," George said. "Tell us how the war's coming along."

"Maybe she doesn't want to talk about work," Sam said. "This is the first weekend she's had off in eight months."

"Oh, rot that," the Major said, still smiling.

"I don't mind," Anne said to Sam. She gave George O'Phelan her brightest smile. "The war's going absolutely swimmingly."

"Swimmingly?" George said. "Does that mean we're winning—or we're getting ready to stomp the little bastards with both feet?"

"George!" his wife shrieked. "I warned you about your language!"

" 'Scuse me."

"Depends on who you talk to," Anne said. "Everyone has a theory."

"And what's yours?"

"Personally, I think the American advisors are going to be there a lot longer than six more months, which is the official line."

"Wunnerful!" George said, gulping bourbon.

"You don't want us to win the war?"

"Not jush yet, I don't."

"Why not?"

"Cuz I've got part ownership in two dozen gravel quarries here. I'm making a fortune off the Thai government. They get American tax dollars, and after the generals and the bureaucrats get their cut the rest goes to roads and bridges and airstrips. I hate to think how much money I'll make if the war drags on a few years."

"So you're in the gravel business," Phil Greene said. Anne had already forgotten he was there. Another quiet American.

"Thas right. Try making concrete without it."

"And what brings you to Bangkok, Phil?" Anne said.

"I just started a job with U.S. AID—the Agency for International Devel—"

"Flushing American tax dollars down the toilet!" George roared.

"Lissena you," his wife said. "S'okay when American tax dollars wind up in *your* pocket."

"What will you be doing?" Anne asked Phil.

"We've already started a new program to inoculate children in rural areas. It's very exciting. You wouldn't believe some of the poverty out there—"

"Honey," Jill O'Phelan said, slamming her highball glass onto the table, "you oughta start telling these Thai kids to stop swimming in that filthy river. Just yesterday George and I were coming back from the floating market in a longboat and we saw a bunch of kids *bathing* in that filthy water. Garbage all over the place. Dead rats. I don't know how they survive." Suddenly she reached out and clutched Anne's arm. "Wha'd you say your name was again?"

"Anne. Anne Sinclair."

"Well you sure are pretty you wanna join us for dinner?"

Anne looked at Sam, panicky.

"That's very kind of you, Jill," Sam said. "But I've already made reservations for the two of us at the Pearl. Maybe tomorrow night."

"Oh, phooey on both of you," Jill O'Phelan said, releasing Anne's arm and swatting the air.

"I saw you swimming today," George told Anne. He patted his paunch. "I need to start getting some exercise. The only exercise I get these days is making money." This got a lukewarm laugh and Sam used the lull in the conversation to order a fresh round of drinks for the others and slip out the door with Anne.

As they went sailing through Chinatown in a *tuk-tuk,* one of the motorized, three-wheel taxis that were the latest addition to Bangkok's kamikaze traffic, Anne gripped the side rail and braced her foot against the back of the driver's seat. Every time he hit the brakes the rig lit up with dozens of red lights, then he would twist the throttle and shoot through an impossible gap in the traffic.

"Hey, this is *fun!*" Anne shouted over the roar of the engine.

"I thought you might like it," Sam said. "Listen, I'm sorry about that scene back at the hotel."

"It wasn't your fault. George and Jill are quite a pair."

"She'll be going back home to Houston in a couple of days, thank God. She should've stayed home—or gotten a room at the Oriental with the rest of the fat cats. Her idea of great dining is a steak sandwich and a perfect Manhattan."

Anne didn't say anything. She couldn't take her eyes off the traffic. She was in the grip of that same exhilarating terror she felt the first time her father took her on the Matterhorn at Disneyland, torn between wanting to bail out and hoping it would last forever. From time to time she had to close her eyes.

"Jill hasn't stopped bitching since she got off the plane," Sam went on. "The streets are so *crowded.* Everything's so *filthy.* The food's so *spicy.* The room isn't *air-conditioned.* Everything *smells* bad. And George just paid another month's rent in advance. I'm beginning to worry he's never going to leave."

"Tell me, do Rat and Jiap ever stop smiling?"

"Oh yes. You should hear them when they fight—a couple of cats in a sack."

"The Major seems like an . . . interesting man."

"The Major's a prince. He's been in Thailand almost forty years, and unlike most of the Europeans you meet—all white people are 'Europeans' here, by the way—he actually understands the Thais and loves them."

The *tuk-tuk* skidded to a stop in front of a huge open-air restaurant on the riverbank, in the rumbling shadow of the Pinklao Bridge. Sam paid the driver and led the way inside, where a tall hostess with shoulder-length hair gave him a big showy kiss on the cheek and led them to a table in the corner that was separated from the river by a bed of red hibiscus. When the hostess was gone, Anne said, "I think she likes you."

"She? Look a little closer."

When the hostess walked by the table and saw Anne studying her, she smiled and brushed against her arm.

"You mean—she's not?—that's really a *man?*"

Sam laughed. "It certainly is."

"But she's—he's gorgeous."

"I know. Sometimes it's hard to tell for sure. But notice the scarf he's wearing on his throat? That's to cover up the Adam's apple, which is a dead giveaway. Nowadays more and more *ka-toeys* are getting their Adam's apples surgically removed. Then it can get downright impossible to tell."

"A *ka-toey* is a transvestite?"

"Yes. The Thais have very open minds about sexual matters. As long as you're not hurting anyone, you can pretty much do whatever you want. Unlike all those pious Protestants in America, Buddhists don't waste a lot of time worrying about sin."

A waiter came and Anne told Sam to go ahead and order for both of them—"anything but bull penis or dog meat." He asked for two Singha beers with ice, spicy beef slices called *nam tok,* a papaya salad, and the house specialty, a sea bass stuffed with chilis, lemongrass and herbs.

"You seem to be very fond of this place," Anne said after the waiter bowed and withdrew.

"I love the way they do the sea bass."

"No, I mean you seem to be fond of Bangkok. Of Thailand."

"Yes, I am." He was looking out across the glittering black river. "But sometimes I wonder if I'm fond of it because I have no other choice."

"Why don't you have any other choice?"

He looked away from the river and into her eyes and she saw it again, that thing she'd noticed at the airport, the darkness, the weariness, the eyes of a man who had seen too much too soon.

"It's simple," he said. "I can't bear the thought of going back to the States."

"Why not?"

He looked back out across the river and she realized there was something he wanted to tell her, but he was reluctant, possibly afraid. It was too early for her to push him. She bit her lip and waited.

"I suppose . . ." He took a drink of beer. "I suppose I don't want to have anything to do with the country that's responsible for what's happening in Vietnam. There. I've never put it into words before, but that's it."

"You mean the war?"

"Yes."

"What's so awful about trying to stop the spread of communism? Don't you think the South Vietnamese would rather live under a democracy than communism?"

"The ones who speak French would, sure. But I think about those Montagnards who thought Buddhism was a disease. I think about those peasants you talked to who have no idea who Ngo Ding Diem is. You'll never convince me that the majority of the Vietnamese give a damn about democracy or Ngo Ding Diem or Ho Chi Minh—as long as they've got enough to eat, a roof that doesn't leak, and nobody's burning their village or stealing their food. They want to be left alone, just like people all over the world. But America won't even leave the poor bastards alone. In fact, that's the whole problem. We're not there to help the Vietnamese people, we're there to show the world how big our balls are. Pardon my French. We want the communists—and everybody else—to know that we're tough guys. What a joke."

"So why don't you try to do something about it?"

"It's like I said at lunch today—I don't want to have anything more to do with that mess as long as I live. It's bigger than I am. I did my duty and got out and it's no longer my problem. I refuse to take sides."

Their food arrived. Sam deftly filleted the fish. It was served with the head and tail attached, with red and green chilis and the light green stalks of lemongrass spilling out of it and sending a cloud of perfumed steam into the night air. The papaya salad and the sliced beef surprised Anne with their fire. She ate in a state of sweaty ecstasy. It didn't take her long to appreciate the wisdom of putting ice in the beer.

"You sound like Fowler," she said.

"Who's Fowler?"

"A character in a novel I'm rereading, an English correspondent in Saigon in the early fifties, during the French war. He was very proud of the fact that he wasn't involved. 'Let them fight,' he would say of the Vietnamese. 'Let them love, let them murder, I would not be involved. I don't take sides.' "

"Sounds like a wise man." Sam's eyes were watering.

"You really think so?"

"I really do."

"Well, he wasn't able to remain uninvolved, no matter how hard he tried. Eventually he wound up becoming *engagé*, as he put it. Eventually he had to take sides. Eventually we all do." She helped herself to more rice and beef and salad. "I've got this theory. Want to hear it?"

"Sure."

"A minute ago, when I asked you about why you can't bear the thought of going back home, you got this look on your face—it was the same look when I asked you at lunch about your marriage. It was like your whole life was passing before your eyes."

Sam grunted. "Not a bad analogy."

"And both times you wound up holding back. It's like you've got secrets you're determined to hold on to."

"We've all got secrets. We need secrets in order to live."

"Maybe so. But some secrets are poison. They'll eat you alive if you don't get rid of them."

He didn't respond. He gave her a look that said she had gone as far as she was going to go for now. She accepted this. She watched waiters sail out of the kitchen carrying trays loaded with exotic dishes. She watched children and cats dart around the restaurant. The *ka-toey* passed back and forth repeatedly, giving her a personal show. When the large loud party of Chinese men at the next table got up to leave, one of the cats hopped up on the table and began picking at a fish carcass. No one shooed it away. A breeze had sprung up and the smells of the river—fish and diesel exhaust and garbage—came to her. She felt sated by the food, a humming warmth, and was mildly, pleasantly tipsy from the gin and beer. She understood that something had begun to grow between her and this man. It would grow slowly, but it had begun its life. She plucked a red hibiscus from the bush and stuck it above her left ear.

"It looks good on you," Sam said, pushing his plate away, patting his mouth and face with a toilet-paper napkin. "But remember—never wear a red hibiscus to a religious ceremony in Thailand,"

"Why not?"

"Very bad form. Executioners used to wear them when they performed executions. And another thing. Never, never, never get a haircut on a Wednesday. Very bad luck."

"There's a lot to know about this place, isn't there?"

"There's no end to it. I'm just beginning. I guess that's another reason I love it here—there's no end to it."

They split one more beer, watching the river, not saying much. He was the first man she'd ever known who wasn't afraid of silence.

On the *tuk-tuk* ride back to the hotel, the driver took the turns at full throttle, shoving his passengers back and forth against each other. Sam felt strong against her side, and as they whizzed through the treacherous streets she imagined he would never allow any harm to come to her.

Jiap was waiting for them at the desk in the hotel lobby. She had stopped smiling. "Message for you, Anne," she said. "You call Jon Mellon at this number right away now in Saigon. He say very urgent." Jiap handed her a slip of paper with a telephone number on it.

Anne dialed the number on the office phone. Jon answered on the first ring and got right to the point. Yesterday in Hue, a group of Buddhist priests and laymen had surrounded the radio station to protest the government order banning them from flying their religious flags on Buddha's birthday. Things got out of hand, there was some sort of explosion, and government troops fired into the crowd. Nine people were killed. The government was trying to blame the Viet Cong, Jon told her, but no one was buying it. He'd been on the phone all day. Reporters were on their way to Saigon from Hong Kong, Melbourne, and San Francisco, and he needed Anne to help him handle the coming crush. "There's an eight o'clock flight in the morning. I hate to do this to you, but I've booked you a seat . . ."

"I'll be on it."

"I'll make this up to you, Anne. I promise."

She found Sam sitting alone at the bar in front of two snifters of cognac. The only other people on the porch were the Germans she'd seen earlier at the pool. They were at a candlelit table in the corner drinking beer, not saying a word.

"Bad news?" Sam asked, sliding a snifter over to Anne.

"Of course," she said, climbing onto the barstool. "The government pulled another incredibly stupid stunt yesterday—and I've got to fly back at eight o'clock in the morning to help handle the press." She took a long sip of cognac, then another. "Maybe you've got it figured out, after all . . ."

"Got what figured out?"

"The war. Not taking sides. Let 'em murder each other."

"You're too young to be talking like that." He was staring into his snifter as though he hoped to find something, some answer, in that pool of flame-colored liquid.

"Oh?" she said. "And you're a wise old man who's earned the right to talk like that?"

"That's right."

"I'm not even going to ask."

"Good. Don't. Not yet."

She watched the lights of the boats moving on the river. It never slept, the seamless life of Asia. "So when do I get to ask?"

"When we know each other better." He hadn't looked up from the pool of fire cupped in his hands. "Will you be coming back?"

"I hope so. But it'll depend on how things go in Saigon."

"Do you need a ride to the airport?"

"Yes. In a pink-and-black Buick, preferably."

He smiled but he did not look happy. She leaned over and took his face in her hands and pulled it to her. She kissed him lightly on the lips. "I've had a wonderful time. I'll come back as soon as I can."

He brightened. "Next time I'll take you to a little island I know—far away from here, a place with no telephones and no Americans and no war."

"Is that a promise?"

"Yes. We'll cook fish on a fire and sleep in a hut and watch the moon rise out of the jungle."

She kissed him again, more slowly than the first time. Then she left him alone at the bar with his cognac and his secrets and she went upstairs and stretched out naked on her bed. She could hear two people making love somewhere in the night. As she drifted off to sleep her eyelids were alive with pictures of a fire on a beach, a huge fire that crackled and spit sparks and licked the sky as a fat moon rose out of the jungle and bathed them in its bone-white light.

14

Though he knew she would keep him waiting—it was as much a part of her style as the stiletto fingernails, the lacquered coiffure and the acid tongue—Charlie Malloy showed up at Saigon's Gia Long Palace at 10 o'clock sharp for his first scheduled interview with Madame Ngo Dinh Nhu.

The wife of the president's brother, reviled as the Dragon Lady by the American correspondents and universally despised by the Vietnamese, she had agreed to grant Charlie a series of exclusive interviews for a profile that was to be a *Time* cover story in late June. The decision to put the unofficial First Lady of South Vietnam on the magazine's cover was a sign of New York's growing interest in the war; and Madame Nhu's decision to pluck Charlie Malloy from the pool of foreign correspondents who hounded her for interviews was a sign that *Time* was the only publication whose coverage of the war lived up to her exacting standards. Also, Charlie's interview requests always carried a pointed reminder that if she agreed to talk with him, her picture would be seen on the cover of an influential magazine with a worldwide readership in the millions, a magazine whose recent covers had carried the portraits of

President Kennedy, General Harkins, Khrushchev, Nehru and Joan Baez.

When she heard this, Madame Nhu's eyebrows rose a notch and she said, "Hmmmmm. Joan Baez is very hot right now."

Charlie felt sure it was this—and not his incisive coverage of the war—that had won him the coveted entrée to the palace that morning.

As he presented his press credentials to the grim guard at the gate, Charlie noticed for the first time that the palace looked like a toy version of the White House. He wondered if the French, with their terrific wit and sense of irony, had done this intentionally. After all, they were responsible for the Statue of Liberty and for the rigorously illogical layout of Washington, D.C. The palace's haphazard sidewalks were still puddled and smoking from a morning downpour, and the meticulously barbered grounds were dotted with tamarind trees and conical shrubs and surly sentries on the lookout for snipers, grenade throwers or signs that another coup was about to erupt on the far side of the iron fence.

As soon as Charlie stepped into the palace, though, the illusion of Gallic grandeur vanished. Ceiling fans failed to stir the heavy air. The place smelled damp, mildewed, like a cat box in August. Did the Ngo family keep cats? It would be very un-Vietnamese—and therefore just like them. He made a mental note to ask Madame Nhu about it.

A girl in a black *ao dai* was waiting for him in the reception hall. Without a word she led him up a broad, curving staircase, down the long front portico—where they made ideal targets for a sniper, Charlie thought—and into a suite of corner offices. The girl motioned for Charlie to sit in a ridiculous chair embossed with fake gold leaf, then she left to fetch him *café sua*, the sweet iced coffee he craved on these hot mornings. The room was airless and dim, dominated by an unlit crystal chandelier. Fortunately, light leaked through the shuttered windows, and Charlie took out the book he had brought as a hedge against the inevitable wait. It was a gift from Les Gallagher, an AP photographer who'd just returned from a long weekend in Hong Kong.

Charlie looked at the cover: *The Spy Who Came in from the*

Cold, by John Le Carré. Charlie had never heard of this new author, but Les, a fellow aficionado of spy novels, had given it his highest recommendation. After the girl in the *ao dai* brought him his glass of potent *café sua*, Charlie settled in to read. But he couldn't get started. His mind kept veering back to the Rex last night, when Les Gallagher presented him with the book and touched off a chorus of jeers from the Sunset Club.

"Don't be giving him a goddam book to read," bellowed Ned Saunders of UPI. "He doesn't have time to read."

"Damn right," chimed in Peter Arnett, a pug-faced New Zealander with AP. "He's going to be busy for the next two months licking the Dragon Lady's bum. Ain't that right, Charlie?"

Charlie didn't join in their laughter. He found Arnett's remark cutting and out of character. Usually the Aussies and the Kiwis could be counted on to be good sports, unlike the Americans and the Europeans, and yet here was Arnett, a decent, hard-working if unspectacular correspondent from some hellhole at the ass end of the world, making a remark that had a distinctly caustic edge.

"Tell us, Charlie," Arnett went on when the laughter died down, "did she lay down any stipulations for the interviews?"

"Stipulations?"

"Don't play dumb, mate. You know perfectly well what I'm talking about. Will you have to service her the way all the diplomats do? What's it going to be?—whips? riding crops? the trapeze? Come on, quit holding out on us!"

The others picked up the bait and the conversation degenerated into an airing of the rumors everyone had heard about what went on inside the palace—kinky sex, drugs, séances, orgies featuring boys, girls, even animals. Ngo Dinh Nhu smoked opium around the clock. Madame Nhu was a dominatrix with a stable of willing sex slaves. President Diem was a bachelor for the simple reason that he was a card-carrying homosexual. Political rivals were targeted for assassination in nightly lottery drawings. There was animal sacrifice. When Charlie couldn't bear to listen to another word, he stood up, drained his drink, and walked to the elevator.

It was obvious to him that the correspondents' bawdy banter was their way of masking their jealousy. He had been chosen and they had not. He had access to the most colorful personality in the war and they did not. She was the dream interview: She never hesitated to make her feelings known and, having traveled abroad extensively, she spoke fluent English and French. All a reporter would have to do was wind her up and sit back and watch the fireworks.

And yet, as he gave up trying to read John Le Carré and closed the book on his lap, Charlie had to admit he did feel some sort of abstract attraction to Madame Nhu. He'd tried to tell himself it was merely the result of the twin facts of his present life—his growing fatigue with the grasping, hard-nosed, brutally unromantic bar-girls, and the realization that Anne Sinclair was never going to amount to anything more than a pretty face to look at across a candlelit dinner table. He wondered if his brother had better luck with her in Bangkok. And yet he knew there was something about Madame Nhu that made his heart race, made his groin tingle, something he'd noticed the first time he met her at a reception at the French Embassy. There was something about the way her hands floated so delicately even though her fingers were tipped with the sharpened, blood-red claws of a hawk, something about the way she looked like she'd just stepped out of a beauty salon, as fragile and flawless as a porcelain doll, much too pretty to be running this vicious little war. There was something about the way she hovered on five-inch heels and rode around Saigon in a chauffeur-driven black Mercedes, the way she walked in a crowd, swiveling slowly to her right, then to her left, waving, beaming, basking in the imagined adulation of the masses. She walked the way a dictator was supposed to walk. Beneath her delicate veneer of Chanel perfume and *ao dais* and cotton-candy coiffures, she was as mean as a snake, a combination that made her the most brazenly sexy woman Charlie Malloy had ever met.

"Madame Nhu will see you now. This way, please."

It was the girl in the black *ao dai*. Charlie was surprised by her impeccable English. She was holding open a door that led into a suite of offices, and suddenly Charlie felt unprepared. He wished he'd had more time to cool off, more time for the sweat stains on his shirt to dry. Quickly he patted his face with a handkerchief. He realized he should have shaved before leaving the Caravelle, but he didn't want to be late. And now the girl was holding the door open and the look on her face made it clear that Madame Nhu did not expect to be kept waiting, certainly not by a sweaty, wheezing, overweight American.

Charlie picked up his novel and his notebook and entered the office. Madame Nhu was seated behind another ridiculous piece of furniture, a massive wooden desk that appeared to have been sprayed with gold paint. It was chipped in spots, revealing white plaster of Paris. She was wearing a pink *ao dai* and holding a white telephone receiver in her left hand while a woman buffed the fingernails of her right hand. She was speaking in Vietnamese, barking orders. He stood in the middle of the room, under another unlit chandelier, feeling like a piece of furniture. Suddenly Madame Nhu slammed the receiver down, shooed away the manicurist and with a radiant smile fixed on her face, stood up and came around the desk to greet her interviewer. Silk swished as she moved. She was wearing platform shoes with five-inch heels, and Charlie guessed they brought her height to five-three, maybe five-four. She weighed well under one hundred pounds.

"Mr. Malloyyyyy," she purred, taking his right hand in both of hers. "I am so sorry to keep you waiting. But these generals . . ." She glared at the white telephone. "Sometimes I think they don't know how to order a meal, much less an invasion." She giggled at her little joke, released Charlie's hand. "Will you have another *café sua*?"

"Um . . ."

"I prefer hot tea in such weather."

"Tea would be fine, Madame Nhu."

She turned to a white-jacketed man Charlie had not noticed. *"Deux thés, tout de suite!"* she said, and the man vanished. She motioned toward the corner of the room, where a sofa and a high-backed chair were arranged around a low, glass-topped table. It looked to Charlie like the scene of a thousand interviews, a million lies. "Let's sit where we can be more comfortable," she said, motioning for Charlie to take the sofa while she perched on the edge of the chair. Her spine was as straight as an iron rod.

The waiter reappeared and set a tray with a silver teapot and two cups on the table, then he bowed so low Charlie thought he was trying to chew the frayed Persian rug. Thus bent, the man backed out of the room, closing the door behind him.

As Madame Nhu poured the tea, Charlie noticed bags under her eyes. Was the pressure of running the war getting to her? Or had she been up late last night, indulging in the sort of sport that fed the relentless Saigon rumor mills, from the roof of the Rex to the Rue Catinat bars to the gambling dens in Cholon? She dumped three heaping spoons of sugar into her tea. "Sugar for you?"

"No, thank you."

She handed him his cup. Her hands were trembling. She crossed her legs—a brazenly Western gesture, more swishing of silk—and with her head cocked and her eyes focused somewhere far beyond Charlie's left ear, she said, "Before we begin, Mr. Malloy, I want to tell you a little secret. Would you like to know a secret about Madame Nhu?"

"Yes, of course I would."

"I feel like I am sitting right now on—how do you Americans say it?—like I am sitting on the edge of a volcano."

"Why is that?"

"Because so many people will read what you write."

"I'll write the truth."

"I am sure you will try. But we are both human. I may not express myself well. Already I have decided that if there are mistakes in your article, the fault will be with me or with the rewriting man. Is that how you say it?—The 'rewriting man'?"

"Yes, close enough." Charlie had come here knowing these interviews were going to be strange, stranger and more important than any in his career, and it had taken her all of five minutes to throw him off-balance. She was prepared to blame any inaccuracies on the rewrite man in New York, the very man who had dressed up Charlie's earlier dispatches, always toning down his criticisms of the Ngo family, soft-pedaling allegations of official corruption and brutality and ineptitude, turning military defeats into victories, doing his best to convince the American people that the official line was the truth and the war was a beautiful success. And now here was Madame Nhu telling Charlie she was prepared to lay the blame on the man who had, with the help of Clem Zablocki and the Proprietor, done more than anyone in America to make her look like a human being.

"Very well," she said. "You may begin, Mr. Malloy. I am prepared to tell you things I have never told anyone else before. What is it you would like to know about Madame Nhu?"

Charlie opened the notebook on his knee. Before he got into his prepared questions, he decided to take a chance. "Do you keep cats here in the palace?"

"Cats?" For an instant her smile cracked. It did not crumble, but Charlie noticed a distinct crack and in that instant he saw the light in her eyes change the way the light changes when a cloud passes swiftly in front of the sun. It chilled him. When her smile was restored to its original radiance, she said, "I do not understand your question, Mr. Malloy."

"I know it sounds silly, but I thought I sensed the presence of cats when I entered the palace today. And I was wondering if you or your husband or the President—or if the staff—keeps cats."

"I am sure that some of the servants keep cats. As you know, we have a terrible problem with rats in Saigon, even here in the palace, and one of the best weapons against them is cats. Actually"—suddenly she seemed to warm to the idea—"I am very fond of cats."

"Oh? Why is that?"

"Because cats must depend on cunning and intelligence to survive, not brute strength, just like Madame Nhu." She was looking past Charlie's ear again, seeming to read her script on the wall behind him. "Yes, please include that in your article—Madame Nhu is a great admirer of cats because they must use their wits to survive, just as the government of President Diem must use its wits to defeat the communists in the countryside and the schemers in Saigon."

"Who are these schemers?"

"There are thousands of them, too many to count. Students, Buddhists, spies, selfish generals, freelance politicians, American correspondents—other than yourself, of course—all the dupes who wish to tear down the government so the communists can march in and take over and destroy the entire country."

The mention of the Buddhists reminded Charlie of his prepared questions. He checked his notebook, took a deep breath, and said, "Tell me, Madame Nhu, are you pleased with the government's response to the killing of the Buddhists in Hue?"

That tripped her button. Charlie spent the next two hours scribbling in his notebook, trying to keep up with the torrent of words. She raged against the Buddhists and against her spineless brother-in-law for acquiescing to even their mildest demands. President Diem never should have replaced the officials thought to be responsible for the killings, for it was as good as an admission of guilt. And they were blameless! The explosions that triggered the killings were far too powerful to have been set off by government troops; in fact, she had received reliable reports that the CIA had set off the bombs. As for the sixty-seven students who were injured yesterday during protests of the killings, she hissed, "The soldiers should have beaten them ten times harder." She paced. She shouted. Sometimes her words were accompanied by a spray of saliva—"like cobra venom," Charlie wrote in his notebook. He couldn't tell if she was angrier at the Buddhists for causing a disturbance or at her brother-in-law for failing to crush them with sufficient force. She said she was preparing a resolution for the National Assembly that condemned the Buddhists as "communist dupes." Her pacing was accompanied by that swishing sound, that maddening swishing sound, and whenever she turned her back Charlie found himself staring at her. Finally, when her anger was spent and Charlie's hand was beginning to cramp, she collapsed into her chair.

"That's one thing you American reporters don't understand," she said wearily. "In times of peace the Vietnamese are Confucians, but in times of war they suddenly become Buddhists."

Charlie had no idea what she meant by this. As he was writing her words in his notebook he heard her say, "This has been a terrible week for me. I am very tense. Come here, Mr. Malloy."

This was not a request. Charlie found himself dropping his pen and notebook, rising from the sofa, and walking toward her.

"You seem like a nice man. Rub between my shoulders . . ." And she twisted slightly in her chair, dipped her chin, offered her back to him. He pressed his thumbs between the shoulder blades and began to knead the muscles. The bones beneath the silk were the bones of a bird. He could feel the tension melting. "Ohhh, yes, that's it, Mr. Malloy. Not quite so hard. A little to the right. Yes, that's much better. Right there. Oh yes, yes, yes . . ."

She sagged against his leg, and for the next twenty minutes Charlie found himself serving as the unofficial masseur of the unofficial First Lady of South Vietnam. He was conscious of an erection trying to stir in his poplin suit pants, but through a major act of will he tamed it. Madame Nhu purred, let her left hand fall against his left leg. "Oh, Mr. Malloy, I pay Vietnamese good money to do this, but they do not have your touch. And I have always thought of the Americans as Ivanhoes. I can see that you are different . . ." And then she shook her head and shoulders and sat up straight, signaling that his duty was done.

He returned to the sofa and picked up his notebook and pen. "That will be all for today," she said. "I will see you again at 10 o'clock next Thursday morning."

Charlie stood up. The situation in his pants was under control.

"And Mr. Malloy."

"Yes, Madame Nhu?"

"Be sure you shave before you come to see me next Thursday."

As he walked down the portico to the stairs he noticed it was raining again and the streets were nearly empty. Already time for the midday siesta. He'd been with her more than four hours. *Be sure you shave before you come to see me next Thursday.* As he climbed into a trishaw Charlie accepted her words for what they were: the command of a lover.

15

After Anne Sinclair returned to Saigon, Sam couldn't get her or the war out of his head. He tried everything—swimming laps, getting drunk, going to the movies, even reading the serious books the Major was forever pushing on him. None of it worked. In desperation he let Rat take him to Gaysorn Road, that gaudy, seductive, nearly-forgotten part of their shared past where everything and everybody was for sale and where Rat's wit and wisdom were always in fullest flower.

Rat's favorite pastime was to sit on a barstool next to Sam and comment on the international mating rituals taking place around them, rituals he knew intimately from a lifetime of hustling on the Bangkok streets. He'd started out as a shoeshine boy and drug runner, graduated to busboy, then waiter, then bartender in the tourist hotels, where he learned English and German and enough phrases of French, Italian and Tamil to conduct a little business on the side. He wound up, naturally and inevitably, as a freelance pimp in a city that offered endless opportunities to "put people together," as he liked to say.

He had learned, firsthand, that Chinese men were looking for big-boned girls, preferably white, preferably German or Australian; that American men were looking for their daughters; that Japanese men were looking for their mothers; and that German men were looking for anything that walked and could be induced to lie down.

Rat knew most of the bar girls, and they all knew him either personally or by reputation. One night at the Boom Boom Room they buzzed all over Rat, and after Sam got a little too deeply into the Scotch he decided what the hell and agreed to go upstairs with one of them, a tall willowy Thai teenager with no breasts and a bucktoothed smile that made his heart melt. She gave him a "mussudge." She rubbed his feet with warm oil for half an hour. They took a steambath together. But when it came time to do business Sam found he had no interest. She was crushed. She should not have been.

It was Anne Sinclair and it was the war: They would not leave him alone.

He got a note from her a week after she returned to Saigon, thanking him for his hospitality, apologizing for having to leave so abruptly, and raging against the South Vietnamese thugs who shot up a bunch of women and children in Hue. She closed with: "I hope your invitation still stands—I'm dying to see all the sights of Bangkok and that island you mentioned. Sounds intoxicating . . . Anne."

Yes, the invitation still stood. He read the note until he had it memorized, and he kept replaying their conversation at dinner that night under the Pinklao Bridge. She was the first person, other than Rat and the Major, who had gotten him to talk about the war. He thought of that English correspondent she had mentioned in the book—Fowler?—and how he had refused to take sides in somebody else's war. Eventually he broke down and took sides. "Eventually we all do," Anne had said. As young and fresh as she was, how could she know such things? How could she be so sure? And when he'd told her we all have secrets, that we need secrets in order to live—it was the most fervently held belief in his world, he realized as he said it, the one thing that kept him going—she came right back with words that had stayed with him like a toothache: "Some secrets are poison. They'll eat you alive if you don't get rid of them . . ."

No matter how hard he tried—and as a last resort he even let the Major drag him to the new Elvis movie, *Girls, Girls, Girls*—he could not shake the feeling that she was right. There truly were two kinds of secrets inside every human soul: life-giving secrets, those private moments, experiences, accomplishments, revelations that were ours alone, that made us unique in a world determined to grind us all into identical dust, treasures we must never surrender to that world; and then there were those poisonous secrets, dark or dirty or horrifying, things we locked away in order to survive even though they kept us from being fully alive, even though, as Anne put it, they ate us alive.

He had never thought of secrets in this way before. But on one of his late-night walks he found himself standing on a footbridge over Klong Saen Saep, not far from the famous home of the Major's American friend, "the silk king," Jim Thompson. As he became hypnotized by the rhythmic clicking of the weavers' looms, Sam realized that he and his mother shared the first kind of secret, the kind that would keep him alive as long as he kept it to himself. A nearly full moon wiggled on the oil-black water of the klong. Garbage and hyacinth blossoms floated past. The silk weavers were working by the light of kerosene lanterns, and Sam could see their bolts of shimmering fabrics drying on racks. Those colors reminded him of fall days long ago, of the day he saw Vivien McNair for the last time and signed the divorce papers in that hallway reeking of cat piss and then fled the building and started walking north.

He had no destination. Every time he came to a bar he ducked in for a belt, and after several blocks he was suffused with a glowing sense of relief. He was on his own and he was on his way to Virginia to become a Frogman and have the first genuine adventure of his life. The future, like the city, seemed wide-open, limitless, all his. As he looked back, the decision he made next still struck him as strange. He was sitting in an Irish bar near Penn Station, bathed in the gangrenous warmth of a neon shamrock, drinking a beer and a shot of bourbon and watching the faces flash past on Eighth Avenue, grim preoccupied faces, city faces. In the back of the bar there was a steam table full of limp Irish fuel, corned beef and cabbages and spuds. Everything in the room was sweating—mirrors, people, barstools, the beer bottle in Sam's fist. He was getting drunk, but one of those thoughts popped into his head that left no room for hesitation or debate: His bus didn't leave for Virginia until the morning and it was a glorious fall afternoon: He should say a proper goodbye to his parents.

He bought a pint of bourbon for the train ride and left early enough to beat the afternoon crush. He put his feet up on an empty seat and uncorked the bottle and watched Long Island unfurl outside the window. The trees were turning to copper and rust and blood, the sun was yellow, the sky unbearably blue. This had always been a confusing time for him as a boy, the days growing shorter and cooler, something dying, but basketball season was coming, his time to shine. Now, as the train rocked out to the suburbs he looked at the blazing trees and the smoke from burning leaves and he did not see death. He saw only the dawn of his own life, a life that was beginning late, perhaps, but a life with a future as cloudless as that blue drum of sky.

The sun was already dipping into the trees when he got off the train at Hicksville. He could smell salt water, wood smoke. He realized he was hungry. In the Depot Diner he ordered a huge breakfast even though everyone else was eating dinner, and he drank four cups of black coffee and felt so sober and alert he decided to walk the three miles to Levittown.

It was dark when he reached Lindbergh Street. There was the smell of mown grass and burning leaves and the sea, and there was evidence of children: The lawns were littered with abandoned bicycles and Hula Hoops, footballs and headless dolls. Lights were burning in all the houses, but in the seven driveways on Lindbergh Street he counted only two Buicks. The Zimmers' turquoise-and-white Century was already dull and beginning to show freckles of rust. Next door, the Deckers' red-and-black Century was rearing back, its front end up on jack stands. An oil change? Something more serious? Where were the other five Buicks? Had people already traded them in? Wrecked them? At Sam's house the basketball hoop was hanging from the garage by a single bolt. This made him angry, then sad, and then he smelled meat cooking and found himself marveling at the elaborate techniques human beings had developed for fighting off hunger and darkness and death.

His father's yellow-and-black Buick was gone, but his mother's old blue Ford station wagon was parked in the driveway. It was listing to port. The tires were as bald as cueballs and they needed air and there was a new spiderweb crack in the windshield. He took a deep breath, tried to steady himself before going to the kitchen door.

Halfway up the driveway he stopped. The curtains were pulled back and he could see the living room in vivid detail. Nothing had changed since he'd followed Vivien to New York three years earlier. The wallpaper was still the color of year-old newspapers; the boomerang coffee table still dominated the room; and the full set of World Book encyclopedias was still arranged neatly on the shelf Jim Zimmer had built one Saturday afternoon while Sam's old man sat around drinking beer and giving instructions that Zimmer wisely ignored. Sam loved that set of encyclopedias, the way they made such a perfect row, the way the gold lettering shimmered on their spines. So pretty and so sane.

His father bought them in Yonkers several years before he moved the family out to Levittown. Even then, at the ripe age of thirteen, Sam wondered what had come over his old man. A jackleg mechanic who was always fretting about money and who never read anything heavier than the back issues of *Field & Stream* at the barbershop, he had let the traveling salesman romance him into buying a full set of World Books (on time, of course) plus a Year Book every year for the next five years, when Sam would be a senior in high school. What brought on this sudden grand gesture? Whisky? An unusually fat pot at his weekly poker game? A bogus transmission overhaul for one of those rich Scarsdale broads who brought their Cadillacs and Packards to his Yonkers garage?

Whatever it was—and Sam never did figure it out—the salesman with the bow tie and the too quick laugh caught the old man at the perfect moment and Sam suddenly found himself spending hours sprawled on the livingroom floor exploring worlds he had only dimly imagined—the Middle Ages, outer space, ancient Rome, the ocean floor, the exploits of Genghis Khan and his Mongol horde. But he loved the maps best, loved the pale blue oceans and the pastel nations, the way the world fit together and made such perfect sense, Mongolia cradled in the palm of China, the impossible skininess of Chile, the blazing whiteness of Antarctica, the way Mississippi and Alabama reached out to touch the Gulf of Mexico, the importance of land meeting water. He learned to draw all forty-eight states from memory. He learned that New York is on the same latitude as Madrid and Peking. He read that it was possible to see seven states from a lookout tower in southeastern Tennessee. He read that South America had once been attached to the dented west coast of Africa. His brother Ed would come in from the garage, grease up to his elbows, and chide Sam for turning into a bookworm: "Why'ncha come out and help me tear down this transmission 'steada spending all day with your nose in a book?"

But their mother rose to Sam's defense. After shooing Ed back out to the garage, she said to Sam, "Don't pay any attention to him. There's no reason a boy shouldn't be allowed to love sports *and* books. You're already a wonderful ballplayer—so you go ahead and read as much as you like. Look at Ed. He can fix anything in the world, but he couldn't write a grammatical sentence to save his life. And Charlie's even worse—writes like a dream but can't tie his own shoes . . ."

Her words had set him free. Until he discovered those encyclopedias and maps—and until she told him he was free to live under their spell—the only times he'd felt truly focused and alive were when he was playing sports. Boxing and wrestling and surfing were good, but basketball was by far the best, the floorboards gleaming with varnish, the black lines so precise and final, the neat orange iron hole with its lacy white skirt of net that popped like a dream after a perfect shot, the red dots of the scoreboard numerals telling you exactly where you stood and exactly how much time you had left to get where you wanted to go. An orderly, understandable world, a world with knowable boundaries, just like the world of maps.

He tried the kitchen door. Of course it was unlocked. One of the reasons his father moved the family to Levittown was because the real-estate agent promised "it's gonna be the kinda place where a kid can grow up with grass stains on his pants and you never have to lock your doors." Sam expected to step into a cloud of cooking smells—he assumed the meat he'd smelled from the street was one of his mother's notorious shoe-leather pot roasts—but the oven was cold and dark. He thought of his father's worn-out quip about his mother's cooking: "Where there's smoke, there's dinner." It was certainly possible that Margaret Malloy—Marge to her husband, Maggie to her friends, Mags to her youngest son—was the worst cook in the world. But Sam loved her for it as much as his father was driven to distraction and, as often as not, to drink by it. She accepted her husband's insults and ugly jokes gracefully. She seemed to find it amusing that she had trouble boiling water. Her amusement was linked in Sam's mind, somehow, to her defense of his boyhood passion for encyclopedias and maps. Mother and son understood each other.

Sam stepped into the kitchen and held his breath. Silence at first, then the hum of a wall clock and the distant murmur of a television set. He crossed the kitchen, went down the knotty-pine hallway that was barnacled with his dusty sports trophies, then stopped in the doorway that opened onto the back porch. His mother hadn't heard him come in. The first thing he noticed was that she'd gained weight, grown even puffier. She was sitting in a bulky redwood chair with flowery cushions, a piece of furniture that belonged on a patio or pool deck. Walter Cronkite was on TV, whispering the evening news. A paperback best-seller, *Requiem for a Blonde,* was open on his mother's lap. But she wasn't watching the news or reading the book. She was gazing out the windows even though there was nothing to see but a curtain of shiny black glass.

There was a half-eaten bag of Fritos on the coffee table, and it occurred to Sam that growing up in Mags's household had been one long parade of brand names. It was Kellogg's or Quaker for breakfast, Campbell's for lunch, Bosco and Fig Newtons and Lorna Doones after school, the Jolly Green Giant or

Rice-A-Roni on the dinner table. It was Bon Ami on the bathtub, Clorox on his sneakers, Windex on the windows. In times of sickness there was Vick's and Bayer and Robitussin. She even bought her books at the drugstore, and at night she lost herself in the worlds of brand-name authors like Jack Webb, Art Link-letter and Norman Vincent Peale or, when she was feeling ambi-tious, Boris Pasternak and John Updike. The carafe of white wine at her elbow looked like a urine sample. Byron, the ratty springer spaniel who showed up shivering at the kitchen door one bitter winter night during Sam's last year of high school and promptly insinuated his way into Mags's heart, was asleep under her feet, snoring and twitching. So her life had come down to this: cheap books, cheap wine, a largely absent hus-band, and a decrepit, largely asleep dog.

"Knock, knock," Sam said softly, tapping the doorjamb with his knuckles.

His mother started, spilling her novel on the floor and waking Byron, who yawned and went right back to sleep. "Sam!" she cried. "What's the big idea sneaking in on me like this?" She held out her arms and he bent down and hugged her, kissed her cheek. She smelled like wine, Bon Ami, dog. "What did they do to your hair?" she squealed, and only then did he re-member that he was fresh out of Navy boot camp, freshly di-vorced, and on his way to UDT training in Little Creek, Virginia.

"All gone, Mags," he said, rubbing the stubble. "Where's the old man?"

She seemed surprised by the question. "What day is it?"

"Tuesday."

"Then I guess he's playing poker." She waved at the air as though shooing a fly. "I don't know. He never tells me any-thing anymore."

"Have you had supper yet?" Sam asked.

"No . . . I haven't had much appetite lately. Sit down, sit down, and tell me all your news. If you want a beer there should be some in the fridge."

He got a beer—his father was still drinking Blatz, would surely go to his grave drinking Blatz. The chair facing the televi-sion set was covered with the Sunday *New York Times*. As a boy

Sam had thought his mother's attachment to the Sunday *Times* was the height of highbrow—until he realized she bought it not for the book reviews or art news or even the crossword puzzle, but for the ads in the back of the Sunday magazine. Those ads fed her fantasy life. But instead of the predictable fantasies about hundred-thousand-dollar Westchester and North Shore estates, she fantasized about useless crap like heel lifts, table pads and bird feeders, military schools and music camps and smoked hams. He knew this because while most Levittown moms were busy clipping supermarket coupons, Mags clipped these ads and tucked them in a drawer in the kitchen. Sam loved her for this, too, for her delightfully skewed fantasy life.

When he cleared the *Times* off the chair and sat down, his eyes landed on the far wall. There was a new picture there—a framed copy of the *Life* magazine's two-page photo of all seven Lindbergh Street Buicks. "Where'd you find that?" Sam asked.

"Oh, that," she said, squinting. "I found it in one of my drawers. Jim Zimmer framed it for me. I think it's real cute."

"Does the old man still have the Buick?"

"Of course he does. He gripes all the time that he can't afford to keep it running—he had to buy a new set of tires just the other day—but he wouldn't trade that car in for the world."

Looking back, Sam realized the only reason his father bought the Buick in 1954 was because the neighbors shamed him into it. If any one of the seven residents of Lindbergh Street failed to buy a new Buick Century, they said, *Life* magazine would have canceled the article. Sam's father was the second-to-last man on the block to buckle under to this fierce neighborly pressure and the equally fierce salesmanship of Hayes Tucker Jr., the local Buick dealer. It was the only new car Sam's father had ever owned.

Sam told his mother about boot camp, about how excited he was to start Frogman training, about how relieved he was to be rid of Vivien McNair. He'd expected his mother, a devout Catholic, to disapprove of the divorce, but she surprised him by saying, "Good riddance. I never had any use for her or her phony family."

Then she started talking about Sam's father. It was obvious

she was not on her first carafe of wine as she rambled about how remote her husband had become, how he'd started sleeping in Sam's old bedroom, drinking more, staying out for days at a time, then coming home and staying in bed for two, three days at a stretch. Sam noticed a tone in her voice he had never heard before, something beyond weariness or sorrow or hurt: It was metallic, empty. It was, he realized, the sound of despair.

"He's really quite lost," his mother said. "At first I thought it was just that he didn't know what to do with himself after handing the business over to Ed—you know how some men get after they retire. But he's had a few bouts of depression lately that've been frightening."

"He didn't get violent, did he?"

"God no. When he gets like that it's all he can do to get up a couple of times a day and go to the bathroom."

"Has he seen a doctor?"

"I keep trying to get him to go see Dr. Sheffield, but he says he doesn't need a doctor. Says he just needs to catch up on his rest and cut down on the booze. You know how he is. Big tough Irishman. Ex-Marine. Stiff upper lip and all that shit. Jesus . . ."

Sam had never heard his mother swear before, and it stunned him, announced they were on new ground. He went into the kitchen for another beer, and when he returned to the porch he realized the beer was acting like a booster on what he'd drunk in the afternoon. His skull felt buzzy and hot. He watched Walter Cronkite's lips moving. He looked at the print of the Van Gogh self-portrait behind his mother's head. When he was a boy he was afraid of that picture because the whites of Van Gogh's eyes were a milky green, which made him look deranged and dangerous.

After a long while he heard his mother say, "There's something I need to ask you, Sam. Are you aware that I had breast cancer?"

His eyes ricocheted around the porch, from Byron to Walter Cronkite to the Buick picture to Van Gogh. Finally his eyes settled on his mother. She was staring at him, waiting. She had once been very beautiful. Beside her bed was a picture of a sleepy-eyed young woman with swept-back, chestnut hair and full, glossy lips. Even as a boy Sam could see that those lips were meant for kissing. But by the time he got to high school she had begun to change, to slide, and in the few short years since he'd left home she'd grown puffy in the face, thick through the middle, as though she no longer cared. She still had that handsome shock of chestnut hair and that high forehead and those full lips, but all Sam could think of was how sad it was that she no longer cared.

"Mags, really . . ." His face was on fire.

"Don't be embarrassed. I need to know the truth."

"Yeah, I know."

"How'd you find out?"

"Mags, please . . ."

"Sam!" The iron in her voice told him he was a goner.

"Well . . . I . . . saw you."

"When?"

He looked away from her, into the green whites of Van Gogh's eyes. "I must've been in the first or second grade. The old man was away, so I guess it was during the War—and I was taking a bath in the old house in Yonkers. I was playing with a rubber battleship and a rubber bi-plane—I'll never forget it—and the bathroom door was open a crack and your bedroom door was about halfway open and I . . . well, I looked up and couldn't help but see you."

"What did you see?"

"You were getting dressed. All you had on was a pair of plaid shorts. I can still see them. Butterscotch-colored with a red and green pattern. You were bending over, putting on socks. You didn't have a shirt or bra on, and I could see that you had only one breast."

"And what did you think?"

He took a long drink of beer. What did he think? What a hell of a question. "I was . . . ashamed. That's the only word for it. I was ashamed."

"But why?"

"Why? Because I felt like I'd seen something I wasn't supposed to see. Something sinful. It's bothered me ever since."

"Those goddam nuns and their goddam guilt!" she shouted,

bringing the palm of her hand down with a smack on the arm of the redwood chair. Byron grunted in his sleep. "I was against sending you boys to Catholic school all along, but your father insisted. Said the discipline would be good for you. What he meant was the *sports* would be good for you. Christ, the sick things we do to the ones we love . . ."

And then it happened. The events of the long day—the break with Vivien, his exhilarating ramble through New York, the drinking, the train ride, the painful unearthing of these long-buried secrets—suddenly it all brought out of him one of those statements that is unpremeditated, unthinkable, and yet utterly true. "It's funny," he said. "When I finally learned that you'd had a mastectomy, my immediate reaction was to resent the old man."

"Resent him? For what?"

"Because I realized that after your operation he allowed the romance between you two to die. And something in you died when he let that happen. He shouldn't have done that. I guess I still resent him for it."

"You know it's not that simple, Sam. Nothing is."

"I suppose not. But that's how I've felt for years. This is the first time I've been able to put it into words. I resent the living hell out of him."

Suddenly she smiled. "You're the only person in this family who's capable of having such a thought, Sam, and I love you for it. You've made me very happy."

"Happy? How could that possibly make you happy?"

"Because you've helped me figure out why you've always been my favorite. Mothers like to know these things."

They sat there for a long time without talking. A lopsided moon had risen and was visible through the glare of the storm windows, just above Walter Cronkite's head. They both admired it. That was another thing Sam loved about his mother: Much as she loved to talk, she wasn't afraid of silence.

Finally she poured the last of the wine into her glass and said, "Did you know that I say a prayer every morning as soon as I wake up?"

"Yes, I've seen your prayer." It was taped to her bathroom

165

mirror. It was along the lines of *Thank you, dear Lord, for letting me wake up one more time.* When he first saw it, Sam realized that since her surgery she had lived every day with her scar, with her secret, with her dread of a relapse.

"Can you keep a secret, Sam?"

"Of course."

"No, I mean *really* keep a secret?"

"Yes."

"You'll be the third person in the world to know—and I don't want anyone else to find out. Not your father. Not your brothers. No one. Ever."

Sam found himself hoping she was having an affair, a wild and carefree love affair with a bright young man who treated her like a queen and made her feel alive again, more alive than she'd felt in years, more desired, more loved. Sam smiled. "No one'll ever find out, Mags. That's a promise. Who's the other person who already knows?"

"Dr. Sheffield."

The name was like the blow of a fist. Sam actually had trouble breathing. "What is it?" he managed to say, though he already knew.

"He found a new tumor. The cancer has already gotten into my lymph system. He told me this afternoon I've got six months, maybe less."

Sam could not speak or move. After a time—he wasn't sure if it was a minute or half an hour—he stood up and walked over and knelt beside his mother. He put his arms around her waist and laid his head on her lap and wept. He wept the way he'd wept into her apron as a boy when they stood at the kitchen sink in Yonkers and watched the trees bending from the front edge of a hurricane and he understood, truly understood for the first time in his life, that one day he would die.

Once again his mother held him and rocked him and let him cry. She let him know, without saying a word, that there was no rush. Finally, when there was nothing left inside him, no more tears, no more resentment, no more anger or fear, she said, "Gene Milacki's been calling every day for you. He finally got the job playing piano in the cocktail lounge at the Embers. I promised him you'd stop by next time you were in town."

"I'm not going anywhere."

"Don't be silly."

"You shouldn't be alone."

"I've got Byron to look after me." She rubbed the dog with her bare feet, and he moaned.

"I'm not in the mood for a cocktail lounge right now, Mags."

"Please go. Gene's dying to see you. And I need some time to myself."

That did it. Sam stood up, accidentally stepping on Byron's paw. The dog snapped at his shoe, then went back to sleep. Sam could see that his mother had been crying, too. But she cried silently.

"Sam, before you go, promise me one more thing."

"Yes. Anything."

"Promise me you won't ever let yourself get into a rut like your father and I did."

"I promise."

"And promise me you'll be true to your dreams. You don't have to be a big famous foreign correspondent like Charlie or a filthy rich fool like Eddie—just be true to your dreams."

"That's what I'm doing, Mags."

"Good. And one more thing. Don't blame your father. It's not entirely his fault. He did the best he could."

"Okay."

"And remember. Don't tell anyone our secret. Ever."

"I won't. Trust me."

"Kiss me goodbye."

He bent down and for the first time in his life she kissed him on the lips.

He left then, drove his mother's old Ford station wagon to the Embers Supper Club out by the Parkway. Sure enough, the man at the black ebony grand piano in the cocktail lounge was Gene Milacki, that great buzz-cut slab of a Polack who played center for the Hicksville High School Hurricanes and always led the league in rebounding because of his brute strength and soft hands. It didn't surprise Sam that Gene had passed up several basketball scholarships to pursue his first love, the piano. There he sat in the pink gloom of the cocktail lounge, trussed up in a tuxedo that appeared to be made of whorehouse wallpaper, tickling out background music by Nat King Cole and Pat Boone and Mel Torme. Everyone ignored him and paid attention to their cocktails. This struck Sam as unfair and sad, and he sat at a booth in the far corner and ordered a beer and a shot of bourbon. When he realized he had nothing to say to Gene Milacki, he gulped the drinks and slipped out the door. On the way back to Levittown he had to fight off the urge to drive the Ford into a tree.

He made it home safely. Still no Buick in the driveway. When he opened the kitchen door he nearly stepped on Byron, who was usually long gone by this hour. But now the dog sat there whimpering, breathing hard.

Sam bounded up the stairs three at a time, suddenly agile and cold sober. Byron struggled up the stairs after him. The master bedroom light was on, but both beds were empty, untouched. The first thing Sam noticed when he walked into the bathroom was that his mother's prayer was gone from the mirror. Water was running in the sink. Then he looked down. His mother, dressed in pink pajamas, was sprawled on the floor between the tub and the toilet. She was on her stomach, head turned sideways. Her eyes were wide-open, unblinking. She was cold to the touch. She had no pulse.

Sam started searching the bedroom. There was no blood, no sign of a struggle. On the night table he found what he didn't want to find: an amber pill vial. The label read: "DALMANE— Take one before bedtime to aid sleep." It was prescribed by Dr. R. S. Sheffield that day, and it was empty.

The vial was resting on a handwritten note: "Remember what I said about your dreams and our secret, Sam. And don't worry, this is my choice and it's for the best. Please destroy this note. I love you."

Sam sat on the edge of his mother's bed to collect his thoughts. After a few minutes he called Dr. Sheffield at home and woke him up. "I'll be right over," the old man growled. "Don't touch anything." Byron sat at Sam's feet, nervous, alert, still breathing hard. Dogs understand everything, Sam thought. He realized he still hadn't decided what he was going to tell Dr. Sheffield, so he put the empty vial and the note in his shirt pocket.

Fifteen minutes later Dr. Sheffield came through the kitchen door without knocking and hurried up the stairs. He was carrying a black bag and was dressed in chinos, a rumpled pajama top, loafers, no socks. He needed a shave. His frizzy, uncombed hair reminded Sam of Bozo the Clown, and to his surprise Sam started laughing.

"You okay, son?" the doctor said, looking at him sharply.

"Yessir." Sam stood up.

The doctor went into the bathroom, and when he came out a minute later he was crying, crying without making a sound, just as Mags had cried earlier that night. He sat on the bed and Sam could feel him shuddering. It lasted a long time. When it stopped, Sam said, "She told me."

The doctor looked at him more sharply than before. His eyes were shiny and red. Sam thought he smelled whisky, or maybe it was just the sour breath of sleep. "She told you what, son?"

A trustworthy man, Sam thought. "She told me about the new tumor. She told me you gave her six months to live, maybe less. She said she and you and I are the only people who know—and she made me swear never to tell anyone, not even my father." Sam took the empty vial out of his pocket and handed it to the doctor. "I found this on the table."

Dr. Sheffield studied the vial and sighed, as though relieved to have a dark suspicion confirmed. He pinched the bridge of his nose and closed his eyes. His body started to shudder again. When it stopped he said, "You find a note?"

"No sir." That secret was Sam's to keep.

The doctor was staring at the lifeless body. "She was a wonderful woman. One of the bravest people I've ever met—and I've met a few in my day. But what I admired more than her bravery was her humility. She was humble enough to be grateful every time she woke up in the morning. Not many of us have that, I'm afraid." He sighed again. "No use kidding ourselves. It's pretty obvious she didn't want to drag the family through a long, painful and costly death that—"

"Yes, but you and I are the only ones who know that."

The doctor looked at him. He squinted, as though he was having trouble focusing. "Yes, that's true," he said.

"And no one else *needs* to know."

"What are you saying, son?"

"I'm asking you to do my mother one last favor, Dr. Sheffield. Couldn't you list the cause of death as natural—a heart attack or something—and avoid an autopsy?"

The doctor's bloodshot eyes held Sam's for a long moment. Then he looked down at his hands, strong old hands laced with blue veins and liver spots and smelling of soap. The hands of a healer. "Yes, son, I suppose I could do her that one last favor. I'll take care of the death certificate and make sure there's no autopsy. Of course, that has to stay in this room, or I'll lose my license."

"Yessir."

"Is there any Scotch in this house?"

"Yessir."

Sam made two stiff drinks while the doctor called the funeral home. Then they sat down together on the porch to wait for the hearse to arrive.

16

That, clearly, was one secret that would remain locked inside of Sam Malloy forever.

But every afternoon, as he walked the half mile to the Oriental Hotel to buy the latest international newspapers and magazines, he became more convinced that Anne had been right about the other kind of secret, the poisonous kind. This conviction grew in him slowly, alongside his newfound fascination with the war.

He devoured every story with a Saigon dateline. Whenever a "knowledgeable American source" was quoted, Sam pictured Anne Sinclair in the back of a Rue Catinat café, talking in lowered tones with an American correspondent, praising the new American helicopters or the strategic hamlets, or arguing that the South Vietnamese Army was getting tougher by the day. Did she really buy this official horseshit? It was clear to Sam that most of the correspondents did not. Their stories tended to have a pessimistic tone, and they confirmed something he had believed for years—that no amount of American money or manpower or distaste for communism could inspire the sorry South Vietnamese Army to defeat an enemy as tenacious and wily as the Viet Cong.

Then Sam began noticing something more subtle in the coverage. It was almost as though each publication had its own set of beliefs and the reporting was tailored to fit those beliefs. His old buddy Halberstam from *The New York Times*, for instance, never seemed to have met a South Vietnamese general who could lead or a South Vietnamese soldier who could fight, and he seemed to take a strange pleasure in reporting the latest example of the Viet Cong outwitting and outfighting government troops. The Associated Press and UPI reporting had a similar edge, and a *Newsweek* correspondent named Beverly Deepe had a knack for capturing the smoky nature of the war by always brightening the "bad" news and darkening the "good" news. When she wrote that 30,000 Viet Cong were killed in 1961, she was quick to point out that recruitment and infiltration had replaced those battlefield losses and, furthermore, that significant numbers of government militia were deserting or defecting to the communists rather than defend the despised strategic hamlets, those fortified villages that the government regarded as a glorious success and that most peasants regarded as prison camps.

And then, of course, there was Sam's brother. Charlie Malloy worked for *Time,* and whenever Sam read the magazine he saw that just as *The New York Time*'s reporting was tailored to fit an institutional distaste for the war, *Time*'s reporting reflected fervent support, almost a love, for it.

This finally came home to Sam one muggy afternoon when he was returning from his daily stroll to the Oriental Hotel's newsstand. He ducked into Holy Rosary Catholic Church just as a rain shower burst from the sky. For someone who had renounced his Catholic religion years ago, Sam found the church strangely comforting. It reminded him of his mother. The pale yellow walls and orange-tile roof did not belong here on the bank of the Chao Phraya; they belonged near the Mediterranean, possibly in the south of France, or Portugal. Inside, the floors were black-and-white tile, the stations of the cross were ornately carved wood, and a spiral staircase led up to a canopied pulpit. There were gold pillars behind the altar and a plush red carpet around it. Yes, this was old Europe, not Asia, and Sam loved to stop in here with his latest haul of periodicals in the afternoon, when the church was quiet and dark and empty and he could sit in one of the pews and listen to the rain and read by the watery light seeping through the stained-glass windows.

The article that finally awoke him to his brother's real mission appeared in early June. It was in "The Press" section under the headline "Foreign Correspondents: The View from Saigon." It began: "For all the light it shed, the news that U.S. newspaper readers got from Saigon might just as well have been printed in Vietnamese. Was the war being won or lost? Was the Buddhist uprising religiously inspired or Communist-inspired? Would the government fall?

"Uncertainty out of Washington is not exactly news," the article went on, "but one of the curious aspects of the South Viet Nam story is that the press corps on the scene is helping to compound the very confusion that it should be untangling for its readers at home."

Come on, Charlie, Sam thought. You're asking your esteemed colleagues to figure out a way to put smoke into a bottle.

"Much of the press corps' failure can be traced to its solidarity. Foreign correspondents, wherever they are stationed, are tempted to band together into an unofficial club; they are their own closest connection with home. When they have finished covering a story, when they have examined it from every angle, they find it pleasant to relax in each other's company . . ."

Sam thought of the Sunset Club. He remembered the Martini & Rossi vermouth billboard and the white mice directing traffic and the girls floating along Le Loi on their bicycles. He remembered the night his blood rose to a murderous boil and he came so close to breaking Halberstam's jaw. He remembered the way he felt back then, dislocated, angry, afraid, a time bomb brimming with secrets and icy rage. It was a year ago and seemed like ten.

To his credit, Charlie also wrote: "At the battlefront, both U.S. military observers and the Vietnamese brass blatantly contradict evidence obvious to the journalists' eyes." But then he reverted to form: "Their reporting is prone to distortions. The complicated grays of a complicated country fade into oversimplified blacks and whites."

And what about Anne Sinclair? Surely she was caught in withering crossfires of her own. He thought of that evening when she'd come down late to have a drink at the White Elephant's bar and had promptly gotten grilled about the progress of the war. As she stepped barefoot onto the porch, Sam could see instantly that she'd been asleep: She was still puffy around the eyes, still under the spell of her dreams. Her face was freshly scrubbed, free of makeup, and in that moment she looked defenseless, gorgeously vulnerable. Sam understood that she had not yet acquired the armor and weaponry of an adult, that she was not quite complete. She was still in the process of becoming a woman. Her edges were still soft. Yes, that was what made her so beautiful: She was unfinished, and the dew was still very much on her.

Was it possible for such a woman, if she possessed enough ambition or patriotism or simple loyalty, to believe the lies she was getting paid to tell the Saigon reporters? Not likely, Sam thought. She called the propaganda films she'd recently worked on "amusing." She'd asked half a dozen peasants what they thought of Ngo Dinh Diem, and she was plainly amused by their mystified response. He'd detected a glimmer of irony when she talked about the "glorious patriotism" of Diem. She'd said she didn't buy the official line that the Americans would be going home in the next six months, and she'd expressed amazement over the inner workings of the U.S. Embassy.

No, Sam thought as he left the church and trotted through the sizzling drizzle to the hotel, it was unlikely that such a woman could believe so many lies. And it was even less likely that she would be able to keep telling them much longer.

Rat and the Major were playing chess in the bar. Rat was hunched over, his nose inches from the board, his face contorted with concentration. The Major was sitting back, sipping iced tea, obviously delighted that he once again had his star pupil tied in knots. They'd been sitting there two hours earlier when Sam had left for the Oriental, and it was possible they would be sitting there for several hours to come. Time simply didn't matter to either one of them. It was another example of how the Major had allowed himself to be seduced by the ways of the Thais. A day spent reading or playing chess or flying kites was a day well spent because today was a replica of yesterday and a dry run for tomorrow. No one worried about changing the world because the world never changed, it was unchangeable, and besides, Buddha taught that such things don't matter. As a result, Thais were free simply to live, and they had used that freedom to turn the simple act of living into a work of art. And now the Major was using that freedom to turn Rat into a quivering, demoralized wreck.

"The newsboy returneth," the Major said when Sam dropped the magazines and newspapers on the bar. The Major picked up the tongs and dropped a fresh ice cube into his tea. "Did you get me the *Times*, old boy?"

"Yessir," Sam said, digging for *The Times of London*. He hadn't looked at any of the newspapers yet. "How's the game?"

"Perfectly lovely," the Major said.

"Perfectly shitty," Rat said. He was resting his chin on his fists, and Sam could see the scar tissue razoring the knuckles, badges of a lifetime of fighting.

"He's in the soup, all right," the Major said. "My Christ, what a head I've had all afternoon! Must've been that bloody red wine I had with dinner—"

"Or that quart of gin you had before dinner," Rat said.

"My dear man, is it quite playing the game to point out such trifles? But perhaps you're right. Perhaps it is time for some hair of the dog." The Major turned to the bar. Jarusit was combing his hair and reading a comic book. The Major clapped his hands and spoke sharply, in Thai: "Put down that silly book and bring me a bottle of gin and a bottle of tonic and a lime and the tallest glass you can find. And be quick about it."

By the time the Major had fixed himself a drink and was basking in its first healing rinse, Rat still had not made his move. Sam wouldn't have the patience for one of these marathons, but the Major seemed unperturbed. He was incapable of impatience. "Anything in the news?" he asked Sam.

"I just glanced at *Time* magazine. My brother's got a story

175

about how the American correspondents are distorting coverage of the war."

"That's news?"

"Yeah. He seems to think it's a bad idea for them to get together and drink after work."

"What on earth are foreign correspondents *supposed* to do after work?"

"Good question. I know what my brother does."

"What does he do?"

"He gets together with the other correspondents and drinks."

Chuckling, the Major unfurled *The Times of London* and instantly sat bolt upright. His jaw sagged. "Good Christ," he muttered. "Have you seen this picture? How perfectly ghastly . . ."

Sam walked around behind him. Even Rat pried himself from his misery and came to look. There, above the fold on the front page, was a photograph of a bald man in a robe sitting in the lotus position in the middle of a city street. A crowd surrounded him, recoiling in horror but unable to look away. It took Sam a moment to understand the source of their horror: The man was on fire; he was being swallowed by a soaring tongue of flame. His face showed no emotion, no pain, nothing.

Sam read the caption out loud: "Thich Quang Duc, a Buddhist bonze, is consumed by flames after setting himself on fire in a busy Saigon intersection yesterday afternoon. The self-immolation was an act of protest against the policies of the government of Ngo Dinh Diem, the Catholic president of South Vietnam." Sam searched for the agate type beneath the bottom right corner of the picture, thinking he might recognize a name from the Sunset Club. When he read it, he gasped.

The photo was taken by Charles Malloy.

"Not that shit again," Rat said, returning to his chair.

"What do you mean, 'again'?" the Major asked. He couldn't take his eyes off the picture. Neither could Sam.

"The Vietnamese. They are more worse than the fucking Japs. Their mandarins is kill themselves for a hundred of years. Whenever they can no decide what is more important—loyalty to emperor or the will of heaven—they kills theirself. Swords, disembowel, burning. A hundred of years. Now the Buddhist monks is do it. They think they got problems? They should look at this board." He pushed his lone rook forward two squares.

"Checkmate," the Major said, still staring at the photograph. "What in hell—!?"

The Major put down the newspaper and slid his queen diagonally three squares. "Elementary, my boy. You let your pawns get overextended and your defense turned into a sieve. If I've told you once, I've told you a thousand times—your pawns must work in concert."

"Shit and fuck. You too good, Major." Rat had already forgotten the whipping by the time he picked up the newspaper and studied the picture of the burning monk. "Does not look good for the good guys, eh Sam?" he said.

The good guys, Sam thought. He was not surprised by Rat's scorn for the Vietnamese. It was a very Thai sentiment. But he was surprised by Rat's knowledge of Vietnmese history. How did he know about mandarins and their ritual suicides? As Sam sifted through the pile of papers, he saw that the same picture of the burning monk was on the front page of every one of them. Since when did Charlie learn how to use a camera and start getting out of the air-conditioning and down into the steamy and dangerous streets of Saigon? And this question led to another: If the killings during the Buddhist protest in Hue had turned Anne's life into "a living hell," as she claimed in her letters, what would happen to her life now that a monk had burned himself alive on a busy Saigon street and the image had been beamed all over the world? Her living hell, he suspected, was about to get a lot hotter.

17

The weeks following her return from Bangkok were an escalating series of crises for Anne Sinclair and her co-workers at the U.S. Information Service. Anne's only escapes were swimming laps at the Cercle Sportif and drinking wine with Lois DeVries, pursuits that now acquired an almost manic urgency. One night Lois uncorked a second bottle of Chablis and looked at Anne's glass. "You good?"

"No."

Lois refilled their glasses to the brims. "Now where was I?"

"You were telling me about Henry Cabot Lodge," Anne reminded her. The more wine Lois drank, the more she needed such prompting.

"So. It's all but settled," Lois said, picking up the thread of her story. "Lodge is in and Nolting is out as Ambassador. A cable from Walt Rostow arrived today. They think the transition will be complete in six to eight weeks, though they're guessing, just like always."

"What do you hear about Lodge?"

"Nothing I particularly like. Keeps his cards close to his vest, doesn't trust anyone. I got a call from a friend in Washington yesterday who heard he's planning to bring two or three of his own people to handle all the cable traffic. He's very secretive, absolutely paranoid about leaks, apparently. If so, he'll fit right in with the Kennedy crowd."

"But the cable traffic is your job, Lois."

"I know that, honey. That's why I'm not in a particularly good mood tonight."

Lois was never in a particularly good mood, and yet Anne found herself craving these nightly visits. Two nights earlier, Lois had poured out her juiciest discovery to date: "Listen to this! You aren't gonna believe it! In May of '61 Kennedy secretly ordered four hundred Special Forces sent to Vietnam. Their mission—and this is a direct quote from a McGeorge Bundy memo—was 'to form networks of resistance, covert bases, and teams for sabotage and light harassment.' I love that part—*light harassment*. It's like saying *a little bit pregnant*. The memo went on to say they were to target railroads, highways, bridges, and train depots in North Vietnam and—you ready for this?—in Laos."

"My God. You mean we've been fighting in Laos for the past two years?"

"Pretty incredible, hunh? They've been doing all kinds of nasty things—training Montagnard tribesmen and South Vietnamese commandoes, most of them fresh out of high school. They've even used Thai Rangers to help blow up bridges and railroad tracks. The CIA's in on it too, of course."

The mention of the Montagnards was like an electric shock to Anne. She remembered Sam Malloy saying the recruitment and training of the tribesmen was old news, and now she was learning just how old it was: It was almost exactly as old as the Kennedy administration.

There was so much to learn, and Lois's wine-fueled monologs were proving to be the ideal crash course. Lois seemed to crave these sessions even more than Anne did. In the past two weeks she'd failed to show up at Anne's apartment only once, and on that night Anne had accepted an invitation from Ray Seward, the cameraman who shot the USIS propaganda films, to go to the weekly barbecue thrown by the Officer's Club on the roof of the Rex Hotel annex. Usually Anne avoided such affairs because she found that when Americans gathered in large groups their worst sides took over. They bitched about the heat and the lazy, inefficient, corrupt Vietnamese; they told gook jokes; they pined for home, for baseball and cheeseburgers and telephones that worked. Worse than their longing, to Anne, was the success with which they re-created a little slice of America right there in the heart of downtown Saigon.

She and Ray arrived at the Rex at dusk, after the Christmas lights ringing the roof had been lit and the limitless supply of iced Budweiser had begun to go to work. Steaks were sizzling. Spirits were rising. The war was on its way to being momentarily forgotten. The tile roof of Gia Long Palace, visible just two blocks away, might as well have been on the moon.

Anne went to the bar and asked for a beer and noticed that the jacketed barman and waiters were not even trying to mask their disdain for the proceedings. She thought of *The Quiet American,* of the night when the British correspondent, Fowler, took his Vietnamese mistress to the Chalet in Cholon and saw a dignified Vietnamese couple on the dancefloor. They owned themselves completely, Fowler thought; they never dressed carelessly, never said the wrong word, were never prey to untidy passion. And now she studied these three Vietnamese men with their starched white jackets and their polished black hair, standing stiffly against the wall, taking in this sea of carelessly dressed, loud, sloppy Americans.

Someone had rigged up a hi-fi and a litany of familiar hits washed over the crowd—"Big Girls Don't Cry," "Surfin' Safari," "Green Onions"—and dancers had begun pairing off, flailing and jerking to the beat. Finally there was a ballad, a song Anne loved, Sam Cooke's "You Send Me," and the dancers pressed close and swayed against each other. Then Jimmy Dean's "Big John" came on and all the men bellowed: "Big John, Big Johhhhhhhhhhhhhn, Big bad John . . ." It could have been a frat party at Berkeley, Anne thought, this sea of well-fed young Americans, working so feverishly to forget where they were.

When Ray went off to talk to some military photographers,

Anne retreated to the shadows to drink beer and study the crowd. She recognized about half of the faces. Every day, it seemed, fresh American faces were showing up in Saigon. She was no longer able to keep track of what all these people did. There were the soldiers who called themselves advisors, of course, and flacks like herself and reporters and Embassy types. But there were also agricultural experts who knew how to breed superior pigs and turnips, there were teachers, accountants, mechanics, even disc jockeys. There were technicians who tested the new high-velocity rifles and needle bombs and the infra-red cameras that could see through camouflage netting. There were businessmen who imported weapons, medicine, milk, gasoline, whisky, fertilizer and drugs. And of course there were spies, spies to spy on the Viet Cong, spies to spy on the South Vietnamese, spies to spy on the Americans, and spies to spy on the spies.

Anne finished her first beer and got a second from the unsmiling barman and returned to the shadows. Otis Redding's "These Arms of Mine," another of her favorites, was playing and the dancers were locked together again, slowly shuffling. Anne wondered why these people joined the military or the Foreign Service or the Peace Corps or the CIA if they had such a deep craving for the comforts and rhythms of America. These barbecues were a weekly ritual for most of them, probably a nightly ritual for some, so it wasn't a matter of occasionally missing life back home; it was a stubborn refusal ever to let go of it. They should have stayed home, she thought. They would have saved everyone, including themselves, a lot of trouble.

"Excuse me, are you Anne Sinclair from USIS?"

Startled, fearing a request to dance, she turned to her left. Looking up at her from the shadows, from the approximate height of her armpit, was an American with a tangled mop of black hair and thick eyeglasses. He had the magnified eyes of a guppy. "Yes," she said, "I'm Anne Sinclair . . ."

"Morey Caan." He held out his right hand, and she shook it. "I'm an old friend of Jon Medlin's."

"Yes . . ."

"I'm working on a freelance article about the Commercial Import Program. I don't know if Jon mentioned it or not—"

"Oh yes, of course he did."

"Jon says I need to talk to you. He says you know everything there is to know about the C.I.P."

One of Anne's first assignments in Saigon had been to learn the intricacies of the Commercial Import Program so she could brief reporters, diplomats and visiting congressmen. It was an elaborate Rube Goldberg contraption that propped up the South Vietnamese economy—and lined more than a few pockets—by using U.S. dollars to pay for imported goods, most of which wound up on the black market. Just the other night, during one of her monologs, Lois DeVries had taught Anne something new about the program: Ambassador Nolting was under instructions from Washington to impress on President Diem that if the persecution of the Buddhists didn't stop, the faucet of C.I.P. funny money might get turned off. Ah, Vietnam, Anne thought, where carrots turn into hammers . . .

"Well, Morey," she said, "I don't know *everything* about the program. But I'd be happy to help you in any way I can. Why don't you call me at the office tomorrow and we'll set something up." She gave him her business card.

"Um, I was wondering . . ." He slipped the card into his shirt pocket and glanced around to make sure no one was within earshot. "Do you think it might be possible for us to meet somewhere other than your office?"

"I suppose so. But why on earth—"

"It's just that I'm a lot more comfortable interviewing government staffers when they're not sitting behind a desk, if you know what I mean."

"No," she said, "I'm afraid I don't know what you mean."

"It's not what you're thinking. It's just that . . . it's just that I've got this thing about bugs."

"Bugs?"

"You know, listening devices. Taps. This city's full of—"

"You think I would secretly record our conversation?"

"No, no, no!" he said, visibly flustered. "I've known people whose offices were bugged for months before they found out about it. I'd just feel a lot more comfortable if we could meet in a restaurant. Or a park. Or wherever you like."

"I see." She made a mental note to ask Lois about this. "Well, just give me a call tomorrow and we'll set something up."

She considered getting another beer but couldn't stomach the thought of standing in the shadows making small talk with a bug-eyed, paranoid reporter and watching dozens of Americans dance the night away. She finished her beer and shook Morey's hand and left for home.

It wasn't until she got to the office the next morning and read *The Times of Vietnam* that she learned how lucky she had been. Moments after she left the roof of the Rex, the barman, who proved to be a Viet Cong agent, rolled a home-made grenade onto the crowded dancefloor. The explosion critically injured five Americans and killed three, including a freelance journalist from Washington named Morey Caan, who died instantly when a chunk of jagged, rusty metal sliced into his brain, just above his bushy black eyebrows.

18

After that, her second close call, the paranoia settled into Anne's bones and stayed there. She understood that she could die at any moment, by plan or by accident. Now she believed every rumor she heard about wiretaps and bugs and booby-trapped pay phones, about Viet Cong agents infiltrating hotel staffs and American news organizations, even the Saigon police. Every rumor was true until proven false. Every Vietnamese was the enemy until proven friendly. She trusted no one.

She didn't realize how far gone she was until two days after the Officer's Club attack, when she stopped by the *Time* magazine bureau to drop off a press release about the suspension of powdered-milk imports. This was the first time the Americans had used the carrot of the Commercial Import Program to put pressure on the Diem regime, and therefore, strictly speaking, it qualified as news. But Anne knew the story would get scant attention on the wires and would be of little interest to the daily papers and weekly magazines. The real reason she stopped by the *Time* bureau was because she needed a break, and she was hoping Charlie Malloy would ask her out for a nice long quiet liquid lunch on Henry Luce's tab. Drinking during office hours was no longer one of her taboos.

When she entered the *Time* office, Charlie's Vietnamese assistant, a gaunt, high-strung chain-smoker named Dang Sy, was talking on the telephone in a cloud of cigarette smoke. She thought he lowered his voice and turned his back when she entered, but she wasn't sure. He was speaking in French. Charlie was sitting inches from the window air conditioner, his woven tan Italian loafers propped on the desk. He was reading the American baseball scores in *The International Herald Tribune*.

"I come bearing news for the almighty Luce empire," Anne said, dropping the press release on Charlie's desk. Dang Sy gave her a dark look and continued murmuring into the telephone.

Charlie ignored the press release. "The Mets have positively got to be the worst team in the history of the game."

"Who are the Mets?" she said, sitting on the edge of the desk.

"My dear girl, the Mets are the new baseball team in New York. They're the reason my father wakes up in the morning. They play in a stadium near La Guardia Airport and they do everything wrong—which is why my father, a connoisseur of ineptitude, wouldn't dream of missing a game. Here it is the middle of June and they're in dead last place in the National League, eleven and a half games out of first and sinking fast."

"Charlie, I bring news of the war."

"Hold your horses. Listen to this . . ."

Anne noticed that Dang Sy was watching her out of the corner of his eye. His hand trembled as he held a match to a fresh Gaulois.

". . . they lost to the Cardinals yesterday, six-two," Charlie was saying. "That might not sound so bad, but they committed four errors, left eleven men on base and gave up two home runs in the ninth inning. Jesus, what a joke!" He tossed the sports page into the wastebasket and swung his loafers off the desk and picked up the press release. When he finished reading he balled it up and dropped it on top of the sports page. "How about lunch?"

"I thought you'd never ask."

"I found a new place over by the docks on Duc Thang," Charlie said, standing up and reaching for his jacket. "It's called Le Palais and they do a marvelous steak tartare. After last night

I need some red meat. We can sit outside and watch the boats if you like."

Dang Sy was still on the telephone, still smoking, still watching her when she followed Charlie out of the office. As soon as they got outside, Anne turned to Charlie. "Do you think we could go someplace besides this Palais place?"

"I'm telling you, their steak tartare is out of—"

"I'm sure it's wonderful, Charlie. It's just that I . . . I . . ."

"You what? Come on, spit it out."

"You're going to think I'm being silly, but I was uncomfortable with the way Dang Sy was watching me and listening."

"Oh no, not you too. Listen, he'd jump in front of a gun for me. He's completely trustworthy."

"Charlie, can we please go somewhere else? I'm sure he's fine—but I'd feel a lot more comfortable."

As soon as he'd consented to take her to the courtyard restaurant at the Continental, she felt like a whiny little girl, a typical spoiled American brat. But Charlie didn't seem to mind. He was quite fond of the broiled chicken at the Continental.

"Cholly!"

They turned. Dang Sy had just burst out of the bureau and was running up the sidewalk toward them, carrying a notebook and a Canon camera. A cigarette with an inch-long ash dangled from his lips. "Just got a tip from top reliable source. He says big news about to happen near Xa Loi. Must not miss. Come, I drive."

"Not another Buddhist demonstration," Charlie said with the same scorn he'd summoned for the New York Mets. "Can't this wait till after lunch?"

"Must go now." Dang Sy shooed away three boys who were waxing a black Peugeot parked at the curb. He tossed the camera and notebook into the back seat and climbed into the driver's seat and fired the engine. *"Now,* Cholly! Must go!"

Charlie turned to Anne and shrugged. "I guess duty calls."

"When did you get a car?"

"Couple of weeks ago. New York's finally beginning to realize there's a real-live war going on around here. You want to ride along? We'll get a bite as soon as this nonsense is over with."

Dang Sy was honking the horn. Suddenly Anne was deeply uneasy again. She was certain they were being set up, but she was also hungry and something in her rebelled at the thought of allowing herself to become a prisoner of her suspicions and fears. She wasn't going to let these bastards run her life. She climbed into the back seat.

Dang Sy grinned when he saw her sliding into the car, then he gunned the engine and lurched into traffic. He drove like a lunatic, constantly honking the horn, never using the brakes, forcing bicycles and pedestrians and food carts out of his path. He cackled with glee when a girl in a white *ao dai* had to ditch her bicycle onto the sidewalk to avoid the hurtling Peugeot.

Anne rolled down her window and tried to relax. Though a fine drizzle was falling, the sun was out, a greasy yellow egg yolk that turned the streets into a steambath. The air wobbled. Dang Sy bounced up and down on the driver's seat, exhaled smoke like a locomotive, honked the horn, poured out a torrent of Vietnamese profanity. It occurred to Anne that maybe he wasn't with the Viet Cong, after all. Maybe he was just hopped up on drugs. Or out of his mind.

After passing the Ben Thanh Market, they turned north, away from the river, and raced through the park. Anne glanced at Charlie. He was gripping the back of the seat and mopping his sweaty brow. He looked like he needed a drink. She had to close her eyes when the speedometer needle climbed past ninety kilometers per hour.

With her eyes shut and the hot wind blasting through the car, her thoughts drifted back to that day, two weeks ago, when she and Jon Medlin had gone to Xa Loi to see what all the fuss was about. The pagoda looked like a Chinese version of the Leaning Tower of Pisa. It had become the headquarters for the protesters who'd been galvanized by the massacre of the Buddhists in Hue. On the day Jon and Anne visited, they were surprised to find souvenir stands doing brisk business outside the pagoda compound. Inside they were greeted by the crunching of mimeograph machines and the chiming of brass gongs and the smell of joss sticks and tea and boiling cabbage. An orange-robed monk bowed in greeting and said, in perfect English, "You are Mr. Medlin and Miss Sinclair from the United States Information Service, yes?"

"That's correct," Jon said, bowing and shaking the monk's hand. Anne, aware that monks were not allowed to touch women, merely bowed.

"Tell me, how is the play?" the monk asked.

"The play?" Jon said.

"Yes—are we making the front page in the American papers?"

Jon and Anne exchanged a look of disbelief. Jon told the monk, "Yes, you're making the front page in many American papers."

"New York Times?"

"Yes, most days."

"Excellent. Please follow me. There is a press conference in progress that you might find interesting."

The monk led the way into a room that was packed with monks and nuns, stiflingly hot, and very quiet. Anne smelled raw sewage and overpowering body odor. Someone was talking, and Anne had to stand on her tiptoes to see that it was a monk with a shaved head and a skeletal face. He was sitting at a low table with his back against the wall, surrounded by a dozen reporters, all of them scribbling in notebooks. On the wall was a banner with a command written in English: YOUTH OF VIETNAM BE READY TO SACRIFICE YOURSELF FOR BUDDHISM! Anne couldn't make out what the monk was saying.

The souvenir shops, the mimeograph machines, the publicity-conscious monks, the banner written in English for the benefit of the Western reporters—it all left a sour taste in Anne's mouth. Jon was convinced the communists were running the Buddhist protest and manipulating the American reporters like a pack of marionettes. Anne had seen nothing at the pagoda that day to convince her he was wrong.

Now the Peugeot squealed to a stop and Anne opened her eyes. They were not at Xa Loi but at the corner of Le Van Duyet and Phan Dinh Phuong, near the Cambodian Embassy, not far from Anne's favorite Indian restaurant. The sidewalks were packed, everyone chanting. The intersection had been cleared of all pedestrians and vehicles, and a column of monks was coming up Phan Dinh Phuong, marching silently.

Anne followed Charlie out of the car. "Is the camera loaded?" he asked Dang Sy.

"Yes, ready to shoot. Roll of twenty-four."

Anne followed Charlie into the chanting crowd. Someone was talking into a bullhorn. Anne saw Dang Sy get out of the car and squat on his haunches in the shade and offer a cigarette to Nguyen Ngoc Rao, the Vietnamese stringer for UPI. She also saw a few familiar American faces—David Halberstam, Peter Arnett from AP, Neil Sheehan from UPI. None of them seemed to be carrying a camera.

Anne was thinking about lunch. She loved fiery curries and shrimp vindaloo, and she hoped Charlie would agree to Indian food. She was wiping sweat from her forehead with the back of her wrist when a gray Austin sedan pulled into the intersection and stopped. At first she thought it was her roommate, Rosalyn. But three monks got out of the car, and several marchers, moving like well-drilled soldiers, formed a circle around them. One of the monks, a wispy old man, placed a square cushion on the street and sat in the lotus position while his two companions removed a large can from the car and splashed him with some sort of pink fluid. Anne was thinking about shrimp vindaloo when she smelled it: They were dousing the seated monk with gasoline.

He calmly removed a match from inside his robes and, as the other monks backed away, he struck it and burst into a bright ball of flame.

Anne heard a low moan rising from the crowd and she realized she was moaning, too. The monk's eyes remained shut, and his face remained serene and he did not make a sound. From him there came only that smell, a smell Anne would remember for the rest of her life, the acrid synthetic smell of burning human flesh.

Now the chanting had stopped and people were wailing and sobbing and the man passed in front of Anne with the bullhorn, droning in English: "A Buddhist priest burns himself to death . . . a Buddhist priest becomes a martyr . . . a Buddhist priest burns himself to death . . . a Buddhist priest becomes a martyr . . ."

Anne was so shocked by the man's use of English that she hadn't noticed the screaming arrival of a fire truck and police vehicles. She looked to her right as monks charged from the crowd and lay down on the street to prevent the fire truck from reaching the burning monk. There was a constant clicking sound to her left. It was Charlie Malloy feverishly snapping pictures.

A groan rose from the crowd as the monk toppled onto his side. Sparks shot into the air, he twitched, then he was still. Half a dozen monks approached. They lifted the charred remains and placed them in a wooden coffin. As they hoisted the coffin onto their shoulders and started walking toward Xa Loi pagoda, Anne could see black sticks protruding from the coffin—arms? legs? They were still smoking. And then Anne was doubled over, vomiting into a bush as the firemen began hosing the stain from the middle of the intersection and the crowd began to disperse.

19

Jarusit, the prettiest and laziest busboy in all of Bangkok, brought the day's mail to the godown just as Sam was replacing the last spark plug in the Malibu Blue Buick, the replica of the chariot that carried Anne Sinclair to her senior prom.

This Buick had belonged to the Zimmers, the family that lived at the far end of Lindbergh Street, and it carried memories of its own for Sam. During Christmas vacation of his junior year in high school, Vivien McNair and her family had gone to West Palm Beach and so Sam, forced to freelance, had spent New Year's Eve on this very front seat listening to the Times Square madness on the Sonomatic radio and coaxing Nancy Zimmer out of her sweater, then her blouse, and finally her bra. Her nipples were as big and tough as pencil erasers. They were delicious. He'd been working on Vivien for months and hadn't gotten this far with her. Nancy Zimmer was a sophomore, a chubby girl with freckles and mud-brown hair who, according to the intelligence on the walls of the Hicksville High School boys' rooms, made up for her lack of looks by giving skull-popping blowjobs. Sam was about to find out if Nancy's reputation was merited—she was tugging at his belt—when the garage light came on and Mrs. Zimmer, in curlers and bathrobe, started shrieking at them through the car's fogged windows, waking Mr. Zimmer and the dog and sending Sam trotting home with an aching groin and a wet spot on his jeans.

"Put the mail on the roof," he told Jarusit now.

"The roof?" The boy looked quizzically at the rafters.

"The roof of the car, numbnuts."

"Oh." He set the mail on the Buick's roof. "What is this new word 'numbnuts,' Khun Sam?"

Sam came out from under the hood, wiping his hands with a rag. " 'Numbnuts' is an American word that means 'beautiful intelligent friend.' "

"Nummmmmmm-nuts."

"Numbnuts. Say it quick."

"Numbnuts."

"So, numbnuts, have you cleared the lunch dishes yet?"

"No, numbnuts, I have not."

"Well then, numbnuts, get your lazy ass inside and do it."

"Yessir, numbnuts."

"Wait a second. What's that on your ear?"

The boy came close to show off his new earring—a tiny jade flower pinned through the left earlobe. He must have spent every baht he made on jewelry, clothes and haircuts, Sam thought. The fingernail on his left pinkie was an inch longer than the others, one more badge of the peacock. Sam watched him bop up the alley, humming some inane pop tune to his beautiful and worthless self.

A letter from Sam's father was on top of the stack of mail.

Dear Sam,

By now you've probably heard that your big brother is up for a Pulitzer Prize for a picture he took of a monk burning himself to a crisp. What a screwy country. I'll be glad when he gets the hell out of there.

Got some great news yesterday. After jerking me around for years, the insurance company finally paid in full on your mother's life insurance policy. They said they didn't have to pay because Doc Sheffield didn't order an autopsy. What a bunch of pricks. I finally had to get an expensive sheenie lawyer from New York to hold their feet to the fire before they agreed to pay up. I'll use the money to fix the roof and pay off the mortgage and I might have some left over to loan to Eddie so he can expand the restoration business. By the way, how are those Buicks?

I haven't missed a Mets game all season. They're pitiful! I love 'em! Most days I feel like Saint Anthony, the patron saint of lost causes. When are you coming home?

Love, Pop.

So the insurance bastards finally paid up. Good, Sam thought. Fuck 'em. He was glad he'd gotten to Dr. Sheffield and talked him out of an autopsy, which would have revealed the true cause of death and given the insurance company a legal excuse for not paying up. Though that was the furthest thing from Sam's mind that night, he now saw it as one more example of the necessity and beauty of certain secrets. His father, after spending his life up to his elbows in other people's grease and grief, deserved the money. Now he was free to enjoy his retirement and his wretched baseball team.

Sam flipped through the rest of the mail. Bills, party invitations he would regret, postcards and thank-you notes from satisfied hotel guests who'd moved on to Nepal and Tokyo and Sydney. The last envelope bore a Saigon postmark and no return address. He tore it open. The letter was written in green ink in a girlish, curlycuing script:

Dear Sam,

I thought this place couldn't possibly get any more insane, but I was wrong. I'm sure you've heard about your brother's famous picture by now, the picture of a monk's suicide by fire. I was with Charlie when he took it. It was the most horrible thing I've ever seen in my life.

That's the bad news. The good news is that I'm learning new things every day—amazing things, disturbing things. You and I need to sit down and have a little talk, compare notes. With things so crazy here, though, it will probably be weeks before I can get away.

It sure would be nice to get a letter. I hope you and the Buicks are doing well. I MISS you!

See you soon, Anne.

He reread the letter half a dozen times. Every time he got snagged on the words *I'm learning new things every day—amazing things, disturbing things. You and I need to sit down and have a little talk, compare notes.* He felt a stab of panic. A woman in her position, with her connections and her brains, could surely learn a great many things. The only question now was: What would she do with the things she was learning?

"Hey, numbnuts!"

Sam looked up the alley. Jarusit was standing by the iron gate, smiling and waving. "You have telephone call long-distance!"

"Where from?"

"Saigon!"

Sam hurried up the alley and through the gate. Shwe Winn was squatting in the shade by the kitchen door, smoking one of her hand-rolled cigarettes. Sam hardly noticed her anymore. She was like the furniture or the weather—merely there, implacable, eternal. She spit bits of tobacco at Sam as he passed.

He went into the office and sat in the swivel chair and put his feet up on the desk. He was surprised by how thrilled he was that her call had finally come. He tried to sound calm. "This is Sam Malloy."

But the voice that knifed through the low grumble of static did not belong to Anne Sinclair. It belonged to a man, a Southerner with a heavy drawl, a hick. It belonged to Vestal Embry: "Well, I de-clare, if it ain't the biggest pencil-dicked, shit-for-brains, goat-fuckinest Frogman that ever drew a breath. How you be, Mr. Sam?"

"Vestal! What the fuck?—"

"Just calling to say 'Hey.' "

"How'd you track me down?"

"Weren't nothin' to it. You know ole Vestal can find anybody

anytime anywhere. And with that big brother of yours so famous in these parts, why, it was like rollin' off a greased log."

"These parts? You're in Saigon?"

"That's a roger."

The syrupy drawl, the country idioms and military slang—it
carried Sam back to Little Creek, Virginia, where he and Vestal Embry were made "swim buddies" on the first day of
UDT training and proceeded to spend their days becoming
brothers and their occasional nights of leave carving a wide
swath through the thickets outside the amphib base, the go-go
bars and pool halls, the car lots with their snapping pennants
and blinking signs ("E-Z Credit E-2 and Up! We Tote the
Note!"), the tattoo parlors and hamburger joints and pawnshops
that were all designed to separate sailors from their money in
this lonely place that felt like it was a thousand miles from
home. Within five minutes of their first meeting Sam had Vestal
sized up as a snuff-dipping, catfish-frying, Pabst-swilling
cracker from the Georgia low country who didn't get his first
pair of shoes until he'd finished elementary school and never
did learn to read or write worth a damn. As first impressions
go, this one was startlingly close to the truth.

Trouble was, it didn't go nearly far enough. Like so many
Yankees—and Sam was to learn that people in places like Eulonia, Georgia, still speak of Yankees and Rebels, as though the
Civil War ended last week and not one hundred years ago—
Sam made the mistake of assuming that since Vestal grew up
backwoods-poor, he was therefore a dumbass. He was not. He
was better equipped to survive than anyone Sam had ever met.
He knew how to shoot, trap, net, hook, gig, grow and steal
food, how to fight with weapons or bare hands, how to find his
way out of thick wilderness, and he could fix absolutely anything, from a radio to a refrigerator, from a V-8 engine to a .45-
caliber grease gun. He could run or swim for hours without
seeming to tire, and he once stayed underwater, in a throng of
jellyfish in the Chesapeake Bay, for three minutes. No one knew
how he did it, and he wasn't telling. He could sleep anywhere,
too, in trees, in tunnels, on a barstool, and by the time the two
swim buddies pulled each other through the blood-curdling joys

Bill Morris

of Hell Week, they were bonded together for life. Waterproof, as Vestal liked to say, a couple of chrome-plated, bulletproof, gen-u-wine Frogmen who never ate and never slept and could fuck all night and breathe underwater and see in the dark and fly.

"What the hell you still doing in Saigon, Vestal? You didn't go and re-up, did you?"

"Shee-it no. I guarangoddamtee you I ain't *that* crazy. Here, I'll let my new business associate tell ya all about it. Say hello to my ace boon coon . . ."

There was laughter, then the unmistakable bullfrog voice of Wes Bledsoe, the only member of Underwater Demolition Team 7 who didn't have to blacken his face and hands when they went out on their fun-filled, nighttime hop & pops. Wes was already as black as a chunk of wet coal and, unlike most Frogmen, he was short, compact, thickly muscular. A super-ego Negro, as he liked to say, an inspired widow-maker.

"Sam the man, whuddup, whuddup?"

"What's this shit about business associates, Wes?"

"Ain't no big thang. Ves and Wes is proud to announce the opening of Saigon's hottest new bar. We calls it The VW Club."

"The VW Club?"

"Yeah, man. VW, like Volks Wagen, like Ves and Wes. You dig?"

"Yeah, Wes, I dig. What happened to all your talk about going back home and helping with the civil rights movement and all that noble shit?"

"You remember where home is for me?"

"Sure. L.A.—Lower Alabama," Sam said, repeating one of Wes's stock jokes.

"Thas right. Just outside of Mo-fuckin-bile, Ala-goddam-bama, to be exact. I went back home soon as me'n Vestal got discharged. I went there hummy, man, I was ready to change the world. Didn't quite work out that way, though. I didn't last a month."

"What happened?"

"What happened? You read the newspapers?"

196

"Sure, a monk in Saigon just torched himself, Pope John the Twenty-third just checked out—"

"Fuck the dead Pope, man, I'm talkin' about what's happenin' in *America*. Two days after I get home, a cousin a mine gets killed in Birmingham when a buncha crackers firebomb her church. Her *church*, for chrissakes! And just yesterday in Mississippi they gunned down a brother named Medgar Evers in his own front yard—thirty-aught-six in the back—while his wife and chirren watched. Medgar was a good friend of my baby brother's. Why would any nigger in his right mind want to stay in a country like that? So I can get my ass bit by police dogs and rinsed with fire hoses and shot all to hell? No fuckin' thanks. I'm stayin' put. 'Sides, I'm startin' to dig this place, Sam."

"Saigon? You used to hate Saigon."

"Love the womens. Love 'em. I went back to Alabama and all them black bitches' butts look like two bulldogs in a bag. Fuck that shit. Fact is, I'm startin' to like slant pussy even better'n I used to like gray pussy."

"Slant pussy, Wes?"

"Yeah, you know—Vee-yet-nam pussy. Best I ever had. Walk on your back, pop your toes, suck you dry. Your wish is their command." There was a moment of reverent silence. Then Wes added softly, "'Sides, Sam, after what we all been through together out there . . . I dunno, man . . . somehow goin' back home and gettin' up with a buncha Toms and ditty-bobs and fightin' for the right to sit down next to some cracker at a lunch counter—somehow that just don't get it. You dig me?"

Yes, Sam dug him. He thought of that night under the Pinklao Bridge when he'd tried to explain to Anne why he couldn't bear the thought of going home again—and here Wes Bledsoe, of all people, had just done an eloquent job of it. *After what we all been through together out there . . . somehow going back home just don't get it.*

"So when you comin' to see us, boy?" It was Vestal again.

"Hard to say, Vestal. I never seem to get caught up around here. And to tell you the truth, that place makes my skin crawl."

"Well, we got ways to take care of that. Wes 'n' me live

upstairs from the bar. We got plenty of spare room. Come stay as long as you like. All the free booze and pussy you can handle—which, if I recollect correctly, is one whole hell of a lotta both. Here, now write down the address and phone number."

Sam wrote it down. He knew the block. It was near the river, just up the street from the café where he used to do his drinking in private, the place where he bumped into Morey Caan and received the inspiration for importing the Buicks to Bangkok. He gave Vestal the address of the White Elephant, and they promised to keep in touch.

Weird, Sam thought as he hung up the phone, positively weird. He had never met two people with less in common than Vestal Embry and Wes Bledsoe—the easygoing yokel from Georgia and the angry young Negro from Alabama—and of all the guys on UDT Team 7, they were the last two he would have expected to stay in Asia after their discharges. But there they were, in Saigon running the VW Club, up to their eyeballs in slant pussy and, no doubt, running all sorts of lucrative scams on the side. By now Vestal had probably cornered a piece of the black market, buying and selling something insanely valuable, like transistor radios or blasting caps or Marlboros. God bless them both, Sam thought. And he found it comforting to know that he wasn't the only one who'd been changed, changed forever, by what they'd all been through together out there.

20

When Anne Sinclair showed up for work the next morning there was a copy of *The New York Times* on her desk along with a note: "See page 17. Then see me. Jon."

On page seventeen she was greeted by a full-page ad dominated by a large blowup of Charlie Malloy's famous picture. The caption read: "The Buddhist priest Rev. Quang Duc has just set himself on fire. He died to protest South Vietnam's religious persecution of Buddhists (70% of the population)." Then, in bold, inch-tall letters: "WE, TOO, PROTEST."

The statement was endorsed by twelve priests, ministers, rabbis and theologians. The only names Anne recognized were Reinhold Niebuhr, of New York's Union Theological Seminary, and James Pike, the Bishop of California and an old friend of her father's. They were protesting four things: "1. Our country's military aid to those who denied Rev. Quang Duc religious freedom. 2. The immoral spraying of parts of South Vietnam with crop-destroying chemicals and the herding of many of its people into concentration camps called 'strategic hamlets.' 3. The loss of American lives and billions of dollars to bolster a regime universally regarded as undemocratic and unstable. 4. The fiction that this is 'fighting for freedom.' "

In small type at the bottom of the page was an excerpt from a June 17 *Times* editorial:

> A majority of South Vietnam's people are Buddhists, yet the ruling oligarchy, dominated by members of the Roman Catholic Ngo family, has discriminated against Buddhists in many spheres . . . The official political ideology, enforced on everybody, is derived from Catholic philosophy. Restrictive social legislation, such as bans on dancing, contraceptives, divorce, and polygamy, runs counter to the customs and beliefs of the majority . . . It is time Mr. Diem realized that he cannot discriminate against the majority of the people of South Vietnam and win his war against the Communists. If he cannot genuinely represent a majority, then he is not the man to be President. He seems to feel that since he is supported by large-scale American aid he does not have to be supported by the Vietnamese people. No more dangerous error could be made.

Readers were urged to voice their support for these sentiments by writing to President Kennedy and their Congressman and by signing the protest and sending it to the Ministers' Vietnam Committee in New York.

Anne paused to collect her thoughts. So much was happening so fast and so little of it was good. She supposed she was in for another one of Jon's grueling, closed-door sessions on the fine art of damage control. Looking at the ad one last time, she had to admit it was stunning. It was stunning not because it appeared in the lordly *New York Times,* but because a group of esteemed clergymen had taken the unheard-of step of speaking out against their own government, openly declaring their passionate opposition, on moral grounds, to the war. It would be impossible to dismiss this as the work of erratic young reporters or misinformed editorialists who were soft on communism. No, this was America's graybeards talking. This was going to require some highly creative damage control.

Anne scooped up the newspaper and headed for Jon Medlin's

office. As she closed the door behind her, she decided to try to keep things light. No sense letting themselves get dragged into the mud by this. After all, it wasn't their fault.

To her surprise, Jon greeted her with a smile. As usual, everything was in its place: The American flag hung limply on its tall pole in the corner; the pudgy Smith-Corona typewriter was on its rolling stand; the gleaming desk was adorned with a telephone, a stapler, a glass ashtray and a green blotter with a single sheet of pink paper on it. But Jon's smile couldn't hide the fact that he was exhausted.

"Before we get started," he said, still smiling, "I have to tell you a quick story. Remember the fifty-thousand matchbooks we got printed up with President Diem's picture on the cover?"

"Sure. I chose the picture myself."

"Well, I'm afraid it was a waste of time."

"Let me guess—someone stole the matches and is selling them on the black market."

"No, nothing so predictable. The matchbooks got to the villages and into the hands of the peasants. But it seems there was a small problem nobody thought of. Care to guess?"

"The peasants don't know how to strike a match."

"You got it. Most of them had never seen a book of matches—and of course they had no idea who the fat man on the cover was. So they burned them. Jesus, what a fucked-up country . . ."

They shared a mirthless laugh.

"I've got some more news for you," Jon said. He had stopped smiling. "I dropped by the medical examiner's office yesterday. Guess what killed Morey Caan."

"I read in the paper it was shrapnel from the grenade."

"It was a tin roof."

"A tin roof?"

"To be precise, it was a shard from a tin roof in a strategic hamlet."

"I don't understand."

"I didn't either—until I called Lou Conein at CIA. Seems that nowadays whenever the Viet Cong overrun a strategic hamlet they don't just burn the place to the ground—they make the villagers pull down the new tin roofs and the barbed wire, chop it all up real fine, then pack it in homemade bombs and mines and grenades."

"Like the one that killed Morey."

"If you want to get technical about it, Morey was killed by a piece of tin manufactured in Wisconsin, paid for with U.S. tax dollars, then shipped to Vietnam where it was supposed to help win the hearts and minds of the Vietnamese people. Instead it wound up killing two American servicemen and one American journalist."

Anne watched Jon shake his head. He appreciated irony, but this was too much even for him. She could see that the man on the far side of the gleaming desk was already a goner.

"So," he said at last, "did you happen to catch Radio Australia this morning?"

"No."

"They had an amazing piece about Tick Tack Toe," he said, using the popular USIS moniker for the late Thich Quang Duc. "Apparently, the only part of him that wasn't consumed by the flames was his heart. Which all the Buddhists agree is a miracle. So the other monks put his heart in a glass jar, and now it's on display at Xa Loi pagoda in its very own shrine. They say it's the hottest tourist attraction of them all."

Jon picked up the pink sheet of paper on his desk. Anne expected him to start talking about the ad in *The New York Times,* but he surprised her again by saying, "I've just received a memo from the Ambassador. Before he returns to Washington he has a little project for us. As you know, he's not pleased with what he's been reading in the American press, and he wants us to prepare a major white paper that proves our policy has been—and I quote—'badly hampered by irresponsible, astigmatic and sensationalized reporting'—unquote. He goes on to say he doesn't condemn all the reporters. He has high praise for Marguerite Higgins and Joe Alsop and your buddy Charlie Malloy—even though he's pissed off that Charlie had the bad judgment to put that picture of Tick Tack Toe on the wires. So. What I need you to do, Anne, is go to our library and go through every TV transcript and every newspaper and magazine article that's come out in the past six months—since the Battle of Ap Bac—and compare them with the official reports from the Embassy and the CIA and the advisors in the field. I want you to pay special attention to the cases where there are discrepancies, not only between what the government said and what the reporters wrote, but also between what various reporters wrote. You with me so far?"

"I think so. You want me to document instances when Alsop and Halberstam write completely contradictory accounts of the same event."

"Correct. It shouldn't be too tough. Sometimes it's hard to believe Alsop and Halberstam are writing about the same goddam war. To give you a head start I've already prepared a file of all the official reports you'll need." He reached in a drawer and took out a foot-tall stack of papers and set it on the desk. "Everything you'll need is here—field reports from CIA, MAAG, ARVN, USMOG, even intercepted VC radio transmissions and documents. There's plenty of ammunition. Of course you're authorized to talk to anyone in the mission, from the Ambassador on down. I'll need the report two weeks from today so I'll have time to edit it and give the Ambassador a chance to sign off on it before he leaves. Any questions?"

"Yes, Jon, I do have a question."

"Shoot."

"Aren't you going to help?"

He looked up from the memo. He had a strange look in his eyes, a lost look. Yes, he was a goner, all right. "I'm afraid I can't, Anne."

"But Jon, this is a massive job for one person—especially if you need it in two weeks."

"I know it is. I'm asking you to do it as a personal favor to me."

"Why can't you help? Are you busy with something else?"

"Yes and no. I'm writing an analysis of the Buddhist crisis for Secretary McNamara. But that's not really it."

"Then what is it?"

"It's . . . it's just . . . I don't know quite how to say it, Anne. I guess I can't bring myself to do my own lying anymore."

And then Jon Medlin did something Anne had never seen him do before. He brought his hands to his face, and he wept.

That meeting was the beginning of the worst two weeks of Anne Sinclair's life. Until then, the lying she'd been ordered to do had had a harmless, almost amusing flavor to it. It was hard to believe that anyone could take the PI-REPs seriously—that anyone with a functioning brain could believe that a pilot buzzing a battlefield at treetop level was capable of counting the bodies of the dead and wounded. And while the propaganda films she'd helped produce were venal and misleading, they were certainly no worse than the communists' propaganda. If anything, they came closer to some sort of truth, and they'd given her a chance to get out of stifling Saigon and see a little bit of the country, places like the old imperial capital in Hue up on the coast; the hill town of Dalat, a favorite destination for honeymooners; the Mekong Delta, which seemed magical to her, timeless, the land as flat as a plate, the paddies turning to molten copper in the late-afternoon sunshine as children fished in the canals and rode on the backs of lumbering water buffaloes. It was unlike anything she had ever seen. It was a page out of the Old Testament. No wonder these people had so little use for democracy or communism or matchbooks decorated with a picture of a moon-faced mandarin in a sharkskin suit.

But now, as she waded into the job of cataloging the hundreds of instances where news accounts contradicted official government reports, Anne understood that the stakes were suddenly much higher. This white paper would be carried to Washington by the departing Ambassador and it would be read by the most brilliant and powerful men in the United States government, men who would sit around a polished conference table and mull over the American correspondents' sins and take them as confirmation of the rightness of their own beliefs, as reassurance that it was only a matter of time before they won their lovely little war. Worst of all, Anne's boss had admitted he was asking her to lie.

Jon was right about one thing: He'd given her plenty of ammunition. Marguerite Higgins of *The New York Herald-Tribune*, who'd won a Pulitzer Prize for her reporting on the Korean War, had just spent a month in Vietnam. She concluded that the Buddhist protest was a sham put on by publicity-hungry monks, that Diem was winning the war, and that the eager young reporters in Saigon were guilty of something bordering on treason. "Reporters here," Higgins wrote, "would like to see us lose the war to prove they're right."

Joseph Alsop visited briefly, long enough to conclude that the young huns were hurting Diem in much the same way correspondents in World War II had hurt Chiang Kai-shek—by calling attention to the unpleasant fact that his regime was corrupt and incompetent. Alsop wrote: "The constant pressure of the reportorial crusade against the government has also helped mightily to transform Diem from a courageous, quite viable national leader into a man afflicted with a galloping persecution mania, seeing plots around every corner, and therefore misjudging everything." Anne could see that the writings of journalists such as Alsop and Higgins were built on the premise that the "loss" of China to the communists in 1949 and the debacle in Korea were two blunders no American president dared to see repeated during his watch.

Then there were Charlie Malloy's dispatches. They not only appeared in a prestigious magazine, but they provided some rare balance, which made them doubly valuable to Anne. Charlie admitted to flaws in the Diem regime and to setbacks on the battlefield, but he took the reassuring long view that Diem was essentially a decent man and that the war was being won. And finally there were the Hearst newspapers, most notably *The New York Journal-American,* which came right out and accused Halberstam and Company of *the* cardinal sin: They were soft on communism.

Anne spent an entire week gathering ammunition. As her arsenal grew, she was dogged by a pair of related realizations. First, she noticed that the writers who criticized the resident correspondents tended to be older, they tended to believe whatever the government chose to tell them, and they rarely ventured out to the battlefield. And second, there were remarkable similarities between the written and broadcast reports of those who did venture out to the battlefield, who "got down in the mud," as they liked to say. Those reporters unearthed a remarkably similar set of facts, facts that the Diem government and the U.S. Mission disliked but rarely managed to refute convincingly. Was this a coincidence? She had few illusions about the Buddhist monks' motives or methods, and she was no fan of the brash, pushy young correspondents. But she had to admit that while they got together for drinks every night, they were also fiercely competitive, almost vicious in their drive to beat one another with a scoop, an exclusive, a fresh insight. And how could she explain away the thread that ran through the reports of the seasoned Asia correspondents who were coming to Vietnam more and more frequently? Was it a coincidence that the reporting of the young huns was being echoed by such respected veterans as Bernard Kalb of CBS, Pepper Martin of *U.S. News & World Report,* and Stanley Karnow of *The Saturday Evening Post?*

One story in particular gnawed at her. It appeared on the front page of the March 1 *New York Times* under the byline of David Halberstam. It claimed, in unusually well documented detail, that South Vietnamese Army commanders were using intelligence provided by American advisors to *avoid* contact with the Viet Cong and were actually faking operations. It stated that Diem's forces were unwilling to engage the Viet Cong even when they had a "7 to 1 advantage, or greater." It offered this scathing indictment of a typical ARVN exercise: "In one of these operations last week, 2,000 troops were used. One guerilla was killed; one woman and one child were killed in air strikes, and another woman and child seriously wounded by aircraft fire."

One American advisor, Halberstam wrote, was so incensed by this farcical incompetence that he wrote a blistering report that sparked an investigation by General Harkins's staff. "The only thing wrong with what he wrote," Harkins's investigator said of the angry advisor's report, "is that all of it is true."

Anne vowed to find out who this advisor was. She asked Charlie Malloy over drinks one night, and he said a lot of the news coming out of the Delta earlier in the year came from an advisor whose name he couldn't remember—Jon Mann? Paul

Gann?—some sort of renegade lieutenant. But Charlie heard he'd already been rotated back to the States.

When several other inquiries turned into dead ends, Anne decided to go directly to the source. It took her two full days to work up the nerve to call Halberstam's office. To her surprise he answered on the first ring and was cordial, almost jovial. He was on a deadline at the moment, but he agreed to meet her the next afternoon. He suggested a new place on Thi Sach, not far from the river. "It's so new," he said with a laugh, "that the Viet Cong don't even know about it yet. I'm sure we'll be safe there."

Anne showed up fifteen minutes early. The place had a red door and no sign. It was a cavernous air-conditioned cave, and to Anne's delight the only customer was a Vietnamese woman sitting on a stool at the far end of the bar. Her hair fell halfway to the floor. She was wearing a short red skirt and white high heels and she was talking softly to the man behind the bar, a muscular Negro whose face almost disappeared in the gloom.

The walls were decorated with Volkswagen hubcaps and with black-and-white magazine ads for VW beetles. This was some weird new breed of homesickness, Anne thought as she slid into one of the booths that ran along the wall.

"Whatcha havin'?" the Negro called to her in a distinctly Southern drawl.

"Just a Coke, please." On the back wall there was a chalk-board with the Daily Specials written in English and Vietnamese, but the light was too dim for her to read it.

The Negro brought her Coke and hovered above her until she started to feel uneasy. She looked up at him. His skin was almost blue, and his neck was draped with gold chains. The muscles of his chest and arms threatened to split his shirt open, and he was stroking a fuzzy excuse for a goatee. "Lemme guess," he said. "You're a TV reporter with one of the big networks."

"Sorry. I'm just a lowly government clerk. Thanks for the Coke." She opened the folder she'd brought with her—it contained all of Halberstam's articles and several pages of her own notes—and she began leafing through them. Taking the hint, the Negro drifted back behind the bar.

The door opened and a well-dressed Vietnamese couple came in and took seats at the bar. To Anne's surprise, the Negro spoke to them in Vietnamese. As he was fixing their drinks, she noticed they were looking the place over in a way that was not casual. Viet Cong agents casing the place, she told herself, and she realized she was no longer ashamed of her own paranoia.

Three Cokes and almost an hour later, just as she was despondently gathering up her clippings and notes, the door flew open and David Halberstam came charging in off the street, shoulders hunched, like a linebacker looking for someone to tackle.

The first thing Anne noticed as he approached was that his white, short-sleeved shirt was spattered with blood, dried blood, more brown than red. Sweat was pouring off him, dripping from his nose. He slumped on the bench facing her and, without a word of introduction, stabbed a finger at her and said, "Those bastards are gonna pay for this!"

"Who?—What happened?"

He started spitting his words like bullets. "There was a big demonstration up by the Chantareansay Pagoda this morning—lots of chanting and shoving, nothing out of the ordinary. I look up from my notebook and see a couple of Nhu's plainclothes thugs grab Arnett and start stomping him, smashing his camera all to hell, really working him over. I wade in and get the little bastards off him. Fortunately Mal Browne got pictures of the whole thing. I swear to God, Nhu's boys go nuts whenever they see a camera. It's been like that ever since Malloy got that picture of the burning monk."

"Are you hurt?" Anne asked, looking at the bloodstains.

Halberstam looked down, seeming to notice them for the first time. "That must be Arnett's. I'm fine. Shit. There goes a brand-new Arrow shirt. Five bucks down the drain."

The Negro was looming over the table. "Whatcha havin'?"

Halberstam squinted at the chalkboard on the back wall. "Good God! You've got home cooking!"

The Negro laughed. Teeth like sugar cubes. "You like home cookin'?"

"No, I *love* home cooking. Look at this menu!"

"You don't sound like no Southern boy to me."

"I'm not—I'm Jewish and I'm from the Bronx. But when I worked for the newspaper in Nashville they sent me all over Tennessee and Alabama and Mississippi. I couldn't get enough of the stuff. You've even got greens!"

The Negro was beaming. He turned to join Halberstam in admiring the chalkboard. "They ain't nothin' up there that ain't cooked from scratch. It's all my momma's recipes . . ."

Halberstam ordered the fried chicken with fried okra, kale and pinto beans, plus iced tea. While waiting for his food, Halberstam poured three spoonfuls of sugar into his tea and set about establishing that he was sitting across the table from something he had never encountered before—a USIS official who was actually interested in hearing the truth. Anne assured him that this was the case.

When his food arrived, Halberstam started talking and eating like a man possessed. Anne had never seen anything like it. His big beefy hands were in constant motion as he answered her questions and shoveled home his lunch, which included great bricks of cornbread. Halberstam's hands chopped the air, his fists pounded the table, his fingers stabbed out to emphasize a point. His face was shiny with sweat and chicken grease and ecstasy. The thick lenses of his glasses were tinted gray, and Anne could see that his eyes were softer than the rest of him, almost gentle.

Only when Anne asked him about his March 1 article on the faked operations did Halberstam balk. He put down a half-demolished chicken breast, ran a paper napkin across his face, licked his fingers. "I'd really rather not tell you the source on that one," he said.

"Was it a lieutenant named Mann?"

"Look. I promised to protect my source on that story, so I'm not going to tell you who it was. Period. But it's no big mystery. I'm sure even a numbskull like Harkins has figured it out by now. Besides, the guy's back at the Pentagon." He picked up the chicken breast and resumed eating. Bones popped and snapped. "Here's what happened. In late February this guy takes me into his operations room down on the Delta, closes the door, and points at a huge map of Division One. He then spends the entire afternoon laying it all out for me, the size and location of every Viet Cong unit, specifics about their weapons and strength and leadership, examples of ARVN commanders going where they know they won't have to fight. You see, Diem hates to hear that his troops have suffered casualties, so the commanders have figured out that the way to win advancement is to avoid casualties. And the best way to avoid casualties is to avoid fighting."

"What a way to fight a war."

"Tell me about it. And you'll notice that nobody—American or Vietnamese—has been able to discredit my story. It's not like they didn't try, though."

"What happened?"

"I just got word from my editor that President Kennedy took our publisher aside at a luncheon in Washington the other day and asked him to replace me with another correspondent."

"You're kidding."

"I got that from the foreign editor. He's not a big practical joker."

"Tell me about this advisor who fed you the story down on the Delta. Did he try to pass his information up the chain of command?"

"He sure as hell did," Halberstam said, pushing his plate away at last. "Just like Ap Bac. Now *that* would make one hell of a story."

"What would?"

"His after-action report on the battle of Ap Bac. He wouldn't show it to me, but he told me it was ninety pages long, with maps and a chronology of the battle, and it was endorsed by Colonel Dan Porter. It doesn't get any more airtight than that."

"What happened to it?"

"Nothing. That's the story. It got passed on to Harkins and a copy went to Nolting at the Embassy—and nobody's heard of it since."

"So this source of yours is back in Washington?"

"Yeah, and from what I hear they've got a good tight muzzle on him." And then, as Halberstam tucked into a wedge of pecan pie with a snowball of vanilla ice cream on top, he offered a piece of free advice: "If I had friends at the Embassy, as I'm sure you do, I'd damn sure try to get my hands on a copy of that Ap Bac after-action report. I'm sure it would make for some interesting reading."

Anne watched in silent amazement as Halberstam polished off the pie and ice cream. Just watching him eat made her want to take a nap. As he called for the check Halberstam said, "I'd like to stay and talk, but I've got to go write my story about the brawl this afternoon and try to find a pigeon."

"A pigeon?"

"A carrier pigeon."

"Cut it out."

"I'm serious. We're using them more and more. Whenever the government censors at the telegraph office get a story or a picture that's the least bit controversial, they carve it up so bad it's usually not worth sending. So we've started sending sensitive stories and pictures out of the country with people flying on commercial airlines. When they get to Bangkok or Hong Kong or Singapore, they hand them over to wire service people, who transmit them to the States for us."

"I had no idea . . ."

"It's been going on for a while. And my guess is it's going to get worse before it gets better."

Anne thanked him for his time and advice. She watched him walk back out into the midday glare. Only when he was gone did she realize the Vietnamese couple at the bar had been listening to every word Halberstam said.

That night, when Lois DeVries dropped by Anne's apartment for her regular monolog and wine-swill, Anne broached the subject of the Ap Bac after-action report. Yes, Lois said, she'd heard of it. But it was classified, and it would take some doing to get at it. Anne started begging and didn't let up. Halfway through the second bottle of wine Lois succumbed to Anne's persistence and to her own disgust with the whole stinking mess. Waving her wineglass, she said, "Aw, why the hell not."

Shortly after 1 o'clock the next afternoon, as the city melted into its midday siesta, Anne walked into Lois's windowless cubicle on the second floor of the U.S. Embassy.

"Close the door and lock it," Lois said. Then she reached in a drawer and took out a large green envelope labeled "Top Secret: Ap Bac After-Action."

"You've got exactly twenty minutes," Lois said. "I'm going across the street for an ice cream. Lock the door behind me. When I come back I'll knock three times. Don't open the door for anyone else."

When Lois was gone, Anne removed the Instamatic camera from her purse. It would be clumsy—she would probably have to read the photographed pages with a magnifying glass—but it was the best she could do. It took less than twelve minutes to photograph the entire report, all ninety pages. She had it back in the envelope and tucked in Lois's desk drawer long before she heard the three knocks on the door.

She took the film to the Kodak shop on Le Loi, near Ben Thanh Market, where she knew the staff. She waited while they developed and printed the three rolls, idly chatting with the proprietor about the rain, the Buddhists, the car bomb that killed four people last night outside the Diamond in Cholon.

When the film was ready, Anne took a taxi to her apartment and locked the door and spread the pictures on her bed. She began reading them with the magnifying glass her roommate kept beside her *Oxford English Dictionary*.

It was, as Halberstam promised, some fascinating reading. It was the work of sixteen American advisors who were directly involved in the battle at Ap Bac. All names were blacked out. The first entry was a twenty-one-page summary that was written in dry military prose but left no room for doubt: Ap Bac was when the Viet Cong came of age, when they stood and fought and won a set battle for the first time; and it was a disaster for Diem's army and a dark omen for the Americans. There were maps. There was an hour-by-hour chronology. It was a portrait of almost unimaginable ineptitude, bungling and cowardice on the part of the South Vietnamese.

And the world knew nothing about it.

And General Harkins, who surely had read it and discussed it with the authors, had blithely told the world that Ap Bac was a victory for the South Vietnamese and their American allies.

In that moment things clicked for Anne, the pieces fell into place like tumblers in a lock. She understood that her discovery of these truths carried a responsibility with it. She must get the truth out somehow. She must put an end to the secrets and the lies before it was too late.

The most obvious course would be to leak the report to one of the American reporters—Charlie Malloy and Halberstam came immediately to mind—but she had promised Lois she would not release it. To do so now would be to toss Lois to the wolves. That would be wrong. Besides, Lois was still a vital source of information, and Anne realized she must be careful not to do anything that would cut off the flow.

She got a knife from the kitchen and cut out the pages in the middle of her book of O. Henry short stories and tucked the photographs of the Ap Bac report into the hollowed-out book. Then she placed it on her bookshelf, next to *The Quiet American*. It was, she had to admit, the most innocent-looking bomb in all of Saigon.

21

Sam Malloy kept drifting in and out. He was sitting on the brick terrace outside the legendary house of Jim Thompson, one of the Major's oldest friends, the American who had single-handedly revived the Thai silk industry. Overhead was a canopy of flame trees in full crimson bloom, a jungle of coconut palms and ferns and dangling creepers. Sam was trying to pay attention to the guest of honor, a mousy little American in a white linen suit who was describing how he'd gotten Marlon Brando to spill his guts when he'd interviewed him in Japan during the filming of *Sayonara*. The resulting article had appeared in *The New Yorker* magazine, and to hear the little man tell it, the world had not been the same since. The Major, Kukrit Pramoj, Rat, Jiap and the dozen other guests were riveted by the story, but the man's high-pitched, sing-song voice was like a dying radio signal to Sam, strong one moment, weak the next.

"... I used the oldest trick in the book. You tell someone your problems long enough—and believe me, honey, I can go on all night about mine—and pretty soon they feel this strange ob-li-*gation* to tell you theirs . . ."

Sam found it hard to believe he was sitting in the middle of

Bangkok. This jungle was lit by pinpricks of fire from coconut oil torches, and in the far corner of the terrace a traditional Thai orchestra, dressed in ornate silk costumes, was pumping waves of trilling Thai music into the heavy air. Sam looked up. The red peaks of Thompson's century-old teak house soared into the starry sky. Before World War II there had been thousands of these houses in Bangkok, but "progress" had wiped most of them out, replaced them with American ranch houses and European villas and boxy apartment buildings. From the far bank of Klong Saen Saep came the clicking of the weavers' looms, a sound Sam knew well.

". . . the most amazing thing about it," the little man was droning, "was that he was just *dying* to admit he was queer. And he kept using these ridiculous big words, and all I could think of was that he sounded like some sort of educated Negro . . ."

Sam excused himself and went off to find a bathroom. A cockatoo and a black spaniel watched him cross the terrace, which was made of 300-year-old bricks. A Thai servant led him upstairs to the master bedroom and pointed to a door. There were no screens or glass in any of the windows, another traditional Thai touch, so Sam was surprised to find a Western-style flush toilet in the bathroom instead of a porcelain hole in the floor and a bucket of water and a dipper. As he filled the toilet bowl with the golden foam of half a dozen Singha beers, he realized the reason he'd been drifting in and out all night was the phonecall that came from Saigon just before he'd left the White Elephant to come to this party.

As soon as he'd picked up the receiver, Anne Sinclair had started babbling, and she babbled for ten solid minutes about suicides and coup plots and faked missions and the white paper. Sam couldn't get a word in. He had the good sense not to try. His job at that moment was to listen. Finally she said, "Sam, you've got to get me out of here!" And then, as abruptly as she'd started talking, she stopped.

It took Sam a moment to think of something to say. "Where are you, Anne?"

"I'm in my fucking office. I just heard an explosion over by

215

the cathedral. I can hear sirens. I'm afraid to walk home. You've got to get me out of here!"

He was familiar with this manic edge. He'd first seen it in the weeks after his discharge from the Navy, when Charlie dragged him to a performance of the Martha Graham dance troupe in Saigon and then to a reception full of U.S. Mission bigwigs and their wives. The women all wore beautiful bright dresses and they were dripping with rubies and emeralds and they were pouring down the booze like a bunch of sailors because they were bored half to death. The ones who'd been in Saigon long enough had gone beyond boredom—they were frightened and distracted, frantic about being caged in a city where suddenly grenades were blowing up in restaurants and movie theaters, and a sense of doom, a physical presence, something they could taste, had settled into the wet sticky air.

"Listen, Anne," Sam had said on the telephone, "why don't you give the war a rest? Come see the sights of Bangkok—"

"Oh Sam, you've got no idea how much I'd love that. After you show me the sights, can we go off to that island you told me about? The one with the bonfires and the moon?"

"Of course we can."

"And there won't be any reporters or press conferences or bombs?"

"No reporters or press conferences or bombs."

"Promise?"

"Promise."

"And we can talk?"

"As much as you like."

"I mean, will you talk, too?"

"If that's what you want."

"I'm serious, Sam. I need to tell someone about the stuff I've been learning—but you've got to tell me about what you learned when you were here."

"Fine."

"Don't *fuck* with me, Sam Malloy!" she shrieked, and suddenly she was sobbing.

Then it was Sam who talked for ten minutes without letup, assuring her that he wanted to hear her stories and would match them with stories of his own, true stories, stories that would make her see that what she was going through now was nothing new, that it had all been going on for years and would probably keep going on for years to come because that's the way it worked when governments had so much to lose. It occurred to him, even as he was telling her this, that it was probably the last thing she wanted to hear. But his words had the desired effect. Soon she was saying, very softly, "Remember what I said that night we had dinner in Bangkok?"

"You said a lot of things that night."

"Remember what I said about secrets?"

"Yes. You said some secrets are poison—and they'll eat us alive if we don't get rid of them."

"And what do you think about that?"

"I've thought about it a lot and I've decided you're right."

"Do you mean that?"

"Yes."

"Good. Now listen to me. They're going to change Ambassadors soon, and everyone's going to take at least a week off. They're going to put the war on hold, like it was a phonecall." She gave a hollow laugh and promised to let him know her travel plans as soon as they were set.

When Sam returned to the terrace, the little man in the white suit was still talking. Sam didn't hear a word he said. Instead, he listened to the music and the chorus of tree frogs and the distant clicking of the looms. He wondered if Anne would hold him to his vow of an even swap of secrets. A woman in her state would surely try. The strange thing, he realized, looking up at the stars and the crimson blooms, was that he no longer feared an exchange of intimacies. For the first time there was something in his life more valuable than his secrets. If sharing those secrets was the only way to get through to this woman, then he would do it. And he would do it with abandon.

22

Charlie Malloy shaved twice on the morning of his third and final session with Madame Nhu. This time he wanted to be perfect in her eyes, beyond reproach. He got his best poplin suit pressed, got his oxblood loafers shined, bought a new silk necktie, even got a haircut. He had made the mistake of shaving only once before his last interview and she had kept him waiting all morning and most of the afternoon, and by the time he was ushered into her corner suite, a 5 o'clock shadow had begun to darken his jowls. She noticed it instantly and was not pleased. This time he was taking no chances.

As he left the Caravelle he noticed that the Indian money changers on the sidewalk were offering 400 piastres for one U.S. dollar, nearly double their usual rate. The Indians and the Chinese never ceased to amaze Charlie—no matter where they went in the world they carried some sort of sonar, some gene that kept them attuned to the true value of money. Today's wildly inflated exchange rate was a sign that the money changers believed the long-rumored coup was coming at last, and they were terrified that they might wake up tomorrow and find that their stacks of piastres weren't worth the paper they were printed on.

Charlie hoped the Indians were jumping the gun. If today's interview went well, he could finish writing his article tonight and ship it in the morning. His first cover story was within reach, and the last thing he wanted was for a coup to push Madame Nhu's gorgeous face off the red-rimmed cover of *Time* magazine.

The same girl in the *ao dai* greeted Charlie inside Gia Long Palace and led him up the broad staircase and down the long portico to the suite of corner offices. As he settled onto the sofa in the dim waiting room, Charlie could hear Madame Nhu on the telephone, speaking in French. He cocked an ear, but just as he began to pick up the drift of her words—she was booking a seat on a Pan Am flight to Los Angeles—he realized he was not alone. A Vietnamese officer was sitting in the far corner of the room, ramrod-straight, his hands on the knees of his starched khakis. The hat on his lap was roped with gold brocade. His face was a stony mask of terror. A man about to face a firing squad, Charlie thought. Worse than a firing squad: the fury of Madame Nhu.

To his surprise, Charlie was summoned to the inner sanctum before the officer. Madame Nhu must have decided it would be crueler to let the man sweat a little longer. Another surprise greeted Charlie in the office: Madame Nhu was as immaculately coiffured and made-up as ever, but instead of an *ao dai* and high heels, she was wearing a simple pink silk robe and satin slippers. She looked smaller, much less regal.

"Mr. Malloyyyyy," she purred, her smile as radiant and false and sexy as ever. "Please sit down. You are very handsome today." She barked for the servants to bring their usual, hot tea and *café sua*, and she lit a cigarette and started pacing. "Now, where were we, Mr. Malloy?"

"Let's see," Charlie said, opening his notebook. "You were telling me about your marriage . . ."

"Ah yes," she said, continuing to pace, her eyes catching fire. "At home I am known as *noi tuong*, General of the Interior. Nhu is a good man, but he is weak—just like his brother—and since I know this, people say I do not love him, that I do not even like men. But that is not true, Mr. Malloy. I have no reason to

219

dislike men. They have always been nice to me. It's just that I have never had—how do you say?—a sweeping love . . ."

Charlie could already tell he was in for a long day. He knew the symptoms: the cigarette, the pacing, the stream-of-consciousness monolog. He was determined not to let her ramble today. "Madame Nhu," he said sharply. "I want to ask you about the suicide of the Buddhist monk Thick Quang Duc—"

"That was not a suicide," she said, lighting a fresh cigarette from the butt of the first one. "That was a barbecue. I happen to know for a fact that it was paid for by your CIA and television networks. There will be more barbecues. Good. Let all the bonzes barbecue themselves. When they are all gone we can devote our attention to the job of defeating the communists . . ."

As she rambled on about the most effective way to fight the Viet Cong, Charlie checked his list of prepared questions. He needed to ask her about some of the more enduring rumors— that she owned a theater on the Champs Elysées in Paris, that she owned all 6,000 taxis in Saigon, that she owned most of the downtown bars and had a hit list of American journalists targeted for assassination. ". . . please make your readers understand one thing about the Ngo family, Mr. Malloy."

"I'll certainly try."

"Explain to them that President Diem is not comfortable in large crowds, that it is not natural for him to visit the villages and shake the hands of peasants the way American politicians do. We Vietnamese do not like to be told what to do. Not by Americans, not by anyone. Even when I was a little girl, if someone told me to stand up I would sit down, even if I wanted to stand up. I have always been this way. It is the Vietnamese way. It is President Diem's way. It is— Come with me, Mr. Malloy . . ."

Charlie looked up from his notebook. She was standing in a doorway behind her desk, holding her hand out. He crossed the room and took her cool hand and followed her down a corridor, through a tall door that gave into a sort of library. There were floor-to-ceiling shelves, but very few books. Sunlight poured through tall windows. Charlie blinked at the brightness, then slowly turned a full circle. The wall opposite the bookcases was covered with the heads of large game animals—tigers, lions, gazelles, wild boars—and Charlie realized he was standing on the hide of a zebra. He was bewildered. There were zebras in Southeast Asia?

"This is President Diem's study, Mr. Malloy. It is his favorite room in the palace. Tell your readers about this room. It will help them understand the man."

Charlie started writing down the contents of the walls and floor. He found it hard to believe Diem was capable of stepping on a cockroach, much less bagging a roomful of trophies that would have made Ernest Hemingway drool. As he was writing he was startled to feel Madame Nhu press against his back and slip her arms around his waist. Her pencil-thin arms barely circled his girth. "Yes, that's it, Mr. Malloy. Write it all down . . . Tell the world . . ."

Charlie looked down. There was a pup tent in the pants of his poplin suit, and though Madame Nhu could not possibly have seen it from where she was standing, her hands slid down and began massaging his groin.

As he lost hold of his notebook, he felt her arms forcing him to turn and face her. Her hair brushed his chin. It had the texture of steel wool. He felt her claws working up his back to his neck, digging in, pulling his face down to hers.

After that Charlie remembered being pushed backward until he fell onto the sofa. As Madame Nhu began undressing him, her robe fell open, revealing tiny pert breasts, the breasts of a girl, and skin that was not brown, not even yellow, but waxy and white, skin that had never been touched by the sun. And then she was climbing onto his lap, swallowing him inside herself, and he forgot about his story and the war and the animal heads staring down at him, forgot where he was and why he was there because all that mattered was that she was thrashing against him with a fury that was frightening, and she was biting his neck until she drew blood and finally, in ecstasy, began to scream.

23

As the turquoise-and-white Buick came up out of the stinking Sargasso of the east Bangkok slums and unwound on the open road, Anne Sinclair stuck her head out the passenger's window and gulped the hot wind and laughed out loud.

"What's so funny?" Sam shouted.

"Everything! Nothing! I'm happy!"

She couldn't remember feeling so happy. When she arrived at the White Elephant three days earlier she was delighted to find that Sam had saved the same room for her—already she thought of it as her room, with the proprietary air common to travelers who've been away from home too long. The parquet floor was cool on her bare soles, and there was a fresh bouquet of orange and yellow canna blossoms by the bed, a gift from Rat and Jiap, who, like the rest of the hotel's residents and staff, were delighted by her return. Beside the flowers was a book of Joseph Conrad's short stories, a gift from the Major, who overheard her tell Sam during her first visit that she loved to read at night but never remembered to pack a book. The hotel was quiet. Most tourists had been driven from Bangkok by the cloying humidity and daily downpours that pimpled the river and thrashed the trees and sometimes turned the streets to impassable rivers of gray soup.

Sam, as promised, gave her a tour of the city. They spent one day in a longboat, passing Jim Thompson's house and the weaving village on Klong Saen Saep, then crossing the Chao Phraya and visiting the floating markets in Thonburi. They passed teak houses, set on stilts, that seemed to float on the rioting vegetation. There were men wading in the black water, stripped to the waist and carrying white porcelain bowls. Sam explained that they were panning for gold.

When the boat returned to the Chao Phraya, Sam ordered the boatman, a barefoot Thai with skin like brown shoe leather, to head downriver, south. Soon they were skimming past the Oriental. An ugly modern tower shouldered against the elegant old hotel, once home to Somerset Maugham and Rudyard Kipling and more ghosts than Sam could name.

Outside the Grand Palace the next day they came upon men tending birds. The Buddhist faithful bought the birds and set them free, thus building merit for the next life. Anne was enchanted. The palace grounds were every bit the Buddhist Disneyland Sam had promised, a world of spiky, gold-plated *chedis*, scowling statues, murals, mirror-studded walls, white elephants and finally the Emerald Buddha, which, Sam whispered, was actually jasper or jade, depending on which story you believed. It was surrounded by unsmiling guards and by lamps with ringed shades that looked to Anne like they'd been lifted from the set of a Buck Rogers movie.

In Lumpini Park they watched snake handlers drain cobra blood and gall into shot glasses, which Chinese men knocked back with cognac in the belief it would enhance their virility. In the sprawling Chatuchak Market they passed vendors selling human skulls, silk and such wildly popular pets as monkeys, pythons and squirrels, more squirrels than Anne had ever seen, flying squirrels, striped squirrels, tree squirrels, ground squirrels. With their clipped nails, filed teeth and fluffy tails, they struck Anne as far more sad than beautiful.

Sam led her through the choked streets of Chinatown, where each block was devoted to a specific commerce, offering coffins or woks, noodles or knives. On the third day they rose in the dark and took a boat across the river to Wat Arun, the Temple of Dawn, where Anne scrambled up the cliff-like steps ahead of him, not even bothering to hold on to the ropes that most people clutched for dear life. He joined her just in time to see the sun punch up out of the flat earth to the east of the city, igniting the gold roofs of the Grand Palace and the belt of haze and smoke that lay on the city like a soft silver blanket.

It seemed they never stopped eating. They eased into it, starting with soups at noodle shops, stopping at hawkers' stalls for spring rolls and phad Thai, a fried-noodle dish laced with bits of egg, bean sprouts, shrimp, turnips and chilis. They sampled sticky rice wrapped in banana leaves, watermelon juice, coconut ice cream topped with lotus seeds. Then, without a word, they became more daring. She ate a whole bag of lychees, hairy red fruit the size of golf balls that yielded a sweet white pulp. She ate guava, mango, jackfruit, fried mussels, coconut pudding, fish balls. Not even a stabbing bout of diarrhea could slow her down. By the third day she was ready for fried locusts and a bowl of bird's nest soup. She didn't meet her match until she tried durian, a fruit that smelled like a marriage between dirty sweatsocks and rotten eggs. At durian she drew the line.

"What are you so happy about?" Sam shouted to her now across the Buick's front seat.

She pulled her head back into the car. Her hair looked like a tornado had touched down in it. "What am I so happy about? This!" She slapped the Buick's dashboard. "And that!" She motioned toward the hot flat world flashing past. "I'm happy because I feel like a little girl on the first day of summer vacation." And she stuck her head back out the window.

Yes, she realized, gulping the wind, that was it. Being with this man made her feel like a girl again, young and carefree, eager to explore the world, a feeling she hadn't known since she arrived in Saigon. When she was in high school and college she ached, as all teenagers ache, to be an adult; and then suddenly she was out of school and in Saigon and her life was deadly serious and her youth was gone. But now, driving away from Bangkok and into the midday heat, she felt she was regaining something precious, something she must never give up as long as she lived. She was a child again and she believed that the flawless gift of this afternoon would be followed by an infinite number just like it and that she must spend those coming afternoons as she had spent the past three afternoons, exploring new worlds, becoming amazed, full of wonder, becoming once again a child.

They stopped for lunch at an open-air restaurant on the far side of Chonburi, a small town thirty miles east of Bangkok. Sam parked the Buick in a grove of coconut palms, where it was cooler, and a flock of giggling children immediately materialized from the shadows. They were all barefoot and as brown as the earth, and their faces glowed with an inner light. They approached the car slowly, as though it were sacred, or possibly dangerous. "What beautiful children . . ." Anne said. And Sam agreed that, yes, they were.

He ordered a seafood platter, and he had to eat fast to get his share from the smoking mound of shrimp, squid, mussels and cockles. When it was gone Anne was still hungry, so she ordered a bowl of scalding tom yum soup and a bottle of beer. By the time she stopped eating, her face was glazed with sweat and her lips were on fire and she was having delightful hallucinations.

They returned to the Buick. The fruit and bottled water on the back seat were undisturbed, but there were hundreds of tiny handprints on the car's dusty exterior. The children had vanished.

Within five minutes, Anne, drugged by the food, the heat and the car's motion, sagged against Sam and dozed off. She snored like a chainsaw. Sam smiled at this—there seemed to be no end to her surprises—and he gunned the Buick toward the storm that was building in the east.

Anne awoke when the first sheets of rain began pelting the car. She sat up. They were passing a rubber plantation, and she marveled at the trees, their long branches and majestic height, all in perfect rows, all tilted at the same angle as though bowing to a breeze. These trees reminded her of the day she was returning to Saigon from Tay Ninh and saw the two Marines and their Vietnamese girlfriends blown to bits by the Viet Cong mine. In her drowsy state she was powerless to fight off this thought of the war. Rubber trees, she realized, were what the war was all about. Rubber trees embodied all the bad history, all the West's abuse and misunderstanding of the East, all the resulting rage and devious killing. Tens of thousands of Vietnamese were worked to death on the Michelin plantations so white men could get rich making tires. And now the Americans, with no apparent knowledge of this or any of the rest of Vietnam's colonial nightmare, had replaced the French. How could they expect the love or even the loyalty of the Vietnamese? They thought their good intentions and their democracy were enough. And already she understood that they were wrong.

"Good morning."

She looked at Sam. He was smiling. His head was bobbing up and down, back and forth, like a boxer dodging punches. He was trying to catch glimpses of the road as the windshield wipers struggled to clear away the sheets of rain. The wipers worked on some sort of vacuum. When he let off the gas they jumped, and when he accelerated they died. A Buick quirk, Anne thought, a charming Buick quirk.

"You okay?" Sam asked.

"I'm fine. Just sleepy."

"You snore like a drunk sailor, you know that?"

"I do not."

"You sure you're okay? You look a little funny."

"I was just thinking about . . . about rubber trees." She made herself stop. Raindrops were slicing into the car, cooling the air, stinging her right arm. She watched the wipers struggle, jump, and die, then struggle, jump, and die again. "Why are all those people standing on the other side of the road?" she asked.

"They're waiting for the bus to take them to Bangkok. What a shame."

"Why is that a shame?" She was relieved to be talking about something other than the war.

"Because all those people are going to Bangkok for jobs. It's the almighty dollar talking. The U.S. is pouring money into this country to make sure it doesn't go communist and that it'll be available if the war in Vietnam heats up."

"Available?"

"For air bases. They're getting ready to expand half a dozen bases in Thailand. Right now most of the money's in Bangkok—with a fair share going into the pockets of the military boys who run the show. That's why all these people are leaving the villages—they can make a fortune working as construction workers and waiters and prostitutes in the big city. That's something I'll never understand about the Thais."

"What is?"

"They're so proud to be the only nation in Southeast Asia that's never been colonized by the white man. They've fought off the Chinese, the Burmese, the Japanese, the Khmers, the Vietnamese—and for what? So they could sell their souls for the Yankee dollar? The word is that Sarit Thanarat, the Prime Minister, is worth well over a hundred million dollars. If that's not the American tax dollar hard at work, I don't know what is."

"Jesus. A hundred million."

"Of course, he needs it."

"What for?"

"They say he has more than a hundred mistresses—and something like three hundred children. Imagine what his grocery bill must be like! Did you happen to see that story about him in *Newsweek* a few months back?"

"Must've missed it."

"It made him out to be some sort of crusader—just because he's fighting the Laotian communists and made his cabinet ministers sell their opium dens and whorehouses. What a joke. The only reason he's fighting the communists is because it's making him filthy rich."

They rode in silence until the rain stopped and the sun broke through the clouds. Soon the car was dry and the ground was steaming and the air was hotter than ever.

"What is it with these Asian rulers?" Anne said without thinking. "I understand Madame Nhu has a few notches in her bedpost, too. And she's Catholic—"

She caught herself, but it was too late. They were talking about the war again and there was nothing she could do to stop it.

"You're telling me the president's sister-in-law messes around?" Sam said.

"Big-time. They call her the Dragon Lady. Are you ready for the latest rumor?"

"Sure."

"I can't believe I'm telling you this. I hear she seduced your brother."

"Charlie!?" Sam laughed so hard the left front tire hooked on the shoulder of the road and he had to fight the steering wheel, barely avoiding a motor scooter with a man driving and a woman riding side-saddle, a graceful Thai couple unfazed by the proximity of death. "You're telling me Charlie got lucky with the president's sister-in-law?" Sam was pounding the steering wheel, howling. "I didn't know the old goat had it in him! How do rumors like that get started?"

This one got started by Col. Tran Van Duong of the South Vietnamese Army, who'd spent a recent morning and afternoon in Gia Long Palace waiting for an audience with Madame Nhu and saw Charlie Malloy emerge from her offices with mussed hair, flushed face, and a wobbly walk that meant one thing. When Colonel Tran got drunk at the Cercle Sportif that night, he let this slip, and soon the story of the *Time* correspondent locking loins with the Dragon Lady was being broadcast on "Radio Catinat," the relentless Saigon rumor mill.

After a while Sam stopped laughing and seemed to lose interest in his brother's latest conquest. As the Buick passed through the dusty frontier town of Trat and continued on to the fishing village of Laem Ngop near the Cambodian border, Anne concentrated on the lush scenery and managed to banish all thoughts of the war.

An hour later Anne was looking over her shoulder at the vanishing mainland. She felt an unshakeable terror that she would never see it again. They were on a porous, orange-and-blue fishing boat that was throbbing out onto the turquoise platter of the Gulf of Thailand. The sky to the west was pale orange. The sun was ripening from yellow to red as it fell toward the water.

"You okay?" Sam asked, rubbing her arm.

"I'm fine," she lied. "Boats make me a little queasy."

They were headed for the island of Ko Chang, a distant green dot, the place where Rat grew up, a place, Sam assured her, where there was not a single telephone or paved road, no electricity or running water, no traffic and no tourists and no war. The twentieth century became a dim memory when you stepped onto Ko Chang. This moment was everything she'd yearned for in Saigon—the water was smooth, the sunset was stunning, the air was as soft as a kiss—so why was she feeling so anxious?

It was Sam's knee, she realized, glancing over her shoulder to discover that the mainland was now gone. He had changed into shorts at Laem Ngop before transferring their supplies from the Buick onto the boat, and for the first time she had seen his scar—an angry pink thunderbolt of tissue that started on the inside of his right thigh and ran down past the kneecap. The source of his limp, she thought. His war wound, his secret. And then the futility of it all hit her, the impossibility of running away from the war. The farther away she got, the more it oppressed her. For the first time she understood that there was no place in the world that would allow her to run away and forget.

Sam was watching the water, his eyes picking up its turquoise light. He seemed content with the sunset and the salt air and the throb of the boat. He was unlike any man she had ever met. Other men were so pushy, so wordy, so eager to please. But he was different. He loved to talk, yet he appreciated silence. He possessed secrets—she glanced at the scar—yet he seemed to have no need to share them with the world. She considered her own secrets and her need to get rid of them. There was the day she helped Lois DeVries carry the old cables to the storage locker in the Embassy and stumbled on Ambassador Durbrow's suggestion, made way back during the Eisenhower administration, that if Diem didn't shape up, it might be time to consider alternative courses of action and alternative leaders.

That cable was the beginning of the end for Anne; the gall of it still stuck in her throat. No one knew that she knew it existed. No one knew that she knew that all those brilliant men in Washington viewed Vietnam as little more than a personnel problem. And no one knew that she knew they were wrong.

Then there was the day she saw the two Marines killed in the ambush on the way back from Tay Ninh—deaths the U.S. military never officially acknowledged because to acknowledge them would be to admit that the road to Tay Ninh was not secure, after all, and the Viet Cong were knocking on Saigon's door.

Then there was President Kennedy's secret order, back in 1961, that sent 400 Special Forces to Vietnam with orders to train Thai Rangers, Vietnamese commandoes and mountain tribesmen to infiltrate neutral nations and perform acts of "light" harassment and sabotage.

Then there was Charlie Malloy's whispered admission that he had allowed himself to be seduced by Madame Nhu—"right there on the presidential sofa!"—a secret that was terrifying to him because he knew that if it ever got back to New York, his career was over. It was so terrifying, in fact, that he was unable to live with it alone and so one night he'd blurted it out to Anne, a woman he trusted, after five double scotches in the eighth-floor bar at the Caravelle.

Later that very night, after Charlie had staggered off to bed, she'd had another surprising and informative conversation. Richard Holloway came in off the rooftop patio and plopped down on the barstool next to Anne. He, too, was inhaling Scotch and itching to talk. He was about Anne's age, fresh out of college, one of the eager recruits in the Saigon office of the U.S. Agency for International Development. He was working on the rural "pacification" program. He'd taken Anne out to dinner once, then out dancing, and then they'd wound up having a nightcap in his apartment. When she asked him why he was in Vietnam he stared at his hands a long time and said, "I guess you could say I came here to try to make a difference."

Anne found this charming, a refreshing change from the cynicism so prevalent in Saigon. He was an idealist, like she used to be, and he wasn't ashamed to admit it. Richard explained that he'd been sent down to the Delta to run the strategic hamlet program in Ba Xuyen province, a critical area where the Bassac River flowed into the South China Sea.

"What an eye-opener!" he cried, motioning for the barman to refill his glass. The Americans in Saigon were reporting to Washington that there were 324 strategic hamlets complete in Ba Xuyen, with 400,000 people under government control. But when Holloway tried to find these completed hamlets, he learned that many of them existed only on paper or else were protected by nothing but a picket fence or a few punji sticks. At night they belonged to the Viet Cong. He gulped Scotch. He said he used to believe everything the U.S. government told him, but not anymore.

Anne asked him what he was doing back in Saigon, and he said, "I'm on my way up to the highlands to solve a little problem they're having with the Sidge."

"What's a Sidge?"

"Oh, sorry," Richard said. "Government acronym. It stands for Civilian Indigenous Defense Groups. Basically it's the Montagnards."

The problem, he explained, was that the Americans had promised the Montagnards that in return for their service fighting the North Vietnamese and Viet Cong, they would get back their tribal lands. But someone had decided to keep a short leash on the Montagnards, who the lowland Vietnamese scorned as *kha*, or slaves. And so Richard was headed north to herd the tribesmen into strategic hamlets.

"The official line is that they'll get as much food as they can eat and as much betel as they can chew," Richard said. He slapped his empty glass on the bar. "But no one seems to understand that these are tribal people, for chrissakes. They'll go nuts inside strategic hamlets. Oh Christ, this is going to be one ugly mess . . ."

Then there was Lois DeVries's belief, based on her intimate knowlege of the Embassy's cable traffic and on recent conversations with sources in Saigon and Washington, that by replacing Ambassador Nolting with Henry Cabot Lodge, the Kennedy administration was giving the green light to the dozens of coup plotters in South Vietnam. According to Lois, Lodge's first day on the job was going to be the beginning of the end for Ngo Dinh Diem.

And finally there was the after-action report on the battle of Ap Bac. She had read it a dozen times, and every time she became more astonished by its detail, by the frustration and cool rage of the American advisors in the Mekong Delta. Of all her secrets, Anne believed the Ap Bac report was her trump card, her one piece of concrete proof that America's conduct of the war was built on the quicksand of duplicity and lies. This gift from David Halberstam and Lois DeVries and the nameless American advisors who wrote the true story of the battle—this gift was also a burden. It conferred power and responsibility. It was likely to be her one chance to alter the course of the war.

The boat rounded the tip of the island and turned its stern on the sunset, now a cauldron of scalding copper. Anne wondered if she was wasting her time coming to this remote island with this silent, self-contained man. When she'd telephoned him from Saigon a few weeks earlier he'd agreed to swap secrets with her, but she'd been borderline hysterical at the time. Maybe he was just humoring her, trying to calm her down. She hoped not. God, she hoped not. She told herself she would find out soon enough.

They had entered a large cove. They were approaching a dock with a fleet of fishing boats tied up to it and, beyond, the village of Khlong Son, a cluster of several dozen thatch buildings that climbed the hillside and melted into the jungle. The buildings actually looked like part of the jungle, Anne thought, like furry brown plants bristling in the dying light. As the boatman cut back on the motor and Sam tossed a line onto the dock, Anne could see that the entire crowd on the dock—every man, woman and child, every betel-spitting crone, every toothless old man and naked infant—every last one of them was beaming from ear to ear.

"My God," Anne whispered, "would you look at this welcome . . ."

"They worship Rat," Sam said as the boat thumped the dock. "He's the only islander who ever went away to war—and went to a foreign country and got wounded and won medals. They treat him like a god. And since we're friends of his . . ."

He held out his hand. When she hopped from the boat onto the dock, a cry went up from the crowd. The children rushed forward to touch her and tug the peach fuzz on her arms and stroke her blond hair. The adults kept their distance, *wai*'ing in unison. Then the men surrounded Sam, jabbering excitedly as a boy took their bags from the boat and placed them on a tricycle that was fitted with a luggage rack and a bench for two passengers: the village taxi.

Sam distributed gifts—ornately carved teak boxes for the village elders, silk shawls for their wives. When the greetings were complete, Sam joined Anne on the tricycle's bench and the crowd parted and the tricycle bounced the length of the dock, then through the twisting paths of the village and onto a dirt road that led into the jungle. As soon as they entered the trees it was midnight. Anne was blind for a moment, but the boy pedaling the tricycle never slowed down.

"Where we headed?" she asked.

"Heaven. You'll see."

After a quarter of a mile the road ended at a large bungalow. It was built on an outcropping of rock, the southern point that guarded the mouth of the cove. Sam led the way inside. The large central room, with plank floor and thatch walls, was lit by dozens of candles and burning joss sticks, and there were sprays of fresh-cut flowers, crimson, lavender, gold. Sam stepped onto a covered porch that floated above a strip of white beach, as phosphorescent as sugar. The sunset was fading, the last colors bleeding away, and the water had turned into jade. Anne stood beside him and watched the sky, listened to the waves licking the sand. They stood there, speechless, until darkness swallowed the world.

They were the guests of honor that night at a banquet held in the largest building in the village, a long house with no walls and a tin roof and a single table that seated three dozen. Sam and Anne sat in the middle of the table with a view of the docks and the bobbing boats and the sparkling black water. It took Anne a moment to realize everyone in the place was already uproariously drunk.

When a woman offered a tray of ceramic cups brimming with amber fluid, Anne said to Sam, "What is it?"

"They call it Mekong whisky," he said, taking a cup and bowing slowly to the woman. "It's actually sugar moonshine, closer to rum than whisky. It goes down smooth, but remember—it's got a kick like a government mule."

"I can see that," she said, looking around the table before taking a cup and bowing to the woman.

Sam raised his cup and offered a toast in Thai, and everyone at the table raised a cup and shouted in unison and tossed off their drinks. Music poured in from outside, metallic and percussive and hypnotic, and Anne could see a throng of children in torchlight staring at her, pointing and twittering like birds. When she waved they ran away, shrieking with terror and delight. She took a second cup of whisky and turned her attention to the food.

They ate for an hour without stopping. There were bowls of soup, fat prawns swimming in a spicy paprika broth, salads made of cucumber, onion, white cabbage and mint, steamed kale, curried bananas, salted fish, sticky rice, sliced coconuts and steaming piles of peppered crabs and lobsters. Whenever a platter was cleaned off, another instantly took its place. As the whisky and the spices lit up Anne's brain, the music seemed to pick up in intensity. A *ramwong*, Sam called it, music that managed to be both urgent and sweetly relaxed, perfect music for a land where there is more bloodshed than neurosis, where people are happy to live a full short life, then die without regrets. The music was a drug. When Anne finally stopped eating she realized she had sweated through her cotton dress and the music seemed to be coming from the jungle itself and everyone at the table was too drunk to stand up. One man fell off the bench and everyone roared and left him lying on the floor.

When they got back to the bungalow—a feat Anne could not have accomplished without Sam's support and a ride on the boy's tricycle—she found herself standing barefoot on the beach under a white coin of moon, facing a pile of logs that was taller than Sam.

"Where'd thac'm from?" she asked. Before he could answer she added, "Phew, I'm sweating pure garlic—and goddam if you weren't right about that fucking moonshine."

Sam struck a match and within minutes they were backing away from flames that crackled and shot into the starry sky. In her drunkenness she thought she had seen all this before—it was like a vivid flashback—but then she realized she had merely dreamed of it that night at the White Elephant when she'd kissed Sam Malloy for the first time and had gone to bed alone imagining a fire on a beach spitting sparks at the stars as a fat moon rose out of the jungle. And now here she was, living that dream.

"I gotta siddown," she said.

Sam guided her to a quilt that was spread on the sand and draped over the trunk of a fallen tree. There were bottles of water on the quilt and she reached for one and guzzled most of it and doused her face. The water was cold and she felt better instantly. Her head began to clear.

"You gonna make it?" Sam asked.

"I'll be fine. Just needa restaminute."

They watched the fire as it roared higher. Halfway through her second bottle of water Anne said, "Do these people always celebrate like that?"

"Every chance they get. They'll do it if someone has a baby, if someone catches a big fish or puts a new roof on his house or comes into town with a cartload of pomelo. That was tame compared to what happens when Rat comes home."

The music of the *ramwong* drifted through the jungle to them, and though it was faint at this distance she could tell it was more frantic than before. She supposed it would go on all night—or until the last musician fell down. There were fishing boats sliding along the horizon, their running lights strung together like tiny pearls. Anne leaned back against the log and sighed.

"Didn't I tell you it was heaven?" Sam was looking up at the stars.

"Yes, you certainly did." She spent a long time admiring the stars and screwing up her courage. Finally she took a deep breath and blurted it out, a command, not a question: "Tell me what happened to your knee."

He didn't hesitate. He kept staring at the stars. "We were on a routine mission into Laos. There were nine of us, plus the two-man crew, in an H-21 helicopter. A real dog of a chopper, but this wasn't supposed to be a long or complicated mission."

"You say it was routine? Americans went into Laos a lot?"

The question seemed to break his concentration, irritate him. "Americans have been poking around in Laos since the fifties, mostly CIA freelancers sent there to study how the French used the native Hmong and Meo tribes to fight the Viet Minh. By '58, when the communists started moving goodies down the jungle through Laos on the Ho Chi Minh Trail, the CIA had a nice little army of Meo bushwhackers working for them. Beautiful ambush artists, the way I hear it told. They'd go out with old Enfields, Springfields, Jap Nambu rifles, maybe a crossbow or blowgun—and even if they only had four rounds of ammunition, they'd never fail to hit two or three bad guys. The communists were going nuts. I've heard more than a few Americans say that those were the good old days, before the clowns and the idiots showed up in their green berets and started passing out M-2 carbines like candy and fucking everything up."

"So back to your story. You're on this helicopter."

"Me and two other Navy Frogmen, Rat and another Thai Ranger, two Vietnamese commandoes and two Hmong—a nice little unit. We were on our way to take out a bridge over the Se Kong River, not too far from the Vietnam border. Piece of cake, we thought. The enemy hadn't figured out how to hit the helicopters yet, so we rarely encountered any ground fire. We were to approach from the northwest, insert one click upstream from the bridge, drift with the current to the site, set charges, let 'er rip, then continue downstream one more click to the pickup site. We weren't supposed to be on the ground more than an hour. But as soon as I saw the river—I've got good night vision and we were flying at treetop level—I knew something was wrong. I'd studied the maps, you see, I've loved maps since I was a kid, and I knew we were coming in way too far downstream. There were steep hills on the riverbanks there, and we were supposed to insert where the banks were flat. And then I saw the bridge and knew we were fucked. It should have been on our right, not our left, and much farther away. I shouted to the cockpit crew—a Thai and an American—but I don't know if they ever heard me because right then some kind of rocket tore into the bottom of the chopper—ba-*boom!*—knocked everyone on their ass—and when I came to my senses I knew we were going down. The rotors were silent, everyone was pressed to one side, and I had that sick feeling you get at the top of a rollercoaster. I got to the door and saw we were about halfway across the river, headed straight into a cliff. I ordered everyone to insert—"

"Insert?"

"Jump into the river. I figured we had maybe five seconds before the chopper hit the cliff. Everyone got out except Rat, who'd gotten wounded when the rocket hit and couldn't stand up. I threw him out the door and went out after him. Just before we hit the water I heard the explosion. It was so bright—it was like noon, even underwater. When I came up for air, sparks and pieces of metal were still falling out of the sky. My first thought was that I wouldn't have to go after the pilot and co-pilot. By the time I found Rat—he was struggling, gasping for air—I realized something besides pieces of helicopter was hitting the river. Up on the bridge there were dozens of men firing at us. I got hold of Rat under the armpits and got our asses out of there."

"Where'd you go?" Anne was sitting upright, staring at him.

"We were trained in the event of this kind of fuckup to proceed to the pickup site. As soon as I got out of range of the men on the bridge I crawled onto the bank to examine Rat. He'd taken shrapnel in the hip and was bleeding pretty heavy, but he was conscious and coherent. He kept apologizing for not being able to move his right leg, urging me to leave him and get out. I got the wound cleaned and bandaged the best I could, and then we were back in the water. I really didn't think he was going to make it. It was all I could do to keep his head out of the water. For such a little fucker, he weighed a ton. He wouldn't stop apologizing and finally I had to order him to shut up."

"Did you find the rest of your men?"

"Everyone was right where they were supposed to be. Not a scratch on anyone. Wes, this muscular spade who was our radioman, had already called for evac and set up a perimeter. We knew we'd be getting company before the chopper arrived. About an hour later, while I was cleaning Rat's wound and rewrapping it, I heard the first faint sound of the chopper. Damn, that sounded good! Just as I started to set up a signal flare I heard Rat's 9-millimeter go off—two quick pops—and a little guy in pajamas with a rifle fell out of the bushes at my feet. He'd gotten through our perimeter somehow and was about to wax us. I smiled at Rat and he smiled back. I knew he was relieved. He'd repaid his debt to me and now we were even."

"But your knee—"

He didn't hear her. He was still on that riverbank. "I sent the craziest guy up the ladder first—this squirrelly little Georgia cracker who's the best shot of anyone I ever met. I wanted him up there working the 50-cal machinegun in case any more bad guys showed up. He was halfway up the ladder when the jungle lit up with small-arms fire, sounded like a bunch of firecrackers. Then I ordered Wes up after I attached Rat to his back. As commander I was the last one up. I thought I had it made, I was two, maybe three rungs from the chopper door and Vestal was laying down steady fire and Wes had his hand out for me and all of a sudden my right leg was on fire. Like someone had stuck a hot poker in it. Turns out the bullet went in right here"—he pinched a handful of scar tissue behind the kneecap—"and went clean through the leg. Thank God Wes had me by the wrists or I'd've dropped like a stone. He pulled me on board and we got the hell out of there. I woke up in an Army hospital in Ubon Ratchathani, Thailand. Eventually they transferred me to Saigon for more surgery—they had to rebuild the knee—and then after recuperation and rehab I was a civilian again."

"What happened to Rat?"

"Nothing. They removed a chunk of helicopter floor from his

hip and he was good as new after a few weeks in the hospital. We both got loaded down with medals. But suddenly we were civilians again—and that was the hard part."

"So you looked up your brother in Saigon."

"Yeah, I tracked old Charlie down at the Caravelle. But the city gave me the willies—too many ghosts, too many noisy Americans—so I went over to Bangkok and went into the hotel business with Rat."

"And you've never been back to the States."

"And I've got no desire to go back. It's like I said before—I don't want to have anything to do with the country that's responsible for what's going on in Vietnam. Besides, I happen to love living in Thailand—the food, the people, the way they move through life."

"Sam, come here." She was holding out her arms when he turned away from the fire and the stars. He crawled across the quilt to her, let her wrap him in those long brown arms. They lay there without speaking while the fire burned low and the stars burned brighter. She ran her fingers through his thick wet hair. "How does it feel?"

"That feels nice. Don't stop."

"No, I mean how does it feel to have one less secret inside you?"

"Fine. Very nice. I like it."

But even as she held him she understood that his story of the night he and Rat saved each other's lives was not the end; it was barely the beginning. There was more, much more to know about what he did during the war. She could feel the tension in him. He was still on guard. This was not the time to press, she told herself, so she pulled him closer and kissed him long and slow and deep. After a time they went up to the bungalow and crawled under the mosquito net and drifted off to sleep in each other's arms.

24

They awoke at dawn. Their skulls were throbbing, and despite the mosquito net their bodies were freckled with red bites. Sam kissed her and said, "Good morning" and stripped off his shirt and walked out of the bungalow and into the water. She slipped out of her dress and, wearing only a bra and panties, followed him.

After breakfast—someone had stocked the bungalow with fresh fruit and juices and a ceramic pitcher of hot tea—the boy arrived with his tricycle. Sam filled a knapsack with fruit and bottles of water and beer, and they started off down the dirt road that ran along the western rim of the island.

Anne's headache was gone. The sun had climbed over the rocky peaks to their left, and a breeze was blowing in off the water and the air was so soft she couldn't feel it against her skin. She had become part of the jungle they were skimming through, as organic as a plant, made of equal parts salt water and fruit pulp and garlic and whisky and sweat and sunshine and blood, alive in this moment and no other. She had never felt so at-home in her body, so at-home in the world. For the first time in her life she was fully happy.

The road was badly rutted in spots, and it rose and fell sharply. When the climb was too steep for the boy, they all walked. On some of the downslopes Anne held on like a girl riding a rollercoaster and closed her eyes and tasted the wind and shrieked with glee.

After half an hour they came to a footpath that branched off the road, ran past a shack and led into the jungle. Four men were playing mah-jong on the porch of the shack. Sam told the boy to wait with the men. The boy smiled and pushed his bike toward the shack.

Anne followed Sam along the path that cut through shoulder-high grass, then crossed several dried-out riverbeds. Entering the jungle was like entering an enormous vaulted room draped with ropes of vines, bristling with deep green ferns and vegetation, the floor damp and soggy. Birds flitted and cried. The sun was a muffled yellow dot, but she felt clammy and suffocated. She'd worn a clean yellow cotton dress and tennis shoes, and already she could feel the dress clinging to her damp back, could feel her feet slipping inside the sneakers. A lizard darted across the path, startling her, and suddenly she was conscious of the danger of snakes. Everything was alive—the ground, the brush, the trees, the air. She could imagine the horror of slogging through such a place carrying a backpack and a rifle, terrified of booby traps and mines and snipers and snakes. She noticed that Sam moved very methodically, looking up, then down, then up again, careful where he placed his feet. She was glad he was leading the way. She found herself stepping in his footprints.

As suddenly as the jungle had swallowed them, it released them and they were in a clearing split by a dry creek bed. The sunlight was briefly blinding. When Anne was halfway up the far bank of the creek bed, she froze.

Something in the air—the taste of the dust, the feel of the sunshine on her sweaty skin, the faint smell of pine trees— something was trying to make her memory speak. There was something deeply familiar about this moment: It was that hint of turpentine, the taste of that powdery dust; it came from her youth and suddenly she was there again, up in the highest meadow above her family's ranch house, up where the grass turned to gold and late in the day the shadows of the live oaks became pools of oil.

There was never any rain from the spring to the fall, and from up there the hills looked like parts of a human body, always a woman's body, a series of smooth thighs, a pair of plump buttocks, a single pert breast tipped with an ancient oak, its green nipple. Late in the afternoon their shadows stretched and flattened, and in her imagination the oaks turned into animals, gigantic grazing cows, or horses, or dinosaurs. That world tasted of dust and pine sap and sunshine. There was a secret swimming hole up beyond the last ridge, known only to her and her father and the few ranch hands who had to ride up there to bring in the unbroken horses every spring. It was a cold green pool surrounded by rock cliffs, the perfect place for a plunge after a day of riding or doing fieldwork. Anne could feel that cold green water on her skin now, and as she felt it she realized this was what she had lost, this feeling of being alive in the moment, this faith that her youth would last forever and no place would ever be closed to her as long as she had the courage to go there.

In Saigon she had begun to sense that this feeling was gone and would never come back. But now, standing in the dusty gravel of the creek bed, it was upon her again. *The heat of life in the handful of dust* was how Joseph Conrad had phrased it in the short story she'd read the night before leaving Bangkok, *the feeling that I could last forever.* Suddenly she had that feeling again, and she vowed she would never let it grow dim, grow cold, would never let it die.

"You coming?"

She looked up. Sam was standing on top of the slope, holding out a hand. He was smiling.

"Yeah," she said, "I was just remembering something . . ." She scrambled over the last of the rocks and followed him back into the jungle. It was no longer menacing, that enormous vaulted room. An untouchable calm had filled her, and it stayed inside her until she stepped out of the jungle and looked up at the waterfall.

It started hundreds of feet up in the air, a single silver strand, then it flared and flashed in the sunlight and crashed against rocks, painting them black and flaring even wider and starting to come apart just before it spattered into the pond. After the ripples ironed themselves out, the pond was smooth, polished like ice. Anne was stunned. Without a word she peeled off her dress and bra and panties, kicked off her sneakers, took two steps, and dove. The water was warm, which surprised her, and it took her a moment to realize she was not in the swimming hole high in those golden California hills—she was in a jungle halfway around the world and the only human being within miles was the man she had left standing on the rock. She held her breath and swam underwater until her lungs were on fire, then she came up for air and did it again. By the time she reached the far side of the pond she was winded. She was able to stand on the bottom, and she was surprised that after tumbling such a distance the waterfall was gentle, like a warm summer drizzle. She closed her eyes and let it wash over her. When she opened her eyes Sam was standing a few feet away. The sizzling water came up to his chest. She felt like they'd been caught in a summer downpour and didn't give a damn.

She took two steps toward him and put her arms around him and they kissed. He, too, was naked, and she felt him stirring against her thighs. As she listened to the gentle roar of the waterfall and felt the heat of this man against her skin, she realized this was the first truly erotic moment of her life.

They kissed until her lips ached. She had never been kissed like this before, by a tongue that probed along her lips and nibbled her earlobes and skated up and down her neck and then, after he'd lifted her up by the armpits, a tongue that was hot against her hard wet nipples. When she couldn't bear it any longer she gasped, "Sam, I want to make love."

"I didn't bring anything . . ."

"You don't need anything."

"But what if—"

"I'm taking birth control pills. Trust me, it's safe." She gripped his shoulders and wrapped her legs around his waist. She was so aroused he could have slid into her in a single quick thrust, but he was slow about it, gentle. He brought her to him slowly, as though he wanted this moment to last forever, and he rocked her gently for a long time, then he was all the way inside her and the tempo increased and eventually the water around her was churning until it caught fire, turned to lava, burned her, burned clean through her, burned her until it melted her bones.

They spent the afternoon lying naked on towels on the sunny rocks, eating the fruit and drinking the beer Sam had packed in the knapsack. Neither of them spoke. It was as though the power of speech had been taken from them and rendered pointless. When he drifted off to sleep she slipped back into the water and swam for an hour, until her arms and legs and lungs gave out. Only when she climbed back onto the rocks, panting and exhausted, and saw him lying there naked did she realize she was falling in love. A switch had been tripped; it was like waking up one morning and understanding that your life will never again be the way it was.

He opened one eye, yawned, saw her standing over him. "What are you looking at?" he asked with a smile.

"You. You're gorgeous even when you're asleep."

He patted the towel. "Come sit down. It's your turn to tell me some secrets."

She knelt down and kissed him, dripping water on his face and chest. Then she lay on her back and rested her head on his stomach and watched the sky as she told him about the day she saw the Marines and their girlfriends killed by the mine; told him about her other close call the night the grenade blew up on the roof of the Rex annex; told him about her meeting with Halberstam and the Ap Bac report and Lois DeVries's prediction that soon after the arrival of Henry Cabot Lodge, a U.S.-sanctioned coup would topple the Diem regime.

As she talked, Sam stroked her wet hair and watched the sun slide behind the trees. The words poured out of her for an hour, garbled at times, eager to get out of her and become part of the larger world. Sam didn't say a word. When she finished she sagged against him. After a while she said, "Well?"

"Well what?"

"What do you think about my stories?"

"None of it surprises me, I'm sad to say. I'm glad I'm here now and not in Saigon. I'm glad you're here with me."

"But I have to go back there."

"No you don't, Anne. You don't have to do anything. Remember that."

She didn't respond. She rolled her head sideways in time to see his face change. She thought she saw the elation go out of him. Already they were being pulled back from this moment, back into the everyday world of responsibility and duty and consequences, where the events of this afternoon would only make things more complicated. She didn't know what to say. She didn't want to destroy this magic. She kissed his stomach where her hair had made his skin wet. He tasted like that swimming hole in California, green and weedy, another taste of what it had been like to be a girl. She rested her cheek on his wet skin and listened to the thudding of his heart and made herself think of nothing.

After a long silence he said, "We'd better start back. We don't want to get caught out here after dark, believe me."

They walked back through the jungle without speaking. It was darker than before, but Anne barely noticed. All she could think of was that the magic of this afternoon had been extinguished and she would soon be torn away from this man. She heard his voice over and over: *You don't have to do anything.* The thought was overwhelming, terrifying, and so she banished it and followed his footsteps out of that jungle where she had started to fall in love for the first time in her life.

She went to bed as soon as they got back to the bungalow. She crawled under the mosquito net naked and fell asleep instantly and slept the sleep of the dead. She was awakened by the smell of woodsmoke and the cries of birds. The sun was up, and Sam was on the porch drinking tea and watching the water.

She called to him and he joined her under the mosquito net and they made love again, as slowly as before, but this time when they were finished she was crying. He didn't ask why. He simply held her until it stopped.

That afternoon the same blue-and-orange fishing boat took them back to Laem Ngop. The Buick was waiting on the dock, gleaming in the sunshine. Someone had washed it. All the tiny handprints were gone.

Sam hardly spoke on the ride back to Bangkok. For the first time the drive oppressed him. The world seemed to deteriorate as they moved through it—lordly rubber and eucalyptus trees giving way to fields of sugar and sisal, which gave way to rice paddies and gravel quarries, then the industrial buildings and half-built highways on the outskirts of Bangkok. Anne was tucked against his side. He drove with his left hand on the wheel and his right arm cradling her. She felt smaller than she had on Ko Chang.

The Bangkok air felt like wool against his skin, a cruel reminder of how sweet the air had been on the island, and of course the traffic was murder. He was exhausted by the time they reached Don Muang Airport. No, he thought as he walked across the parking lot holding Anne's hand, this was not exhaustion; this was despair.

In the airport Anne was all business, almost frosty, as though she was determined to make their parting surgical and painless. She spent half an hour in the bathroom, brushing her hair and applying mascara and lipstick and changing into espadrilles and a sleeveless blue linen dress that fell to her knees. When she emerged she pecked Sam's lip. He tried to pull her to him, but she pushed him away. "Please, Sam. Don't."

He watched her stride across the tarmac to the Air Vietnam DC-6. She trotted up the stairs, and just before stepping into the plane she turned and waved, an anonymous gesture to a faceless airport terminal. But he accepted it: It was better than nothing.

Driving back to the White Elephant, he relived the weekend, minute by minute. He dwelled on the stories she had told him, the secrets that had been eating her alive. He was surprised by how unsurprising it all was. Least surprising of all was the news that Washington was now in favor of a coup. Puppets, after all, were interchangeable.

He parked the Buick in the godown and shut off the engine and listened to it tick and ping as it cooled. He realized he hadn't told Anne much of anything about what really happened to him during the war—and this made him realize how much he already missed her. He looked through the windshield at Prince Prem's old villa. It looked like an ice cube to him now, like an igloo, a cold jail, and for the first time in his life he felt marooned and he understood what it meant to be in exile, and alone.

PART THREE

25

Rat brought his new Zenith television set down from upstairs and placed it on the bar so all the guests and staff at the White Elephant could watch the special evening newscast. The papers that morning had contained the first sketchy reports of the latest horror in Vietnam, and all day radio bulletins had fleshed out the appalling details.

In the early morning hours of August 21, uniformed troops had surrounded Xa Loi pagoda in Saigon. For the next two hours, while helpless monks rang the pagoda's gong and beat on pots and pans, the troops kicked down the doors, smashed furniture and windows, sprayed the compound with gunfire, beat the monks and nuns and then herded them into trucks and hauled them off to prison. There were unconfirmed reports that two monks escaped over the pagoda's wall, that thirty were wounded and nine were missing. Similar raids were taking place simultaneously in pagodas all over South Vietnam, with arrests of monks and nuns totaling 1,400. The bloodiest scene was in Hue, birthplace of President Ngo Dinh Diem and now the personal fiefdom of his eldest brother, Ngo Dinh Thuc, a Roman Catholic archbishop. There, thirty monks and students were shot or clubbed to death and a revered statue of Buddha was smashed.

Originally the Diem government claimed that the raids were carried out by the South Vietnamese Army acting spontaneously, without orders from the palace. But this was quickly refuted by Western journalists who'd witnessed the Xa Loi raid and reported that the troops wore the berets and camouflage fatigues of the CIA-trained Special Forces, and that they were joined by the Combat Police, also trained by the CIA, and by the white-uniformed National Police.

President Diem immediately declared martial law and imposed a 9:00 P.M. curfew. Anyone on the streets after that hour without proper authorization was to be shot on sight.

"And now," the announcer, a jowly Australian, said, "we take you to Saigon's Tan Son Nhut Airport, where Henry Cabot Lodge, the new American Ambassador to South Vietnam, is about to deplane. Lodge's arrival in the capital, originally scheduled for next week, was pushed up because of the worsening crisis."

The camera cut to a DC-6 parked on a shiny, floodlit runway. A light drizzle was falling. The plane's door opened and out stepped a statuesque man in a white suit. He was holding a straw hat.

Lodge strode down the steps and started shaking hands with the small crowd that had been allowed to come out after curfew to greet him. He seemed surprised by the television lights, but as soon as he was through with the formalities he approached the clot of reporters. Microphones were jammed in his face. Unfazed, Henry Cabot Lodge started talking blandly, as ambassadors are supposed to talk, about the need for democracy in South Vietnam and the importance of a free press in any democracy. He was drifting off on a reminiscence of his first trip to Vietnam, back when he was a young reporter for *The New York Herald-Tribune* and found Saigon a "bewitching" city. Suddenly Rat sprang off his barstool and pointed at the television screen and shouted, "Look! There's Anne! Standing right behind Cabolodge!"

They all leaned closer to the set. Sam squinted and saw that, yes, it was Anne Sinclair. She looked different. At first Sam thought she'd had her hair chopped off, but then he saw that she had pulled it tight against her skull and tied it in a ponytail. The next thing he noticed was how tall she looked—she was almost as tall as Lodge, who towered over most of the reporters and all of the Vietnamese dignitaries.

The next surprise was at the end of the line of reporters—a rotund man in a light suit. It was Charlie Malloy. Sam had to smile at the sight of him, sweating like a wheel of cheese in the steamy evening air, looking like a man who was deeply dismayed at having to work so late into the anointed cocktail hour.

As soon as the newscast ended, the crowd in the bar returned to the more customary pursuits of card games and cocktails and conversation. The Major challenged Sam to a game of rummy, but Sam begged off. He climbed the stairs to his room, where he would try to read himself to sleep but most likely would wind up lying in bed with the light off, watching the ceiling fan. At least tonight he would take a small consolation to bed with him. For the past two weeks, since that day Anne had waved goodbye from the doorway of the DC-6, he'd been trying vainly to reach her by phone. His mind had begun playing horrible tricks on him. Now, at least, he knew she was alive and safe. And even more beautiful than he remembered.

26

Lois DeVries, true to form, had indeed found a way to get around Henry Cabot Lodge's long-anticipated and much-dreaded obsession with secrecy. When he stepped off the plane at Tan Son Nhut, Lodge was followed down the steps by three hand-picked assistants. Leading the way was Lt. Col. John Michael Dunn, who reporters had already begun describing as "omnipotent" and a "hatchet man" because of his fierce loyalty to the ambassador and the fervor with which he carried out orders. Lois called him "the bulldog" because he guarded the Embassy's cable traffic as if it were his personal bone. Under the new system, Dunn and the other two assistants were supposed to be the only people who saw the cables emanating from Lodge or directed to him personally from Washington. Some highly sensitive cables were even being sent through CIA's more secure line. Lois was given only the most routine traffic.

"But I've beaten them at their own game!" she crowed as she swept into Anne's apartment two weeks after Lodge's arrival. It was past 8 o'clock, which meant if they got into the wine Lois would miss curfew and have to spend the night. Anne didn't mind. Her roommate had gone back to Danang to work on her article about the orphan boy, and Saigon was so quiet at night, so moist with fear and the taste of doom, that Anne welcomed the company.

"So let's hear how you did it," Anne said, bringing two glasses of wine out to the balcony. The new Dave Brubeck record, which her brother had just sent from California, was on the turntable. Usually Brubeck's brand of bright sprinting jazz lifted Anne's spirits, but now, looking down at the streets, where only a few bicyclists and pedestrians hurried to beat curfew, where no candles burned and no children played, the music had a tinny sound that deepened Anne's gloom.

"Nothing to it," Lois said. "Keys were the key, as usual."

"Keys?"

"For starters, Mike Dunn thought he was pulling a big surprise his first day on the job when he demanded that everyone turn in their keys to the cable room. He knew there were six keys out, so when he got six keys back he figured he'd secured the cable room. What he didn't know was that I'd expected him to pull something like that, so I'd had a copy of mine made weeks ago. So now I can get into the cable room anytime I want—which is usually about this time of night, when everyone's gone home and the early-morning traffic from Washington gets cranked up. A few times I've stayed past curfew and picked up some very juicy tidbits. Only problem with staying past nine is that I have to sleep on the sofa in my office. But it's been worth it every time."

"You said keys. There's another key?"

"About a year ago Nolting's secretary came down with a bad case of dysentery and I had to fill in for her. One day I took her keys with me when I went to lunch and had a copy of the ambassador's office key made. No particular reason. Just figured it might come in handy someday."

"And that day has arrived?"

"Yes it has. Turns out Lodge dictates all of his cables into this huge tape machine he keeps on his desk. Then he has them typed by one of Dunn's goons, he proofreads them, initials them, and they're sent to Washington. So if I want to know what he's telling Washington, all I have to do is slip into his office at night and play back the tape. Piece of cake."

Anne was hooked. "So what is Lodge telling Washington?"

Lois reached into her briefcase and took out a long yellow legal pad. She flipped through several pages. "Let me see . . . where the hell? . . . ah yes, here it is. Lodge hadn't been in town two days when he got this cable from the State Department: 'U.S. government cannot tolerate situation in which power lies in Nhu's hands . . . Ambassador and country team should urgently examine all possible alternative leadership and make detailed plans as to how we might bring about Diem's replacement if this should become necessary . . . Needless to say, we have held knowlege of this telegram to minimum essential people and assume you will take similar precautions to prevent premature leaks' . . . blah blah blah.''

Lois burst out laughing and Anne found herself laughing along with her. This was so delicious—beating these powerful men at their own game.

"So what was Lodge's response?" Anne asked.

"The next day, here's what he cabled to Rusk and Hilsman at State: 'Believe that Diem's chances of meeting our demands are virtually nil . . . therefore propose going straight to Generals with our demands, without informing Diem . . . Would tell them we prepared to have Diem without Nhu but in effect up to them whether to keep him . . .' ''

"That's awfully thoughtful of him."

"Isn't it, though?"

"Who are these generals?"

"From what I hear there are three generals behind the current plot. Lou Conein, the oldest spook in town, has been chatting them up like crazy. Let's see." She flipped through the legal pad. "There's Duong Van Minh, they call him 'Big' Minh because he's probably the only man in Vietnam who's taller than you are. Then there's Tran Van Don, who's gorrrrr-geous. And finally Le Van Kim. I don't know much about him, but I hear he's sort of an egghead. They all belonged to the French Army at one time. I will say one thing for Lodge—he doesn't let any grass grow under his feet. And he understands the importance of 'face' to Asians better than any American I've ever seen. He never misses a chance to insult Diem and Nhu."

"How does he do it?"

"His first day on the job he stopped by the AID office, which is where the two monks ran after they jumped over the wall of Xa Loi the night of the pagoda raids. Not only did Lodge tell them they were welcome to stay as long as they wished, but he ordered fresh vegetables brought to them every day. I'm sure Diem had a fit. Just yesterday Lodge topped that. He ordered us to clear out a conference room so the monks could move into the Embassy. They're living two doors down from my office. Holloway called from AID to thank me personally for getting them out of his hair."

"Richard Holloway?"

"Yeah, you know him?"

"I know him to see him," Anne said. The mention of Richard Holloway reminded her of the Montagnards, and that in turn reminded her she hadn't heard a word from Sam Malloy since her return from Thailand. At first she was angry, then hurt. But the night before the pagoda raids Diem or Nhu had cut the phone lines at all U.S. installations, and service was still erratic. Surely Sam had tried to reach her. She ached to talk to him. Of all the things she'd told him that day at the waterfall, she'd forgotten the most important thing of all—Richard Holloway's story about the Montagnards and the strategic hamlets. She knew, cold knew, that the story would unlock the rest of the secrets inside Sam Malloy. Private phones were rare in Saigon, but she vowed to find one in the morning and get through to Bangkok.

"Well," Lois was saying, "Richard's back in Saigon. Says he had a horrible time in the highlands, herding the Montagnards into strategic—"

The rest of her sentence was drowned out as the 9 o'clock siren began its maddening crescendo, a growl that rose to a pitch so shrill people covered their ears and every dog in the city joined in a chorus of mournful baying. By the time the siren died the city was a ghost town, the only signs of life the occasional rumble of a Jeep or the distant crack of a rifle. Some poor soul who didn't make it home on time. Another faceless casualty of war.

27

Not only had Jon Medlin agreed to let Anne use the telephone in his apartment, he'd also insisted she come over early enough to eat breakfast and watch the "CBS Evening News" from New York. The network was expanding its newscast from fifteen minutes to half an hour, and Walter Cronkite was scheduled to interview President Kennedy. Vietnam was sure to come up, and Jon wanted Anne to hear the President's remarks.

She left her apartment shortly after curfew was lifted. Lois was still snoring in the other bedroom, still fully dressed. The night before she'd stormed into the apartment just before the 9 o'clock siren carrying a bottle of bourbon and bursting to unload her juiciest revelations yet. Anne had never seen her so manic. She talked non-stop as she cracked the bottle of bourbon, filled two glasses to the brims (no ice, no water), and led the way out to the balcony. Her voice grew steadily more agitated as she read the newest jottings from her legal pad.

"Lodge dictated this cable to Rusk last Tuesday: 'We are launched on a course from which there is no respectable turning back: the overthrow of the Diem government . . .' "

"Jesus Christ," Anne whispered.

Lois held up a hand, gulped bourbon, and continued reading: " 'There is no turning back in part because U.S. prestige is already publicly committed to this end in large measure and will become more so as the facts leak out. In a more fundamental sense, there is no turning back because there is no possibility, in my view, that the war can be won under a Diem administration, still less that Diem or any member of the family can govern the country in a way to gain the support of the people who count, i.e., the educated class in and out of government service, civil and military—not to mention the American people . . .' "

"That Brahmin son of a bitch!" Anne shouted. A dog started howling in the alley. "The people who matter to Lodge are the educated class. My roommate's going to be thrilled when she learns just how right she is to call the people she's writing about 'the ninety-five percent who don't count.' This is insane, Lois."

"It gets better. Lodge finishes with this prediction: 'The chance of bringing off a Generals' coup depends on them to some extent, but it depends at least as much on us.' "

Anne was speechless. To her surprise, Lois was too. She sat there with the legal pad on her lap and the half-empty glass of pale warm whisky in her fist and a stunned look on her face. Of course, Anne thought. This is my first job out of college; but this is Lois's life, this is the culmination of her career, and for the first time in that long and unswervingly devoted career she has begun to see how the game is actually played and she is appalled. Devastated. Anne wondered what Lois intended to do with the dynamite she had discovered on Henry Cabot Lodge's tape machine.

"The National Security Council met shortly after receiving Lodge's cable," Lois continued slowly. "Here's what Rusk cabled back to Lodge: 'The U.S. Government will support a coup which has a good chance of succeeding but plans no direct involvement of U.S. armed forces.' "

"That Rusk—what a shrewd operator."

"Tell me about it. And here's Lodge's reply: 'Agree with you that getting the Nhus out is the prime objective . . . This surely cannot be done by working through Diem. In fact, Diem will oppose it. He wishes he had more Nhus, not less. The best chance of doing it is by the Generals taking over the government lock, stock, and barrel." Then Lois tossed the legal pad on the floor. In a very small voice she said, "Anne, I don't know how much longer I can go on." She then proceeded to drink herself into a reasonable facsimile of a coma.

As Anne walked the three blocks to Jon Medlin's apartment now, the sun was beginning to brush the city's orange-tiled rooftops. She loved Saigon at this hour, before the shops opened and the traffic got berserk, before the heat and the war returned, when the city was still a drowsy and unkempt whore and it was easy to see that her decay was what gave her her charm.

To Anne's surprise Jon was not alone when the maid admitted her to his apartment. David Halberstam was sitting on the sofa in a blue bathrobe, groggily drinking coffee. Sitting next to him was Nguyen Ngoc Rao, the Vietnamese reporter in the UPI bureau who had the best police sources in town and always looked like he'd just stepped out of the shower. Someone was in the kitchen shouting into the telephone—she instantly recognized the voice of UPI's Neil Sheehan. Jon's walkie-talkie, the U.S. Mission's new defense against another telephone cutoff, crackled in the corner of the room.

The sight of Halberstam reminded Anne of her little secret tucked away in the hollowed-out book of O. Henry stories. She supposed Halberstam would give up his first-born male child for a look at those photographs. Maybe she would give him the chance.

"I believe you've met my new roommates," Jon said, handing Anne a cup of coffee.

"But boss, I thought these guys were supposed to be the enemy."

"Oh, they're still the enemy," Jon said with a smile. Halberstam grunted into his coffee cup and switched on the television set. "They're also on Nhu's hit list. And I'll be damned if I was going to turn them away when they knocked on my door at five minutes before nine."

"Nhu's hit list?"

"Haven't you heard?" Halberstam said, settling back onto the sofa. "Nhu's got a list of people he plans to have assassinated—

and Rao and Sheehan and I are right up near the top. Ain't that right, Rao?"

"That is correct," Rao said in a voice that told Anne this fact was of no greater or lesser importance than any other fact.

"I guess congratulations are in order," Anne said. "If Nhu wants you dead, you must be doing a hell of a job."

"Thanks," Halberstam said with no trace of a smile. Rao's face was blank.

"Here's the President," Jon said, turning up the volume.

Anne had brought a notebook, and she opened it now on her knee. But she did not write in it. She was riveted by the man on the television screen, the young President who looked even better than he'd looked that day he came to lunch at the ranch in California. He was still tanned and boyish and sleek, but he'd aged in a pleasing way. He looked wiser, more mellow, like a man in control of his destiny, and he talked as though he relished his upcoming re-election campaign and knew he would win in a landslide. He was so full of confidence that when the subject turned to Vietnam, Anne forgot to write down a word he said—until she heard him say: "This war belongs to the Vietnamese. In the final analysis it's their war. They are the ones who have to win it or lose it."

Even as she wrote down his words, though, she was thinking of last night and wondering why she was going to the trouble.

When Sam came on the line Anne thought he was drunk, but then she realized the connection was bad. Her great fear was that he hadn't given her a thought since she left Bangkok and that he would be mildly, and not pleasantly, surprised to hear from her. But he sounded ecstatic. He talked in such a garbled rush that she had to keep telling him to slow down. He said he needed to see her soon, right away, now; they needed to talk. When she told him she couldn't possibly get away, he said he was going to book the next available flight to Saigon.

28

The Saigon Sam returned to was a city running a high fever. This came as no surprise. After watching Henry Cabot Lodge's televised arrival at Tan Son Nhut, Sam hadn't missed a single evening newscast or international newspaper or magazine. He'd also started receiving long, erratic, richly detailed letters from an obviously distraught—and probably drunk—Charlie Malloy. The stories Sam was hearing and reading were so fantastic he figured they had to be true.

Henry Cabot Lodge, according to one, had received so many death threats that he kept a loaded revolver in his desk. Thousands of Vietnamese, according to another, were flocking to a lake in Hue where a magical fish was said to surface periodically and utter dire prophecies about the future of the war. In the central highlands, thousands more climbed a remote mountain where a nun was said to perform miracle cures—especially for deformed babies afflicted by the diabolical American chemical that killed every tree and plant it touched. Now Buddhist nuns had joined the monks in immolating themselves on busy Saigon street corners. Western reporters were regularly set upon and beaten by troops and police and Nhu's thugs. The universities were closed and thousands of student protesters had been thrown in jail. When the anti-Diem protests spread to the high schools, they too were closed and high school students were beaten, arrested and jailed. Sam read one unconfirmed report that grade school children had been beaten. Tran Van Chuong, Madame Nhu's father and the regime's ambassador in Washington, had resigned in protest; so had his wife, who was South Vietnam's official observer at the United Nations. There were reports, still unconfirmed, that a Viet Cong agent known as the "Tiger Lady" rode around Saigon on a scooter blasting American officers with a .45-caliber pistol. It was said she had killed a dozen Americans, all officers, in the past month. It was also said that Ngo Dinh Nhu had a hit list that included several prominent American journalists.

The spectacle was astonishing, "like watching a snake swallow its own tail, eat itself alive," as one BBC radio broadcast put it.

The day before Sam returned to Saigon, Viet Cong sappers had had their greatest score to date. At night they swam under the popular My Canh Floating Restaurant and rigged it with limpet mines. That evening, at the peak of the dinner rush, there were two explosions, which killed no one but caused a mad rush for the ramp that led to the quay. When the ramp was packed with panicked diners it erupted into a massive yellow fireball, hurling bodies into the air and the river and the trees; forty-two people died and more than one hundred were seriously injured. After that, the terror sank in deep.

So Sam was not surprised that he and the dozen other passengers on the Thai Airways flight were marched across the tarmac at Tan Son Nhut by a platoon of soldiers, their faces grim, their bayonets fixed. Inside the terminal Sam was questioned sharply for half an hour, then given a long list of instructions, reminded of the 9 P.M. curfew, and told he must leave the country within ninety-six hours.

He hailed a taxi, haggled with the driver, and finally agreed to a price that was double what he'd paid the last time he was in town. But he wrote it off to the fever. The driver chainsmoked and yammered in bad English as they entered the city.

He cackled, pounded the Renault's steering wheel, pointed out spots where VC bombs had gone off, where curfew violators had been shot, where monks had burned themselves, where the Tiger Lady had blown the head clean off one luckless American officer.

Sam tuned him out. He was busy studying the streets, checking to see if he was being followed, noticing the prevalence of troop trucks. Those sorry bastards, he thought. They should be down in the Delta fighting the Viet Cong, not hanging around Saigon getting drunk and laid and waiting to defend Diem against the inevitable coup. He counted a dozen American GIs blithely strolling the streets. The ones who weren't in uniform wore Bermuda shorts and Hawaiian shirts. Sam wondered why they didn't go ahead and paint bull's-eyes on their backs.

He told the driver to take him to the zoo, not to the Caravelle Hotel as originally agreed. This produced such a typhoon of outrage that Sam balled up a 500-piastre note and tossed it onto the front seat just to shut the guy up.

At the zoo Sam spent an hour strolling around the grounds, which were nearly deserted. Zoos had always depressed him, and this one was appalling. All the tigers and egrets and snakes looked ratty and underfed, listless. Even they seemed to feel the doom in the air.

As soon as Sam felt confident he had not been followed he slipped out the side gate and took a zigzagging route through alleys, working his way toward the river, constantly checking over his shoulder. The Vietnamese shrank from him.

He came out of a long, crooked alley and found himself on Thi Sach, not far from the river. It took him a moment to get his bearings. His old watering hole, Nguyen Tat Thanh's café, was across the street and one block up. Sam considered stopping in for a beer and the latest gossip with old Thanh, but he decided against it. Anne would be getting off work in two hours, and he had business he wanted to get out of the way.

He turned right and walked toward the river. Everyone recoiled at the sight of him, even the shoeshine boys and lottery sellers and cyclo drivers. No one tried to sell him anything or hustle him. Terror has its virtues, he was thinking just as he spotted the door.

It was painted fire-engine red and flanked by a pair of Volkswagen hubcaps. There was no sign. Sam pushed the door open and stepped into air-conditioned darkness, such a change from the street that he had trouble breathing at first. He shivered. When his eyes adjusted to the gloom he stepped forward and saw that the place was empty except for a Vietnamese girl sitting alone at the far end of the long bar.

Sam cupped his hands to his mouth and shouted: "Vestaaaaaaaaaaaaal! Wes-leeeeeeey! You goat-fuckers got company!"

The girl vaulted off her barstool, shrieking. It took Sam a moment to see that she was pointing a nickel-plated revolver at his chest.

"Put that fucking thing down!" he shouted.

She put the pistol on the bar. She had straight black hair that fell to her waist, and she was dressed all in pink: pink haltertop, pink miniskirt, pink high heels, even pink lipstick. This, no doubt, was slant pussy deluxe.

A beaded curtain parted with a clatter and Wes Bledsoe came charging out of the back room like a locomotive. He wrapped Sam in a bear hug and squeezed so hard Sam expected to hear his ribs crack. When Wes released him, Sam felt Vestal Embry's leathery hands clamp onto his right hand and pump it like a bumper jack. Vestal's skinny arms were sunburned halfway up the biceps, then the pink flesh turned abruptly to marshmallow white. Sam looked from those pink arms to Wes's coal-black face and thought again of "boiled shrimp and anthracite" and he laughed out loud.

"What's so motherfuckin' funny?" Wes boomed, and he slapped Sam's hand and hugged him again.

"Nothing, Wesley. Put me down, goddammit."

"You want a beer, numbnuts?" Vestal asked.

"Hell yes I want a beer. Who the fuck you think you're talking to?"

And so, after introducing Sam to his Vietnamese girlfriend—"Her name's Phuong and she don't speak English too good"—Wes took three beers to the back booth and the old Frogmen got down to some serious drinking and catching-up and reminiscing. As the forest of empty bottles grew larger, Sam told them about the hotel in Bangkok, about the American girl who had lured him back to Saigon, about his utter lack of desire to return to the States; and they told him about the craziness in Saigon, how the curfew was killing their business, how they hoped all the coup rumors would come true so people could start living again.

As he listened to them bemoan their bad luck, Sam kept trying to imagine what had inspired this odd couple to undertake this odd enterprise. He figured Vestal, being Vestal, decided to stay in Saigon because it beat the hell out of going to work at the local minnow farm, or whatever it was that decorated war heroes did when they went back to Eulonia, Georgia. But Wes was different. Wes was pathological. Wes was the most ingenious bushmaster, the most brilliant killer Sam had ever had the pleasure of accompanying on nighttime patrols. Maybe you had to be pathological to stay in Saigon voluntarily, Sam thought. Or maybe you just had to be willing to settle for very little. Or maybe you had to understand that there was no place else in the world that offered anything more, certainly not home sweet home Alabama. Or maybe you simply had to be one of those people—and Sam knew from experience that Wes Bledsoe was one of those people—who viewed danger as the ultimate drug. Some people had to be near it in order to be fully alive. Wes did everything for a reason and he was passionate and thorough about everything he did, whether it was blowing up a bridge or chasing a skirt or breaking a man's neck with his bare hands.

"Help me out here, Wes," Sam said. "You already explained to me that you went home to Alabama and didn't like what you saw—the police dogs, the firebombings, all that good shit— and you explained how you've learned to appreciate the charms of Phuong and company—"

At the mention of her name she swiveled on her barstool and smiled. Wes said she didn't speak good English, but Sam had his doubts.

"But it doesn't add up," Sam went on. "If Alabama's so bad,

you could go live in New York. Or Detroit. Or Senegal. Of all the Swans, you hated this country the most. You couldn't wait to rotate back to the States."

"I'll try to make it simple for you, my man," Wes said. Even in this frigid room his face was glistening with sweat. Sam couldn't imagine how he survived their jungle hop 'n' pops. "I got me a kid brother who's in school at Tuskegee Institute. He's involved with an outfit that calls itself the Student Non-Violent Coordinating Committee. Ever hear of it?"

"Can't say that I have."

"Me neither," Vestal said.

"Well, this baby brother of mine writes me these long letters—he's a very sensitive, very intelligent cat. He's sat in at more lunch counters and registered more voters and spent more nights in jail than I can count—and he's still a motherfuckin' teenager. He just got back from D.C., where he attended that huge-assed March on Washington."

"I saw some pictures," Sam said. "Looked like a lot of folks."

" 'Bout a quarter million brothers and sisters comin' together to hear speeches and carry on and rattle whitey. Made headlines all over the world."

"Was that the 'I got a dream' guy?" Vestal said.

"That's right," Wes said. "Martin Luther King gave his 'I Have a Dream' speech. And you know what my baby brother said about the whole thing?" They waited. "He said it was nothin' but a pep rally for President Kennedy. He said the FBI wrote the script. He calls it The Farce on Washington. So here's where I'm at—when a cat as sharp as my brother says the greatest moment in the civil rights movement is a farce, then I got no use for none of it. Whitey's fightin' the niggers and the niggers are fightin' whitey and now they got the niggers fightin' the niggers. Fuck it. I'm stayin' right here. Fuck it all to hell."

From there the conversation drifted onto less somber terrain. They reminisced about the time Rat gave them a guided tour of Bangkok's underbelly during their first R&R; about Hell Week in Virginia Beach, when they were fused together as a unit; about the night Wes saved their lives by carrying Rat into the hovering helicopter and then pulling Sam aboard.

Finally, after they'd told all their war stories and finished a case of beer, Vestal leaned close and whispered to Sam, "Before you run off, there's something we'd like to show you. Out back."

Sam followed them through the kitchen, where a Vietnamese woman was boiling something in oil in a huge wok. Sam thought it looked like a spaniel. They went out the back door, down a reeking alley full of clucking chickens, and into a cinderblock building. They climbed a rickety staircase and walked down a long, dimly lit hallway. Vestal produced a key ring and unlocked three dead bolts on a metal door. Sam followed him into darkness, and after Wes relocked the dead bolts he switched on a lightbulb.

At first Sam thought the walls were covered with hunting trophies, snakes, animal heads, racks of antlers. In the next instant he understood how wrong he was. The walls were covered with an arsenal. Sam recognized most of the weaponry—M-16s and AK-47s, .45-caliber grease guns, .38-caliber pistols, and 9-millimeter pistols with hush puppies (for quiet killing). There were Motorola walkie-talkies like they used to carry on missions, boxes of grenades, starlight scopes (to aid night vision), and guns and ammunition Sam had never seen before.

"What the fuck are those?" Sam asked, pointing at three sleek pistols.

"Beretta 92-SFs," Vestal said. "They fit into these nifty thigh holsters and take 15-round clips of Hydra-Shok hot loads that'll tear off your head."

Sam had forgotten about Vestal's deep love for the technical aspects of killing. Now Sam pointed at an elaborately retrofitted machine gun. "What in the—?"

"That's a specially modified Heckler & Koch MP5 submachinegun. Takes 30-round magazines of jacketed hollowpoints. We got about 600 rounds lying around here. Supposed to get a couple hundred more tomorrow. Ain't she a beaut?"

"Where are you guys getting all this shit?" There was even a radio console for monitoring military channels.

"We got friends all over town," Wes said. "And if you have

the money, you can get anything you want in this town. Ain't that right, Vestal?"

"That's a roger."

"What's it for?" Sam asked.

"What's it for?" Wes snorted. "It's for when the shit hits the fan. This city's about to blow, my man, and we intend to be ready when it does. 'Sides all that, this shit'll be worth a fortune in the States. To hear my baby brother tell it, the race war's fixin' to crank up any minute now. I know some brothers in Alabama and De-troit who'll pay a small fortune for what you're lookin' at."

Sam had seen enough. He led the way out of the building and back into the restaurant. The place was half-full, mostly Americans who'd finished another rough day of shuffling papers and were now furiously pouring down the booze in the few hours left before curfew.

Sam thanked Vestal and Wes for the hospitality and the beer. Phuong rose from her throne at the end of the bar and smiled brightly and said, "Nice from meeting you."

"Same here." Sam wondered if she knew about the arsenal out back. Hell, she probably helped procure it. He promised to keep in touch, and as he opened the fire-engine red door he had the chilling feeling it was not an idle promise.

After the air-conditioning, the heat on the street was even more vicious than before. The rainy season had ended, and now the evenings would hang on the city, heavy and oppressive. He was sweating before he got across the street.

He stayed close to the walls and took alleys whenever possible and kept checking over his shoulder. As he walked he thought of the strange scene in that cinderblock building. So Vestal Embry had turned out to be everything Sam had expected—and then some. He was a Georgia cracker, a shrewd black marketeer, a gun nut and gizmo junkie, and, like Wes Bledsoe, a very good man to know in Saigon in the dying days of 1963.

Sam found the apartment building without difficulty and knocked on the door three times, then once—their code. The door flew open and Anne Sinclair hurled herself at him, wrapping her arms and legs around him and squeezing him every bit as hard as Wes Bledsoe had squeezed him inside the VW Club. She buried her tongue in his mouth. He fumbled with her dress and got his hands under it and cupped her ass cheeks. She was not wearing panties. She pulled her mouth away from his long enough to gasp, "Bedroom," and then her tongue plowed right back in. Holding her like that, he waddled into the apartment, elbows and knees banging the walls, then followed her head signals to the doorway in the corner of the living room. He kicked it open and she pulled him down on top of her—landing on the bed was like landing on a cloud—and she began tearing at their clothes.

It wasn't until after the curfew siren had sounded and darkness had fallen that they finally lay still, pooled with sweat in the scrambled bedsheets, spent, content to let the waves of cool air from the ceiling fan wash over their drying skin. When the room began to glow with the light of the streetlamp at the end of the alley, Sam said, "I trust you're still taking that pill."

"Yes, of course I am."

She sagged against him, all animal warmth and perfume, and he understood that his concern for practical matters at a moment like this meant he was falling in love with this woman.

Later she gave him a pair of black silk pajama pants, and though they were freighted with the very worst memories, he said nothing and slipped them on. The cool silk felt good against his skin. She wore the short-sleeved pajama top, nothing else, and led him out to the balcony.

He couldn't believe how quiet the city was. The distant growl of artillery fire, the barking of a single dog, the wail of a faraway siren. It was almost—the word made him smile—peaceful.

Anne went into the kitchen and returned with a huge bowl of vanilla ice cream and two spoons, a bottle of Mumm's champagne and two long-stemmed glasses. "I didn't have time to get to the store. I hope you're not hungry," she said, popping the cork and filling the glasses.

"No, this is fine. It's perfect."

"I got the ice cream at the PX. The champagne's a gift from your brother."

"God bless Henry Luce. So you told Charlie I was coming to town."

"No, I didn't tell anyone you were coming. Charlie just likes to give me things."

"I see." He was glad she hadn't told anyone. It was somehow important that this moment was theirs, and theirs alone.

They sat there without speaking, simply listening to the occasional rumble of a Jeep or troop truck, watching tracer fire wink and die way down over Cholon. They wolfed the ice cream and drank the cold bitter champagne. Sam had not known such peace was possible—and it made perfect sense that he had found it in the middle of a war. He didn't care if he stayed in that chair forever, and in fact he doubted he could have stood up if he'd tried: The marrow in his bones had melted. He watched a squadron of rats scurry down the alley as he dipped his finger in champagne and rubbed it behind Anne's left knee, in that taut pocket where the tendons stretch the flesh smooth and tight. She shivered and sighed. Her whole body was on fire. Everything he touched—lips, earlobes, nipples, neck, thigh, the salty thatch between her legs—it all lit her up.

Just then a man came sprinting up the alley, the tire-tread soles of his sandals slapping the pavement. He was followed, a moment later, by a Jeep full of White Mice. The Jeep skidded to a stop at the end of the alley, then there were shouts, three rifle shots, silence.

"Come on, Sam. I can't stand it."

Anne was standing in the doorway, holding out her hand. He rose and took her hand and followed her back to the bedroom. She unbuttoned her pajama top and peeled off his pajama bottom and pushed him onto the bed. She crawled on top of him, began licking his earlobes. She had taught him that this was one of his on-off switches, and within minutes he was inside her again, surprised to be there, surprised by her appetite, then delighted to be tumbling once again into the bottomless ocean of ecstasy.

29

When he awoke the room was aglow with lemony sunlight and she was gone. There was a note on the bookshelf beside the bed: "Had an early appointment. There's juice and coffee and croissants in the kitchen. I'll be home by six. Love, Anne."

After breakfast and a bath he went down to the corner market, then returned to the apartment and spent the day on the balcony drinking beer and reading the dog-eared copy of Graham Greene's *The Quiet American*. The novel was set in Saigon in the early 1950s, but Sam found it uncannily similar to what was happening in Saigon today. The only difference was that ten years ago it was the French misreading the Vietnamese and today it was the Americans. He read the book in a state of rising joy, the joy that comes to a man who has discovered a prophet, even a prophet of doom.

He couldn't put the book down. The thing he liked best was that it was a cleverly disguised whodunit: Not until the end does the reader learn that Fowler, the jaded British war correspondent, has helped engineer the murder of Alden Pyle, the quiet American. It's impossible to tell if Fowler acts because he wants to put an end to Pyle's gruesomely botched attempt to bring democracy to Asia, or because he wants to prevent Pyle from stealing his Vietnamese mistress. Fowler's motives are messy and unclear. Just like war, Sam thought, just like life. The one sure thing is that Fowler, despite his claims to indifference and neutrality, takes a stand; he acts; he becomes *engagé*, as he puts it, and as a result he winds up with blood on his hands. Better that, Greene seems to be saying, than to stand aside, detached and inert, and let the killing of innocents continue unchecked.

Anne returned to the apartment shortly after 6 o'clock carrying groceries and two more bottles of champagne. Before she got half of the groceries put up she found herself sitting on the kitchen table with her dress hiked up around her waist as Sam, the black pajamas sliding to the floor, entered her with slow, gentle thrusts. From the kitchen they adjourned to the sofa, to the livingroom floor, to Rosalynn's room, then to Anne's room, where she wound up kneeling on the edge of the bed and twisting the sheets in her fists and cursing as he stood behind her, gripping her hips, pumping furiously. They came together one last time and collapsed on the bed just as the curfew siren began to wail.

After the ceiling fan dried their skin, she fetched a bottle of champagne and two glasses from the kitchen and returned to the bedroom and lit a dozen candles. Sam was lying on his stomach, still breathing hard. She was frightened, for an instant, by how out of control she became with this man. In the candlelight she saw for the first time that he had a tiny tattoo high on his right buttock. When she touched it, he flinched.

"I'm sorry," she said, leaning closer. "What is it?"

"It's a swan."

"What does it mean?"

"It was the name of our Frogman team—Number Seven was known as the Swans. We all got the tattoos one night in Bangkok when we were drunk as a bunch of monkeys."

They listened to the familiar silence of the city, punctuated from time to time by a rifle report, an explosion, a siren—the same sad nocturne.

When the champagne glasses were empty, Anne refilled them

and knelt beside the bed and kissed the scar on the back of his right leg. This time he did not flinch. "Sam, there's something I need to ask you."

"Yes . . . ?"

"Remember the night you told me about getting wounded here?" She kissed the scar again.

"Yes . . ."

"You didn't tell me everything. There's more to your secret, isn't there?"

To her surprise he didn't hesitate, he simply started talking in a deliberate monotone, as though he'd been rehearsing this speech for a long time and was relieved to get the chance, at long last, to deliver it.

"About two months before the night Rat and I got wounded, we got sent on a mission that everyone knew was going to be a goat-fuck . . ."

For the next two hours he talked nonstop, in that same monotone, about Team Seven's assignment to spend three nights and two days way up north on the Ho Chi Minh Trail. Instead of their customary "blow and go"—rigging an objective with explosive, blowing it up, then vanishing—they were under orders this time to plant the charges on a bridge, then lie low nearby for the next two days and two nights cataloging all traffic that crossed the bridge.

"It was no longer enough for us to interrupt the flow of goodies coming down from the North," Sam said. "Now Washington wanted information, too. I've got to believe McNamara was behind it, as nutty as he is about numbers."

The mission was so delicate that the Swans were not even told where they were being dropped. Only the helicopter's pilot and navigator knew. Sam found, to his surprise, that this was a relief. Sometimes, too much knowledge just got in the way. His obsession with maps had always made it important for him to know exactly where he was being sent to kill, but now, for the first time, he was being dropped into a void. As the chopper left Tan Son Nhut at dusk and headed north, Sam felt calm and light, clean, very nearly pure, as though he'd been absolved of all responsibility for the first time in his life.

They rode in silence for three hours, which, by Sam's rough reckoning, put them well north of the DMZ, over North Vietnam, or possibly Laos. The briefer had told them they were to insert into a broad, jungle-lined river, just upstream from swift rapids. "Based on our recon the water there is plenty deep for you to insert from one hundred feet," he said, "but I'm ordering the pilot to go down to fifty, just to be sure." What a sweetheart, Sam had thought. This asshole has never left the air-conditioning or set foot in a jungle or heard a shot fired in anger.

A few seconds before the chopper's pilot turned on the green light, Sam spotted the rapids glittering in the moonlight. He stood by the door and held up his right hand and everyone sprang into formation without a word. Some of them had been dozing, but they were instantly crystalline, good to go.

Sam was the first one out the door. He went into the water feet-first, ready to absorb the shock of the river bottom, but it never came. The briefer, for once, knew what he was talking about. When Sam bobbed out of the water the chopper was already gone. Its faint throb turned to a murmur, then the silence of the night swallowed it. The only things overhead were a lopsided yellow moon and the jagged black outlines of the jungle where it reached the riverbank. Sam's night vision was so good he preferred to operate on moonless nights, but such decisions were not his to make.

They gathered on the north riverbank to count noses. All nine of them made it in. This was the finest group yet, Sam thought, three teams of three—one Frogman, one Thai Ranger, one Montagnard per team—the most proficient killers Sam had ever worked with. At Sam's signal they eased into the water—it was surprisingly cool—and at fifty-yard intervals they moved downstream. They hugged the riverbank until they cleared the rapids and then, after the river's second graceful bend, they came upon the bridge.

It was right where it was supposed to be, a solid cable job anchored by tree-trunk pylons, sturdy enough for heavy machinery. It was thirty yards long, as expected, but it was much higher than the briefer had led them to believe, maybe sixty feet above the river, not the advertised twenty. But at least they were so far north that Charlie was likely to have a false sense of security, and there would be little danger of mines or booby traps. Even so, Sam was taking no chances. He never took chances. Taking chances could kill you or, worse, kill your men. He ordered Vestal to probe the cliffs on the north side of the river while his 'Yard probed the south side. Everyone else slipped into the brush to swallow mosquitoes and wait.

After three hours Sam began to worry. He decided to give them thirty more minutes and then go after them himself. As soon as he made this decision, Vestal and the 'Yard popped out of the water, grinning. Their teeth glowed in their blackened faces. Sam hadn't even heard them coming. Good boys.

Vestal crawled into the brush and whispered into Sam's ear: "Both banks had three trip wires on each side of the bridge. There was even a wire on the cliff on my side of the river, about ten feet under the bridge. Surprised the living shit out of me."

He was close enough for Sam to smell the Doublemint gum he was chewing. Vestal always chewed Doublemint when they went out on missions. Said it helped keep him calm and focused.

"You both go barefoot?" Sam whispered.

"Course we did."

They'd learned from the 'Yards that if you were barefoot it was much easier to sense the wires, as invisible as strands of a spiderweb, which the Viet Cong stretched across trails and attached to charges, devious surprises for the uninitiated or the unwary.

"Sounds like Charlie doesn't want anybody fucking with his bridge," Sam whispered.

"I'd say that's a roger."

"Any guards?"

"One at each end of the bridge. They both acted a little dopey, though, like they aren't expecting company. They have Enfield rifles, believe it or not." Sam registered this bit of intelligence. The Viet Cong felt the bridge was so remote and so safe from attack that they equipped the guards with antiquated Enfields. The good weapons were headed south, where they would be put to better use.

"Anybody see you?"

"Fuck no, Sam. You know me better'n that. I'm invisible."

"We'll wait thirty minutes." He checked his watch. "Get some rest. You're going to need it."

Exactly thirty minutes later they were saddled up and ready to go. Wes Bledsoe and his two teammates had volunteered to carry the party favors—three thirty-five-foot lengths of rubberized Mark-8 hose, two inches thick and packed with fifty pounds of 70/30 Composition A-3 and aluminum powder. To ensure detonation, both ends of each hose contained a booster of seventy-five grams of granulated TNT. Each length of hose weighed 150 pounds, a genuine bitch, but Wes and his boys hefted their loads without complaint.

They spent the rest of the night laying the charges. Vestal, the most nimble climber in the group, tied the first length of hose to his belt, then crawled along the bottom of the bridge, his back to the river, looping the hose through the bridge's cables. When he had the hose centered he came down for the other two lengths and attached them to the ends of the center hose. It was almost thirty-six yards of continuous charge—enough to turn the bridge and its pilings into thousands of matchsticks and chew huge divots out of both riverbanks. It was a much bigger bang than was needed, but Saigon wanted to make sure Charlie would have to rebuild his bridge from scratch. Besides, big bangs left more lasting impressions.

For the rest of the night and the next two days and two nights, the Thais and the 'Yards melted into the jungle to set up a perimeter while Sam and Ves and Wes took turns cataloging the traffic that passed sporadically over the bridge. Periods of intense activity were followed by hours of silence. Boredom was the true enemy—it could make you careless and get you dead. Even worse than the boredom and the mosquitoes were the green ants that rained out of the trees, like needles on the skin. The men learned fast to keep the collars and sleeves of their black shirts buttoned tight.

The trucks that passed over the bridge were loaded with boxes of rifles, grenades, barbed wire, artillery shells and sacks of fertilizer, most likely the same fertilizer that had blown up that culvert and killed those Marines the day Anne was returning from Tay Ninh. There were coolies pulling carts loaded with medical supplies, and there was a steady stream of men, each one dressed in black pajamas and sandals and conical hat, each one carrying a spanking new AK-47 rifle, compliments of Nikita Khrushchev. This procession, all this silent obedient toiling, reminded Sam of the stories he'd heard about Dien Bien Phu—how Giap's men had dismantled entire cannons and howitzers and hauled them piece by piece through the supposedly impenetrable jungle, then reassembled them and rained the worst sort of surprise on the "invincible" French fortress.

At night Vestal and Wes wore infrared goggles. Sam didn't need them. The light from the trucks' headlights and the torches at the ends of the bridge was good enough for him.

At 0300 on the third night, Sam relieved Vestal and began the last shift. They would set the charge at dawn and then the chopper would return to extract them.

Just as the sky began to show its first sheen of blue, Sam heard the distant roar of truck engines. Soon the bridge was sagging under the weight of a fresh convoy of trucks, wagons, coolies, soldiers and then—Sam blinked, he thought his eyes were playing a trick—a long column of girls, no more than ten years old, each one balancing a twenty-kilo sack of rice on her head. They walked in single file, like zombies, and Sam imagined they'd been marching all night, possibly for days. They kept pouring out of the jungle and onto the bridge, like ants. It occurred to him that they might keep coming forever.

For the first time in his career Sam panicked. He did not know what came next. He checked his watch; the green numerals glowed 0442. He was due to trip the charge in eighteen minutes. He reached into his shirt flap for his radio—then remembered this mission was under strict radio silence. Besides, he was within earshot of the guards and the girls on the bridge, close enough to read the lettering on the rice sacks.

He returned the radio to its pocket. Deep breaths, he told himself. Concentrate. Stay focused.

His head began to clear. He simply could not go through with this mission, not with those girls on the bridge. He had to report this to headquarters and get instructions. When the guard turned his head, Sam took a deep breath and slipped into the river and swam upstream. When he got around the first bend he crawled into the brush and took out his radio and whispered into it: "This is Swan-Seven to base, over."

The crackling that came back was so loud he jumped. "This is Echo-Two, Swan-Seven," hissed the voice of Lt. Chet Lahr Jr., the son of an admiral, an Annapolis man, the cigar-chewing ass-kicker in charge of all Navy Frogmen in Vietnam. It was obvious he was not pleased with this breach of radio silence. "This better be good. Over."

"We're twelve minutes from blowing," Sam whispered, "and the bridge is full of girls. Please advise. Over."

"Did you say girls? Over."

"Roger. Girls. Children—carrying sacks of rice. Hundreds of 'em. Over."

"Proceed with mission as planned. Over."

"Sir! Some of them aren't even ten years old! Over."

"That's an order, sailor. Proceed with mission as planned. Over and out."

The radio went dead. Sam lay there face-down in the mud of the riverbank, shivering. Five minutes passed, then ten. He checked his watch. He had exactly 120 seconds to make up his mind. He sweated and shivered and sweated some more. He had to bite down hard to keep his teeth from chattering. He bit down until he tasted his own blood. His mind raced. They were children, for chrissakes. But they were helping feed soldiers who were killing Americans. They probably packed bombs and planted mines and stuffed culverts with fertilizer, too. But they were children. Girls. Someobody's daughters. If he didn't follow orders, he would go to prison. Those girls were killers, just as deadly as men with AK-47s. He had no choice, he told himself. This was not the time to wrestle with the right and wrong of it; this was the time to follow orders and get out. As he drifted back downriver, a solution came to him: He would not trigger the charge until the girls were off the bridge, even if it meant delaying the extraction and risking his teammates' lives.

To his horror the girls were still pouring out of the jungle.

There were dozens of them on the bridge now, along with groaning trucks and grim silent coolies.

Just then Sam picked up the throb of the helicopter. The people on the bridge must not have been able to hear it over the roar of the trucks' engines. But seconds later the last truck of the convoy moved onto the bridge. His noise cover was about to expire, and he had already waited past the appointed time.

He slipped the radio out of his pocket and punched up the code and pressed the red button.

The bridge turned into a long roaring rope of fire. Trucks spun into the air, then toppled drunkenly into the river. Arms and legs and bags of rice splashed into the water alongside burning boards and truck tires. For what seemed like a long time, the sky rained pieces of scorched meat. The sound of that meat hitting the water was something Sam knew he would never forget as long as he lived. The jungle sang with the shrieking of hundreds of terrified girls.

Sam heard rifle fire as he slipped into the water and swam upstream as fast as he knew how. The helicopter was hovering over the water just past the rapids, but there was no one on the ladder. They were already up there, waiting. As soon as Sam stepped onto the bottom rung of the ladder the helicopter jerked skyward, shoving his guts down into his feet. When he got to the helicopter's door, Rat was there to pull him aboard.

The next thing Sam remembered was landing at Tan Son Nhut in a lashing rain squall. His body and mind had shut down. He hadn't stopped weeping during the entire three-hour flight.

After releasing these secrets to Anne, Sam simply dropped off. One moment he was talking in that numb monotone; the next he was gone, snoring softly, absolved at last of the things he had been made to do.

He awoke several hours later and for an instant did not know where he was. A lamp was on. He rolled to his left and found Anne sitting up in bed, a look of deep worry on her face as she studied a stack of photographs with a magnifying glass.

"What're you doing?" he said with a yawn, burying his face in the slope above her hipbone, nibbling the soft flesh.

"There's something I need to show you."

For the next hour he peered at the photographs through the magnifying glass and read the after-action report on the battle of Ap Bac. The surprising thing to Sam was not that General Harkins had buried the report where he thought the world would never find it; the surprising thing was that men in the U.S. military had stuck their necks out so far in the interest of the truth. This was not the way to win promotions. But these men had put the truth ahead of their own careers. Brave fools, Sam thought. Brave, admirable fools.

When he finished reading the report, Anne told him about the latest coup plot, which everyone believed would unfold soon, possibly within the next two weeks. There were three generals involved, she told him, and Ambassador Lodge and the White House had given them their blessing—"the green light," they called it. The two major concerns in the U.S. Mission were that the coup must be a success and that the Americans must be able to deny any involvement. This must appear to be a thoroughly Vietnamese affair.

"They've actually got a word for it," Anne said with a mixture of disgust and disbelief.

"What do they call it?"

"Deniability."

"Deniability," Sam said, testing the sound of the word.

"Isn't that rich?"

"Yes, it's rich. And very typical." Then he asked her why she had photographed the report and why she had showed it to him.

"Because, Sam, I need to know the truth. And now that I'm learning the truth I want the rest of the world to know about it too. I want to stop these bastards."

"Hold on. How is the rest of the world going to find out about this?"

"I'm not sure. I'm thinking about leaking the report to your brother."

"Jesus. And how do you propose to stop these bastards?"

"I'm not sure about that either. But this is crazy, Sam. The United States government is involved in a plot to overthrow the government of a fucking ally. And they've got no earthly idea who'll run the country if the coup succeeds—or what'll happen if it fails. Can't you see how insane this is?"

"Yes, Anne. Believe me, I can see how insane this is. I've known for a while."

"Then don't you think you have a responsibility to do something?"

He considered her question for a long time. He thought of that burning meat hissing as it hit the river on the Ho Chi Minh Trail. He thought of Thomas Fowler seeing to it that Alden Pyle wound up face-down under a Saigon bridge with a stab wound in his chest and his lungs full of mud. But those thoughts carried no answers with them. They carried only possibilities, the possibility of caring enough to take action, the possibility of once again becoming involved in a war he thought he had left behind forever. He couldn't imagine how he might become involved in it again.

When Anne grew tired of waiting for his answer, she said, "Well, I think I have a responsibility to do something. I can't just keep this to myself, Sam. And as much as I hate to say it, I don't think I could have any respect for someone who could know so much and not do anything about it."

They didn't talk after that. Anne returned the photographs to their hiding place in the hollowed-out book, then she turned off the lamp and allowed Sam to hold her. Making love was out of the question. Their minds were going too fast, going over the possibilities that lay before them, trying to figure out how they had arrived at the edge of this cliff from which there was no turning back.

Sam's flight to Bangkok left at 10 o'clock the next morning. He awoke at dawn, feeling clammy and tired, and took a bath. When he emerged from the bathroom Anne was dressed for work. They drank coffee on the balcony, watching the city come back to life, the bicycles and the bells and the smoke and the frenzy, and they said very little.

Sam walked her to the end of the alley and kissed her goodbye. She didn't say a word and suddenly the prospect of being shut off from this woman became very real, and unbearable. He watched her melt into the crowd. She never turned. She didn't wave. Already he had ceased to exist.

Instead of hailing a cab and going directly to the airport, he crossed the street and headed toward the river. He could not bear the thought of losing this woman. Before leaving Saigon he decided to pay a quick visit to his friends at the VW Club. They, of all people, would understand that the things he knew carried a responsibility with them, a responsibility to act, a responsibility to do something to stop the spiraling madness of this war. Vestal and Wesley would be able to tell Sam what he had to do.

PART FOUR

30

The VW Club was bombed three weeks later.

The only person injured was a young American lieutenant who'd been in-country less than four hours and lost all the toes on his right foot. No one was killed. This miracle was the result of two uncanny pieces of good luck. The first bomb, the one that separated the lieutenant from his toes, rolled under the long metal bench that ran along the wall; the bench absorbed most of the concussion. And the second bomb was a dud.

Vestal and Wes were out back in what they now called the "O.R." (Ordnance Room), taking delivery on a box of American grenades from Phuong's brother, who'd bought them from a Viet Cong agent, who'd stolen them right off an American supply ship that was tied up across from the Majestic Hotel on the Saigon River pier. "Iron pineapples," Vestal called them affectionately. Surplus from World War II, but good to have around and worth every penny.

Phuong was sitting at the bar drinking a Coke when the sappers entered the club. She disliked the looks of them instantly, the way they sized up the room before the door shut behind them. They were shifty-eyed, hungry-looking, plainly dangerous. One of the men walked toward her, not seeming to see her, as the other man bent over and rolled two bombs across the floor. As the men turned to flee, Phuong reached under her purse and smoothly drew out her nickel-plated .38-caliber Smith & Wesson and aimed it at the back of the nearer man's legs and fired twice.

He went down just as the bomb exploded, sending glass sailing through the air like nails and sending people scrambling and shrieking for the door. Phuong calmly walked over to the sapper and placed a high-heeled shoe between his shoulder blades and placed the barrel of the pistol behind his right ear and told him to shut up and be still. He was whimpering and writhing in pain. One bullet had entered the back of his right leg and torn away the kneecap.

She told the hysterical cook to go get Vestal and Wes. The club had emptied, and only then did Phuong hear the moaning. A young buzz-cut blond American in uniform was sitting on the long bench cradling his right foot. The tip of the shoe was missing, and she could see bloody meat inside.

Vestal spotted the dud bomb as soon as he came out of the kitchen. To everyone's surprise it was not a homemade Viet Cong job; it was a regulation U.S. Army hand grenade, the same vintage as the freshly delivered box of iron pineapples up in the O.R. It probably came off the same supply ship.

It took them three full days and nights, but Vestal and Wes, past masters at the art of interrogation, learned from the wounded sapper that he was not Viet Cong, as they originally assumed, but was on the payroll of the CIA—venerable old Lucien Conein, to be exact. This puzzled the interrogators. They knew from their network of street sources that Conein, one of Ed Lansdale's old guard, one of the spooks who'd helped elevate Ngo Dinh Diem to the presidency in 1955, was now actively wooing the three generals who were plotting Diem's overthrow. So why had Conein paid this sixteen-year-old boy to bomb a club owned and patronized by Americans? Eventually the boy told his interrogators that the bombing was part of a CIA campaign designed to elevate the pitch of terror in Saigon and hasten the collapse of the Diem regime.

As subversive campaigns go, this one was a flop. Three days after the bombing of the VW Club, the sapper was found floating in the oil-black waters of the Saigon River by a woman washing clothes. His body was badly burned and he was missing his testicles, his right kneecap, eight fingers, both eyes, and his nose.

Vestal and Wes shuttered the club and retreated to the O.R. to listen to their military radio and plot their next move. The coup was about to unfold. They wrote a letter to Sam Malloy and sent it to Bangkok with a Navy Frogman headed there for R&R. They let Sam know they were ready to help him execute the plan they'd hatched the morning he'd stopped by the club on his way to the airport.

All he had to do was say the word.

31

The letter from Anne Sinclair arrived two days after Vestal
Embry and Wes Bledsoe's declaration of war against the United
States of America.

Sam got a huge kick out of his old teammates' outrage. Their
letter was written by Wes in a curiously girlish script, very neat
and ornate, with beautiful grammar. It went into great detail
about the bombing of the club, including Phuong's part in ap-
prehending the sapper and the three days the unlucky boy spent
giving up his secrets, one body part at a time.

"He did not make a pretty corpse," Wes wrote, and Sam,
knowing what this meant, felt pity for the boy. The surprising
thing to Sam was that Lou Conein was behind the terror campaign. Conein, the shiftiest old operator of them all, should have
known better than to fuck with a couple of old Frogmen. The
letter closed with an open invitation for Sam to return to Saigon
and stay in the building behind the VW Club as long as he
liked and make full use of "the facilities," as Wes put it. The
letter was signed with Vestal's chicken scratch and Wes's flowery full name, Wesley Prince William Bledsoe.

Anne's letter also arrived by courier, but it was much less

amusing. She was plainly nearing the end of her rope. The letter was garbled—a cry for help, an ultimatum, a news update. She wrote that her best sources at the U.S. Embassy believed the coup would begin no later than the end of October and that they felt its chances of success were excellent, though there was still no one in town with any idea as to what would happen if the coup did succeed. She, too, closed her letter with an invitation for Sam to return to Saigon and stay as long as he liked. "I meant what I said on your last night in town," she wrote. "In fact, I feel more strongly about it than ever. I could not have any respect for someone who knows as much as we know and who did nothing with it. I have some ideas. Do you? I still haven't shown the Ap Bac report to anyone yet. I'm going to wait to see what happens with the coup. I hope to hear from you soon. I'm scared, Sam. I miss you. Love, Anne."

There was a guest staying at the White Elephant, a Frenchman involved in some sort of import-export business, who was returning to Saigon on that evening's flight. Sam wrote a quick letter to Anne and gave it to the Frenchman. Sam instructed her to call him at the White Elephant at noon, Bangkok time, the day she received the letter. He told her to make sure it was a secure line.

For the next five days he locked himself in his office from 10 o'clock in the morning until 2 o'clock in the afternoon. At noon on the fifth day the phone rang. He pounced on it.

"Anne?"

"Yes, it's me."

"Are you all right?"

"I guess so. My nerves are shot, but I'll live. This place gets crazier every day, Sam. Did you hear about what happened at the VW Club?"

"Yeah, heard all about it. You sure this phone's secure?"

"Positive. It belongs to the woman who mops the floors in my office. She lives in Cholon. Even Nhu couldn't possibly care about her. I'm sorry it took so long for me to call, but she was reluctant to let me use her phone. I finally had to pay her off."

"Listen to me carefully. I'm coming back to Saigon—"

"You are!? When?"

"I'm not sure. Soon. I need you to do me a favor. Do all the people in your office have the same kind of ID card?"

"Yes . . ."

"Does it have your picture and signature on it?"

"Yes . . ."

"Do you have a list of all the people in your office who've got clearance to enter Gia Long Palace?"

"I'm sure I could get one. But I think just about everybody's got palace clearance. Why?"

"Just listen. I want you to get the signature of some man in your office—someone who's not well known at the palace—and bring it home with you. Do it today so you don't forget."

"What do you want a man's signature for?"

"Don't ask questions. Just do it. I'll see you in a few days."

"Sam?"

"Yes."

"You're scaring me. Please tell me what this is all about."

"No reason to be scared." He thought the lie sounded good. "I'll see you soon. Just a few more days."

"Sam, there's one other thing."

"Yes?"

"I love you."

"I love you too, Anne. That's why I'm doing this."

32

Sam checked into the Continental Hotel shortly before noon on October 29th and set about establishing his cover. He was a tourist, he told the Frenchman at the reception desk, on his way from Bangkok to Hong Kong, and thought he'd stop in for a few days of sightseeing and some good food. He put out this story in case Nhu's boys came around. He asked the Frenchman to recommend a place for lunch, and this, as Sam expected, lit up the little man with the waxed mustache and the shiny bald head. He described half a dozen restaurants, each more laudable than the last, before insisting that Sam go to the Trocadero, down by the river, for the steak tartare. He actually closed his eyes and kissed the fingertips on his right hand when he said, "Their steak tartare is *incroyable.*" Sam gave him the look a Frenchman would expect from an American tourist, a look that said he knew what steak tartare was but had never tried it and this by God was going to be the day. The Frenchman was delighted by the look on Sam's face because it confirmed everything he believed about Americans.

"*Merci beaucoup, monsieur,*" Sam said in his most atrocious French.

"My pleasure, Mr. Malloy. Please don't hesitate to let me know if there is anything else I can do to make your stay more enjoyable." Then he slapped the bell and turned away.

Sam tipped the bellhop too much and set about unpacking the clothes he had borrowed from George O'Phelan—loud sportcoats, slacks, a dinner jacket—as well as a pair of his own swim trunks even though he wasn't sure the Continental had a pool. He spread his toiletries in the bathroom, tossed a shirt carelessly over a chair, mussed the bed. He did all this methodically because he understood that in the coming days such little details could be a key to whether he lived or died. Then he hung the DO NOT DISTURB sign on his door and pocketed the key and slipped out the hotel's side door.

Sam passed in front of the whitewashed General Assembly building, that mockery of democracy where Madame Nhu's puppets rubber-stamped her whims. He skirted the Caravelle Hotel, fearing he might bump into his brother or one of the other American correspondents. That would be disaster. From a distance he noticed that the Indians and Chinese were feverishly changing money, shouting, waving their arms—a sure sign, according to Charlie, that something big, most likely a coup, was in the wind.

Sam thought he was being followed by two men, so he took a zigzagging course through familiar alleys. He walked briskly, then slowed, then picked up the pace again. The men stayed with him, about twenty yards back. When he reached the birdshit-slicked statue of the hero-emperor, Le Loi, he sat on a bench in the shade of a tamarind tree and waited for the men. They passed a few feet in front of him, smoking, chatting, still pretending to be unaware he existed. They wore black leather jackets, despite the syrupy heat, and pointy-toed French shoes— the uniform of Nhu's thugs. As soon as they passed, Sam stood up and, walking fast, doubled back the way he'd come. Within minutes he lost them.

Vestal and Wes were locked inside the Ordnance Room listening to their military radio transmitter and playing checkers. They sprang to their feet when he gave the secret knock—three quick raps, then two, then one. He sensed they'd been fighting some severe boredom. That made sense. Sitting around waiting for the South Vietnamese army to make up its mind and actually do something could put anyone to sleep. Sam noticed a new color-coded map on the one wall that was not covered with weapons. It showed where military units—presumably disloyal troops—were stationed. Saigon was surrounded. Things did not look good for Ngo Dinh Diem.

Wes called for coffee on an intercom and within minutes Phuong arrived, dressed in skintight Capri pants, high heels, a baggy camouflage T-shirt knotted at her navel. She had a very flat tummy. She smiled at Sam and bowed and withdrew. The coffee cut through the first wave of fatigue from Sam's early flight and from the anxiety of being back in this city full of bayonets and rumors and fear. Until now it had all seemed like a dream, but the sight of Vestal and Wes in this room bristling with weapons brought it all home for Sam. He was back in the war.

"Did you get the maps of the palace tunnels I asked for?" Sam began, refilling his cup. His armpits and skull felt hot from the coffee, buzzy. Much as he hated to admit it, the French did do a few things right.

Vestal rummaged in a file cabinet and dug out a large blueprint, which he spread on top of the desk. True to the rumor Sam had heard from an old friend in the CIA, there were three escape tunnels radiating from Gia Long Palace, part of Ngo Dinh Diem's contingency plan for ruling a country where coup plots were as inevitable as the monsoon. One tunnel ran from the palace reception area, under the tennis courts, and let out in an alley two blocks away. The other two let out on the street that ran in front of the palace. Since there were sure to be tanks and troops clogging that street, Sam decided the first tunnel was best suited to his purposes.

"Is Rat with you?" Wes asked.

"He begged me to let him come, but I decided against it."

What actually happened was that Sam and Rat had stayed up late the night before on the roof of the White Elephant, drinking and talking. Rat lined up three one-liter bottles of Singha beer on the edge of the roof. Sam drank straight from a bottle of Courvoisier. They sat up there for hours as Sam laid out what he intended to do when he got to Saigon. He wanted to hear himself say it. He figured any flaws would reveal themselves if he heard himself say them out loud to Rat. When he finished he felt good, felt it was airtight. Rat took a long pull of Singha and said, "You are a crazy. You know that?"

Suddenly Sam had realized what it was he loved about Rat's English. Most people heard only the mangled syntax and malapropisms, but Sam heard a heightened form of expression, a deeper understanding of the world.

"Yeah," Sam had said, "maybe I am a crazy. But that's what I'm going to do."

And then Rat had asked him why he was going to do it, as Sam knew he would, and Sam tried to explain. It wasn't easy. He wasn't doing it for love, exactly, though he never would have considered it if Anne Sinclair hadn't looked at him across her tangled bedsheets, the blue vein throbbing in her neck, and told him she couldn't possibly have any respect for a man who knew as much as he knew and refused to do something about it.

But that wasn't the reason, not really. That was just the beginning. On top of that, Anne had made him understand the depth of his own rage and disgust, his anger over what his government had done to him and what it had made him do to others, particularly to those little girls on that bridge in the middle of nowhere, girls who could not possibly have visited any harm on the United States of America.

But that sounded like revenge, and revenge wasn't the reason he was going back, either. There was more to it than that. He tried to explain to Rat that he had come to agree with Anne— and with the Thomas Fowlers of this world—that a person who knows the truth has a responsibility to act on that knowledge. He tried to explain that a person who knows the difference between right and wrong has a responsibility to act when he sees a wrong about to be committed. "Unluckily for me," Sam had told Rat, "I happen to know that a wrong is about to be committed and I'm in a position to do something about it. So I have no choice, really. I simply have to go back."

Finally Sam had tried to explain that he was acting out of so many motives that he couldn't say exactly what was drawing him back to Saigon. And then he came full circle and took a gulp of Courvoisier and admitted that, yes, he supposed he was doing it mainly because he loved Anne Sinclair and couldn't bear the thought of losing her.

"It is about high time you make some sense," Rat had said. "She is a very beauty. Worth the risk."

And then Rat had said he wanted to go along for the ride and Sam had said no, definitely not, this was personal. And that was the end of that.

Now Sam could see that Vestal and Wes were staring at him, their eyebrows raised a notch. "Look," he said. "You both know Rat wanted in on this action. Bad. I just decided the fewer people got involved the less chance for a fuckup. It's gonna be plenty hairy as it is."

They nodded, seeming satisfied.

"So," Sam said, glancing at the wall map, "what's the latest word on the coup troops?"

Vestal went to the map and explained that by listening to all five military frequencies, to the CIA channel and their dozens of street sources, they'd learned where the rebel units were stationed. Sam had been right: Saigon was surrounded. The rebels outnumbered loyal troops at least four to one. Vestal said things would probably break on November first, certainly no later than the second. If it hadn't happened by then, it was off. That bastard Lou Conein from CIA had been in daily contact with the three Generals behind the plot, especially Major General Tran Van Don. They met either at the Joint General Staff headquarters at Tan Son Nhut or at the office of Don's dentist. The Generals had agreed to give Conein advance notice of the coup, and they wanted him at rebel headquarters as it unfolded. Lou Conein was to be the plotters' insurance policy in case the coup failed.

"We even know the radio code Conein's gonna use to alert the CIA station that it's under way," Wes said, obviously pleased. "He's gonna say, Nine, nine . . . nine, nine . . . nine, nine . . .' He's even got twelve Special Forces with his wife and chirren—ready to get 'em out of the country in case there's a fuckup."

"Shit," Sam said. "Is this going to be a cluster-fuck?"

"I don't see how they could blow this one," Vestal said. "They've got too many units and too much firepower on their side—and everybody in the country hates your little moon-faced buddy in the sharkskin suit. Not to mention his brother and the Dragon Lady. In fact, you might be the only guy in-country gives a rat's ass about them."

"You guys going to be able to get me that I.D. card printed in the morning? I'll need it to get into the palace."

"All set," Wes said. "You got the original on you?"

"I'm picking it up at Anne's tonight. I'll drop by with it first thing in the morning."

"Cool. Printer says it shouldn't take more'n half an hour."

"He can take my picture?"

"No problem. Got his own darkroom."

"One last thing. Who's going to drive me?"

Vestal and Wes exchanged a look. "We were just discussing that," Vestal said.

"We were thinkin' you oughta have a local drivin' you," Wes said. "You know, case you get in a tight spot once the shootin' starts."

"Got any candidates?"

They exchanged another look. "We were thinkin' Phuong's brother might be a good call," Wes said.

"You trust him?"

"He ain't fucked up nothin' yet. Course, it'd be nice if you had Rat along . . ."

"Well, I don't have Rat along."

"Pham's a good boy," Vestal said, a little too fast for Sam's taste. "He'll do you right. He watched what we did to that sapper who bombed the club."

Wes chuckled at the memory.

Sam promised to return first thing in the morning, but as he left the cinderblock building and started up the alley, dodging chickens and two naked baby boys, he had a hollow feeling in his stomach. He wished he had let Rat come along. He knew nothing about Phuong's brother. He cursed himself for leaving something to chance. On a mission like this, as he knew so well, leaving something to chance was the kind of mistake that could leave a man good and dead.

When Anne Sinclair got home from work at dusk she was surprised to see a lamp burning in her living room. When she saw the balcony doorway blocked by the shadow of a man—a man much too large to be a Vietnamese—she gasped and started backing out of the apartment.

"Anne, it's me. Sam."

"Sam!" She dropped her briefcase and her bag of fruit and raced to him. As they hugged, she said, "You scared me half to death! How did you get in?"

"An old Frogman trick."

"When did you get to town?"

"This morning."

"Why didn't you tell me you were coming so I could—"

"Shhh." He gripped her elbows and held her at arm's length and admired her. "You look lovelier than ever." It was true. The tension and fatigue were beginning to show. There was a new darkness around her eyes, and her features were sharper, some of the softness melted away by the weeks of not having much appetite and not being able to sleep right. She looked older in a pleasing way, more substantial. There wasn't quite as much dew on her.

"Sam, I've missed you so much . . ." They kissed again and held each other a long time, just pressing against each other, rocking back and forth. They could both feel it: Just being together again was enough. For the first time since he'd walked off the plane at Tan Son Nhut that morning he felt sure he was doing the right thing.

It was too close to curfew to go out to a restaurant, so she made omelettes with scallions and Brie cheese and *pommes frites* and a salad. She brought the food and a bottle of burgundy onto the balcony just as the curfew siren sounded. They watched the city as they ate. They hardly spoke.

When they finished eating, Sam took the dishes to the kitchen and refilled their wineglasses. When he returned to the balcony he saw tracer fire across the river and imagined it was a fireworks show, the Fourth of July at Civitan Field in Levittown, Long Island, a thousand summers ago. When the lights died he said, "You have your I.D. card with you?"

She went into the bedroom. He heard her rummaging in her purse. He noticed a new strand of violet bougainvillea crawling along the balcony's iron railing. To top everything off, she had a green thumb. Did it ever end? She came back onto the balcony and handed him her I.D. card.

It bore her picture, a grim one, like she was in a police line-up, along with her signature, the USIS logo, and an official-looking Vietnamese stamp. It was laminated with plastic.

"How about that man's signature?"

She went back into the bedroom and returned carrying a sheet of unlined paper with Hugh Prescott's signature on it. She'd told Hugh, the newest guy in the office, a Yalie, that she was studying handwriting analysis and wanted to try to read him. He'd been bugging her all week for the results.

Sam told her he needed to borrow the I.D. card and the signature for a couple of hours first thing in the morning. She asked him why. Instead of answering he said, "Do you think you can arrange an audience for the two of us—I mean for you and Hugh Prescott—with President Diem?"

"I could try. As a matter of fact, I just finished a new propaganda pamphlet and my boss wants me to show it to the president."

"Perfect. Can you arrange it for late in the morning of November first?"

"I suppose so. You mind telling me what this is all about?"

"Not yet. You'll know when you need to know."

"Sam, I don't like this. Are you sure it's legit?"

"No, it's not legit. It couldn't possibly be less legit. But you said you couldn't have any respect for a man who knows what I know and refused to act. So I'm getting ready to act."

"Sam, you're scaring me. Please tell me what you're going to do." She sat beside him and rested her head on his shoulder and ran her fingers through his hair. "Please."

He waited a long time, then took a deep breath. "Look, it's no secret that a coup is about to happen—"

"Yes . . ."

"—and let's just say Vestal and Wes and I have a little plan. A plan for short-circuiting the coup."

"How?"

"The less you know, the better off you'll be. All I can tell you is that we're going to try to do something we used to be very good at. Hopefully we still are."

"Like blowing up bridges?"

She was afraid she'd pushed him too far, but he spoke softly: "Nothing's going to get blown up. I'm here to save people, not kill them. I've done enough killing for one lifetime."

Already he'd told her more than he intended to, and he lapsed into silence. There was more tracer fire, and again he thought of fireworks when he was a boy. When machinegun fire started near the river, Anne blew out the candles and led the way through the darkened apartment to the bedroom. They stripped off their clothes and lay in bed naked, hugging, nuzzling, but they did not make love. The air was too heavy—too heavy with rumors and questions, too heavy with their own doubts and fears.

33

The gray Austin pulled up at the main gate to Gia Long Palace a few minutes before 11 A.M. on November 1, All Saints' Day. In an hour the midday siesta would begin. Though few knew it—including the Roman Catholic president inside that stout white palace—the coup had already begun.

Anne Sinclair and Sam Malloy climbed out of the Austin. She was wearing a pale blue linen suit with a white blouse and a strand of pearls. She had decided on black shoes with flat heels. No sense in making the President feel any smaller. Sam was wearing a navy-blue suit and carrying a briefcase full of pamphlets recently produced by the U.S. Information Service, which explained how a new hydro-electric dam near Dalat built jointly by the governments of South Vietnam and the United States would soon bring electricity to the region for the first time. People would be able to enjoy electric lights, refrigeration, even air-conditioning. The pamphlet, written in Vietnamese, English, and French, made it sound as though the electricity were a personal gift to the Vietnamese people from President Ngo Dinh Diem.

"Anne Sinclair and Hugh Prescott from the USIS," Anne told

the unsmiling guard at the gatehouse. "We have an eleven-o'clock appointment with President Diem."

"Identification," the guard snapped. He took their I.D. cards, studied their pictures, then their faces, then their pictures again. As he compared the signatures on the cards with the signatures on his clearance list, Sam felt a single bead of sweat gallop down his spine to the small of his back, where he had the 9-millimeter pistol tucked under his belt. Its handle was wrapped with rubber bands to keep it from slipping down into his pants. That was Vestal's touch, said he picked it up from a fellow car thief back home in Eulonia. Vestal had done all of Sam's outfit-ting: the 9-mill with the rubber bands; the flat Beretta strapped to his right shin and loaded with a 15-round clip of Hydra-Shok hot loads; the long knife with the pearl handle strapped to his left shin; and the snub-nosed .38-caliber Smith & Wesson insur-ance policy tucked into his left armpit, under his shirt.

The guard handed back their I.D. cards and motioned toward Sam's briefcase. "Open." Sam opened the briefcase and the guard sifted through it, removing one of the pamphlets and skimming it. "Air-conditioning," he said with disgust, snapping the briefcase shut and handing it back to Sam. He unlocked the gate and jerked his head toward the palace.

Before moving toward the open gate, Sam turned and looked back at the Austin. Rat was at the wheel, pretending to read a newspaper. The sneaky little bastard had been sitting in Sam's room at the Continental that morning when Sam returned from breakfast. Rat was drinking a can of 333 beer and cleaning his fingernails with a switchblade knife.

Sam had looked at him and said: "Son. Of. A. Bitch." And then they both burst into laughter. Sam didn't even pretend to be angry or try to hide his relief. No one was better at watching your back than Rat.

Now Sam nodded and Rat dropped the Austin into gear and drove off.

Sam and Anne trotted up the palace steps. His heart was pounding. He knew there wasn't much time left. Just before they'd left the Ordnance Room to pick up Anne, they'd heard

Lou Conein's signal over the supposedly secure CIA net: "Nine, nine . . . nine, nine . . . nine, nine . . ."

After they picked up Anne at the USIS office, Sam tuned in to Vestal and Wes's network of lookouts posted throughout the city with walkie-talkies. They reported that Conein was on his way to Tan Son Nhut with a sack full of American dollars to pay off the Generals; that units of the Seventh Army Division were already on the outskirts of Saigon, moving to block off the main road to the airport and potential routes for reinforcements or escape; and they were being joined by three battalions of tough, American-trained Marines.

As he hurried up the palace steps Sam had two fears—that Diem already knew about the troop movements, or that he would keep them waiting and would get word and all would be lost.

But a smiling girl in an *ao dai* greeted them in the reception area and led them briskly down a long hallway to a suite of offices. The place smelled like a basement to Sam, moldy and mildewed. A male secretary with watered hair rose as they entered and led them to a doorway, opened it, and motioned for them to enter.

Ngo Dinh Diem was sitting at an ornate, gold-leafed desk reading correspondence and smoking a cigarette. The first thing Sam noticed was that his tiny feet barely reached the Persian rug. The room, gloomy and high-ceilinged, seemed to swallow him whole.

He rose to greet them. He was beaming. He gripped Anne's right hand in both of his and bowed from the waist. "Miss Sinclair, it is always such a great honor to have you visit the palace."

"Mr. President, I would like to introduce Hugh Prescott," Anne said. "He's new on our staff."

Diem gave Sam a curt handshake and no bow. Then he turned to a jacketed waiter and barked at him in Vietnamese. The man vanished. Sam heard a distant thud—a tank shell?— and his groin tingled. But Diem seemed not to notice. He motioned his guests onto a pale red velvet sofa. Its stuffing was beginning to burst from the seams.

The waiter returned with a coffee service, and the President poured three cups and offered sugar and lit a cigarette, a single fluid motion, doubtless one he had repeated thousands of times. "I have had a most productive morning," Diem announced, blowing smoke at the distant, unlit chandelier. His sharkskin suit glowed in the weak light. "Ambassador Lodge and Admiral Felt just paid a surprise visit on me."

Anne and Sam locked eyes. Admiral Harry D. Felt, commander of all U.S. troops in the Pacific, was supposed to be in Honolulu. Was this some sort of smokescreen to mask U.S. involvement in the coup? And didn't Lodge know the coup was planned for today?

Anne said, "I didn't even know Admiral Felt was in Saigon . . ."

"Neither did I!" Diem laughed, a single puff of smoke. "Naturally I told him we are whipping the communists like dogs and that I know there is going to be a coup—but this time I do not know who is going to do it. They have really concealed their sources on this one."

"Yes, Mr. President," Anne said. "We brought the new pamphlet about the dam in Dalat to show you."

He didn't seem to hear her. "Admiral Felt is at the airport right now speaking to reporters. I think I made him understand the importance of my brother's counsel—"

"Is your brother busy?" Sam cut in. Diem gave him a startled look. Sam said, "I would like very much to meet him. I'm a great admirer. If he isn't too busy, of course . . ."

"Yes, of course." Diem, clearly flustered, waddled to the desk and picked up a telephone and said something in Vietnamese. Lighting a fresh cigarette, he returned to his chair. "Where was I? Oh yes. I asked Ambassador Lodge to remind President Kennedy that I am a good and frank ally . . ."

Sam heard the distinct thump of mortar fire. He thought he saw Diem cock an ear, but the President kept talking.

". . . and I would rather be frank and settle our differences now than talk about them after we have lost everything."

"I'm sure the Ambassador will pass the message along," Anne said.

Sam reached for the briefcase just as a door behind him opened. He heard a man enter the room, coughing moistly. Sam turned to face Ngo Dinh Nhu. He was wearing a white shirt opened at the throat, revealing crinkly wattles of flesh. His cheeks were sunken, his black hair hanging into his eyes, into his pink wet eyes. He had the wrists and arms of a girl. Yes, Sam thought, this skeleton loves his opium pipe.

Sam and Anne rose in unison. As Anne was shaking Nhu's hand, Sam reached back and removed the 9-millimeter pistol from his belt and pointed it at Diem's face. The President's eyes grew wide as he rose from his chair, as though tugged by a string. Sam heard Anne gasp, but he couldn't see her.

"Mr. President, Mr. Nhu," Sam said, "I have come to inform you that a coup is under way at this moment, led by three of your own Generals—"

"I just received word," Nhu said. Turning to his brother, he added, "I was on my way up to tell you when you called." There was nothing in the voice. No bitterness, no hysteria, not even concern.

"I have come to take you to a safe haven," Sam said, the gun still aimed at Diem's face. "I'm afraid the palace will soon be heavily shelled."

"You are representing the government of the United States?" Diem asked.

"No."

"The CIA, then?" Nhu said. He was smiling in a way that unnerved Sam.

"No, I'm acting on my own. I'm a civilian, an American citizen. My government is behind the coup and I believe it's wrong."

"Sam! What are you doing?!" It was Anne. He looked at her for the first time. The blood was gone from her face.

He told her, "I'm taking them through a tunnel that runs under the tennis courts. Then to a safe place. If necessary, we'll get them out of the country." He turned back to the brothers. "Please cooperate. I'm doing this for your own safety. If you try to resist, I'll shoot you."

Nhu laughed. "I am always amazed by you Americans—shooting people in order to save them."

Sam picked up the briefcase and slipped the pistol into his right jacket pocket. With it pointed at Diem's back he ordered the brothers to start walking and followed them out of the office, down the long hall and into the reception area. Anne was beside him, hurrying to keep up. They encountered no one. In the distance they could hear sirens and machinegun fire. Diem pushed a wall panel near the staircase and it swung open and he led the way into the tunnel.

It was lit with flickering lightbulbs spaced at fifteen-foot intervals. The floor was wet. Sam heard water dripping and he tried not to think about rats.

"Where do you intend to take us?" Diem asked. His voice boomed in the dank tunnel, but Sam could tell he was relaxed. He stuck a cigarette between his lips and his brother lit it without having to be told. They were so casual, as though another coup were all in a day's work.

"Some friends of mine have a safe place nearby. They have radios—"

"No!" Nhu had stopped walking. "You will take us to our refuge in Cholon. We have radio and telephone communications set up there for an emergency such as this. This is not negotiable. If you refuse, you will have to shoot me."

Sam looked into the wet red eyes. "Keep walking. Please."

Nhu didn't budge. "If the situation in Saigon is bad, we will go to Vung Tau after dark and wait for several days. Then loyal troops will descend on Saigon and crush the rebels. This plan is brilliant. We will use it to trap the friends of the Americans in a dead shell of a capital city."

Sam put the barrel of the gun against his forehead and they resumed walking. Diem reached the exit first. He unlocked one lock with a key, then slid four heavy dead bolts and pushed the door open. The first thing they heard was the roar of a tank, very close by, and a quick burp of machinegun fire. The gray Austin was parked outside the tunnel exit with its right doors open.

Sam ordered the brothers to lie down in the back seat. He

covered them with a blanket and told Anne to ride in front. She got into the car and said, "Jesus Christ." Rat had the Heckler & Koch submachine gun, an ugly oily thing, resting on his lap. There were half a dozen grenades on the floorboard by his feet. He was listening to the walkie-talkie.

Sam climbed in back, his 9-millimeter still aimed at the lumpy form of the President and his brother.

"Cholon!" came a muffled command from under the blanket.

"What'd he say?" Rat asked, putting the car in gear and guiding it up the narrow alley.

"There's been a change of plans," Sam said. "Drop Anne off—then we head for Cholon."

"Cholon?" Rat said, dodging a frightened dog. "What's in Cholon?"

"Chinese people."

"Don't fuck with me. What's in Cholon?"

"They've got a communications setup there. We'll maintain contact with V and W on our walkie-talkie. What's the latest news?"

"Doesn't look good for your friends," Rat said, gunning the car up an empty side street. The sky was smudged with black smoke. "The rebels have already seize the central police station and naval headquarters. They about got the airport and the central post office. They move on the palace within an hour—I am glad for getting the hell out of there."

Behind them came the concussive thunder of heavy artillery. "What's that?" Anne said, turning.

"Must be coming from the barracks of the Presidential Guard," Sam said. "They got some tanks and big guns. Guess they're putting up a fight."

Just then a pair of T-28 fighter-bombers with rockets under their wings swooped overhead, moving toward the palace. Then came the chatter of *ack-ack* from the rooftop guns. Sam took the walkie-talkie from Rat. "This is Swan-Seven to base. Over."

"Go ahead, Swan-Seven," came Vestal's voice.

"We're dropping Anne with you. We've got both chickens out of the coop and we're taking them to Cholon. Over."

"Cholon?"

"That's a roger. We touch down in three minutes. Be ready. Over and out."

There were a few scurrying pedestrians, but no vehicles or troops on Thi Sach when they pulled up in front of the VW Club. At the end of the block Sam could see something burning. Garbage? Tires? Before the Austin came to a full stop the club's red door swung open and Phuong was there, holding her nickel-plated .38 and motioning for Anne to hurry.

"Go on," Sam told Anne. "Wait for us here. It'll be safer than your apartment. We should be back in a few hours."

Rat gunned the engine. Anne turned to face Sam and said, "I'm coming with you."

"Get out of the car, Anne."

"I'm coming with you. I'm the one who dragged you into this mess."

Sam was still holding the pistol on the brothers with his right hand. He balled his left hand into a fist and for an instant she thought he was going to hit her. But he slammed his fist onto the seat beside her shoulder and shouted, "Get out of this fucking car! Now!"

And then she looked into his ice-blue eyes and saw it—the same thing the Major had seen in Rat's eyes that night on the White Elephant Hotel rooftop with Marlon Brando, the look of a man whose blood was on fire, a man who was capable in that instant of unspeakable things. She looked at Rat. His eyes were soft, almost sad, and they told her he hoped she would do them all a favor and get out of the car. She understood for the first time that her life—that all their lives—were in danger.

Reluctantly, and very gingerly, she kissed Sam and got out of the car. As soon as the red door closed behind the women, the car sped off.

34

They were shot at three separate times on the way to Cholon—a burst of machinegun fire near the central market, a sniper on a rooftop, then more machinegun fire—but Rat kept the gas pedal pressed against the floorboard and nothing hit the speeding Austin.

The streets of Cholon were as chaotic and bustling as ever. Word of the coup hadn't gotten here yet, Sam thought. Maybe it never would. The Chinese were too busy making money to be bothered with Vietnamese politics.

He let the brothers get out from under the blanket to give directions, but he kept the pistol on them. Diem ordered Rat to turn left down a side street that was lined with food stalls and noodle shops and vertical red banners emblazoned with Chinese characters. Then another left down an alley that ended at a walled house with a green tile roof.

The men got out of the car. Sam pressed the 9-millimeter against Diem's back and Rat pressed the submachine gun against Nhu's back and they marched through the iron gate and onto the porch. A yellow cat sat in the sun, watching them warily. Chickens strutted and clucked in the dirt courtyard. Sam smelled food and raw sewage.

Diem pounded on the door and almost instantly it was opened by a frail Chinese man dressed in a purple silk skullcap and a long purple silk robe. Wispy white billygoat whiskers, nearly a foot long, fell from his chin. The man reminded Sam of Ho Chi Minh, and he laughed out loud.

No one else laughed. The Chinese man's slit eyes grew wide when he saw that a white man and a Thai were standing behind the President and his brother, pressing guns to their backs. The man waved them into a typical Chinese anteroom with stiff black carved chairs that no one ever used. It hurt Sam's back just to look at those chairs.

The Chinese man led the four men down a long hallway to a large, windowless, teak-walled room. He motioned for them to enter, then he withdrew, closing the door behind him. He hadn't said a word.

The room was equipped with a two-way radio transmitter, several portable transistor radios and six telephones, all of it arranged neatly on a long table. There were three folding chairs and a red leather sofa. One wall was covered by a large map of the Saigon area, from Tay Ninh down to the Delta. It had colored pins stuck in it. It didn't look anything like Vestal's map on the wall in the Ordnance Room.

The telephone lines were hooked up through the palace switchboard, which enabled Diem and Nhu to take calls and place outgoing calls without anyone realizing they had already left the palace. Sam had to admire the subterfuge.

The brothers got down to work without a word to each other, as though they had rehearsed this exercise many times. They tried to reach corps and division commanders, province chiefs, heads of the Republican Youth Movement and the Women's Solidarity League. They got answers from none of these staunch supporters.

Meanwhile Rat turned on a transistor radio. An announcer was reading a statement from one of the rebel leaders, General Duong Van "Big" Minh, which Rat translated for Sam: "The day the people have been waiting for has come! For eight years the people of Vietnam have suffered under the rotten and ne-potic Diem regime, but now the Armed Forces have come to their rescue!" Then the announcer put on a cha-cha record, a flagrant snub of Madame Nhu, who had banned such records and the dances they inspired because she felt they were emblems of Western decadence.

As the day wore on in that cool windowless bunker, it became apparent to Sam that the Ngo brothers' confidence was evaporating and they were beginning to grasp the true extent of their plight. Sam's thoughts turned to the boat. It was tied up across from the Majestic Hotel, but it would be a simple matter to get it here to Cholon. It was a junk with a secret cargo hold that Phuong's brother used for ferrying guns to and from the Delta. They would radio for the boat between midnight and dawn if the coup succeeded, then take the brothers downriver to the South China Sea, around the Ca Mau Peninsula and up to Kampot, Cambodia, where they would wait for the dust to settle and plot their next move. Sam did not look forward to an all-day and all-night boat ride to Cambodia, but it was beginning to look like their only option. Most of the brothers' supporters had defected or vanished. There was still heavy fighting at the palace—no one yet realized Diem and Nhu were gone—but that seemed to be the only genuine resistance. And how long could that last? Even Madame Nhu was unavailable to help. She was on a speaking tour of the United States and was asleep in her ninety-six-dollar-a-day suite at the Beverly Wilshire Hotel in Los Angeles after addressing a convention of adoring Young Republicans.

Late in the afternoon Diem finally got through to Ambassador Lodge at his residence. Sam picked up an extension.

"Some units have made a rebellion," Diem said, "and I want to know what is the attitude of the United States?"

"I do not feel well enough informed to be able to tell you," Lodge replied. "I have heard the shooting, but am not acquainted with all the facts. Also it's 4:30 A.M. in Washington and the U.S. government cannot possibly have a view."

"But you must have some ideas. After all, I am a chief of state. I have tried to do my duty. I want to do now what duty and good sense require. I believe in duty above all."

"You certainly have done your duty," Lodge said. "As I told you only this morning, I admire your courage and your great contributions to your country. No one can take away from you the credit for all you have done. Now I am worried about your physical safety. I have a report that those in charge of the current activity offer you and your brother safe conduct out of the country if you will resign. Had you heard this?"

Sam's spirits rose. Maybe there would be no boat ride to Cambodia, after all.

"No, we have not heard this," Diem said. He pressed the receiver to his chest and looked at his brother and said in English, "We have been offered safe conduct out of the country—"

"A trap!" Nhu hissed. "To hell with all of them, including the big American."

Diem said into the receiver, "You have my telephone number."

"Yes," Lodge said. "If I can do anything for your physical safety, please let me know."

"I am trying to re-establish order."

As soon as Diem hung up, the phone rang again. Sam picked up the extension. The caller identified himself as General Duong Van Minh. They spoke in Vietnamese, then a string of other voices came on the line. When Diem hung up, Sam asked him who the men were and what they had said.

"They were the rebel Generals, calling to tell me that continued resistance is futile. They plan to continue bombarding the palace until I surrender."

"Let them," Nhu said, dialing a number. "We're not in the palace, remember?" Nhu then tried to arrange asylum in Nationalist China, but was rebuffed.

As the night wore on, maids brought tray after tray of dim sum and tea and sandwiches to the bunker. Sam and Rat took turns sleeping and communicating with Vestal and Wes and keeping an eye on the Ngo brothers.

Shortly before dawn a white flag of surrender was hoisted over Gia Long Palace.

Sam awoke on the leather sofa and was surprised to see Diem standing over him. His eyes were glassy, his suit rumpled. He looked like hell.

"Today is All Souls' Day," the President said softly, almost a whisper.

"Yes . . . ?" Sam sat up.

"Are you Catholic, Mr. Prescott?"

"I was as a boy. Not anymore."

"Well, at least you know that yesterday was All Saints' Day and today is All Souls' Day—very holy days for all Catholics. We also call today the Day of the Dead."

"Yes, I know that."

"There is a Catholic church near here. Will you drive us there? My brother and I need to pray. While you were asleep we agreed to surrender with honor."

"Where?"

"At the church. Soldiers will pick us up there in half an hour. They will take us to staff headquarters at the airport for the formal announcement. Then we will be flown to Paris."

"Yes, of course."

Rat was standing by the door, ready to go. The four of them rode through the quiet streets in silence. Just as Sam expected, the coup had not touched Cholon.

Diem directed Rat to the Church of the Sacred Heart, a nondescript pile of pink bricks on a nondescript side street. Sam could smell bread baking. All four men went inside. The brothers knelt in the front pew and bowed their heads in prayer while Sam and Rat retreated to the shadows by the baptismal font to discuss what came next.

"I think it is time for us to start thinking about saving our own two asses," Rat said. "Haven't we done enough?"

"I don't know. I guess so."

"No guess so about it. Let us get the fuck out of here right now."

"I don't guess there's much more we can do."

"Damn right. And if the rebels find us—"

Just then they heard a rumble out on the dawn-dusted streets, a rumble that grew relentlessly louder. They went to a stained-glass window at the rear of the church that opened onto the street. They watched as two yellow headlights—some sort of heavy truck—rounded a corner and approached the church.

Sam looked toward the altar. The brothers, oblivious to the noise, were still bent in silent prayer in the first pew. The vehicle stopped in front of the church, tires squealing, then backed up toward the door. It was an olive-green M-113 troop transport with the logo of the Army of the Republic of Vietnam. The back hatch flipped down and three uniformed soldiers with rifles trotted out and came up the stairs of the church. Sam and Rat crouched behind the last pew. Sam had the 9-millimeter in his right hand and the Beretta in his left hand; Rat had the submachine gun resting on his knees.

The soldiers strode up the middle aisle and spoke sharply to Diem and Nhu. The brothers crossed themselves and rose without a word and led the soldiers back down the aisle and out of the church, heads held high, not in any hurry. Sam and Rat rose to watch through the window. The soldiers were arguing with Nhu.

"What are they saying?" Sam whispered.

"Nhu is very pissed-off. He says a troop truck is not a suitable vehicle for the President."

"He doesn't know when to quit, does he?"

"No, he does not."

They watched Diem and Nhu bend over and step into the M-113, where soldiers forced them to kneel, then bound their hands behind their backs. A crew-cut Vietnamese soldier came around from the cab of the transport. He was close enough for Sam to see that his upper lip was split by a jagged scar and he had close-set, vicious eyes. He walked up behind the brothers and removed a revolver from a holster and without a word he shot Diem, then Nhu, in the backs of their heads. After the bodies had toppled face-down, the soldier removed a long knife from a scabbard and plunged it, again and again, into their backs.

Then he stepped back and wiped the knife on his pants. Sam could see that the backs of the brothers' heads were gone and they were lying in a lake of blood. The assassin ordered the hatch closed, and the soldiers climbed onto the M-113 and it roared off into the dawn.

35

Anne was asleep on the sofa when Sam let himself into her apartment with the spare key. She was still wearing the pale blue suit and the white blouse and pearls, and there was a half-empty glass of red wine on the coffee table. She was barefoot. Sam studied the yellowed map of Vietnam on the wall above the sofa—Tonkin, Annam, Cochin China, the bad old days of the French Empire—then he went into the kitchen and quietly poured himself a tall glass of Scotch, added a single ice cube, and went out onto the balcony. His hands would not stop shaking.

The sun was above the rooftops, and the alleys and streets looked like the aftermath of a mad carnival. The city was littered with wine bottles, flowers, spent cartridges and the frayed casings of fireworks. Yes, it had been an all-night carnival, and Sam had missed it. The revelers were now ransacking the palace.

It was strange, but he couldn't figure out how he felt. He thought of that night when he blew up the bridge with the ten-year-old girls on it, of the shame and regret that would be with him for the rest of his days. He thought of how simple his life used to be. How had things gotten so complicated in such a short time?

And now his hands were shaking and he couldn't even figure out how he felt about what he'd just done. He'd told himself before he left Bangkok that no matter how things worked out in Saigon, he was doing the right thing and that was all anyone could ever ask of a man. He almost tricked himself into believing he was absolved of any responsibility for how things turned out simply because he was doing the right thing. But then he remembered the night the Swans had been flown north into the void, remembered feeling relieved that no one had told them where they were being sent. That should have absolved him, too, and he saw how that had worked out.

As the Scotch warmed his insides, he tried to console himself. He had failed—failed utterly—but at least he had taken sides. At least he had tried to do what he believed was right. Like Thomas Fowler, he had, at the very least, become *engagé.*

So where did that leave him?

The answer came to him from the living room—Anne calling out to him. He went inside and she opened her arms. "I didn't hear you come in. Kiss."

He sat on the floor and kissed her. She had the rotten baby breath of sleep. He kissed her again.

"I tried to stay awake," she said groggily. "Vestal drove me home just before dawn." She looked around the room. "What time is it?"

"A little after ten."

"So what happened?"

"They assassinated them."

She snapped into a sitting position. "They?—Who?"

"Soldiers. They tied up Diem and Nhu and shot the backs of their heads off and then stabbed them. Rat and I saw the whole thing. It happened so fast . . ."

"Oh, Sam, how awful." She rested his head on her thigh and cradled it in her hands.

"The soldiers had promised to take the brothers to the airport and put them on a plane to Paris. We thought we were home free. They say Big Minh's personal bodyguard pulled the trigger. Come to find out the guy's killed more than forty people. They buried the bodies in unmarked graves next to Lodge's house, of all damned places. What a total goat-fuck . . ." And then he started to weep.

Anne cradled his head, rocked him softly. After a long time, she told him, "You did the best you could."

"It was a goat-fuck from the get-go. I should've known."

"You did the best you could," she repeated. "And I love you for it. Do you hear me? I love you for what you've done." She kissed his ear, his cheek, his damp eyelid.

Later, he let her lead him to the bedroom, and they fell onto the bed fully dressed. Only then, with his face buried in her hair, tasting his own tears, did he realize how exhausted he was. He let her hold him and rock him until he melted into the velvety sleep of a child.

PART FIVE

36

Sam Malloy and Anne Sinclair were married two weeks later beside the green pond on the highest ridge above her parents' ranch house in California.

There was a respectable contingent on hand from Southeast Asia—Rat and Jiap, the Major, Vestal and Wesley and Phuong, and Charlie Malloy, whose coverage of the coup and breaking of the Ap Bac story had won him his dream job as *Time* magazine's new White House correspondent. Sam's father and brother Ed called from New York to say they couldn't afford to make the trip.

The morning after the wedding, the bride and groom climbed into the pink-and-black 1954 Buick, which they'd shipped back from Bangkok, and started driving cross-country. They were headed for Alabama. As payment for Wes's help during the coup, Sam had agreed to deliver the car to his kid brother. Sam relished the trip; he was in a frame of mind to forget Asia for a while and see America one last time.

The Major and Rat and Jiap rented a car and drove to Los Angeles, where they planned to look up Marlon Brando, visit Disneyland, and take the tour of the stars' homes. The Major figured it was going to be his last chance to see Hollywood.

On their first day, Sam and Anne drove nonstop to Bill Williams, Arizona, and rented a cabin at the Rustic Courts Motor Lodge. In the morning they awoke to find the Buick and the rest of the world coated with sugar from a freak snowstorm. They spent the morning in bed, making love. In this cold cabin their lovemaking lacked the sweat and fury it had possessed in Bangkok and Saigon, and when Sam mentioned this, Anne laughed. He understood that her laughter meant she was not concerned, that she believed once they returned to Bangkok everything would go back to the way it had been, the way they both wanted it to be, for all time.

They walked through the town, stopping for coffee and waffles, and they wrote postcards until the sun was high and plows had cleared the roads. Then they drove north toward the Grand Canyon. Along the way they saw deer foraging for food on the shoulders of the road. One doe walked right up to the Buick, and when Sam rolled down the window she stuck her quivering wet nose inside the car.

The sky was brushed blue steel by the time they reached the canyon, but the air was still sharp and the world was still covered with that sugary snow. Sam and Anne gazed down at the Technicolor hole in the ground for two hours without saying a word.

They had just passed through El Paso, Texas, when they heard the news on the Buick's Sonomatic radio that President Kennedy had been assassinated in Dallas. Anne slid close to Sam on the big front seat, and he wrapped his arm around her and they rode in silence until they pulled up in front of Willie Bledsoe's home near the campus of Tuskegee Institute.

Willie was tall and thin, his skin the color of café au lait. It was hard for Sam to believe that he and Wes were brothers. But Willie was, as Wes had promised, a very sensitive and intelligent young man. His apartment was spotless, full of books and jazz records, and though the whole nation was in a state of shock over the assassination, Willie seemed to be in high spirits. When Sam asked him about this, Willie said, "I don't mean no disrespect, but I can't see that it makes much difference to the American Negro who happens to be living in the White House."

After listening to Wes tell about Willie's involvement in the civil rights movement—the Freedom Rides, the jail time, the beatings, the church bombings, the murder of his friend Medgar Evers—Sam had to admit he had a point.

That night, though they weren't in a festive mood, Willie insisted on taking them to the Starlight Club to see Carla Thomas and Otis Redding. Sam and Anne were the only white people in the crowd, but they did not feel unwelcome. When Otis launched into the ballad "These Arms of Mine," Anne was back on the rooftop of the Rex annex the night Morey Caan was killed. She started crying and Sam held her and they swayed to the lovely sad music.

"I'm sorry," she whispered.

"Shhh."

"It's the memories—they won't go away."

"Shhh. They'll go away. Give 'em time." Then he kissed her tears, just as she had kissed his damp eyelids on their last morning in Saigon. Later he understood that the taste of salt was what made the ice inside him begin to thaw.

Willie Bledsoe drove them to the Birmingham airport the next evening. The whole way he kept marveling at the Buick's many virtues, its power, its upholstery, its ecstatic gaudiness. As they pulled up to the terminal, he announced he was going to load up the car and get out of Alabama for good.

"Where are you going to go?" Anne asked him.

"De-troit. Got relations up there. Gonna start all over from scratch."

Sam and Anne hugged him and wished him luck. Then they stood by the curb and watched the Buick recede until its four ruby tail lights vanished into the night.

"I'm going to miss that old car," Sam said.

"So am I," Anne said.

"But we've still got six left."

"Yes, we do. Let's get going. I'm dying to see them again."

Holding hands, they walked into the terminal to begin the long trip back to Asia.

37

Rat was waiting for them at Don Muang Airport in Bangkok with the Malibu Blue and white Buick, the car that had taken them on that fateful trip to Ko Chang. They both wondered if Rat had done this on purpose, and then they decided, in their own ways, that it didn't matter. He was smiling, full of sunshine, and as soon as they stepped out of the terminal and into the Bangkok heat, they could feel the last of America melt from their skin. In that moment they understood, without having to say a word, that they were never going back. This was now their home.

In the following months they plunged into their new life. Anne started working in the kitchen at Shwe Winn's elbow, learning the arts of Chinese and Thai cooking. She was such an enthusiastic pupil that the old lady found herself warming up to an *ang moh* for the first time in her life. The tall one was very good with garnishes. After two tries she was able to peel a tomato and turn it into a perfect rose.

Anne was thrilled by the things she was learning. Turning a tomato into a rose—making something beautiful for the sake of making something beautiful—filled her with a joy she had never known before. She compared this to writing white papers full of lies for blind men in Washington, and she found herself laughing out loud.

Sam kept busy with the Buicks and the hotel, and he spent his free hours, especially at sunrise and sunset, up on the White Elephant's roof, watching the light change on the river and telling himself the memories would go away if he just gave them time. Already, to his delight, he could feel them growing dim.

All the while, Sam and Anne tried to ignore the worsening news from Vietnam, but it proved difficult. Lois DeVries turned out to be a ferociously energetic correspondent. She wrote long letters of the latest intrigues, including an impenetrable blow-by-blow of the bloodless coup of January 1964 that saw "Big" Minh deposed by Major General Nguyen Khanh. Khanh, in turn, was soon gone. And soon after that a letter came from Washington describing Charlie Malloy's latest audience with President Lyndon Johnson. The interview took place in the Oval Office several days after Johnson had ordered the bombing of North Vietnam in retaliation for a dubious attack on two American destroyers—and hours after he had rammed the Tonkin Gulf Resolution through Congress.

Sam read the letter late one night, alone on the rooftop. "I'll never forget it," Charlie wrote. "Lyndon Baines Johnson—the President of the United States—leans over close to me and says with a wink, 'I didn't just screw Ho Chi Minh—I cut his pecker off.'"

Sam tore the letter up and dropped it in the trash. Then he took one last long look at the moonlight on the Chao Phraya River and went downstairs to make love to his wife.